# Dead Or Alive

## An Owning Vegas Spin-Off

Kylie Kent

*For the dark romance souls. The souls who fall for the villain, crave obsession and a love that would burn empires to the ground. This is for you, mi alma, the one who sees beauty in the broken.*

# Prologue

Whit e walls sprayed with blood. Art at its finest. I stare at the red splotches and lines, seeing images in the shapes that the blood mixed with brain matter form against the otherwise pristine wall. If you focus hard enough, you can see all sorts of pictures. A cat, a shoe, wings... always fucking wings.

I've spent months trying to figure out the

meaning of the wings. They're certainly not the kind that belong to angels. Nothing good belongs here. This place is hell on earth.

I used to dream about this, about having a father to teach me everything I didn't know. I stopped dreaming when I was eight. I'd give anything to be able to go back to the days when I thought the man standing in front of me was dead. It took him fourteen years to find me. He says my mother stole me from him, denied us the opportunity to be a family, denied me my birthright.

At fourteen, I believed him. I hated my mother for the lies she told me. Hated that she made us struggle when we didn't have to. Now, just two years later, I'm thankful she did what she did. The sacrifices she made to try to give me a normal life. Not that it made a difference. He still found me.

It took three months for me to see my father for who he really was. The devil. The ruthless cartel leader everyone fears. Including myself. The things I've witnessed this man do in just two years... it's what nightmares are made of. Nothing could have prepared me for this life.

"You see where he went wrong, *mijo?*" my father asks, pointing to what's left of the man's face that is hanging from rusted chains in front of the white wall.

"Where, Papa?" I ask him. The title tastes bitter on my tongue. He might be my father by blood, but he will never be *my papa*. No matter how many times I call him that.

"Love," he says. "Made him weak."

I look to the right of the man. The body of his wife lays lifeless on the ground. My father spits at it. "Puta, if it weren't for her, I wouldn't have had to blow the brains out of one of my best men," he says.

"Of course, Papa." I have no idea what this woman did to cause both her and her husband's deaths. Whatever it was, I'm sure it's not worthy of the torture they both received.

"Walk with me, *mijo*." My father put his hand on my shoulder, his fingers digging into my skin as he guides me out of the building.

I don't utter a word. I have nothing to say to this man, unless he asks a direct question.

"I'm glad you were here to witness what love does to a man. It's a weakness that we must kill before it kills us."

My mind goes to my mother, who is still very much alive, in a very nice house in Las Vegas. It's a gilded cage, but it's much better than the alternative. My father doesn't allow her to leave the grounds. He says it's because she's a target. I just think he's a control freak.

"I'm sending you back to Vegas tomorrow, Emmanuel. There is a problem I need you to fix."

I smile before correcting my face. I'm going back to Vegas. I'll be able to see my mother, my friends, *my girlfriend.* I don't even care what the problem is. Whatever he wants me to do, I'll do it. I haven't seen Laura in a month. We haven't spoken or messaged.

"What is it?" I ask.

"There will be a full brief waiting for you on the jet. You have two weeks, *mijo.* Make them count," he says before adding, "And don't disappoint me."

I nod my head. "I won't."

---

I'm so eager to get back to Vegas. I message my friends, Louie, Carlo and Sammie. They're street kids, but I know they're going places.

ME:

I'm coming home. Today. Just boarded the jet.

LOUIE:

You're being let out of the palace?

CARLO:

Party?

SAMMIE:

Do you even know how to party
still, E? You've been gone a while.
Do they party in Mexico?

Ignoring all their stupid questions, I ask the one that's burning in the back of my mind. Laura. I might not have been able to keep in touch with her while I was gone. That doesn't mean I don't keep tabs on her through everyone else I know.

ME:

How is she?

LOUIE:

She'll be happy to see you.

*What the fuck is that supposed to mean? She'll be happy to see me? Does that mean she's not happy now?*

Pocketing my phone, I settle into the plush leather seat and pick up the envelope on the table in front of me. I rip it open and pull out the photos inside. My stomach drops, and it has nothing to do with the fact that the jet just took off from the runway.

Staring back at me is the face of the only person in this world that I love. Laura. What the fuck? I've kept her secret. I've made sure he didn't know about her. How the fuck did he find out? There's a note with my father's handwriting scrawled across it.

*Kill her. Kill your weakness, mijo. If you don't, I will.*

The threat is there. If I don't kill Laura, he will. And what he'll do to her will be far worse than anything I can imagine. But I can't do this...

I climb out of my seat, walk as calmly as I can manage into the bathroom, and slam the door shut. Leaning over the toilet to empty the contents of my stomach.

*Kill her.* He's asking me to do the one thing I can't fucking do. Anyone else but her. I need to figure out a plan. I need to get rid of her, get her away and out of his reach. There has to be a way to do that.

---

As soon as the jet lands in Vegas, I ditch my father's security and go in search of Laura. It doesn't take me long to find her. She always did stand out in a crowd. The most beautiful person I've ever seen.

The words keep repeating in my head. *Kill her.*

*Kill her.* This is going to kill me, because when my father finds out I've betrayed his orders, blood or not, he *will* kill me.

I lean against the wall and watch her. She's sitting on a park bench with one of her friends. Two seconds later, she's looking around until her eyes connect with mine. A huge smile forms on her face and then she's up and running across the street.

The moment she reaches me, her arms wrap around my neck. My lips land on hers. "Fuck, I missed you," I tell her.

"Not as much as I missed you," she says.

When my arms tighten around her waist, I feel nothing but skin and bone. She's lost weight. "You wanna go somewhere?" I ask her.

Laura bites down on her lower lip and nods her head. "Give me a sec. I need to go and say goodbye to Heather."

"I'll be right here."

My eyes never leave her as she talks to her friend. It's not until I watch Laura take a bag of white powder from the other girl's hand that I start crossing the road.

Snatching the bag from Laura's hand, I throw it at the other girl. "Get that shit away from her. If I ever see you give her anything again, I will kill you."

"Emmanuel, stop!" Laura gasps. "I need that."

My glare turns to my girlfriend. "No you fucking don't," I tell her.

"Yes, I fucking do!" she yells at me. "You don't know. You're never here. I need it." She holds out a hand to her friend.

"Do it. I dare you," I threaten the girl, who shakes her head and turns away. *Smart.*

Taking hold of Laura's hand, I drag her away.

"What the fuck, Laura? What was that?" I ask her.

"It's nothing," she says.

"Nothing? You're doing drugs now?" I hiss.

"Pfft, like you're one to talk. You think I don't know where they come from? Who they come from? From your father? *From you!*"

"So what? That gives you the right to throw your fucking life away?"

"I threw my life away the moment I fell in love with you, Emmanuel. Someone I can't ever have, not really. What do you expect me to do? Sit around and wait for the brief moments you come back to town?" she asks.

"It's not always going to be like this," I tell her.

"Yes, it is," she says. "Or... we could run. Just you and me."

"We can't run."

"We can. You have money. We can go anywhere. I can't live this life, Emmanuel. I can't be the girl in a different city, waiting for crumbs."

Does she think it's easy for me? I miss her like fucking crazy every fucking day. But I know that one day, things will change. I'm prepared to endure the hard times now, because she is worth it.

I've been in town for a week. I haven't figured out a way to get Laura away. I need to find her a new identity, get her a one-way ticket and figure out how to tell her she needs to stay hidden until I can come for her. Which could be years.

The identity part I've got. I just picked up her new passport and papers. I've got her a credit card and a bit of cash that will tide her over for a bit. She's a smart girl. She will figure out how to survive wherever she ends up.

"Why do you look like you're about to drown a cat?" Louie asks.

"Who the fuck drowns a cat?" I throw back. "I gotta go see Laura. Catch you later."

I'm fucking pissed that my friends missed the fact that Laura was getting her nose dirty. How the fuck did they not know? I've been with her as much as possible over the last week and she's been clean, as far as I can tell.

I get to Laura's house and climb through her bedroom window. She's not in here but the adjoining bathroom door is slightly ajar. So I walk over, push it open, and find her on the floor.

She looks at me and shifts her body to the side. *What is she doing?*

Then she rolls onto her back and closes her eyes.

"Laura? What? No!" I drop to my knees, pick up her head, and slap her cheeks. Her eyes blink open at me.

"E? You came back." She smiles, her gaze unfocused.

"What did you do?" I ask her.

"What you couldn't... I killed your weakness so you can become the greatest," she says, her words slurred. "I love you."

"What are you talking about? Laura, what the fuck did you take?" I look around the bathroom. That's when I see the syringe sticking out of her right arm.

Just as I'm about to pull it out, her entire body shakes and foam bubbles out of her mouth.

"No!" I scream and hold her against me. "Don't do this," I tell her. "I have a plan!"

There's no response, though. Instead, she goes limp in my arms.

I don't know how long I've been sitting here. But when I finally stand, with the lifeless body of the girl I love in my arms, I smile. "You wanted to create a monster, Papa? Now you have."

I will become the monster he wants. I'll become the monster who destroys him too.

# Chapter One

"You look exhausted, Evie." The concerned tone comes from my employee.

"Well, thanks. That's just the look I was going for, Amy, *tired*. You know it's trending, right?"

I quirk a manicured brow at her.

"I don't mean to offend. Just... if you want to take off early, I can close up here." She waves a hand around the store. It's been a quiet but steady day.

I own a little boutique, Evie's Vault. This shop is my baby. My pride and joy. I love being here, probably more than I like being at home, and more often than not, you'll find me right in this spot.

There's something satisfying about being able to help people find that perfect outfit, being able to offer them advice and make sure all the right assets are flattered in their choice of clothing. Some people would call me vain for caring so much about appearances. They don't get it, though. The right outfit can change your entire day.

If you feel good in what you're wearing, that good feeling sinks right down to your soul, and your entire attitude shifts. If you feel like shit, well, you're going to feel like shit all day. And take it from me, self-doubt isn't easy to live with. Which is why having the right outfit is more important than people realize.

Also, I'm a southern lady. I was raised to never leave the house without looking my absolute best. A real-life beauty pageant queen. That's me. Or at least it was me before I quit the circuit three years ago and opened my shop.

Best decision I ever made. Although it was more of an escape. The glamor and glitter of the pageant world are only there to hide the evil that resides within it. The monsters who disguise themselves as good people.

My mind drifts to my mother. I haven't spoken to her in three years. All I was to her was a meal ticket. She loved my beauty. She never loved me. The funny thing is, that beauty that she loved so much, it's only skin deep. A mask to hide the ugliness underneath.

Like I said, the right outfit shifts your mindset. If you look good, you feel good. For most people, that's true. For me, the right outfit is nothing but a mask to hide the scars that are burned so deep into my soul I will never be free of them.

But I'm okay. I escaped. I have a million things to be thankful for. I have a successful business. I have my two best friends. Rachel and Charlotte, who are more like sisters. The moment I need them, I know they will drop everything and come running.

I've never bothered my friends with my issues, though. They wouldn't understand. They love me and they would try, but they don't know what it's like to live with the memories I have. They don't have to fear falling asleep.

I shake off those thoughts, because those kinds of thoughts don't belong here. In my happy place. I refuse to tarnish my shop with the memories.

"I'm fine, honestly. You go ahead and take off, honey. I'm just going to straighten a few things out," I tell Amy.

"I can stay," she offers.

"No, seriously, go home to that hunky boyfriend of yours. Enjoy your night." I laugh at her reddening cheeks. Amy's boyfriend is the town's most-eligible bachelor. She snapped him up off the market a year ago and there are still women mourning their losses over it.

I have no interest in him. I just like to see her blush whenever he's mentioned. I like sex. Don't get me wrong. I just have no interest in relationships. I'm far too damaged to be worthy of anyone else's commitment. And I've accepted that. I'm okay with it. It's better this way.

"Okay, I'll go. But if you need anything, just call," Amy says as she walks into the back room, returning with her purse a few moments later.

"I won't need anything." I chuckle. "But I appreciate the offer."

The bell on the door rings as she leaves and I heave a sigh of relief. Alone. Sometimes I love just being alone. It's easier. I don't have to pretend. I don't have to wear the fake smile or be the person everyone else needs me to be. I can just be... me.

After locking the door, I turn up the volume on

the radio and start reorganizing the dresses on the sale rack. This is what gives me peace, sorting everything, making sure the store is perfect.

Another two hours and I find myself walking through the front door of my house. It's a small cottage, but it's mine. And just like my store, I'm proud to own it. No one can take it from me. I know I won't be sleeping tonight, so I turn on the television and flick through until I find something I can binge.

Sleep isn't something I do often. I used to try every night, but then I gave up. Insomnia rules my life. When I do eventually fall asleep, I'll be out of it for up to twenty-four hours. That's only when my body can't physically handle being awake any longer. Until then, I don't fight it. I just find things to keep myself occupied.

When my phone rings and Charlotte's name pops up on the screen, I jump to answer it. My friend was supposed to be married this past weekend. She ended up finding her fiancé in bed with her sister instead and then took off to Las Vegas without telling anyone. She just recently turned her phone back on and called Rachel and me, telling us that she was... getting to know some new guy.

It's quick. But honestly, her fiancé was an ass and my friend deserves to be happy. So I've encouraged her to follow through and have fun with this guy in

Vegas. I even offered to come out and see her there. I don't particularly want to. I've avoided that city for years...

"Charlotte, what's happening?" I ask as soon as I answer her video call.

"I messed up," she says, giving me an eyeful of her boobs.

"Okay, but did you do that with clothes on or did that happen afterwards?" I try not to laugh at her.

"Shit! Sorry." I can hear her fumbling with the phone.

"It's fine. What happened?"

"I went out. I was going to just go out by myself after I spoke to you and Rachel," Charlotte explains, which is exactly what we urged her to do.

"Yep, and then what?"

"The moment I stepped outside the casino, Owen was there. He grabbed me and dragged me to the side,"

"He *what*? Are you okay?" I get up and head into my bedroom, pacing the length of the floor.

"I'm fine. I told him to go home. That I knew what he and Melanie did. And then I returned to my room and just went to sleep."

"Okay, so how did you mess up?"

"Louie came home. Saw I was there and brought

me back to his place, but then he saw the bruise," she says in one long breath.

"What bruise?" I pause in my tracks. *Hell no! Some cheating douchebag did not put his hands on my best friend.*

Charlotte moves the phone until I'm looking at the palm-shaped bruise on her arm.

"What the hell, Charlotte? Owen did that?" I yell at the screen.

"Yeah, when he grabbed me. But I'm fine." She nods, her teeth sinking into her bottom lip.

"I'm going to kill him," I tell her.

"I think Louie might beat you to it," she whispers.

"Good. I hope he does." I don't usually wish violence on anyone, but fuck Owen.

"No, Evie, I'm serious. He lost his mind. As soon as he saw my arm, he kept asking me who did it and I told him and then he got dressed and he..." Charlotte trails off. She's not saying something.

"He what?" I swear to God, if he hurt her too, I'm going to be digging holes all over the Nevada desert.

"He has guns, Evie. He opened a safe in his closet. He took guns. Told me to go to bed and that he'd be back," Charlotte whispers.

"Okay, calm down. It's going to be okay. Wait...

Are we even worried about Owen? I mean, he kinda deserves whatever he gets." Also, I hate to break it to her, but we're from the south. We grew up around guns. The fact that this Louie guy has them isn't that big of a deal.

"Evie! We don't want anyone dead!" Charlotte gasps.

"Right. You're right." I nod. "*But*... if anyone has to die, Owen is a good choice," I add with a shrug.

"Evie? Why would someone have a safe full of guns?"

"Ah... I'm not sure, but I have an idea. What did you say Louie's last name was?" I ask, knowing full well she didn't give us a last name. Otherwise I would have already Googled him. I open my laptop, ready to do just that.

"Louie Giuliani."

"Holy shit, I mean, I knew he was hot after that quick peek. But, Sweet Mother Mary, this man is fine, Charlotte." I let out a whistle when picture after picture of Louie Guiliani of Las Vegas fills my screen.

"He really is." She sighs.

"Ah... Charlotte?" I pause, reading the news article I just clicked on.

"What?"

"Have you looked him up, like at all?" I ask her.

"No. Why?"

"He owns casinos, as in *multiple*. On the Vegas strip."

"I know," she tells me.

"There... ah... there are also some articles that suggest he's involved in the criminal underworld." I keep my voice low, unsure why I'm even whispering. It just feels like this is something you shouldn't say out loud.

"What? That's ridiculous. Why would he be involved in the criminal underworld?"

"Why wouldn't he be? He's a casino owner. *In Vegas*. He has a safe full of guns, and he's gone after a cop because the guy hurt you." Holy shit, he might actually kill Owen. My best friend is shacking up with a mobster. And she's in that city all alone.

"Well, when you put it like that, it doesn't sound good. But... he's not a bad person, Evie."

"You don't know him," I remind her. Spending two days with someone does not mean that you know them.

"But I know that he's good. He's... I don't know how I know. I just know that he's not bad," Charlotte insists.

"I think you should come home. I don't like the idea of you being out there by yourself," I say, before adding in a hushed voice, "You're in bed with a mobster."

"Actually, I'm in bed alone right now, and it's the most comfortable bed I've ever slept on." She smiles.

"Probably 'cause it's paid for in blood money." I laugh. "Look, I'm just worried about you. But I'm also excited *for you*. It's been a long time since you've done anything for yourself." I'm torn between insisting she comes home and letting her have... fun?

"I know." Charlotte sighs. I haven't seen her this content in a really long time. Maybe the stories are made up. Surely, he's not *actually* a mobster. But if he is...

"And if it's a mobster you want to do, then just... maybe learn how to shoot a gun or something. You might need it," I suggest.

"Funny."

"I really am booking a flight. I'm coming to see for myself that you're safe."

"What about the store? You can't just leave." Charlotte sits up on the bed.

"It'll be fine. I'm coming. I'll be there tomorrow... or I mean *today*."

After chatting a little longer and booking my flight, I end the call.

"Go to sleep. I'll be there soon," I tell Charlotte. "Love you too."

Shit, I need to pack a bag! I'm doing this. I'm going back to Vegas. My best friend needs me and I'm not going to let her down. I will be fine.

I send a message to Amy to let her know I won't be in for a couple of days. Her reply comes quick with an *okay* and a *have fun and relax.*

Yeah, 'cause that's going to happen. *Relax* and *Vegas* are not two words that belong together.

# Chapter Two

Las Vegas, the city of hell. There was a time when I would have done anything to come back here. Now, all this city represents to me is failure. My biggest failure. If it weren't for my friends, I'd never return.

Them and business. As much as I hate this city, I love money more. I planted my own little spy in my friend Louie's casino six months ago. I got a tip that shit was about to go down in Vegas. People were making moves to take the so-called key to the kingdom from Louie.

That shit was never going to happen on my watch. I always knew my friends would go places. All three of them were way too fucking determined to make a name for themselves not to raise to the top. Which is exactly where they sit now and where I plan on keeping them.

They have no clue as to the trouble that's coming for them. It's better they don't. Besides, my plant is the fucking best in the business. If Lailani can't get them out of the shit coming their way, then no one can. Her five-hundred grand a week paycheck is well fucking earned.

I didn't tell her I was coming to town. It's fun to try to throw her off her game a bit, and honestly, the past six months have been... boring. It's time for some entertainment, and frustrating Lailani is one of my favorite forms of entertainment. She is the single most lethal person I know—other than myself, of course. My enforcers fear her. Which is why, when she's frustrated, anything could happen.

I feel sorry for the poor fucker who dares to fall for that woman, though. He will have his work cut out for him. And with Lailani being part of my trusted inner circle, whoever thinks they can date her better be fucking worthy of her. Although, from what I hear, she's spending an awful lot of time getting to know one of my friends. If anyone was worthy of her, it's Sammie. Even if he has no idea who she really is.

The jet touches down. I wait for the stairs to lower and my men to exit first. They form two lines, leaving a gap down the center for me to walk through. I smile... to hide the fact I'm fucking dying on the inside. I hate being back here.

I greet the man in front of me with outstretched arms. "Louie, it's been far too long, my friend."

"It has. How was the flight?" he asks, returning my embrace.

"Bumpy. Thought I was a goner for a bit there." I laugh, but I really did think that fucking jet was going down. I've already told my second-in-command to have a replacement ready for the return trip.

"Let's get out of here. It's fucking hot." Louie directs me to a line of waiting SUVs.

"Carlo, you're looking old," I say in greeting.

It hasn't gotten past me that someone's missing. Sammie. No doubt Louie has him watching the woman who's suddenly captured my friend's attention. It's why I'm here. I need to make sure this chick is legit and not working with the fucking enemy. Of all people, it would be Louie who'd make the mistake of falling for the enemy.

"Working will do that to you. You should try it sometime." Carlo slaps a hand on my back.

"I'll keep that in mind." I laugh and follow my friends towards the car.

—————

"This city never changes," I say, staring up at the Vegas skyline. I've frequented this city a hundred times and yet it remains the same.

"From your lips to God's ears," Louie replies.

"Where's Sammie? He didn't want to come greet me?" I watch Louie's face. He's good. Not a single thing gives him away. That doesn't mean he's not lying.

"He's working."

"Right. Well, we'll party tonight. Where we going?" I raise a brow. If he's hiding this woman from me, he's gonna want me as far from here as possible.

As expected, Louie says, "Aces." Carlo's home turf while Sammie manages the Wild Card casino.

I stare at my friend. "What's wrong with the Royal? Am I not worthy of being royal?"

Without missing a beat, Louie says some shit about new strippers at Aces. I'm not one to turn down the female form. He's dangling that carrot on a stick, hoping I'll bite. "It's also where the game is set for tonight, if you want to buy in," he adds and then drops, "I've had your bags delivered to Aces."

"I'm staying there too?" It takes everything in me not to laugh. He's trying really fucking hard to keep me away from this girl.

"Yep," he says as the car comes to a stop. "Now, come on. Let's get a drink."

Walking through the casino floor, I spot Lailani working behind the reception desk. She does a double-take when she sees me. I have no doubt she'll message me as soon as she can.

A few minutes later, I'm sitting across from my friend with a drink in hand. I wait. He wants something. I came here under the guise of letting loose, not discussing business. And yet, here we are. Sitting in his office.

"Let's cut to the chase so we can get to the party part of the night. This is Vegas after all," I say, leaning forward. "What do you want, Louie? Why'd you summon me here?"

He didn't, but it sounds better if I make it seem like my being here was his idea. The asshole knows what I've done too. He did call... about four weeks ago. I ignored his request for a meeting then. I was busy. But I'm not now.

Louie pours us each a glass of whiskey, sliding one across the desk to me. "I need more product." He looks me dead in the eye. My face remains a mask of indifference as I wait for him to continue. "The shipments are moving faster than I anticipated. The demand is through the roof."

My lips tilt up at the sides as I bring the glass to them. "More cocaine, huh? I figured as much. How much *more* we talking?"

"Double the last order," he asks, watching me.

I lean back in my chair, the amber liquid swirling in my glass as I consider his request. My father taught me to never show your cards, to always take your time and think about what you're going to say before you say it. "You know the risks involved, Louie. Doubling the shipment means doubling the heat. You really think you can move double?"

He nods his head. "I've got everything under control. My network here is solid, and I've taken extra precautions. This is a calculated decision."

My eyes narrow in on my friend. Now's not a good time for these fuckers to be expanding. They've got no fucking idea what's lurking in the shadows of their own fucking city. Of course I can't tell them that. I'd rather sort the problem out and have them never know it existed in the first place.

"All right. I'll make the arrangements. But know this: If anything goes south, it's your head."

"Understood," he says. "You'll get your payment upfront, just like always."

I raise my glass towards him. "I know I will." Because friend or not, I will remove his fucking head if he tried to steal from me.

When we exit Louie's office, Carlo and Sammie are waiting for us, along with my men. "I'll meet you guys over at Aces. I've got a few things to tie up here," Louie says.

I look at him. He really must like this woman to go to such great lengths. I make a mental note to have Paz dig more intel up on *Charlotte*. So far, her story adds up. A southern girl, a runaway bride, broken-hearted and all that bullshit. I don't like the fact that my friend is making himself so fucking vulnerable, though.

*Love is a weakness we need to kill.* My father's words echo through my head. Fucking asshole, he wouldn't know a thing about love.

Deciding my friend really doesn't trust me to meet his girl, I turn my attention to Sammie, quickly slapping a hand on his shoulder. My pocket vibrates, so I drop my arm and pull out my phone. Smiling to myself when I see Lailani's nickname on my screen.

KILLER WOMAN:

Why didn't you tell me you were in
town?

She insists we aren't friends. Her text would suggest otherwise.

ME:

That seems like something a friend
would do, and we are not friends,
remember?

KILLER WOMAN:

You really need to let that go. How
long are you staying?

ME:

Until I leave.

I pocket my phone and laugh again, picturing how twisted up all the unknowns are making her.

---

I sit at the bar. My eyes glued to the woman on the stage. But I have no interest in the entertainment. What does have my interest is the reason my friend is lying to me.

"Who is she?" I ask, calling him out.

"Who is who?" Louie looks around the room.

"The one who has your balls in her clutches. You haven't even blinked at any of  'em." I wave a hand towards the stage. "And I know you. If you're not interested in anything on the menu here, you have someone else. Who is she?"

"*She* is none of your business," he says with a clenched jaw.

"Ah, so I was right. You went and found yourself a wife. Never thought I'd see the fucking day." I shake my head.

"I don't have a wife." The asshole rolls his eyes at me. He's fucking lucky he's my friend. Otherwise those eyeballs would be rolling around on the goddamn ground.

"If she's special enough for you to want to hide her from your friends, and you clearly aren't interested in other options, then maybe she should be made a wife."

"What the fuck would you know about wife material? Your longest relationship has been... what? Five hours?" he scoffs.

Two years. Laura and I dated for two years before I failed her. "I don't have a need or a want for a wife," I say, instead of correcting him. I don't want to think about her. Especially not in this city.

"And I do?" He raises a brow at me.

"If you found someone willing to put up with

your sorry ass, keep her. She's clearly one of a kind."
My laughter is loud, overtaking the music.

"Fuck off. It's not that serious," he grumbles.

"Sure it's not. Where is she?"

"Not here," Louie grunts.

My eyes close tighter as I stare at him and my hand lifts to rest over my heart. "You don't trust me? I'm hurt."

"I don't trust anyone. You know that." Louie shakes his head.

It's true. It's also smart. "We've been friends for a long time, Louie," I remind him. "There are very few people I would consider a friend. You are one of them. I wouldn't do anything to someone important to you." *Unless they gave me a reason to.*

"Unless you wanted to get at me for something," he says, as if he can read my thoughts. "Women and children aren't off-limits in your organization."

He's right again. No one is off-limits. It's how we stay on top. "Then I guess you best not give me a reason to hurt you." I smile and tap his shoulder. "*Relax.* Things are changing in Mexico. My tyrant father is dead."

It's only half true. Things aren't changing, not as quickly as I'd like them to anyway.

"Yeah, and how'd that go down, exactly?" he asks me.

"Better you don't know. Like I said, I don't want to have to kill you," I tell him. "Now, get out of here. You look sad and you're scaring away the girls."

"I'll catch up with you tomorrow. Welcome back to town." Louie stands and walks out.

I watch him leave before turning my attention to Carlo and Sammie. "Please tell me you two fuckers still know how to party."

"You think you can keep up, old man?" Carlo grins while refilling my glass.

"You think I can't?" I counter.

# Chapter Three

I arrived in Vegas an hour ago, and now I'm giving Charlotte a makeover in a very luxe hotel suite. I know it's going to make her feel like a million dollars. I've always loved playing dress-up with Charlotte. She's a natural beauty, with 1950s pinup curves I could only dream of having one day. Giving someone a makeover when they're already beautiful is easy work.

"You know, you're glowing. Whatever sex you're having, obviously it's good." I smirk at my friend.

"I agree." Rachel's voice comes through the speaker. Charlotte and I video-called her so she wasn't left out. Rachel is a first-year resident at the local hospital back home. She can't just up and leave as easy as I did.

"The best." Charlotte smiles wide, and my heart fills with happiness for her.

She deserves this. To be happy. She was stuck in a dead relationship for years. Rachel and I both asked her if she really wanted to go through with that wedding and she kept insisting she did, so we dropped it and went along with her plans.

It's shitty that it ended the way that it did for her, with her fiancé fucking her sister and all, but I'm not sorry she got out. Because now she can finally be herself. She can finally be happy.

I dig through my makeup bag until I find what I'm looking for and pull out the red lip stain I bought just for Charlotte. It matches perfectly with her dark locks.

I also hope it will be a nice distraction after hearing the news that her ex is dead. He was found in a hotel room, right here in Vegas. Overdose. Which wasn't like him at all. Owen was an asshole, sure. But he wasn't into drugs. Charlotte hasn't said anything, but we're both thinking it. This guy she's been dating, Louie, I'm almost positive he had something to do with it.

I say good riddance, though. That asshole broke my best friend's heart and wasted years of her youth. Do I think he deserved to die? Probably not, but I'm not sad about it either. My emotions are also easily deflected, my walls so high when it comes to caring about anyone that isn't Charlotte or Rachel. I would do anything for those two women.

Even jumping on a plane in the middle of the night to fly across the country. It's not as hard being back here as I thought it would be. There are loads of things to distract me. For an insomniac such as myself, this is the perfect city. There's always something happening. I'm trying out the *glass is half full* thing.

"Blot," I tell Charlotte after painting her lips a bright red and holding some folded tissue up to her mouth.

She does as instructed without complaint. I know she's doing it for me. She actually hates being my Barbie. It helps take my mind off the fact that I'm here. In Vegas. Again. I won't allow my past to dictate my happiness, which is why whenever those thoughts come up, I shove them down and refocus on my friend.

"I think this is my best work yet!" I exclaim, spinning Charlotte around so she can look in the mirror.

"Holy shit." Charlotte gasps the moment she sees her reflection.

I've put her in a tiny white dress with a low-cut neck and a high-cut hem. It fits her like a glove. I packed it just for her. I'll admit I was nervous about putting her in white. I wasn't sure if it'd give off wedding vibes.

"You look fuckable," I tell her. "It's a real shame I'm not into girls."

"I think Louie would kill you if you tried to hit on me." Charlotte laughs and then suddenly stops. Her eyes widen. "I'm a horrible person, Evie." She slumps onto the bed.

"Why would you think that?" I ask her.

"Because Owen is dead, and it's my fault." She sighs before whispering, "And... I really think Louie did it."

"Do you want to go home? I will find a way to get you out of this city without anyone knowing." I don't know how, seeing as she has a fucking babysitter in the living room. But I will find a way.

"That's the thing, Evie..." Charlotte looks like she's about ready to burst into tears.

"What?"

"I don't want to leave. I want to be with him. I want to stay with him. Even if he did it," she admits. "What kind of person does that make me?"

Someone who is blinded by love... or dickmatized. Probably the latter. She can't possibly love this man after just a few days.

"You are one of the kindest, most loyal, most trustworthy people I know, Charlotte. There isn't a terrible bone in your body. I've never even heard you utter the words *bless your heart* to anyone. You are a good person. So who cares if you want to spend some time getting thoroughly fucked by a god? That doesn't make you bad," I tell her.

"He's a murderer, Evie."

"With a good dick," I add.

"Well, yeah, but he killed Owen," she says in a hushed tone.

"First, I doubt he's killing people with his dick, which is the part of him you're addicted to. And second, we don't know that for sure. Neither of us was there. We didn't see anything."

"Just because you don't see something, doesn't mean it didn't happen," she says.

My heart picks up speed. I know better than anyone how true that is.

"I know that." My hands shake. I can feel the sweat on my forehead.

"Shit, Evie, I'm sorry." Charlotte jumps off the bed and wraps her arms around me. "I've been so focused on my own issues I didn't think about what I was saying."

"It's okay," I whisper, holding on to her tighter.

"It's not. But we will be. Both of us," she says.

*She* will be. Me? I'm never going to be okay again. I can fake it, though.

Stepping back out of her embrace, I shake the sadness away and plaster on my best beauty-queen smile. "Right, well, enough of this melancholy. We're in Vegas and we are going to have a good time."

"We are. But you need to change. You are not putting me in a slutty dress and heels while you're staying in Chucks." Charlotte points to my feet.

I peer down at myself. I'm still wearing the denim dress I put on in the airport bathroom. It was the first thing I did after I got off the flight. I went into the restroom, washed my face, and reapplied a fresh layer of makeup. I was not showing up here not looking my best.

"Okay, I'll change, but I need to shower first," I tell her.

"Through there. I'll be out in the living room

with Sammie. Take your time," Charlotte says before disappearing through the bedroom door.

I shut myself inside the bathroom, turn on the hot water, and let the space steam up as I undress. I avoid looking in the mirror. I hate seeing myself naked. Don't get me wrong. I know I'm beautiful. How could I not? I've been told just how beautiful I am throughout my entire life. It's because of that beauty that I hate my reflection. Nothing good has ever come from it.

Actually, that's not entirely true. I could use my looks to my advantage if I wanted to. I never do, or at least I try not to. But I can't help it if people treat me differently based on how I appear on the outside. That's on them, not me.

What I can do is avoid the truth, and that's something I have down to a fine art.

I step into the shower and let the water wash over me, piling my hair on top of my head to avoid getting it wet. I don't want to keep Charlotte too long, and if I have to do a full blowout, she'll be waiting a while.

After cleansing my entire body, I rinse off the suds and repeat the process. I do this three times before I get out my sugar scrub and rub at my skin. I take my shower process very seriously. This routine keeps everything silky-smooth.

Once I'm out of the shower, I tap my skin dry with a soft towel before applying a floral-scented lotion. This is then repeated with a floral-scented body oil. When I'm done, I wrap a towel around myself and wipe the fog away from the mirror.

"Right, time to fix yourself, Evie," I whisper to my bare-faced reflection.

There are days I wish I could go out without a speck of makeup on. What would people think if they saw the tiny freckles that dot my nose? Would they notice that my skin sometimes blotches? Would they treat me differently?

Today is not the day I'm going to find out.

I walk into the bedroom and retrieve my makeup bag, and forty minutes later, my hair and face are perfectly done. Next, I dig into my bag and pull out my black leather shorts and matching black corset. I told Charlotte I would get dressed up just as slutty as I made her. For me, that's easy. I'm used to people staring at me. It doesn't matter what I wear. They still stare.

Sometimes I think they know. That they can see under the mask. But they don't. No one bothers to look any deeper than surface level. Well, nobody other than Rachel and Charlotte. But even they don't know the full extent of my ugliness. Charlotte knows some. Rachel knows even less than that. It's a burden I choose to keep to myself. It's easier that way.

I pair my outfit with a cute red-bottomed ankle boot. Running my fingers through my hair one more time, I check out my reflection from the back. Once I'm satisfied with the outcome, I walk out of the bedroom and go in search of Charlotte.

It's time to show this town how southern girls turn it up.

# Chapter Four

I assisted in ridding this earth of a pig last night. Louie's girlfriend is a runaway bride. Of course, I already knew that part. Her ex turned up looking for her, and when he found her, he made the mistake of leaving a bruise on her, and Louie would never let that slide.

I understand his motives. Me? I just went along for the ride. Besides, killing cops is a fun little hobby of mine. It wasn't until I watched Louie shove a syringe into the asshole's arm that I started having issues with the situation. I was helping Carlo hold the fucker down, but all I could see was Laura on that bathroom floor...

It took everything in me not to fucking crack right then. I held myself together though, because that's what we do. One lesson my father taught me that I'm thankful to him for. No matter the situation, never let your feelings show. I mastered that after I lost Laura. It was easy, because other than her loss, I didn't feel a goddamn thing.

As soon as I parted ways with Louie, I ditched my men and came here. It's where I've been sitting all fucking night. In front of the unmarked grave, knowing that Laura's decomposing body is right below me. No one knows what happened to her. I didn't tell a single person. My father assumed I killed her and I let him think that. Until I knew he was about to take his last breath and I told him the truth. She killed herself.

Not that it matters. She might have pushed that needle into her arm, but she did it because of me. I never found out how she knew what I was supposed to do. I always suspected it was my father, but without solid proof, that's all it is. A suspicion.

I don't know why I come here. To punish myself? Remind myself of my failures? Whatever the reason, it's calming being here with her. It took years for me to realize that whatever Laura and I had, it wasn't love. We were kids. Infatuation, sure. She was and still is the most beautiful person I've ever seen. But she didn't love me.

She killed herself to escape the reality of who she was dating. She didn't know who my father was when we first met, who I was destined to be. I told her the truth about six months later. She didn't seem too fazed at first, but then she'd start to mention little things. About getting out, running away…

At the time, I didn't think much on it. Now, I know she didn't want me to be who I was born to be. Fuck, I didn't want to become who I am today. But this is real life, and I wouldn't change who I am for anyone.

I like that she's dead. I mourned her at first, until realization hit me one day. She's dead. No one else can ever have her. She was mine. She is mine and mine alone. Nobody knows she's here but me. I don't think anything else has ever been completely mine before, and I fucking like owning it. Her.

I get why my father fought so fucking hard to maintain his spot at the top of the food chain. The money, the power, it's addictive. The more I have, the more I want. And I'm not about to let any motherfucker take it from me.

My palm wraps around the handle of my gun the moment I hear the crunching of leaves behind me.

"Jefe, I got you some food." My second-in-command comes into view as he places a Styrofoam box in front of me and then a cup of coffee.

"Gracias." I look down at the box. I'm not hungry. I do pick up the coffee cup, though. "How'd you find me?" I ask him.

"It's my job to know where you are," Paz says, sitting down beside me.

"Did you find anything else out about Charlotte?" I need to know who this woman is, considering my friend was all too willing to kill a cop for her. I need to know everything about her. I will not let my friend fall on a sword he doesn't see coming.

"She's clean, jefe," Paz says. "A real-life southern woman."

"Good. I'd hate to see what'd happen to this city if Louie got his heart stomped on," I grunt.

"Your mother wants to see you..."

"Of course, she does," I groan. The last thing I want to deal with right now is my mother. "She in town?"

"At the house." Paz nods.

"I'll deal with her later. I gotta see Lailani," I tell him.

"Need me to come?" he asks, then adds, "What

am I saying? It's Lailani, of course you do." He shakes his head.

"I'm not scared of her." I laugh.

"You should be," he mutters.

"Make sure everything is set up for the drop. We're leaving here first thing tomorrow."

Now that I know Charlotte is legit and not a threat, I don't need to stay. I do need to check in on Lailani and make sure she's still focused on her job, though.

As I stand, I wipe at the dirt on my slacks. "You did get a new jet, right?"

"Sure did, jefe. It's a good one." Paz smirks.

"Good. Blowing up in a ball of flames is not how we go down," I tell him.

"No, we'll go down in a gruesome war." The psychopath smiles at the thought.

"I have no doubt," I agree. Because in this life, that's how everyone goes out. It's how my father went out. Or at least, that's what the world believes. The only two people who know the truth are me and the old man. And since one of us is dead, that secret will stay in the grave with him.

I send a message to Lailani as I walk towards the car.

ME:

I'm heading to your apartment.
Meet me there.

LAILANI:

Are you summoning me? Because
you're not the boss of me, E.

ME:

Who pays your wage?

LAILANI:

I'll meet you there, but just know
you're cock-blocking me.

ME:

Yeah? Whose cock?

I know it's Sammie. He won't tell anyone about them for some fucked-up reason, though.

LAILANI:

Not yours.

A shudder runs through me. I love the girl but she's more like a sister.

ME:

I'm going to need therapy if you put
that image in my head again.

When I get to Lailani's door, I let myself in. She's not here. So I drop down on the sofa and wait for her to arrive.

"You look like..." I stop talking and grin when she lands me with a glare.

"Please, let yourself in," she says, sarcasm dripping from her lips.

"Nice place." I smirk as I look around the small living room.

"It's a shithole, but it's what a struggling college student can afford." She shrugs. "Is there a reason for this visit, E?"

"Can't a friend just check up on a friend?" I raise a brow at her.

Lailani's lips twitch at the corners. "You don't have friends."

"Ouch." My hand rubs over my heart. "This Charlotte woman checks out."

"That could have been an email." Lailani busies herself in her kitchen making coffee. For herself.

"I didn't want a drink. It's okay," I tell her when she sits down across from me.

"Great, what *do* you want?" she asks.

"I really did just come to check that you were doing okay." I lean forward, my forearms resting on my thighs. "You seem... happy?"

"Orgasms have a way of doing that to a girl." She smirks.

My entire face screws up. "Don't hurt him."

"What if he hurts me?"

I laugh. "I'd say I'd kill him, but you'd beat me to it." I stand and walk over to her. "Stay focused. I'm leaving town tomorrow."

"I'm always focused," she counters.

"Good chat," I say with a wave of a hand and walk out of her apartment, making sure not to be seen by anyone. I don't need my friends knowing that Lailani works for me. Not yet anyway.

---

My mind is playing tricks on me. I've finally lost it and now I'm fucking seeing things. Because standing just a few feet away from me is... Laura. My Laura. Which is insane because my Laura is dead. I'm seeing dead people.

She's standing with Louie and Charlotte— judging by the pictures in the file I have on her. Louie's back stiffens the moment he spots me.

I keep my eyes firmly fixed on Laura's ghost, afraid she's going to vanish if I look away. But the closer I get, the more I realize it's not her. No, this woman might be Laura's doppelgänger but she's not *her*. What she is, is breathtakingly beautiful. And there's a look in her eyes that's holding me captive. She's hiding something and I instantly want to know what it is.

"Louie, are you going to introduce me to your friends?" I ask, stopping a few feet short of his entourage.

"Emmanuel, this is Charlotte, my girlfriend. And this is Evie." He makes a point of putting extra emphasis on the woman's name. He knows as much as I do exactly who she looks like.

I look to his girl. "Well, Charlotte, it's a pleasure to meet the woman who's captured this old bastard's heart." And then my full attention turns to the gorgeous strawberry-blonde in front of me.

*Evie*. Her name rolls around on my tongue. I like it.

"Charlotte, take Evie over to the bar. I'll meet you in there," Louie says. I'm about to order them to stay. I'm not done looking at this girl when Charlotte's thick southern accent has me glancing her way.

"Sure. It was nice to meet you."

"You too." I nod, before returning my gaze to Evie.

Louie spins around, blocking my view. "Don't," he growls.

"Don't what?" I lift a single brow. No one—and I mean fucking *no one*—tells me what I can and can't do.

"I know that look. I've seen it before. Evie isn't her," he says.

"Isn't who?" I tilt my head to the side as I brace myself for what he's about to say. Her name. My friends all know better by now.

"Laura."

I feel my jaw twitch as I look Louie dead in the eye. "I don't know who you're talking about."

"Right, and I'm fucking Father Christmas. Don't fuck with my girl's friend, Emmanuel." His words are meant to be a warning. But come off more as a challenge to me.

"I have no intention of fucking with her. Now, *fucking her*... that's not off the table." I smile at the thought before I make my way over to her.

Evie is like a fucking siren, calling me to my death. And yet, I can't turn away.

I squeeze myself between her and Charlotte and pivot in the seat. "Sorry, mi alma, we didn't get properly introduced. I'm Emmanuel." I hold out a hand.

The moment her skin touches mine, I know without a shadow of a doubt—dead or alive—this woman will be mine.

# Chapter Five

alm. That's the feeling that washes over my entire body when Emmanuel's hand covers mine. Until that calmness is quickly replaced with fire. I feel like every single nerve ending has just been sparked to life.

My throat goes dry as I swallow a lump. On the outside, I'm giving this man my very well-practiced pageant smile. On the inside, I'm burning up with a need I've never experienced before.

"Evie," I tell him, when I realize I've been staring far too long.

Emmanuel smiles, and with that simple gesture, the calmness comes back. He doesn't remove his hand from mine. It takes me pulling away for him to let go. As soon as he's no longer touching me, I regain a bit of my senses.

This man is dangerous. It's not the darkness of his eyes or the tattoos decorating his hands and neck and probably a lot more of his skin if it wasn't hidden by the custom-fitted black-on-black suit he's wearing. None of that is what makes me think he's dangerous. It's the way I want him to cover my hand with his again, the way I want him to smile at me like he is right now and never stop.

Choosing to ignore that thought and shove it way down in a spot never to be found, I turn my attention to Charlotte's boyfriend. I really have been eager to meet the guy who's managed to interest my friend so quickly.

"So, Louie, tell me. How'd you do it?" I ask him.

"Do what?" Louie looks at me.

"How'd you kill Charlotte's ex and make it look like an overdose?" I keep my eyes fixed on his face. His expression. Waiting for any sign that he's uncomfortable with the question. He doesn't give anything away as he assesses me right back.

"He didn't," Emmanuel says. "I did."

His voice... it shouldn't sound so good. Especially when admitting to murder. "Do you just go around killing all of your friends' girlfriends' exes?" I'm sure that he's joking. They didn't really kill Owen. At least that's what I'll continue to tell myself.

"Only the ones who leave bruises on my friend's girlfriends," Emmanuel replies, his gaze firmly on mine. Is he trying to throw me off?

"So, are you like an assassin or something?" I cant my head as I wait for his answer.

"No, but ever heard of the De La Sangre Cartel?"

"Fucking hell," Louie groans from the other side of the table.

Ignoring him, I keep my focus on Emmanuel. Because, well, it's not a hardship. The man is fucking gorgeous. "No, should I have?"

"Probably best you haven't. I run the organization."

"Emmanuel, really?" Louie grunts, shaking his head.

"So, you're supposed to be a big, scary drug lord or something?" I ask Emmanuel. "I don't see it. You don't look that scary."

It's a lie. He's plenty scary—although I would

never have expected a drug lord to be so damn good looking.

"He's full of shit. That's why. We didn't kill Owen," Louie says in a *don't ask questions* kind of way before turning to Charlotte. "What happened?"

*So he's allowed to ask questions. We're not. Got it.*

"Rachel said he was found in a hotel room. Overdosed. But it's strange... I mean, I know the guy was an asshole, but he didn't do drugs. He wasn't an addict," Charlotte repeats what we both heard from Rachel.

It's odd, though. Charlotte was with Owen for years and doesn't seem even the slightest bit upset over his death. I'm not judging my friend. I'm not the least bit bothered either.

"We also didn't think he was *doing* sisters but he did that too," I chime in. "I say good riddance. The asshole broke your heart. I just wish I could have been the one to end him. I even bought a shovel." I didn't, but I'm sure it wouldn't be hard to find one. I bet if I asked the *so-called* drug lord sitting next to me, he'd be able to help me.

"He didn't break my heart. My sister did," Charlotte corrects me.

"Semantics. So, tell me more about this cartel of yours. What exactly do you do other than kill people?" I shift my attention back to Emmanuel, to avoid discussing Charlotte and her sister. I know my friend and she is not ready to open that can of worms just yet.

Before Emmanuel can answer, he's interrupted by Louie. "You hungry? Let's order food."

I ignore him. "So the cartel business pays well, I assume?"

"It does." Emmanuel smirks. "What do you do?"

"I have my own empire too." I smirk. "A boutique. It's called Evie's Vault."

"Impressive. Do you enjoy it?" Emmanuel asks. He hasn't looked away from me once. It's a little unnerving having someone's undivided attention on you.

"I love it. I've always loved clothes," I tell him.

"Okay. Evie, I want to dance." I'm pulled to my feet by Charlotte. And I follow her out to the dance floor that no one is actually dancing on. "I don't think that guy is joking about the cartel," she whispers.

"I don't think he is either." I laugh. It's just my luck that the one guy I actually could see myself with turns out to be undesirable. Although I couldn't really be with him for more than one night anyway. Which isn't the worst idea.

"Stop flirting with him, Evie!" Charlotte shrieks.

"Why? A man like that knows how to fuck, Charlotte."

"This isn't a joke. I don't want anything to happen to you."

My body is pressed tighter against hers as we dance. "So, you're the only one who gets to jump into bed with a dangerous man? It's just sex. I'll be fine." I don't acknowledge the feelings he's bringing to the surface after a single platonic touch.

"Wait... You're already planning on spending the night with him?" Charlotte's eyes widen.

"No, I'm planning on spending a hot few hours with the man and then never seeing him again." I smile when I see my friend's Mr. Tall-Dark-and-Dangerous walking towards us. "Incoming."

"Can I cut in?" Louie asks me.

"Be my guest." I'm quick to escape Charlotte's stern glare. I mean, really, Emmanuel's probably talking nonsense. I've seen movies. Real criminals don't just admit their crimes. Or at least I don't think they would.

---

I don't know who, but someone suggested we go somewhere else, so I file in next to Charlotte as we both follow Louie to wherever it is we're going. The casino is busy, and a lot of people try to stop and talk to him and his friends along the way.

I keep flicking my eyes to Emmanuel, who warms my other side. There's a lot of men in suits gathered around us, a lot of Hispanic men. Maybe he *is* a drug lord. He seems too... clean-cut though and he smells even better than he looks.

Louie is stopped by some French woman, and when I hear her offer to meet him in her room later, I see red. I will not sit back and watch my friend get hurt again.

Stepping in front of Charlotte, I smile at the newcomer. "Oh, sweetheart, you clearly ain't got any of the good sense God gave a rock because you are so barking up the wrong tree right now."

"Who are you? And why are you here?" the woman asks, waving a hand towards me before her glass of champagne is tipped over on my dress.

I don't budge. "Bless your heart. You think a spilled drink is going to bother me?"

Before she can answer, an arm wraps around my waist from behind me, pulling me back. Emmanuel hisses something in Spanish and then two men are grabbing hold of the woman. "Miss, it's time to leave," one of them says in a thick Hispanic accent.

"Emmanuel, no," Louie growls out. "She's the daughter of the French president."

Emmanuel fires off something else to the two men, again in Spanish, and I'm now wishing I had taken the language in school. He then turns to me and his voice softens. "Are you okay?"

I shake out of his hold and glare back at him over a shoulder. "Sticky, but I'm not opposed to having this champagne licked off me." I wink before I rush forward to catch up with Charlotte.

We end up in a bar, somehow playing Truth or Dare, when one of Louie's friends tells me it's my turn.

"Dare," I call out, deciding to be careless. I mean, what could these mobsters actually dare me to do anyway?

Sammie, whose name I recently learned, smirks at me while pointing to a man in a suit by the bar. "I dare you to go hit on that guy and get his number."

I smile. "*Please*, that's like taking candy from a baby."

Did he really think that would be a challenge?

Shit, maybe he can see my ugliness. I'm trapped into the booth by Emmanuel, who doesn't get up to let me out. I don't bother asking him to move. Instead, I climb up onto the table and crawl across. Thankful I'm wearing shorts.

I put an extra swing into my hips and flick my hair over my shoulder as I approach the man. My hand lands on his bicep—*shit, he's ripped.* "Hey there, handsome. You look lonely. How about you give me your number so I can fix that problem for you." I bat my eyelashes at him.

The man in question is frozen, his stare deathly. He removes my hand from his arm like he's disposing of a rotten banana peel. "I'm good," he says.

"What?"

"You're not getting my number. Go back to your friends," he clarifies before turning his back on me.

I am so confused as I make my way over to the booth again. "He's gay," I announce.

"No, he's not." Sammie laughs. "He just wants to keep his head on his shoulders."

"Nope, he's gay. That's never happened to me before. Shit. Am I... Oh my god!" I shriek.

*This cannot be happening.*

"What?" Charlotte asks as I'm climbing back over the table.

"I'm losing it. I'm getting... old," I tell her, horrified by the thought.

"You have not lost it, mi alma. You are the single most beautiful thing I've ever laid my eyes on," Emmanuel says into my ear, and goose bumps erupt all over my skin.

*Holy hell, I want this man whispering all kinds of dirty things to me.*

# Chapter Six

I told Louie I wasn't going to fuck with Evie. Just *fuck her*. I take that back, because I don't have any intention of fucking and then leaving this woman. It's not often something catches my attention like she has, which is why I know she's different.

She's mine.

I could have put a bullet in that French bitch's head. There and then. I showed restraint, like a goddamn fucking saint. I'll keep my word. I won't touch the woman. But I've already instructed Paz to dig up dirt on her father, the French president. Because I *will* end him.

Like I said, my organization is changing. I don't intentionally go after women. That was my father's thing, not mine. Will I do it if need be? Sure. I do whatever has to be done.

My best friend since childhood just got hitched, Vegas-style. How we ended up in a little wedding chapel, I have no idea. But Evie was there, so you bet your ass I was following along.

Like I said, I've made up my mind. I'm keeping her. I don't care what I have to do to make that happen. If I piss off my oldest friend in the process, then so be it. I make the rules. I don't follow them.

Paz was all suited up at the bar, and I watched as Evie tried to flirt with him, thanks to Sammie's stupid fucking dare. Lucky for him, my second knows better and quickly turned her down. He left not long after that, sending me a message about getting shit ready for tomorrow.

We're leaving town. Or at least we were. Now, as I look at Evie and the huge grin plastered on her face as she talks on her phone to one of her friends, I think I've found a new reason to stick around.

It's stupid. The longer I spend in the States, the

more law enforcement I have gunning for me. I'm more than aware that the FBI would love to pin me down, lock me up, and throw away the fucking key. I'm not stupid enough to ever let that happen. That doesn't mean they won't try, though.

"I'm really sorry, Charlotte. I'm crashing." Evie's words catch my attention. I'm about to ask her what she means when Charlotte takes hold of her hand and starts guiding her outside.

"Okay, we'll go back to the hotel," Charlotte tells her. "Are you okay?"

I'm two steps behind Evie. She doesn't answer, just nods her head. There's something wrong. I don't know what, but she looks as if she's ready to pass out.

Charlotte tells Louie that they have to get back to the hotel, and like a lost fucking puppy, I follow them out to the car and climb into the front seat. I keep quiet, hoping that if I don't say anything, Evie might talk. She might let slip what's wrong with her. It crosses my mind to have a doctor meet us at the casino. She looks sick.

When I glance towards the back seat, I see her head resting against the door. She could just be tired.

"You might wanna wake her up. We're almost there," Louie says.

"I can't. She won't wake up for a while now," Charlotte replies.

My head snaps back again. "What do you mean?"

"She has insomnia. She stays awake for days at a time, and then she'll just crash and sleep for hours without getting up," Charlotte explains. "We won't be able to wake her."

The car stops out front of the Royal Flush. And as much as I want to tell them I'm taking Evie home—to my home because that's where I want to keep her—I don't. That would cause issues I don't want to deal with right now. The main one being Louie. The guy just got hitched. He'll be busy consummating his new marriage all night. And me? I'll be coming up with a plan to keep the maid of honor.

"It's okay," I tell Charlotte as I step out of the car. I open the back door, unbuckle Evie's belt, and scoop her into my arms. "I've got her."

It's not the first time I've had her body pressed against mine. But, fuck, does it feel good.

"Are you sure?" Charlotte asks me.

I nod. "Lead the way. Where is her room?" I'm going to assume it's on the top floor, right next to Louie's penthouse. That's where the crazy, obsessed fucker would have put Charlotte.

Sure enough, a few minutes later, we're riding the elevator up to the top floor before Charlotte opens the door to the penthouse suite right next to

Louie's. I set Evie on the bed and watch as Charlotte removes her friend's boots and then covers her with a blanket.

I don't want to leave, but it's easier if I don't have to answer questions. I walk out, get into the lift, and as soon as I'm sure Louie and Charlotte are inside his penthouse, I step into the hall and tap my all-access card against the door. I walk in and make myself comfortable in the chair opposite Evie's bed.

I take in every single feature of her face. She's still wearing makeup. So I stand and make my way into the bathroom. Digging through the huge fucking cosmetic bag until I find wipes. I pull out a few, sit on the edge of the bed, carefully brush her hair away from her cheek, and start wiping at the makeup. I want to see the real her without anything covering her up.

It takes a few of the disposable wipes to get it all off, and she doesn't even stir as I go about cleaning her face. Odd. I thought for sure she'd wake up.

I toss the used wipes into the trash bin in the bathroom before I pull my phone out and snap a photo of her. This is how I want to see her. Bare.

She's even more fucking breathtaking. Little freckles dot her nose, her cheeks have a natural shade of pink to them, and those lips... Fucking hell, pink, plump. I want to taste them.

Forcing myself to sit back down, I glance at my screen and message Paz.

ME:

> Change of plans. We're sticking around. Get my mother out of town. I might want to use the house and don't need her there.

I love my mother. She had a rough few years after my father found us. I believe my father loved her, though. That's why he kept her locked up in that house. I get it now. He didn't want anything to happen to her, and the safest place for her to be was captive.

But I saw how that same captivity broke my mother. It's not something I'd ever want to see happen to another woman I care about. Which is why I'm not grabbing Evie and walking out of here with her in my arms.

My phone buzzes in my hand and I tear my eyes away from her sleeping form again.

PAZ:

> Sure thing. You need anything tonight?

ME:

> I'm good.

Pocketing my phone, I go back to staring at my future. It hits me that I don't know much about this woman, other than the fact that she's from a small, fucking nowhere town and she owns a dress shop.

I bend and snatch up Evie's bag from the floor where Charlotte left it, digging through the contents until my hand brushes across her ID. I tug it out and read the name there. Evie Carter.

"Who are you, Evie Carter?" I ask aloud.

Next, I grab her phone and hold it to her face to unlock it. The first thing I do is open her social media accounts and scroll through them. There are tons of pictures of her with her friends, but none of her with other men. Which is fucking good. I don't need to be flying to the fucking south to kill anyone tonight.

Then I open her emails, making sure not to read any that she hasn't already opened. Most of them are from a girl named Amy, and they're all about her store. Pretty mundane stuff.

I don't get it. How can someone so fucking remarkable lead such a normal life?

---

I've been awake all night, waiting for Evie to open her eyes. When I check my watch, I see that it's a little after nine in the morning. Why the fuck isn't she awake yet?

She rolls over and I straighten, thinking this is it. But still, she doesn't stir. She does, however, start mumbling something I can't decipher. Her head shakes from side to side before she lets out a gut-wrenching scream.

"What the fuck?" I'm on my feet in seconds, but by the time I reach her, she's stopped screaming and is settled back against the covers.

There's only one reason someone would have nightmares like that. Something happened to her.

I storm out of her room and let myself into Louie's apartment. He meets me in the foyer. "Where's Charlotte?" I ask him. She's the one person who will have the answers I want.

"She's asleep. What the fuck are you doing here?" Louie grunts.

"Wake her up."

"I'm not doing that. What do you want, E?" he asks.

I reach behind my back, draw my pistol, and aim it at his head. "Wake her up!"

"I'm not waking up my wife for you." Louie crosses his arms over his chest.

Footsteps sound from the other end of the hall

before they get closer and then his new bride is right in front of me.

"Charlotte, go back to the bedroom." Louie tries to step in front of her.

"Don't move," I tell her, lowering my gun, because I don't actually want to scare the woman. "Something is wrong with Evie."

Charlotte shoves past Louie and stops right in front of me. "What? What happened?" she asks but she's already walking towards the door.

"She's talking in her sleep. I want to know what happened to her. Who the fuck is she talking about?"

The question stops Charlotte in her tracks. She spins around to face me. "She's probably having a nightmare. She has them from time to time. They're not real."

*She's lying.*

"How do you know she's talking in her sleep?" Charlotte glares at me with as much distrust as I feel for everyone around me at the moment.

"I was watching her," I admit while aiming an accusatory finger instead of the pistol that's itching to get back in my hands. "And you're lying to me."

Louie steps between us. "Don't fucking speak to her like that," he growls.

I ignore him. "I'm going to find out. You might as

well tell me, Charlotte. Someone did something to her, and I want to know who it was."

"I think that's something you should ask her. When she's awake, but don't expect her to open up to you. She doesn't talk about her past," Charlotte says.

She really is a loyal fucking friend. I've got a gun in my hand and she still won't tell me what I want to know.

Then something flickers across her face. "But say they were real... If you could find the person who caused those nightmares, what would you do about it?" she asks me.

"You don't want to know what I'll do, because those are the kind of nightmares that will keep *you* awake at night." I smile at the thought.

"Look, I don't know the full story, because like I said, she doesn't talk about it. But I'm sure if you dug into the pageant world, you'd find the reason behind her nightmares. That's all I'm saying. Anything else you want to know, you'll have to ask Evie," she says, and I know that's about as much as I'll get out of Charlotte.

"Thank you. I will ask her. When do you think she'll wake up?"

"I have no idea," Charlotte tells me.

I don't say anything else before I walk out of

Louie's penthouse and return to Evie's side. She hasn't moved. She's still fucking asleep.

I take my phone out and Google *insomnia* and the effects on the body. I want to know how to help her...

This is fucking insane. I don't even know her. Sure, she resembles my dead girlfriend, but that's not why I'm so drawn to her.

Is it? Am I only fixated on her because I want a second go at saving Laura?

I don't think that's it. I've liked knowing that Laura is dead. It's peaceful. No one can hurt her anymore. She didn't deserve to die so young, but it's better that she did.

Evie, though, I'm almost certain I'll do anything to keep her alive. But if I can't, then I will take whatever part of her I can. Even if that's her death.

I will keep this woman to myself. I never have been very fond of sharing.

# Chapter Seven

When I wake up, Charlotte is sitting on the sofa in the living room. She looks like she's just showered and made herself up.

"Hey, you look nice," I tell her as I cross the suite. I don't sleep often, but when I do, I always wake up groggy as hell.

"I've been waiting for you to wake up," she says.

"Let me get coffee first." I head into the kitchen area. There has to be a coffee pot here somewhere.

Charlotte follows me. "Hey, I think you should get an early flight back home," she says.

When I find the already full coffee pot, I thank God that I have good friends. Charlotte knew I'd need it. "Why?" I ask her. I just got here.

"Remember that guy from last night? The one you were flirting with?"

"Emmanuel, kinda hard to forget." I smile at the memory of him I have imbedded in my brain. The sight of him in that suit, the smell of him whenever he got close...

"Yeah, well, I don't think he was kidding around about being a cartel boss, hon. When I woke up, he was holding a gun to Louie's head," she says.

"What?" I gasp, coffee spilling from my mouth.

"He wanted to wake me up and Louie wouldn't do it."

"You mean, the guy you just met had a gun to his head and still wouldn't wake you up? That man is a keeper, Charlotte." Maybe this whole marriage thing *will* work out for her after all.

"Yeah, well, I did marry him. But that's not the point. Emmanuel wanted to know what happened."

"What happened when?" I ask.

"To you," she says, and her voice goes quiet. "He

was watching you sleep. I didn't know. He left after he had carried you up to the bedroom. I didn't know he came back."

My blood goes cold. He was watching me sleep. I take a mental inventory of every part of my body. I don't feel like I was touched. I don't feel like anything actually happened. But I've been wrong before...

"He carried me up to bed? Doesn't matter. What did you tell him?" I don't plan on seeing the man again, but the last thing I need is for him to think I'm broken or have issues. Appearances are everything, remember?

"You were talking in your sleep, Evie. He was adamant on finding out why. I didn't tell him anything other than to look into the pageant world." She flinches apologetically.

*Crap. Fuck. No.*

"It doesn't matter." I shake my head. "I'm sure he's forgotten about it by now. But you're right. I do need to get home."

"I'm sorry. I shouldn't have said anything. I know that."

"It's fine. He can dig all he wants. He's not going to find anything, because there is nothing to find. I'm glad I was here when you got married," I say quickly changing the subject.

"Me too. It's crazy, right?" She sighs.

It's fucking insane, but that's not what she needs to hear right now. She needs support.

"It is, but I think it was for the best. You seem... happy with him."

"We don't even know each other. What if it turns out he clips his toenails in bed or something just as gross? Or what if he wakes up tomorrow and decides he doesn't want to be married anymore?" In true Charlotte fashion, she's spiraling. I reach across the counter to steady her.

"What if he doesn't? What if you spend the rest of your life waking up next to him and you're both sickeningly happy? What if you get to live the dream everyone wants?"

Truth is... I wish I could take my own advice and learn to be happy. Learn to let go of the past.

"I know, but I just worry. It's all happened so fast."

"You know, there are many cultures that have arranged marriages and those work out. Is it fast? Yes, but that doesn't make it wrong," I tell her.

"How did you get so smart?" Charlotte chuckles.

"I don't know, but don't tell anyone because I don't need them all expecting this level of wisdom from me. Now, I'm going to shower and find a flight. He's not still around, is he?"

"Who?"

"Emmanuel?" I need to avoid that man like the plague. He's not safe for me. He watched me sleep, and I have no idea what he did to me while I was out of it. Was I drugged? Is that why I passed out so suddenly?

My hands start to shake. I clench my fists to try to ward off the oncoming panic.

"I have no idea. Want me to ask Louie?" Charlotte asks.

"No, I just want to get out of here without running into him. It's creepy that he watched me sleep... and embarrassing," I tell her as I make my way to the bathroom.

"I'll make sure you don't have to see him," Charlotte calls out from behind me.

After saying my goodbyes to Charlotte, I make my way to the check-in desk at the airport. My heart is beating so fast. I keep counting in my head, trying to calm my nerves. I can't get over the fact that he was in the room with me when I was sleeping.

I went over every inch of my body while I was in the shower. I didn't see any marks. I didn't feel like

I'd been touched, but that doesn't mean he didn't. Why the hell was he watching me anyway?

And to think I was fully prepared to have a few hours of naked fun with that creep. I bet he would have been so good too. Always the way... The ones who can actually make you come are not the ones you should be in bed with.

"Hi, checking in for the flight to Atlanta." I hand over my ID to the young guy behind the counter.

"Thank you, Miss... Carter," he says after reading my name. "How many bags are you checking?"

"Just the one." I left a bag of clothes with Charlotte, considering she came here with nothing.

Once I get to Atlanta, I have to make the drive to Madison, my little hometown. I'll be as far away from the supposed cartel boss as I can get. Although I'm almost certain he's already forgotten about me. Moved on to his next poor victim.

"Thank you." I smile at the guy as he hands me my ticket. It's better than acknowledging the ache I feel at the thought of Emmanuel turning his attention to another woman. I don't want his attention, but I don't really want to lose it either.

Something is very wrong with me. That's nothing new, though. I just need to get home, get back to the store and my normal, boring life. That will reset my... whatever it is that needs resetting to forget all about the tall, dark, dangerously handsome man in a well-fitting suit I'm leaving behind.

"Argh." *I am not doing this. Nope.*

After walking through security, I find a seat at the gate and plug in my earbuds. I turn on the latest Taylor Swift album and lose myself in her music while I scroll through my emails and reply to all of Amy's. The thought of messaging Rachel and Charlotte to get their reassurance crosses my mind. But I don't want them to worry about me, so instead of bringing up my own issues, I message them with a distraction.

ME:

Enjoy your honeymoon @charlotte!

RACHEL:

I still can't believe you got married and I wasn't there. But I've seen your new husband. I get it!

ME:

Right? The man is a goner for her. He's got it bad.

CHARLOTTE:

He's a catch for sure. Thank you for understanding, or at least pretending to.

ME:

Babe, you upgraded. Trust me, this is going to work out for you.

CHARLOTTE:

One day soon, you two will find your own Louies.

ME:

Nope. I want a boring accountant, someone with a desk job. I don't want or need a mobster.

CHARLOTTE:

Or a cartel boss.

ME:

Or that.

When the announcement for boarding comes across the loud speaker, I send the girls one last text and jump up. I'm going home, but it feels like I'm leaving something behind. I just don't know what that something is? Charlotte?

Has to be her.

The entire time I'm standing in line, inching closer and closer to the plane, my stomach turns. And I can't put my finger on why. I get settled in my aisle seat and take a deep breath. I would have preferred the window but beggars can't be choosers, right?

I switch my phone to flight mode. It's midday. I'll

be home around six or seven o'clock tonight. The first thing I'll do is go to the store and make myself busy. After sleeping last night, I know I won't sleep again for at least three or four days.

The plane starts to taxi and I breathe another sigh of relief. I really do hope Charlotte will be happy here. I hate that she's not coming home. Especially considering I'm not sure when I'll be able to bring myself to come back to this city.

"There's a slight delay for take-off, ladies and gentlemen. We are required to return to the gate. We'll get you in the air and eastbound in no time," the pilot's voice comes over the speaker, followed by a wave of audible groans. Nobody likes a delay. I wonder why they're being called back to the gate.

"Do you think there's something wrong with the plane?" the lady beside me asks, her voice sounding a little panicked.

"I'm sure there isn't. It's probably an ill passenger or something. These things happen all the time," I tell her with my best smile. I'm bullshitting out of my ass, but if I can help ease her worry, it's worth it.

The woman nods, appearing relieved.

When we get back to the gate, the doors to the plane open again, and I drop my head against the seat and close my eyes. Whatever they're doing won't take long. I'm sure of it. I try to relax until the quiet shriek from the woman next to me has me jolting upright again. I open my eyes, look to her, and then in front of us.

*No... No... Hell fucking no...*

"Am I asleep?" I ask aloud. I must be, because there is no way Emmanuel Lopez is making his way down the center aisle. His glare fixed right on me. He looks... pissed, and I can feel all the other passengers staring.

"Ma'am, I'm going to need you to gather your things and come with me," he says, stopping next to my seat.

I shake my head. "I'm not doing that."

Emmanuel leans over, his breath bristling the skin on my neck while his hand unfastens my seat belt. "You can either come willingly, or I will throw you over my shoulder and carry your pretty little ass off this plane," he whispers.

"You wouldn't!"

"Fine, we'll do it my way." He smiles, like that was what he wanted.

When his hands reach for me, I shove them aside.

"*Fine*, I'll come with you," I hiss under my breath as I stand on my own, because the only thing worse than being carried off by a man I just met is being escorted off by a federal agent I don't know at all.

# Chapter Eight

The fire in Evie's eyes has my dick hard. I take her bag from her grip and then place my free hand on her lower back, guiding her off the plane. As soon as we're in the tunnel and away from all the prying fucking eyes of the other passengers, Evie shrugs away from me.

"Don't fucking touch me." She turns and seethes.

I smile. "Trust me, mi alma, I plan on touching you a hell of a lot more."

"What the hell do you think you're doing?" She folds her arms over her chest. "I know what you did, creep."

"What did I do?" I keep walking. My hand reaches for her lower back, my fingers clenching around the fabric of her dress when she tries to move away again. "Don't," I warn her.

"Don't what?" she asks me. "And you know what you did. You watched me sleep, and God only knows what else you did. Is that your thing? Touching unsuspecting women while they're passed out and can't say no?"

I chuckle. "No. Touching you, however, is definitely becoming my thing."

"You better find a new thing because you won't have hands left to touch me with if you even so much as think about doing it." Her chest rises and falls in an exaggerated huff. She's mad.

Before we make it out of the tunnel, I press Evie up against the wall. "Are you threatening me? Because I gotta be honest, mi alma, people who threaten me don't live long enough to do it twice."

"Are *you* threatening *me*? I'm not scared of you. Now get the fuck off me, you psycho." Her hands shove at my chest, and I take a step back. Not because I want to, but because I don't need to be making any more of a scene in the fucking airport than what we already have.

"Not threatening. *Educating*. I'd very much prefer to keep you alive," I tell her.

"What the hell do you want with me, Emmanuel?" she says, and the sound of my name on her lips...? Fuck me, I want to hear her scream it for the entire fucking world to hear.

"You," I reply simply.

"Me?" Her eyes widen. "You can't have me. I'm not available."

"You don't have a boyfriend or a husband. You're available." I shrug.

"You don't know that, and just because I don't have a man, doesn't mean I want or need one. Especially not a creep who does shit to me when I'm asleep."

"I didn't touch you," I tell her. She seems really hung up on the fact I watched her sleep. "Actually, I did. I wiped your makeup off your face. But other than that, I didn't touch you."

"You... wiped my makeup off? Why?"

"I've heard it's not good to sleep in that shit. Besides, you don't need it," I say.

"Yes, I do. But... don't do that again. In fact, how about you just don't watch me sleep again either and let me get back on the plane so I can go home."

"I'm not agreeing to those terms." My hand lands on her lower back. This time, she doesn't try to shrug me off.

"Where are you taking me? Somewhere you can have your filthy way with me against my will? Is that what gets you off? Helpless women?"

*And she's back to that.* I roll my eyes. "You're not helpless, Evie, and I wouldn't take you against your will. *When* I take you, it'll be because you're begging me to do it."

"Yeah? Do me a favor and hold your breath until that happens," she hisses.

Paz is waiting for me at the end of the tunnel. He has Evie's luggage.

"You?" Evie stomps over to him. "Are you gay?"

My lips tip up. Paz looks confused. "No, ma'am," he says with a shake of his head.

"Then why the hell wouldn't you give me your number?" Evie asks.

"Ah... jefe?" My second looks to me for help.

"Evie, this is Paz. He works for me. Anything you need, he'll make sure you have it," I tell her.

"Good, I need a new plane ticket home and your number, *Paz.* I have all this built-up sexual energy I could use your help getting out," she says in a sugary-sweet southern accent.

Paz's face visibly pales, and he takes a step backwards.

"He will get you anything but that," I say before dropping my mouth closer to her ear. "Don't make me kill my most-trusted man because you have the hots for him, mi alma. I don't share."

"First, I'm not yours. And second…" Evie smiles wide at me. "You couldn't possibly kill all the men I want to jump because there's a lot of them, Emmanuel. Like a lot, a lot. I have an entire to-do list."

My jaw clenches. She's fucking with me. I know she's trying to get a reaction, and it's fucking working.

"We're going." My hand wraps around hers. When she tries to get away, I tighten my grip and glare at her. "Do not test my patience," I warn. "There is only so much I will tolerate."

"Guess you best be killing me now then. I mean, that's what you'll do eventually anyway. Why drag it out."

Her words hit me hard and sharp. Each one digging a knife into wounds I buried a long time ago. She's right. I will end up killing her. It's what happened to the last girl I took an interest in.

No. I shake my head. I'm not going to kill her. My father isn't here to tell me I can't have her and no one else is gonna tell me shit either. Including the woman herself.

"I'm not going to kill you. I want to talk." I keep my expression neutral.

She narrows her eyes at me. "Talk? About what?"

"You. You have the answers I want to know," I say. I can't get the sound of her scream out of my head.

***

Surprisingly, Evie got into the back of my car without a fight. I don't think she wants to make a spectacle of herself. She's been quiet the entire drive back to the Lopez Estate. I don't come here often, but I want her to myself so staying off the Strip it is.

I don't miss the way Evie's face pales as we drive through the gates, her eyes landing on the men holding them open for our small convoy—more specifically, their rifles.

"Tell them to keep weapons out of sight while she's here," I tell Paz in Spanish. He's sitting in the front passenger seat.

"On it, jefe." He nods as the car stops in front of the house.

"What is this place?" Evie asks.

"The compound," I tell her. "Come on, I'll give you a tour." I hold out a hand, waiting for her to get out of the car.

"The only thing I need to see is the exit," she grumbles.

"Sure, it's that way." I point back at the gates while suppressing my grin.

"Are they going to shoot me if I leave?" She looks at the men in the guard shack.

"No one here will ever hurt you, Evie," I tell her. "And no one is stopping you from leaving."

"Good. I'll catch you... never then," she says as she starts walking towards the gate. A few long strides and I'm right beside her. "What are you doing?"

"I said I wouldn't stop you from leaving, not that I wouldn't follow you wherever you went," I tell her.

Evie stops in her tracks. "What the hell do you want?"

"You," I repeat.

"Nobody wants me, Emmanuel. You don't even know me."

"I can guarantee you every man in this compound would want you if it didn't cost them their lives," I say. "I want you, and you're here so I can get to know you."

"You want what everyone wants. The beautiful

outside. You don't want what's underneath it. Trust me." She shakes her head before adding under her breath, "I don't even want that."

"I want to show you the house." Taking hold of her hand, I lead her back towards the estate and up the stairs. Maria is waiting for us in the foyer. "Maria, this is mi alma, Evie. Evie, Maria is our housekeeper. She'll make sure you're comfortable while you're here."

Maria's eyes light up like she's just found a long-lost friend. "Miss Evie, it's a pleasure to meet you. Are you hungry? Of course you are. I'll get you something," she says, and then she's rushing off towards the kitchen.

"She doesn't need to get me food, Emmanuel," Evie whispers.

"She's going to whether I tell her to or not. If Maria wants to feed you, she's going to feed you." I laugh. "This way."

I guide Evie through the bottom level of the house.

"Why are you showing me every room?" she asks.

"Because I want you to be familiar with the estate. It's big. I don't need you getting lost in the halls." Next, I lead her upstairs and show her the bedrooms, leaving mine for last.

Evie steps inside and takes in every detail. "You're kinda boring, aren't you?"

I laugh. No one has ever called me *boring* before. Not to my face anyway. "What makes you think that?"

"I don't know. I expected your bedroom to be like some kind of sex dungeon. It's just so... plain."

"You want me to build you a sex dungeon, Evie?" I quirk a brow at her. I'm not opposed to the idea.

"No. I prefer to not be tied up. Or passed out," she mutters.

"Again, I didn't touch you," I remind her. "I do want to know who did, though."

Evie's body tenses and her eyes look everywhere but at me. "I don't know what you're talking about."

"You screamed out in your sleep."

"It was a nightmare. People have them. Except you, right? Considering you *are* the nightmare," she throws back at me.

I laugh again. I don't remember a time I've smiled so fucking much. "Funny, but it wasn't a nightmare. It was a memory, and I want to know what it was about. I want to know what happened to you."

"Nothing happened to me," she insists.

My phone rings, and Paz's name flashes on the screen. "I have to take this. I'll be in my office when you decide to stop lying to me." I close the distance and kiss the middle of her forehead. "Maria will come and find you soon."

I leave Evie in my bedroom. I don't need to keep her locked up. I'll know the minute she steps out the front door and tries to leave. I'll also be there to follow her.

"Yeah?" I answer Paz's call.

"We have a problem," he says. "Basement."

"Be there in a minute," I tell him and make my way downstairs towards the one room I didn't show Evie on her tour. I don't need to fill her head with anymore nightmares.

# Chapter Nine

He just left me in this room. His room. What the hell is this guy's problem? I consider walking out, just going right out the front door. The issue with that is the horde of armed men who will be there to stop me. I'd have to go past them. And honestly, that's not something I want to try to do on my own. Without Emmanuel standing beside me.

I shouldn't find comfort in him. Yet his presence

makes me feel almost untouchable. Stupid. It's probably my subconscious's way of trying to cope with the fact I've basically just been taken hostage by a psychopath.

No, *not basically*. I have been taken hostage.

He wants to know what happened to me. He'll be waiting a long-ass time before I give up that information. It's not something I talk about. It's bad enough that Rachel and Charlotte know a little of my story. No way does anyone else need to know too.

Charlotte. I could call her. Surely, Louie knows where Emmanuel lives. They could come and get me. But it's her first day of being married. I don't want to make it about me, when it should be about her.

*What the hell am I supposed to do?*

When I accept I don't have an answer to that, I sit on the floor. Right at the end of Emmanuel's bed, because like hell am I sitting on it. I scrunch up my nose. God only knows how many girls he's had up here.

Argh, why the hell did he have to leave me behind. I'd rather be fighting with him than sitting here by myself.

About ten minutes into my protest (is that what I'm doing?) Maria knocks on the open door. "Oh, *mija*, why are you on the floor?" she asks, a tray resting on one arm while she balances the rest on her hip.

"It seemed like the safest place to sit," I tell her.

"Mr. Lopez would not like you sitting on the floor, Miss Evie," she says.

"Yeah, well, Mr. Lopez needs to learn that he can't always have everything he wants," I fire back.

Maria smiles at me. And I realize how rude I was.

"I'm so sorry. I did not mean to be rude to you, Maria."

"Never mind that. You're not wrong." She sighs. "I'll just leave this over here for you. If you need anything else, just call down to the kitchen." Maria places the tray on a table in the corner of the room, where two small chairs are set up beside it.

"Thank you." I smile. It's not this poor woman's fault she works for a kidnapping asshole.

I don't get up and check out the tray, even though it smells so good. It appears I'm on a hunger strike as well. Because about an hour later, when Emmanuel steps back into the room, I'm still sitting on the floor in front of the bed.

He stops when he spots me. "What happened? Why the fuck are you on the floor?"

I look up at him, and my mouth drops open.

Emmanuel reaches down, scoops up my arms, and lifts me to my feet.

"What happened?" he repeats. "Why are you on the floor? Are you hurt?" His eyes travel all over my body, and I could almost fool myself into thinking he actually cares.

He doesn't. Why would he? He doesn't know me.

As soon as the shock wears off, the sudden spark of him touching me, my eyes catch on the blood on his hands. On his shirt too.

"What happened to you? Are you about to bleed out?" I shake my head. "No, I wouldn't be that lucky." I don't think it's his blood anyway. He doesn't appear injured.

Emmanuel laughs, and I swear the sound goes right to my core. He really needs to stop doing that. "I'm okay. It's not my blood. Thanks for the concern, though, mi alma."

"I'm not concerned," I say, taking a step backwards.

"Why were you on the floor? You don't belong on the fucking floor," he grunts.

"I'm protesting," I tell him.

"What are you protesting?" he asks as he starts undoing his shirt, revealing more of that tanned, inked skin with each button.

My mouth goes dry, but I manage to reply, "Being held captive."

"You're not captive. We've discussed this." Emmanuel drops his shirt onto the floor, and my eyes feast on his bare torso.

Holy shit, I knew this man was dangerous. But this? The way my panties dampen at the sight of him? This is way worse.

Emmanuel turns and heads through an adjoining door. I follow him. I don't know what else to do. Bad decision, because it's a bathroom. I'm frozen to the spot as he drops his pants and steps into the shower, totally unbothered by being completely naked in front of me.

He glances over a shoulder to look at me. "You wanna join?"

"Nope, I'm good." I lean against the cabinet and watch him. If he's not bothered by being naked, then I'm not going to be bothered by looking.

"You sure? I'd make it worth your while." He smirks.

"I'm sure."

"You don't look sure. You look like you're about to pounce, mi alma, which I'm not opposed to either."

"I'm just admiring the art," I tell him. Not only is his skin covered in ink, but his body itself is a work of art. "You have a good tattoo artist. Think they'll do something on me?"

"Not if they want to keep their hands, and I hear those are useful to artists." Emmanuel picks up a loofah and squirts a bunch of shower gel on it before rubbing at his arms and torso.

*Fuck, I should not be in here. I should not be watching this.*

My eyes follow his hands down, down and farther down, until he reaches his dick. There's a nice little V that leads you right to it. He's hard, really fucking hard.

"That looks like it hurts." I grin.

"I've been hard since I first laid eyes on you," he says.

"Good thing your hands work. Want me to leave you to it?" I offer.

"I'm not jerking myself off, mi alma. When I relieve myself, it'll be inside you," he says.

"Well, I hope you look forward to a lifetime of celibacy then, because that's never going to happen." I walk out of the bathroom, for my own sanity, before I take back what I said and join him in that shower. I really do want to experience what he could do with that dick of his.

I'm stubborn, though. So if I say it's not happening, it's not happening. I return to my spot on the floor. I don't know what else to do.

Emmanuel walks out of the bathroom, a billow of steam trailing behind him. "Get up," he growls at me.

"Excuse me?" I raise a brow. I'm not a dog. He can't just bark an order and expect me to follow it.

"I said get off the fucking floor." He stomps towards me and drags me up by my arms again. "You do not belong on the goddamn floor, Evie."

"What is your problem with the floor?"

"It's for people beneath us. *You* are not beneath us." He guides me over to the little table with the tray. "Sit," he says, pointing at the chair.

"No." I cross my arms over my chest. "I happen to like sitting on the floor, and people are not beneath me. I'm not better than anyone else."

"Yes, you are," he seethes. "We have chairs. Sit on chairs. Sit on the bed. Anywhere but the fucking floor." He stalks towards another door.

I don't move. I consider sitting on the floor again. That's what protests are about, aren't they?

If I'm honest with myself, I don't particularly want to risk making him any angrier than I already have, though. I don't think he'd hurt me.

I'm a fucking idiot. He's a cartel boss. He'd hurt me if he had to.

Emmanuel comes out in another perfectly-fitted black-on-black suit.

"Do you buy those suits from Costco? Like in bulk or something?" I ask him.

"You own a boutique, Evie. Tell me, do you really think my suits are from Costco?" He raises a brow.

"They could be," I say, even though I know damn well those suits are custom-fitted.

"Sure. Why didn't you eat?" He eyes the untouched food.

"Hunger strike," I tell him.

"Yeah, that's not fucking happening. Come with me." Emmanuel grabs hold of my hand and drags me out of the bedroom.

"Where are you taking me?" I huff behind him.

"To the kitchen. You're going to eat."

"No, I'm not," I spit.

"I'm not about to sit back and let anyone hurt you, Evie. That includes you," he says.

"Why do you even care?" I don't understand this guy. What is his deal?

Emmanuel stops. We're halfway down the stairs when he turns around to face me. "Why wouldn't I care?"

"You don't know me?"

"Mi alma, I don't need to know you. I know that I want to keep you. That's enough for me."

"What does that mean? *Mi alma?*" He keeps calling me that, and I have no idea what he's saying.

"It means... mi alma." He smiles. "You are mine now, Evie. You are my soul."

"Yeah, I'm not." I shake my head.

"I'll give you time to get used to the idea." He nods. "But right now, we're eating dinner and you are going to tell me what the fuck happened to you."

I keep my mouth shut, sitting when Emmanuel pulls out a dining chair for me. And I continue to keep it shut when he positions himself across from me. Two plates are brought in and placed in front of each of us. I pick up a fork and stare at it.

"Out of curiosity, how hard would it be to kill someone with this?" I ask.

"You want to stab it right here." Emmanuel points to a spot on his neck. "Make sure to get it as deep as you can, then give it a little twist," he says.

"Seems messy." I shrug.

"It is," he tells me.

Instead of trying to make conversation, I eat. My hunger strike lasted right up until I needed a distraction from the man across from me.

"What do you want to do tonight?" Emmanuel

asks. "I know you won't sleep, but we can do something to pass the time."

"I want to go home. I want to be in my store."

"Okay," he says. "I'll take you home, right after you tell me what happened to you and who did it."

"Why are you so interested in my past?" I grumble and regret the words as soon as they're out of my mouth.

"Because I plan on being your future, and for that to happen, I need to know your past."

"You're not going to be my future, Emmanuel. This? It's not happening. You can keep me here forever, and it's still not happening." I gesture between us. Mostly because I'm never going to tell him about my past. And if I did tell him, he wouldn't want me anyway.

Huh, maybe that's my ticket out of here. Letting him see all the ugliness inside me.

"What would you do? Say someone did hurt me, what would you even do about it?" I ask.

"I'd bring you their heads on a silver platter," he replies without hesitation.

# Chapter Ten

"You're a businessman, right?" Evie asks.

I nod my head, but don't say anything.

"Then you understand that I do have to get home? I have a business to run."

"I understand. And I've told you, as soon as you *tell me* what I want to know, I'll have the jet take you home," I say.

Evie glares at me from across the table. I wonder

if she's even the slightest bit afraid of me. Men wouldn't dare to look at me the way she's looking at me right now, let alone speak to me how she does. I don't want her to be afraid of me. I don't think. I want her to talk to me.

The fact that there are people out there who have hurt her is driving me fucking insane. I just spent hours in the basement with some fucking pageant judge Paz picked up. The guy claimed he didn't know Evie. He was full of shit because his face paled the moment I showed him her photo. The asshole took whatever secrets he had to hell with him, though. Because he didn't talk and I didn't stop.

I'd been waiting to get a call that Evie was leaving. She didn't fucking move. She sat her ass on the fucking floor in the middle of my room.

"Why didn't you leave?" I ask her what I've been wondering myself.

"What?"

"When I left you in the room, why didn't you walk out the front door?" I don't get her. She says she doesn't want to be here, doesn't want me, but she's really not putting up much of a fight.

"I didn't want to get shot down trying to walk out of the gates." She shrugs.

"No one here is going to fucking shoot you, Evie," I tell her.

"You have an army of men out there with rifles. How am I supposed to know what they will and won't do?"

"They're not going to touch you," I repeat.

She lifts a curious brow at me. "What were you doing?"

"Torturing a pageant judge," I say honestly.

Her face pales. "You what?"

"He's dead," I tell her. "If you won't tell me what I want to know, I will get those answers elsewhere."

"You can't do that, Emmanuel. Some of those people are innocent!" Evie gasps.

"You see that? You just admitted that someone *isn't* innocent. Who is it, Evie?" I press her.

She shakes her head. Her eyes water. "You can't kill people because of me."

"Actually, I can. And I will." I study her face for a moment, then change the subject. "We should watch a movie."

"You're insane," Evie whispers.

"Mi alma, you have no idea the lengths I'm willing to go to." I stand. My chair slides backwards, and I walk over to her side of the table and extend a hand. "Come on, let's go watch a movie."

"I want to go home, Emmanuel. I have work to do," Evie says.

"You were planning on staying in Vegas for the

entire week before you ran," I remind her. "Give me that week."

I have no intention of letting her go, but maybe if she thinks she'll eventually escape me, she'll relax, and I'll get the information out of her.

"The week? For what?"

"So we can get to know each other." I'm still waiting for her to stand.

"A week isn't long enough to get to know another person," Evie argues.

"Want to make it longer? I don't mind." I smirk. "Besides, a week is just the beginning, not the end."

"I'm not sleeping with you," she says.

"You barely sleep at all, so I'd assume that."

"That's not what I meant." Evie sighs. "You can't watch me sleep. When I do eventually pass out again, you can't be in the room while I'm sleeping. And you can't have anyone else in there either, unless it's Charlotte."

That really is a thing for her, huh? I'd be willing to put money on it having something to do with whatever the fuck happened to her.

"Why are you worried about me watching you sleep?" I ask, because like fuck am I agreeing to not watching her.

"It's creepy and I don't know what you're doing to me," she says.

"You can watch the tapes whenever you want," I tell her. "I didn't do anything to you, and I wouldn't do anything you didn't want me to do."

"I don't want you to keep me here," she mutters under her breath.

"Okay, where do you want to go?"

"Home," she says.

"Fine, we'll go to your place. Give me a couple of hours to get the jet ready." I pull my phone from my pocket.

"That's not... I don't want you to come with me, Emmanuel."

"If you're going, then I'm coming," I say. She *doesn't* have a choice on that.

"Argh, you're so... Argh." Evie stands and shoves at my chest. "Why are you doing this to me?"

Taking hold of her hands, so she can't continue to shove me, I hold them firmly against my chest. "Because, mi alma, I can't get you out of my head."

"Try harder," she hisses.

"I don't want to. I like you occupying my mind. You are much better to think about than what's usually there. You are a reprieve from the hell I have to deal with every day," I admit.

Evie inhales a lungful of air and slowly releases it. She's about to say something when the ringing of my phone interrupts her. I look down at the screen and see Lailani's number.

"I have to take this." I let go of Evie's hands and walk out of the dining room.

"Yeah?"

"Charlotte was just shot. She's being taken to the hospital," Lailani says.

"Where?"

"The casino floor. She jumped in front of Louie. The gun was aimed at him."

"Why the fuck would she do that?" I yell into the phone, making my way to my office. "Find Paz, now," I tell the two men standing guard in front of the door. I sit behind my desk and return my attention to Lailani. "Where's the shooter now?"

"Dead, security got him," she says. "You want me to do anything?"

"Not yet," I tell her and cut the call.

I turn on my computer and pull up the Royal's security feed. It takes ten minutes of scrolling through all the cameras to find Louie and Charlotte, and then I watch as she pushes Louie out of the way. She saw the gun and jumped in front of it. Fucking hell.

I need to find out what's happening with Charlotte before I tell Evie anything. I need to know what we're dealing with.

"Jefe?" Paz walks in, closing the door behind him.

"Someone took a shot at Louie, got his wife," I explain. "I need you to hack into the hospital records and find out what's happening with Charlotte."

"On it." Paz sits on the sofa and grabs his laptop from where he left it resting on the coffee table.

"Did the mess in the basement get cleaned up?" I ask him.

"Spotless," Paz replies.

"Who the fuck would take a shot at Louie?" I grunt as I run a hand through my hair.

"No one who will live to tell the story," Paz says as he taps away at his keyboard. "They got her in surgery."

"Let me know as soon as she's out, not a word in front of Evie," I warn him.

Paz looks up at me. "She's going to be pissed if you keep this from her, jefe. They seem close."

"I'm not keeping it from her. I'm waiting until we know the outcome," I counter. "And get some guys out on the street. I want to know who the fuck is going after our connections."

Paz nods, and then he's back on his phone. I leave him to work and go in search of Evie.

"She went upstairs, Emmanuel," Maria tells me as I pass. So I turn and head up the stairs.

I find Evie sitting on the edge of the bed. *Well, that's an improvement from the floor.*

"What happened?" she asks me.

"Why did you come up here?" I say instead of answering.

"You left me in the dining room. I didn't know what to do." She lifts a shoulder.

"Evie, you don't have to stay in this room. You don't need me to walk around the house. You can go wherever you want," I tell her.

"There're a lot of people in this house," she says. "I can just stay in here."

"I'll kick them all out. If they make you uncomfortable, I'll have them all stay outside, except Maria. We need to eat." I grin.

"You don't have to do that. It's fine. I'm not going to be here long."

"A week," I tell her.

"If I agree to this *week*, what happens? What do we do for a whole week?" Evie eyes me suspiciously.

"Talk. We can do whatever you want to do, Evie," I say, sitting next to her on the bed.

"Talk," she parrots. "About what? I doubt we have anything in common."

"How would you know that? Unless *we talk*?"

"You're a cartel boss from Mexico. I'm a small-town girl with a dress shop. We are not even remotely close to being compatible for anything but a one-night stand. And since you're a creep who watches people sleep, that ship has long sailed." She laughs.

"Good, because I don't plan on being your one-night stand, mi alma." I push to my feet and hold out a hand. "Come on, let's go downstairs."

Surprisingly, she actually takes it, and I lead her downstairs to one of the living rooms. It's the one with the most comfortable sofa.

I turn on the television and pass her the remote. "You choose."

Evie flicks through the channels until she finds some Hallmark movie. I don't complain. I don't care what she's watching. I just need to keep her occupied long enough for Charlotte to come out of surgery. Then I'll take her to the hospital.

"You're going to be bored out of your mind and probably fall asleep. But don't worry, I won't watch you because I'm not a creep," Evie tells me.

I settle back onto the sofa. My arm wraps around her shoulder and I pull her body against mine, so her back is resting on my chest. "I don't care if you creep on me, Evie. Watch me sleep all you want."

"You're not a talker, are you? Because that's going to be a problem. Movies are meant to be enjoyed—*quietly*," she says.

"Lips are zipped." I chuckle.

It's best I don't talk anyway. Less of a chance of her putting that wall up between us again. Because right now, her body relaxes against mine and I feel at peace. My lips press to the top of her head, and I inhale the fruity scent of her shampoo.

An hour later, Paz walks into the living room, and Evie stiffens. I shift her weight and slide out from under her.

"I'll be right back," I say and walk out of earshot with Paz following me.

"She's out of surgery. Still asleep but going to be fine," he says.

I sigh. I didn't know how much I was fucking hoping to hear that. Two people I happen to care about would be fucking devastated otherwise. "Thanks. Get the car ready. I need you to come with me."

Paz nods and walks out towards the front of the house. I go back into the living room. Evie looks up at me.

"What happened?" she asks.

"We have to go to the hospital," I tell her. "Charlotte was shot. She's okay. She's out of surgery and going to make a full recovery."

# Chapter Eleven

All I heard was that *Charlotte was shot.* And I'm up on my feet. "What? No! What happened? OMG, I have to go. Where is she?" My questions are rapid-fired at Emmanuel.

I walk past him towards the front of the house. Gone is my fear of being gunned down by the lunatics he has surrounding this place. My sole focus on getting to my friend.

*Charlotte was shot.* This isn't real.

A pair of arms wraps around me from behind just before I reach the door. "Evie, she's okay," Emmanuel whispers into my ear. He is the last person I want to be taking comfort from. And yet, when he touches me, that's exactly what I do.

My body relaxes into his a little. He's a good hugger. Tight, like I'm wrapped in a protection bubble. That's how I felt on the sofa. I almost protested when he got up to go talk to Paz. I was enjoying the bubble.

"How do you know?" I ask him.

"I had Paz hack into the hospital system. He read her files. She's out of surgery and in recovery. She will be okay," Emmanuel says, his voice soft. Soothing. "Come on, let's go."

Emmanuel holds my hand throughout the entire ride to the hospital, his grip firm. I don't even try to pull away. I can't. I need the anchor. My head is full of images. Dark images.

"It's my fault," I say.

"What's your fault?"

"Charlotte getting shot. It's my fault."

"How the fuck do you figure that?" Emmanuel grunts.

"I encouraged her to stay. I should have talked her into going home." If I had done that, she would have been safe right now.

"That is not your fault. You're not blaming yourself for something you had no control over. Someone took a shot at Louie, and your friend pushed him out of the way. She literally jumped in front of the bullet," Emmanuel says. He seems to know a lot about this.

"When did you find out?"

"Shortly after it happened. I wanted to wait until she was out of surgery before I told you," he admits.

"What? *You knew* and didn't tell me. You let me sit there and watch some crappy movie while my best friend was in surgery. I can't believe you." I snatch my hand out of his. When the car comes to a stop, I try to yank the door open, but it doesn't budge. "Open the fucking door!" I yell.

Emmanuel gets out on his side and slams the door shut. Then he comes around and opens my door, leaning into the car until he's taking up most of my space. "I didn't tell you because I didn't want you to worry unnecessarily. I wanted to be able to tell you after we knew she was going to be fine."

"And what if she wasn't?" I counter.

"Then I would have found a way to break the heart of probably the only person alive I don't want to disappoint," he says, and his eyes connect with mine.

I don't care about his bullshit words. He can't possibly mean them.

"Move! Let me out!" I hiss between clenched teeth.

Emmanuel looks me over before he steps out of the way. But he catches me before I can storm off. "Walk behind me. Paz will walk behind you."

"Why? Scared I'll run?"

"Run and I'll chase you, mi alma." He lifts a challenging brow at me before adding, "I don't know who took a shot at Louie, and if they're stupid enough to try to hit him on his home turf, who knows what else they're capable of. I don't want you taking any stray bullets."

It takes a minute for his words to sink in. "Is Charlotte still in danger?"

"No. Neither are you, if you stay behind me," Emmanuel says. "Don't ever do what your friend did. Move away from bullets, not towards them."

"Pfft, please, I'd be the one waving a red flag over your head so they knew where to aim," I huff.

Emmanuel laughs. "Also, this deal of ours... it stays between us. I'd hate to have to kill our best friends because they tried to take you from me," he says.

Then he just turns and walks into the hospital. And sure enough, as I follow him, Paz follows me.

I turn and look at the guy over a shoulder. "You, I might save." I wink and Paz shakes his head.

The moment Emmanuel pushes through a set of double doors, I hear Louie's loud voice. "Where the fuck have you been?"

"Where is she?" My hands ball into fists and slam against his chest. "What the hell did you do?"

Emmanuel grabs me around the waist and pulls me away from Louie. "Whoa, it wasn't him," he says.

Struggling against his hold is pointless. The man has a firm freaking grip. "If it weren't *for him*, nothing would have happened to her. Where is..." I stop moving when I look through the window behind Louie and spot Charlotte on the bed—wires attached to her body. "No!"

"She's going to be okay," Louie says. "She's going to wake up."

Giving him my best *fuck you* glare, I shake out of Emmanuel's hold (or let's be real... he lets me go) and I walk into the hospital room.

"Oh my god, Charlotte, I'm so sorry. I never should have talked you into staying here. I'm so sorry." I kneel down next to her bed. Close my eyes and hold her hand as I pray. I don't know what else to do. I don't know how to help her.

*Rachel!* I need to call Rachel. She will know what to do. I stand and realize I don't have my phone. *Where did I leave it?*

Louie storms into the room. He sits on the opposite side of the bed and starts scrolling through his phone. "Fuck!" he hisses out.

"Are you okay?" I ask him, not because I care. He could literally burn in hell. But I, for one, do not want to explain to my best friend why her husband was burned alive when she wakes up. Because she will wake up. There is no other option.

"My wife was shot. So, no, I'm not fucking okay," he grunts.

"What happened?" I've heard Emmanuel's version of the story, but I'm not sure I can trust him.

"She jumped in front of a bullet that was meant for me," Louie says, sounding defeated.

"She loves you. You would have done the same thing... if you were the one who saw it coming. Right?" I ask him.

"Of course I would have. I don't know what music she likes. I need to play her music and I don't know what kind she likes." He looks across the bed to me.

I smile. "Charlotte, if you don't wake up, I'm

going to tell him you love Tay-Tay and that's all you're going to hear until you wake up." She doesn't budge. I thought for sure that would do it. "Why isn't she waking up?"

"They said she will, in her own time."

"Well, that time could be now." I look to Charlotte. Still nothing. "She likes country. Just put on any country mix and she will love it," I say, sitting down.

"You think she can hear us?" Louie asks.

I shake my head. "I don't know."

I would like to think if she could, she'd wake herself up. Charlotte is the last person who would want her loved ones worried about her.

***

My butt is numb when I finally stand again. "I'm going to get coffee," I tell Louie.

We've both been sitting here for hours. Watching Charlotte. I don't know what to say to him, and honestly, the quiet has been welcoming. My head is a mess. Everything with Emmanuel and then Charlotte... I don't know what I'm doing.

The minute I step out of Charlotte's room, Paz stands from the plastic chair. "Jefe wanted me to give you this." He hands me my phone.

"Thanks." I smile or at least try to.

"How is she?" Paz asks.

"Still asleep," I tell him. "I'm going to get coffee."

"I'm coming." He walks beside me. A comfortable silence falls over us as we make our way to the Starbucks located at the front of the hospital.

While I'm waiting for my order, I scroll through my missed messages and calls. There's one from a name I don't know. *Mi Amor.* I tap on the message and instantly know who it is.

MI AMOR:

> I had to step out. Call me if you need anything. I'll be back as soon as I can.

ME:

> You left? I didn't even notice. Is what you're doing dangerous?

His response comes immediately.

MI AMOR:

> You worried about me, mi alma?

ME:

> No, but I've heard it's fun to play chicken with bullets. You should try it.

MI AMOR:

> I'll keep that in mind.

I look across to Paz. "What does *mi amor* mean?"

"Ah, it means *my love*." He looks uncomfortable.

"Pfft, *my love*, my ass. What's the Spanish word for asshole?" I ask him.

"Female or male?"

"Male," I tell him.

"Cabrón," he says. "Want help spelling it?" Paz looks over at my screen as I change the contact name Emmanuel put in for himself.

"I've got it." I smirk. I've heard this word once or twice. It's fitting.

"You probably shouldn't be too hard on him. He doesn't know what he's doing when it comes to you, so he's going to fuck up a lot," Paz says.

"Really? And here I thought kidnapping women from planes and keeping them hostage was a completely normal dating ritual." I roll my eyes.

"In some worlds, it is." Paz shrugs.

My name is called out at the counter, and I pick up two venti-sized coffees. I got one for Louie, even though he doesn't deserve it.

"He does care," Paz tells me as we make our way back. "For you."

"Sure he does." How can Emmanuel care about me? He doesn't even know me.

"What if he didn't come back? What if he did

have to play chicken with bullets and got hit? How would you feel?"

"Free," I deadpan before my smile drops. The thought of Emmanuel not actually coming back makes me feel something else. Something I'm not prepared to acknowledge.

"Yeah. That's what I thought." Paz nods and returns to the crappy plastic chair he has positioned outside Charlotte's door.

I pause in my tracks as soon as I walk back into the room. "Oh my god, you're awake. Why didn't you tell me she woke up?" I glare at Louie. He's so not getting his coffee now.

"What are you doing here? You went home," Charlotte asks me.

"I... ah... ran into a little obstacle. We'll talk about it later. I'm just so glad you're awake. You scared the crap out of me. Don't do that again," I tell her.

The doctor finishes checking her over and then leaves the room. Shit, I still need to call Rachel. "What happened? To the guy?" Charlotte says.

"Security got him seconds after he fired the shot," Louie tells her.

I tune out of their conversation and have my own private one with God. Thanking him for not taking my friend.

"Now, you. Why are you back?" Charlotte looks directly at me.

"Shit, it's my mom. I gotta take this." I wave my phone in the air—the one that's not ringing—and basically run from the room.

*Your mom? Really, of all people, that's who you choose?* Charlotte knows I haven't spoken to my mother in years.

# Chapter Twelve

I had to leave Evie at the hospital to go and pick up a drop with Sammie. I wasn't going to make Louie leave his wife. And Sammie couldn't do it alone. I'm fucking glad I was there. When he opened the container, there were four of my own fucking workers aiming rifles at us.

Safe to say I'm now four men down and fucking pissed off.

Now we're back at the hospital. I need to see

*her*. I don't like not having her nearby. I'll wear her down. She will be mine willingly. I just have to be patient and give her time to come around to the idea.

I find Paz outside Charlotte's room. Before I can say anything to him, Evie comes running out, her face flushed. She stops right in front of me, looks up and then back down at the floor.

"Argh!" She stomps a foot—literally stomps a foot like a child having a tantrum—and steps around me.

"Where are you going?" I ask, following her.

"Anywhere you're not," she fires back.

Taking hold of her elbow, I lead her into the next room. Louie had the entire ward cleared. The only patient is Charlotte, which means the place is empty. The door slams behind me.

Evie shrugs out of my hold. "Don't manhandle me!"

I step towards her, and she takes a step back. I repeat the dance until her back is pressed up against the wall. "What happened?" I ask her.

"You mean apart from being kidnapped?" she hisses.

"I've already told you you're free to leave anytime." I press harder against her body, and I'm not doing a damn thing to hide the effect she has on me. "I don't think you really want to leave though, do you, Evie?"

"Of course I want to leave." Her hands land on my chest. I'm sure her intention is to push me off. Instead, her fingers curl around the lapels of my jacket. "I want to leave," she repeats quieter.

I lean down, until I'm a breath away. "No, you don't," I tell her right before my mouth crashes onto hers. My tongue pushes through her closed lips. And then, like I've just flipped a switch, Evie lights up.

Her hands move higher, wrapping around the back of my neck. One of her legs lifts until her knee is level with my hip. I grab on to her thigh, holding it there while I press my cock right against her core.

*Fuck me, I need this.*

"I need..." Evie moans, breaking the kiss.

"I've got what you need," I tell her, grinding my dick against her again.

Her head tips back, her eyes close, and her mouth falls open on a soft moan.

"Say it," I growl.

"Say what?" she asks.

"Open your eyes and tell me you want this." My hand moves between her legs. My fingers rub down the center of her pussy, right over the lace covering her.

"Oh god," Evie groans.

"Say it." I push the lace out of my way. My fingers glide through her wetness.

"I want it, E, please." Her eyes open and connect with mine. This is what I wanted. Her. Every single fucking bit of her, without those goddamn walls she likes to keep around herself.

"With pleasure." I pin her against the wall with my body.

She pushes up onto her tippytoes on one foot while I free my cock and line it up with her entrance. And then, as I'm sliding in, my hands land on her ass and I pick her up. Evie doesn't miss a beat. Her legs wrap around my waist, and she clings to me.

The moment I've bottomed out, I pause. "Mi alma," I whisper, soaking in the feel of being inside her. It's more than I ever expected. My lips find hers again, and I start moving in and out, taking my time to enjoy every single minute I get her.

Evie's hips match my movements. Her fingers tangle in the ends of my hair at the back of my neck, and she holds my face pressed against hers. I swallow every single one of her moans. Her pleasure is mine and mine alone. I'm not sharing any of it, not even her moans.

"I want you to come for me," I say while thrusting in and out of her as hard as I possibly can. I pull back. I want to see it. Her face. I want the moment she finally lets go for me burned into my memories. "Mi alma, you are mine."

My fingers tighten around the flesh of her ass. Evie's body tenses up. Her head falls backwards, hitting the wall, and her mouth falls open into an O-shape.

"Don't you dare let anyone hear your pleasure. I will burn their fucking ears off," I grunt.

Evie tilts her head forward, her gaze delivering me a *fuck you* look. But she doesn't tell me to stop. No, she fucking explodes. Her pussy quivers around my cock as pleasure takes over.

*Fucking beautiful.*

I keep thrusting, drawing out her pleasure for as long as I can before I have to pull back. I walk her over to the hospital bed, sit her ass on top, and fist my cock. I give it a tug, spilling my own release all over Evie's thighs.

She looks down and then back up at me. Her face is flushed, her chest heaving. "That was..."

"Fucking perfect," I finish her sentence for her.

"It was something," she says. "I need to use the bathroom."

"Don't move." I walk into the adjoining bathroom, leaving Evie on the bed. I'm not even the slightest bit surprised when she doesn't listen and follows me. "I told you to stay put."

"Last I checked, I wasn't a dog, Emmanuel, so you can't just bark orders at me," she fires back.

I find a washcloth and wet it. Kneeling in front of her before I lift her skirt.

"What the hell are you doing?" she says, trying to swat my hands away.

"Cleaning what's mine," I tell her.

"This isn't yours," she hisses. "And I can do that myself."

"I clean up my own messes, mi alma," I say as I shift her panties aside before wiping the washcloth along her pussy. I move it along her upper thighs until I'm satisfied that she's clean.

"You are seriously deranged. You know that, right?" Evie grumbles.

"I know. Now, tell me why you were upset before." I stand to my full height, discarding the washcloth in the sink.

"Charlotte asked me why I didn't go home. I didn't know what to tell her and I freaked out, making up some bullshit about getting a call from my mother. Which just made it obvious I was lying because I don't speak to my mother," Evie rambles.

"Why don't you speak to your mother?" I ask her.

"That's not important. What am I supposed to tell Charlotte?" Evie stares back at me as if I'm supposed to have all the answers for her. I fucking love that look.

"Tell her your flight was delayed, then you heard about a shooting at the Royal. When you arrived, the reception staff told you about the incident."

"Do lies always fall from your lips so easily?"

"It's an occupational hazard. I have to think on my feet." I lift a shoulder and refasten my pants. Evie looks down at my hands, and I grin. "You want round two?"

"You wish." She smirks.

"I do actually." I chuckle.

"I have to pee."

"Toilet's right there." I point to my left.

"Get out." Evie shoves at my chest, and I let her push me out of the bathroom, giving her the privacy she needs. It takes her five minutes to come out. When she does, I'm sitting on the hospital bed waiting for her. "You're still here. Why?"

"Because you are," I tell her.

"I'm going to see Charlotte." She walks past me, towards the door.

"Evie." I stop her just before she can open it. "Don't hate yourself for giving into your desires."

"I don't hate myself. I hate *you*," she says.

"You always fuck men you hate?" I counter.

"Yes, because it's easier not to get attached." With that, she opens the door and walks out.

I find Paz sitting in the same plastic chair and fall into the one next to him. "We have to go back home. House needs cleaning," I tell him.

"What happened?" he asks.

"Four of our own were waiting in the container to kill these guys." I nod towards the window. My gaze falls on Evie.

Paz follows my line of sight. "What about her?"

"She's not going to leave her friend like that. I'll make sure Lailani knows her assignment's changed. Evie's safety is above anyone else's."

"She's strong-willed. You really think she's going to come around to your way of thinking?" Paz shifts his gaze to me.

I don't tell him that she did just *come* to my way of thinking. "She will," I say. "She doesn't have a choice."

I knew I wanted to keep Evie before I fucked her. Now that I have, my need for her has just increased tenfold. I hate that I have to leave her here. I need to, though, especially if I ever plan on taking her home with me. I need to make sure there are no fucking threats coming from inside the house.

"I'll get the jet ready." Paz stands from his chair. "You good here?"

"Yeah, I'll meet you at the hangar. Give me an hour," I tell him before making my way into Charlotte's room. "I'm glad you're awake, Mrs. Guiliani."

"Thanks," Charlotte says.

"I would love to stay, but I have matters I must tend to in Mexico." My eyes lock on Evie.

"When are you leaving?" Louie asks.

"Now. I'll be back, though. I have a new fondness for the city," I reply. Then I turn and walk out of the room, leaving my fucking soul behind.

"Emmanuel." Evie's voice stops me as I reach the end of the ward. I pivot to face her, tucking my hands in my pockets. I want to reach out and touch her, pull her into me. I also want her to come to me.

"You're really leaving?"

"Something's come up. I have to go and sort it out," I explain.

"What... Okay. Well, bye, I guess."

"Fuck it." I close the two-step distance between us and wrap my arms around her. My lips press to the center of her forehead. "I'll be back. If you need anything, call me. I've had your bags returned to the Royal for you."

"Thank you," she says. "But how do you know I'm not going to run and hide the moment you leave?"

"Because your friend is going to need you to

hang around for a bit. And there isn't a damn place you could hide that I wouldn't find you, mi alma," I tell her, because I would scour the ends of the earth for her.

"Thanks. Safe flight, or not. If the plane does crash, though, ensure it's big enough to make the news so I find out." She smiles.

"If that happens, I'll be certain to put out a broadcast just for you." Kissing Evie's lips one more time, I smile when she doesn't pull away and then I force myself to step back.

"Emmanuel, is it safe here? Is someone still going to come after Charlotte?"

"You're safe here. I have people everywhere, mi alma, and they've all been instructed that your safety is their number one priority. Nothing will happen to you."

"And Charlotte?" she presses.

"And Charlotte." I nod, even though I have no intention of putting her friend's safety above hers.

# Chapter Thirteen

Vegas at three a.m. is very different from the Vegas a few hours prior. Don't get me wrong. There are still people hanging around, the noise of the slot machines continues to slowly grate on your nerves, and the smell of alcohol, weed, and cigarette smoke lingers everywhere.

I think this is Vegas at its seediest. Hookers are out on the prowl, hoping to get their last client of the night. There're people passed out drunk or just asleep in the most random places. And every man I walk past gives me the damn creeps. I don't know why I came down to the casino floor. I couldn't sleep and got bored.

I didn't want to wake up Rachel, who is sharing the suite with me. And Charlotte got out of the hospital a couple of days ago, not that I could disturb her without her husband shooting me first. Which is how I ended up here. Walking aimlessly. I find an empty sofa and sit down. The moment I do, a waitress comes over.

"Ma'am. Do you need anything?" she asks.

"No, thank you. I'm good." I smile and watch as she walks away. I know I'm supposed to order a drink or something to use these lounges, but it's not like there're a lot of people waiting for one to become available.

My phone buzzes with a text message. I roll my eyes, tempted to ignore it. But if I do that, he'll end up calling or sending one of his henchmen to find me. Emmanuel is persistent as hell.

CABRÓN:

What are you doing walking around by yourself?

I look up and search the room for him. He's not

here. I know that. He's in Mexico. But he has people everywhere—*his words.*

ME:

Stop creeping on me.

CABRÓN:

What's wrong? Why are you down there and not in the suite?

ME:

Because I can be.

CABRÓN:

Mi alma, I'd prefer you go back upstairs.

ME:

And I'd prefer you leave me alone and forget you ever met me. We don't always get what we want.

CABRÓN:

I always get what I want.

I roll my eyes again. The man is insufferable.

ME:

What are you doing? Other than stalking women?

CABRÓN:

Women would suggest there is
more than one. There is only you,
mi alma. One woman who I'm
keeping my eye on.

ME:

What did you do today?

Our conversations always start out with me
telling him to fuck off, him not doing what I want,
and then they always have a way of turning into
something more real. I don't hate it. *Which I hate.*

I've slept once since he's been gone, once in an
entire week. But he seems to always know when I'm
bored, or when I just need something to occupy my
mind. The few times I've tried to ignore his
messages, one of his lackeys has turned up, holding
out a phone to me with a pleading look on their face.
Like their life depended on me taking that call.

CABRÓN:

I bought a house. You'd like it.

ME:

Where is it?

CABRÓN:

I'll show you one day soon. What
did you get up to today?

ME:

I baked a cake. You'll love it. I put extra arsenic in the batter.

CABRÓN:

I'd still eat it because you made it.

ME:

That's really messed up, E.

CABRÓN:

How is Charlotte?

ME:

Getting better. I think I'm going home in a couple of days. I can't stay here. Amy is struggling at the store.

CABRÓN:

When you're ready to go, let me know. I'll have the jet take you.

ME:

I'm not flying on your jet.

CABRÓN:

Yes, you are.

ME:

You can't make me.

CABRÓN:

I will cause air traffic to shut down if you try to fly commercial.

I laugh. There's no way he can do that. Can he? Then again, he did get them to turn my plane around while it was taxiing. I wouldn't put it past him.

ME:

Fine, but I'm bringing Rachel with me.

CABRÓN:

You can bring whomever you want.

ME:

Really? Anyone, because I met a guy today. He was super cute. He'd fit right in too. A genuine southern boy.

Three seconds after I've hit send on that message, my phone lights up, the name *Cabrón* flashing across the screen. "Yeah?"

"Evie, that sleepy little country town you're from will be decimated if you so much as let another man lay a finger on you."

"Emmanuel, shut up. You're being ridiculous." I close my eyes and throw my head back, resting it on the sofa.

"I'm deadly serious, mi alma. No one is going to touch you ever again. No one who isn't me."

"You're not touching me again either." I sigh. "That was a onetime thing."

"Keep telling yourself that, and you might even believe it one day. But we both know what we did, and it's way too fucking good not to do it again."

"Isn't there some hot Mexican woman you can be bothering instead of me?"

"Do you really want that? For me to go and randomly fuck some woman here?" he asks.

I sigh. I want to say *yes*. I want to tell him I don't care who he fucks. But what if he calls me on my bluff and does just that?

No, I want that. Don't I?

"I don't know what I want," I admit.

"I know what you want, mi alma, and I'm going to remind you every day," he says.

"You will tire of me soon, E," I tell him, because he will. Either that or he will notice just how broken and ugly I really am. As soon as that happens, he won't want a single thing to do with me.

"I'm going to have the jet ready to take you home tomorrow night, Evie. I think it'll be good for you to get out of Vegas, get back to your store," Emmanuel says.

I do need to work. "Thank you. Wait... Will you be on that jet?" I ask him.

"Why? Are you missing me?"

"About as much as I'd miss a hole in the head." I laugh.

"You having a hole in the head is not a joke," he grunts before sighing into the phone. "Unfortunately, I won't be on the jet. I have to finish some things here before I can leave."

"Are you okay?"

"I'm tired and I miss being able to look at you." He sounds so brutally honest.

"Hold on." I press the button to switch the call to video. Emmanuel accepts it, his face filling my screen. "Hey."

"Hey," he says with a huge smile on his lips. "Mi alma, fuck me." He shakes his head. "I thought I was dreaming it."

"You thought you were dreaming what?"

"How your beauty takes the breath right out of my lungs," he says.

"It's just skin." I'm uncomfortable with the same praise I've heard my entire life.

"Your beauty goes farther than skin-deep. Your soul is what takes my breath away, mi alma, not your skin," he tells me.

"Where are you?" I take in the moving background behind him.

"In the middle of a meeting."

"Then why are you talking to me?" I quirk a brow.

"Because you're more important than the asshole

I'm meeting with. Now, tell me what I have to do to get you to go back up to the suite. That casino floor is not the place to be at this time of night."

"Don't you have your people watching me? I'm sure I'm completely safe right where I am."

"I do. But that's not the point," he grumbles. "I would just prefer you weren't alone."

"I like being alone," I say. "It's easier."

"Easier than what?"

"Pretending," I admit.

Emmanuel doesn't say anything. He just stares at me through the screen. I see something move behind him, a flash of something silver.

"E, who is behind you?" I try to get a closer look at the screen.

The next thing I hear are gunshots. The phone is dropped, the camera now facing the ceiling. There're two more shots before the phone is picked up and Emmanuel's face fills my screen again.

"Evie, I have to go. Get on the jet tomorrow. Talk soon," he says.

"Wait!" I yell and he must hear me because he doesn't cut the call. "Are you okay?"

"I'm good. The other guy, not so much." He smiles. "Today is not the day you get rid of me, mi alma."

"I'll keep praying then." I smile and hang up. My

heart is beating out of my chest. He could have been shot. We were just talking on the phone, and he could have been killed.

My hands shake as I stand and walk back over to the bank of elevators. "Are you okay, ma'am?" a man in a black-on-black suit asks me.

"I'm okay. Thank you." I smile at him politely. I've come to learn that Emmanuel's men only come out of hiding when they think they need to be seen. They're also always polite to me.

It's on the tip of my tongue to ask him if he knows what his boss is doing, if he's going to be okay. I don't. It's not like they'd tell me anything anyway. And Emmanuel is fine. He didn't get shot.

---

Paz is waiting by a car at the casino entrance. Emmanuel mentioned that he'd sent a car for me. He didn't say he'd sent Paz.

I smile. "You got stuck being my babysitter?"

"I've had worse jobs, Miss Carter," he says, opening the back door.

"Rach, I'll be right back. Wait in the car for me," I tell my friend, who is looking at me as if I've grown two heads. *"Please."*

She nods but I know I'll hear about it later.

"Paz, follow me." I walk out of earshot of Rachel, before I spin around. "Why are you here? Shouldn't you be with Emmanuel? You know, making sure he doesn't get himself killed."

"Miss Carter, I assure you, Jefe is very capable of making sure he doesn't get himself killed."

"What happened last night?" I ask.

Paz grins. "I'm not sure what you're referring to."

"I'm referring to when I was on the phone with him and gunshots started going off in the background. What happened? You really should go back. He needs you more than I do," I say in one, long, frustrated breath.

"Unfortunately, he's the boss, ma'am. I'm following orders. And right now, he can't do his job if he's worried about you, which is why he sent me."

"He's worried about me?" I stop pacing. I didn't even realize I was doing it. "Really?"

Paz appears to consider his response before saying, "He's never had anyone like you in his life before. He doesn't want to lose you."

I blink, words escaping me. "We should go."

"He really is okay," Paz adds as we make our way back to the car.

I slide in beside Rachel, who gives me another look. This one letting me know the inquisition is going to start as soon as we're alone.

# Chapter Fourteen

There are parts of the job I love and others I can't fucking stand. Right now, this is the part I love. Usually, it would bring me a kind of satisfaction most people could never understand. It's not doing that for me, which only pisses me off more.

I want to be back in the States. With her. I want to look at Evie's face. Hear her laughter—or her anger—directed at me. I'll take whatever I can get from her. I'm addicted. I've spoken to her every day either through text messages or phone calls. It's not enough. I need to get to the bottom of the rot within my organization so I can get back to her.

I walk around the limp body that's being held up only by the rope wrapped around its torso, securing it to a wooden chair. Taking a fistful of hair, I pull her head backwards. "Jenna, Jenna, Jenna, you know I didn't want to do this. But you left me no choice."

It's the truth. I hate hurting women. That said, when it's a woman who's been working for me for the past ten years and I've just discovered she's crossed me, I don't see sex. All I see is the betrayal.

"Jefe, please..." she rasps out through a pair of swollen lips. One eye blinks open. The other is swollen shut already.

Ignoring the tearing pain in my shoulder, I yank on her hair again, forcing her face upwards. "You want this to end. I want to not be shot by my own fucking people. We don't all get what we want, now do we?" I lean closer to her ear and whisper, "Tell me what I want to know."

"I... I can't," she whimpers.

"Wrong answer." I rise to my full height and nod to one of my top enforcers.

Alejandro brings over a wet towel and a bucket of water. I take the towel from him and place it over

Jenna's face. She shakes her head from left to right in a lame attempt to get away. There's no point. She's not coming out of this alive, and we both know it.

Alejandro then starts to slowly pour the water over her face. After a while, I pull the towel off.

"Jenna, this could have been so much quicker if you weren't such a *puta*," I hiss at her. "I would have ended you hours ago. *You* made me draw this out. *You* are the only one to blame for your suffering right now."

"F-f-fuck you," she says. "I tried to warn you, Emmanuel. You didn't listen."

"*I* didn't listen? *I didn't listen?*" My laughter echoes against the concrete walls, dying off when the backside of my hand makes contact with her cheek. "I'm listening now, Jenna. Talk. Who else have you poisoned within my organization?"

I went through ten guys before I got to Jenna's name. I know she's the one who started it all. She managed to talk enough shit that she turned my own men against me. Either that or she was just fucking a bunch of them. It wouldn't surprise me.

"You had to know I'd find you eventually. What was your plan?" I grunt at her.

"My plan was to ruin you," she says. "I still will. You can kill me. It won't end, Emmanuel. It'll never end. You're going to die, just like your father, and his father before him."

My foot kicks out at the legs of the chair, knocking it over. And Jenna screams as I jump on top of her. "You think you can ruin me?" I laugh. Smiling down at her, I take the knife from my ankle. "Don't worry. I'll make sure you're remembered. The entire population of Mexico will hear of your death. Your name will be whispered within the streets. You'll be the warning of what happens to fucking idiots who think they can take me on."

"They know about her," Jenna whispers. "You can't save her."

My hand stills, my blade pressing against the skin of her neck. "Who?" I ask.

"The woman you're obsessed with, Evie Carter. They'll take her. Just like they took Laura." Jenna smiles like she's thrown me.

I count in my head. One, two, three. That's how long it takes for the blade to slice from one side of her throat to the other. I don't move, not until I watch the last sign of life drain from her body.

"See you in hell, *puta*," I spit out, wiping my knife against her shirt before I shove it back into its holder on my ankle. I turn to Alejandro. "I want her hanging from a traffic light. Make sure everyone gets a good fucking look."

The sick fuck smirks. He enjoys the kill more than anyone I know. "Sure thing, jefe."

Walking out the door, I dial Paz's number. I sent him to fucking Atlanta with Evie. "Jefe," he answers.

"Where is she?" I ask him.

"At her stop," he says.

"You got eyes on her?"

"Always, jefe," he replies.

"Jenna says they're coming for her." I leave out what she said about Laura. That's not new information. I know my father went after her. He'd ordered me to kill her. But he's dead. I know. I removed his head from his body myself. There's no coming back from that.

"She say who they are?" Paz questions.

"No," I grunt.

"Whoever the fuck they are, they'd have to go through me to get to her, jefe. I won't let that happen," he says.

I need to find a reason for Evie to return to Vegas. I have Lailani there. It's not that I don't trust Paz. He wouldn't be my second if I didn't. I just know how fucking good Lailani is at her job.

"Fuck it. I'm coming," I grunt. I need to see her with my own eyes.

"You do that, and whoever they are, you're giving them the ammunition they need to know she's important to you," Paz says. "I've got her, jefe. She's safe. Honestly, in this little fucking hick town, you're gonna stick out by a mile."

"Want me to send Lailani?" I offer.

"Fuck no! I need to be able to do my job without worrying about what she's doing," he grumbles.

I laugh. It's funny how scared he is of her. I get it. Lailani's dangerous, but his fear is unwarranted. She doesn't tend to just kill for the fun of it. It's more of a job for her.

I head back to the car and instruct my driver to take me to our compound. "I'll talk to you later," I tell Paz.

"Talk or see?" he asks.

"Talk. You're right. I shouldn't go chasing anyone right now." I don't need to put Evie in anymore danger than I already have.

Fucking hell, what was I thinking getting close to her?

I was thinking I had a second chance. As messed up as it is, she is a second chance to get it right. And this time, I'm not going to fuck it up.

Then my mind wanders to what Jenna said about Laura and if I was missing something. Who the fuck got to her? At first, I assumed she meant my father. Now, I'm not so sure. Was someone else at play? If so, who the fuck was it? And why would my father have done their dirty work for them? He wasn't the type of man to take orders from anyone.

---

Stepping out of the shower, I wrap a towel around my waist. And my hand swipes across the mirror to clear the steam from the glass as I pull the wet gauze from my shoulder. Digging through the cabinet, I find some antiseptic and some clean dressings. I take a few moments to patch myself up and then walk out into the bedroom.

It's not the first time I've been shot, probably won't be the last time either.

I quickly get dressed, fastening my cufflinks when an idea hits me. I pick up my phone and send a message to my artist.

ME:

I need a small piece done now.

HECTOR:

Your place or mine?

ME:

Mine.

HECTOR:

On my way.

I toss my phone onto the bed and remove the cufflinks, because Hector is going to need access.

She has managed to bury her way deep into my soul. I always thought people had one person, and for my entire life, I thought Laura was that person for me. I was wrong. What I feel for Evie doesn't compare to whatever it was I once felt for Laura.

Evie is different. I don't want her. *I need her.* The second I hear her voice, my entire mood shifts, and right now, I need that reprieve. I've grown to love this country over the years, taken it on as my own. I love the job I once despised, and I've built this empire to be more than my father ever dreamed it could be.

The power, the money. Having everything at my fingertips. It's a drug like no other. I want Evie to have it all right alongside me. I can't bring her here yet, though, and that fucking grates on my nerves. I should be able to bring my woman to my home and know she's safe.

Thirty minutes later, there's a tap on my door. One of my men pops his head inside to inform me that Hector has arrived.

"Send him in." I stand, remove my jacket, and fold the sleeves of my shirt.

"E, long time," Hector says as he saunters into

my office with an easy *I don't give two fucks* kind of attitude. It's what I've always liked about him. Most people who walk into this office do so in fear.

"I've been busy," I tell him.

"So I've heard. What are we doing today?"

"A name. Right here." I point to the spot on my wrist. "And it goes without saying that this name stays between us."

"Of course. So, who is she?" He quirks a brow, placing his bag on my desk as he prepares his gun.

"Evie." I feel my lips tip into a smile before forcing them down again.

"Not from around here then," Hector comments.

"No."

"Right. What font?"

"Script," I tell him. "She asked me about you, you know. Wanted me to get her an appointment."

Hector's hand freezes mid-swipe as he's cleaning the area on my wrist. "I'm assuming you told her no."

"I told her It'd be a shame for such a great artist to lose their hands." I laugh.

"It would be," Hector deadpans.

"Relax. She's not getting ink from anyone," I tell him. "She's perfect just the way she is."

"If she's managed to take you off the market, she must be something else."

When Hector's finished, I look down at my wrist. I can't wait to show Evie. She's going to fucking hate it. The thought makes me smile.

162

# Chapter Fifteen

It's been two days since I had that phone call with Emmanuel, when I heard the gunshots in the background. I haven't spoken to him since. Not really. There have been a few brief text messages but that's it.

If it weren't for Paz following me around town and sleeping in his car out front of my house every night, I'd start to think Emmanuel was losing interest in me. Which is what I want. Well, 99.99% of the time it's what I want. Right now, I fall into that other 0.01%, where I want him to want to talk to me.

I'm on my way to Rachel's house. She has a couple of days off from the hospital, and I know I'm going to be crashing soon. I don't feel comfortable sleeping in my own house. I need to know someone is there. Someone who won't let anyone else in. Someone I trust, like Rachel.

Tapping the button on my steering wheel to activate the car's voice command, I say, "Call Cabrón," quickly glancing in my rearview mirror. Paz is following me in a dark, nondescript car. It would blend in perfectly if I didn't already know it was him.

He doesn't say much, and whenever he does, he's polite and respectful. But knowing he's right outside my house makes me too damn nervous to sleep there.

The phone rings two times before the call connects. "Mi alma, driving and talking on the phone is not safe," Emmanuel chastises me.

"Neither is talking to a cartel boss, but here we are." I smirk. "Besides, it's the twenty-first century. Phones are hands-free."

"*Suspected* cartel boss, mi alma. Those are merely rumors."

*Shit, am I not supposed to say it out loud?* It's the very first thing he told me. I didn't think anything of it.

"Well, obviously, you're not. I imagine that kind of thing would require someone with a lot of smarts," I joke.

"Exactly. Where are you going?"

"Rachel's house. I just wanted to let you know that I'm probably going to crash out soon. You won't be able to reach me for a bit."

"You're driving while you're on the verge of falling asleep? What the fuck, Evie! Pull the fucking car over now," he yells into the phone, adding something else in Spanish that I have no chance of understanding.

"I'm fine. I'm almost there."

"Paz can drive you."

"I'm not comfortable falling asleep around him," I admit. "If he drives me, there's a strong chance I'll fall asleep in the car."

"Has he done something to you? Said something?" Emmanuel's tone changes almost immediately.

"No, it's not him. It's just... I don't like people being in the room with me or having access to the room while I'm asleep."

"Why?" Emmanuel asks.

"I just don't. What have you been up to? I was starting to think you were finally losing interest in me when I hadn't heard from you much." I pull the car into Rachel's driveway, pick up my phone, and switch the call to video. Emmanuel's face fills my screen. "Guess I'm not that lucky."

"I'm not ever going to lose interest in you, mi alma," he says. "You look fucking gorgeous. I thought you were going to your friend's."

"I am. I just got here," I tell him.

"You know, if you tell me what happened, I can hunt your demons and erase them," he says.

"Some demons can't be killed, E," I whisper. Emmanuel lowers his phone and something catches my eye. A bandage. "What the hell happened to your shoulder? And why are you naked?"

"I'm not naked. I have pants on, and I'm at the gym." Emmanuel pans the camera to show me.

"What happened to your shoulder?" I repeat.

"Remember that game you told me to try out a while ago? Well, I gave it a go. Turns out, it's not as fun as you made it sound." He smirks.

*He got shot? When? By who? What the hell! Why didn't he say something sooner?* I told him to try playing chicken with bullets. I was joking. I didn't actually want him to get shot.

"Are you okay?"

"I'm a lot better now that I know you care enough to ask," he says.

"Pfft, I don't care. I just want to know if I'm

going to need a black dress for your funeral. I got a new line in, you know. I could pick something out tomorrow... or whenever I wake up." I grin. We both know I'm full of shit. I do care. I just can't admit it out loud.

"I told my artist about you," Emmanuel hums, clearly changing the subject.

"Yeah? Did you get me an appointment?"

"Turns out he's fond of his hands, so no. But he did do this." Emmanuel holds up his wrist, and my name stares back at me in cursive writing.

"How many girls named Evie do you know?" I ask him.

"Just you," he says.

"What the actual fuck, E? Why would you put my name on your skin. That shit is forever, idiot. Fucking hell, seriously, what were you thinking?" I yell.

I climb out of the car and start pacing up and down the length of Rachel's front yard. Paz slides out of his own vehicle and stands a few feet away from me.

"I can't believe you would do that. I knew you were insane but this! This is stupid on a whole new level!" I yell before pausing in my steps. "Show me again."

Without a word, Emmanuel holds his wrist up to

the camera. "I am well aware of what things last forever. Are you?"

I turn to Paz and flash him my phone screen. "I told you he needed you there. Look what the idiot went and did! You can't erase that."

"Looks good, jefe," Paz says.

"I know," Emmanuel replies. "Evie, my body, my choice, right?"

"It's not always a choice," I whisper. "I have to go." I cut the call, walk inside, and immediately plop onto Rachel's sofa.

"You okay?" she asks. "Trouble in paradise?"

I tell Rachel all about Emmanuel and his weird infatuation with me, the onetime thing we did in the hospital, and all the messages and phone calls. She listens without judging and promises not to worry Charlotte with any of it.

"The man is seriously deranged, Rach. He got my name tattooed on his wrist," I huff out.

"Oh yeah, he sounds like a real looney." She laughs.

"It's not funny!" I groan.

"You have a rich, hot—did I mention *hot*—guy so into you that he tattooed your name on his *hot* body. How horrible your life must be!" she mocks.

"You missed the part about him being a cartel boss," I remind her.

"Meh, our jobs do not define us as people," she says, and I roll my eyes.

"Sounds like something a doctor would say."

It shouldn't bother me. He's right. It's not my body. But the fact he put my name on him is a big fucking deal. This infuriating infatuation he has with me isn't going anywhere. I agreed to give him a week of getting to know each other. And here we are, three weeks later...

"What am I doing? I'm playing with the kind of fire I know is going to burn me." I sigh.

"Well, it's a good thing I happen to know how to treat burn injuries," Rachel tells me. "You deserve this, Evie. Don't let your past take away something good from your future just because you're scared."

My brows furrow. "I'm not scared of E," I tell her. Because as stupid as it is, I'm really not.

"No, you're scared of letting yourself be happy, of letting someone in. Because you think if you do, they're going to run and then you'll end up alone and hurt again."

"You know, for once, I wish I had dumb friends." I shake my head.

She's not wrong, though. I'm afraid of him learning the truth. Because I know it's only a matter of *when* with Emmanuel. The guy is like a dog with a bone. He's not going to stop until he knows everything that happened to me, and when he does, he's not going to see me as some beautiful trophy he wants to own. He's going to see that beneath all that flawless skin, there's layer after layer of ugly scars.

"You just don't like that I'm right," Rachel says.

"I know," I groan. "Okay, enough of this boring boy talk. Let's watch a cheesy Hallmark movie. I'm about to crash, and I want you to make sure that if I do, no one gets into the bedroom while I'm sleeping."

"Deal, but let's watch it in the guest room. You're not sleeping on the sofa." Rachel stands and then pulls me to my feet with her.

After changing into my favorite sleep tee and washing my face, I get comfy on the bed in her guest room and turn on some Christmas movie.

"I love you, Rach," I say over a yawn.

"Love you too, Evie," she replies, squeezing my hand. "Go to sleep. I won't let anyone in."

"Thank you." I close my eyes and, for the first time in days, sleep overcomes me.

---

When I wake up, I'm alone. I roll over and glance around the room. I'm at Rachel's house. I have no idea how long I've been here. Reaching over to the bedside table, I swipe up my phone.

My eyes widen when I see the date. Two days. I've been asleep for two days! There're a few messages from Charlotte and one from Rachel letting me know she had to go to work, but that she made sure no one was going into my room. She set up a nanny cam and was monitoring it remotely for me.

I smile and send her a message back.

ME:

Thank you. Just woke up. I'm going to shower and head home.

RACHEL:

There's a package waiting for you outside the bedroom door.

My brows furrow. A package? She probably left breakfast, expecting I'd wake up soon.

At the thought of food, my stomach growls and I drag myself out of bed. It's always strange to lose so much time sleeping.

I open the bedroom door and freeze. Not exactly the meal I was expecting but not one I'll be turning away either. Sitting with his back against the wall, opposite the door, is Emmanuel. He looks up at me. But before he can stand, I pounce. My legs straddle his waist and my arms wrap around his neck. Then my lips fuse onto his. My tongue pushes into his mouth. Greedily. Not that he complains.

After a few seconds, I pull back. "Sorry."

I smile, suddenly self-conscious that I just threw myself at him, with morning breath too. Gross. I know that I look like crap. My hair isn't even brushed. *Oh god, what he must be thinking!*

Emmanuel's fingers curl around a strand that slides into my face. "You are fucking beautiful. And, mi alma, you don't ever have to apologize for jumping on me." He smirks.

"What are you doing here?"

"I arrived last night. Paz said your friend threatened to stab him with a syringe filled with enough morphine to take out a horse when he asked to check on you." Emmanuel raises a single brow. "I'm not sure about these dangerous people you're surrounding yourself with." The backs of his fingers brush over my cheek. Light, tender, almost reverently.

I lean into his touch. "No, what are you doing on the floor in the hallway?"

"The only way your friend would let me stay in her house is if I gave her my word that I wouldn't cross the threshold into that room," he explains.

"Yeah, Rachel can be scary." I smile.

"The fact I'm sitting here wasn't her doing,

Evie," Emmanuel says, his eyes connecting with mine.

"What was?"

"You. I want you to know that you can trust me. I want you to know that I wouldn't do anything I knew made you feel uncomfortable."

"Apart from kidnapping." I smile.

"That was a necessary course of action. It's behind us." Emmanuel leans in and presses his lips to mine. "You still owe me a week."

"We've been talking for *three* weeks. That deal has long since passed."

"No, you owe me a week of living with me, of getting to know each other in person." His hands move down to my hips, his fingers pressing into the flesh there. I'm dressed in only an old Taylor Swift shirt and a pair of panties. Charlotte isn't a fan, but I am unapologetically in love with the woman's music.

"I can't just leave. I have a shop to run." I sigh. "And bills to pay and... plants that need watering."

"I can have someone water your plants and handle any bills you have to deal with. As for the shop, tell Amy you'll pay her double to manage it for a week while you're gone. I'm sure she won't complain," he counters.

"Ah, I can't afford to pay her double, and you are not *handling* my bills. And... well, I actually don't have anything to say about the plants. Let me come back to you on that one."

"Evie." Emmanuel looks at me. "Just let go, say yes, and let us have this week." As he says this, he forces my hips to grind down on his cock—his hard cock. "Getting to know each other in person is not the same as over the phone."

No, it's definitely not. Pleasure radiates through my core.

"Okay," I say before I can find another reason to talk myself out of this insane idea. "But where are we going? Mexico?"

# Chapter Sixteen

I would love to be able to take Evie to Mexico. She'd never be able to leave the country without me knowing.

"I will take you home one day, but not now. Now, we're going back to Vegas," I tell her, instead of voicing my intentions of keeping her with or without her permission to do so.

The smile on Evie's face drops slightly.

"You don't like Vegas?" I ask her.

She stands. "It's okay. I'm starving. I feel like I haven't eaten in days. I'm going to have a quick shower and get dressed. Do me a favor and see if Rach has anything edible in her kitchen?"

I push to my feet and follow her when she turns and walks back into the bedroom she just came out of. "Evie, stop. Why don't you like Vegas?"

"I didn't say that. It's fine, Emmanuel. I need to shower," she tells me without turning around. Then she strolls into the bathroom and closes the door.

I'm about to follow her in there too when I hear the lock click. I shake my head. Does she really think a shitty lock will keep me out? I could get in there before she had time to strip down. Instead, I give her the space she clearly needs. Whatever her hangup with Vegas is, I'd put money on it having to do with her past.

I pull out my phone and send Paz a message.

ME:

Get me more Vegas pageant officials. Whatever happened to her, it was done there.

PAZ:

Already on it. Jet's ready whenever you are, jefe.

Opening the fridge, I quickly discover that there

is nothing in there to feed Evie. Well, nothing I'd want to feed her. So I take out my phone again and dial Paz.

"Jefe?"

"I need you to find a café. Get coffee and breakfast for Evie," I tell him.

"Already doing it. Figured she'd be hungry after sleeping for a couple of days," he says.

It fucking pisses me off that he's thinking about her needs before I tell him to. I keep those thoughts to myself, but my eye will be on him. If my second gets too close to her, I will fucking end him. Everyone is replaceable.

I don't reply, cutting the call and walking back into the bedroom. Evie is still in the shower. I can hear it running. I pull out a little pick I keep in my pocket, and the lock clicks within seconds.

"Evie, I'm coming in." I give her a little warning before stepping inside the room.

My feet stop and my heart fucking cracks at the sight of her sitting on the floor under the water, her knees drawn up to her chest and her arms wrapped around her legs. She looks up at me, her eyes red from crying.

My mind drifts to Laura lying on the fucking bathroom floor, and without realizing I'm doing it, I scan every inch of Evie's skin. Looking for any signs of self-harm. When I don't see any, I step into the shower, sit in front of her, and pull her onto my lap. Without a word, she buries her face into my chest.

"You're getting wet," she says.

"I don't care." My hand moves her hair aside, and I pull back a little so I can look down into her eyes. "You need to tell me."

Evie shakes her head. "I can't."

"You know I will find out anyway."

"And then you will see how ugly I am. You will see all my scars and damage and leave me alone."

"Try me." Nothing she can say will make me leave her alone. There's nothing that could make me not want her.

Evie shakes her head. "I'm sorry. I'll be fine. I just…"

"You know you don't need to be fine. It's okay not to be. Because whatever you need, I will find a way to make sure you have it, mi alma. I will be fine so you don't have to be." I stand, making sure Evie is balanced before I let go of her.

"Your suit is drenched," she says.

"It's just a suit." I shrug out of my wet jacket, grab my phone, and send Paz another message.

ME:

I need clothes.

PAZ:

For you?

ME:

Yes.

PAZ:

Clean up?

He's asking if I've left bodies on the ground.

ME:

No, I got wet.

I toss my phone outside the shower, then take my wallet from my back pocket and do the same. Evie stands under the water, watching as I remove everything that's strapped to my body.

"That's a lot of weapons. Are you expecting a war to break out in this little town?" she asks me.

"I always expect the worst," I explain. "It's how I stay alive."

When I remove my shirt, her eyes land on the gauze covering the bullet wound. "Did you expect that one?"

"No," I grunt. I'm fucking pissed off at myself for not seeing Jenna's betraying ass earlier.

"Does it hurt?"

"I've had worse." I smirk. "But I won't stop you if you want to kiss me better."

"Don't hold your breath waiting." Evie smiles at me.

I prefer it. Her smile over her fucking tears. I know she's trying to distract me from seeing her so fucking sad when I walked in here.

Once I've taken off all my clothes, I step forward and pick up the loofah, squirting some soap on top. Then I start wiping it over her shoulders, working my way down her arms. "I've thought about doing this for weeks," I admit.

"You thought about washing me?"

"Yes."

"That's... weird." She laughs.

I don't care if it's weird. "I like to take care of things that are mine," I remind her, moving the loofah over one breast, and then the other. This is the first time I'm seeing her completely naked. It's better than any fantasy I've cooked up in my head.

"I'm not yours," Evie says, watching my hand move farther south.

"Being my girlfriend makes you mine."

Evie laughs. "I'm not your girlfriend, Emmanuel. You haven't even asked me to be."

"If I want something, I take it. I don't ask. And I've never wanted anything more than you." My hand moves down between her thighs, as I push her back against the wall. Evie's legs part as I rub the loofah over her pussy. "Are you going to let me have you, mi alma?"

She shakes her head from side to side, but her legs open wider. Evie places her hands on my forearms. "I don't belong to anyone. I belong to me," she says.

"Wrong answer." I drop my hand away from her pussy and step back.

Evie glares at me. She was on the verge of an orgasm. "Why did you stop?"

I shrug. "You don't want me."

"I didn't say that."

"Tell me that you're mine, Evie, and I'll make you come so hard you won't remember ever not being mine."

Evie smiles at me, a defiant look in her eye as she reaches up and lifts the showerhead from its holder. "I don't belong to anyone but me," she repeats as she moves the nozzle towards her pussy. Her free hand covers one of her breasts, her fingers pinching and pulling at her nipple.

"You think a showerhead can give you better pleasure than I can?" I quirk a brow. "Okay. Show me." I lean my back against the opposite wall, calling her bluff. There is no way that showerhead can do for her what I can. My cock is rock hard. I wrap a hand around it, slowly pumping as I watch Evie bring herself pleasure. "Tell me that feels better than my fingers? Better than my cock?"

"It doesn't, but it's good enough," she fires back.

"You are an exceptional creature, Evie Carter. You should never settle for anything but the best," I say, stroking my cock a little faster.

"And you're the best?"

"For you? Yes." I'm her only fucking option. If she thinks she can find better than me, she'll learn real quick how I'll prove my point.

I can see the moment she's about to come. I step forward and rip the shower handle from her grip before she can fall over that edge of ecstasy. Then I drop to my knees in front of her, running my tongue up her slit.

"Nobody makes you come but me," I growl as I feast on her cunt.

Evie's hands land on the top of my head, and her moans echo off the tiled walls. I fucking love it. When she's come down from her high, I kiss my way up her body. My hand wraps around her throat and I hold her gaze.

"You are mine," I tell her before slamming my lips onto hers, letting her taste herself on my tongue.

Evie jumps up, wrapping her legs around my waist. "I want more."

I reach between our bodies and line up the tip of

my cock with her entrance. "I will give you every-thing you've ever wanted."

"I just want your cock, Emmanuel. Fuck me," she groans.

My lips tip up. "Anytime, anyplace."

My hips thrust in and out while her back is pressed against the tiles. My hand cups her head just as she's about to throw it backwards, breaking the impact of her skull against the wall.

"Fuck, you feel good," I grit out. Better than I remembered, better than anything I've ever fucking felt. I thrust in harder, faster. I want her pussy to feel my cock long after we've finished. I want her to know that I'm the one who makes her feel this good. "Come for me, mi alma. Soak my cock in your juices."

"Oh god, fuck, E!" Evie yells out, her pussy squeezing my cock so fucking good.

I pull out of her at the last minute, my own release spilling all over the wall behind her. "Fuck me, you are something else," I tell her.

"Thank you," Evie huffs out, her lungs working overtime.

"You're thanking me for fucking you?" I laugh.

"No, I'm thanking you for pulling out," she says.

I blink. I don't know why I'm bothered by the fact that she doesn't want me to come inside her. I pulled out on instinct, not because I don't want to come inside her. But I wouldn't do it unless I knew she really wanted it. Now that I know she doesn't, it will become my mission to make her want to be filled with my seed.

"You're not on birth control?" I ask.

"I am," she says.

"So it doesn't matter if I come inside you next time."

"Birth control isn't always enough. Don't come inside me, Emmanuel," she says, unwrapping herself from me. She bends and picks up the showerhead, placing it back on the holder.

"Finish up. I've got breakfast." I decide not to push the subject right now. Leaning forward, I press my lips against the center of her forehead. "Whatever it was that made you cry, I will find out and I will kill it."

"You can't kill memories, Emmanuel," she whispers.

"Watch me." There is nothing I won't do to kill whatever the fuck is haunting her.

# Chapter Seventeen

When I walk out to Rachel's living room, I find Emmanuel and Paz deep in conversation, both speaking Spanish. Clearly they don't want me to know what they're talking about. It's a good thing I have no interest in knowing what they're discussing. Otherwise, I'd tell them just how rude they were.

The minute Emmanuel sees me, the conversation stops. He steps forward with a paper cup in hand, holding it out to me. "Coffee, and there's food on the counter."

"Thank you." I take the cup. "You do know this isn't my house, right? You two can't just waltz in and make yourselves at home." I gesture from Emmanuel to Paz, who just gives me a blank look in return.

If Rachel knew they were in here, just hanging around, she'd have a heart attack. Rachel doesn't like people she doesn't know in her house.

I walk into the kitchen and pick up a blueberry muffin. I'm starving. "I have to go to the store. I don't know what you two are up to today, but you can't stay here," I say around a mouthful of food.

"I'll be outside if you need anything," Paz tells Emmanuel and walks out the front door. I continue to eat the muffin. Because one, it's delicious. And two, I'm hungry.

"How long do you need to be at the store?" Emmanuel asks.

"Why?" I counter.

"Because I have a pilot on standby to take us to Vegas. And if it's going to be hours, I'll let the guy sleep."

Well, now I feel like a bitch. He has people waiting on us?

"I had a shipment that was supposed to arrive yesterday. I need to check the stock and make sure Amy is okay on her own for the week."

"How long?" Emmanuel repeats.

"I should be done by four." That's five hours away. It will give me time to stop at home, get dressed properly, put on some makeup, and fix my hair before I go to the shop. Right now, I look like I've been freshly fucked, which I have been, but it's not the look I'm going for.

"Okay." Emmanuel's eyes bore into mine. He's looking for something. I'm not sure what. "I want to show you something before you go to the store."

My brows furrow. This is my town. What could he possibly have to show me here?

"I need to go home first. I need to change and fix my face and hair," I explain.

"Fix what now?" Emmanuel closes the distance between us, his hand curls around the base of my throat, and he tilts my chin upwards. "This face is fucking perfection, mi alma. There is no need to fix it." His hand then moves to my hair, his fingers twirling around a loose strand. "This hair, fucking perfect. What the fuck could you possibly have to fix?"

I blink up at him. I'm used to being told I'm

beautiful. I've heard it more times than I care to admit. The words lost their meaning for me a long time ago. But when Emmanuel tells me I'm perfect, with that conviction in his voice... Like he really believes what he's saying, there's a part of me that wants to be perfect for him. At least for the week I agreed to. After that, he should lose interest and move on. And if he hasn't, I'll figure out a way to make sure he does. Because us together, as good as it feels, is never really going to work long-term.

"Thank you, but I can't go to work looking like this. How about you tell me where you want to show me whatever it is, and I can meet you there?" I suggest.

"You ready to go?" Emmanuel asks.

"Yep."

I look around the kitchen and living room, making sure I haven't left a mess behind in my friend's house. Then I pick up my bag and keys, and take the hand Emmanuel is holding out to me. There's something very intimate about holding this man's hand. There's also a part of me that doesn't want him to let go. That part I shove deep down into the pits of hell. Nothing good will come of those kinds of thoughts.

Once we're outside, Emmanuel walks towards

where Paz's vehicle is idling by the curb. "Ah, I have my car here." I stop, pulling my hand away from his.

"I'll get Paz to drive it back," he says.

"No, you won't. I'm driving my own car home, E. You can do whatever you want, but I'm driving my car." I turn around and stomp towards the driveway. Before I can reach the driver's side door, Emmanuel catches up to me.

"Keys," he says, holding out his palm towards me.

I raise my brows at him. Is he seriously demanding that I give him my car keys?

"Yeah, that's not how this is going to work. I'm not a dog or one of your lackeys. You can't bark orders at me, Emmanuel." My hands land on my hips.

"Can I have your keys? I'll drive your car, with you in it, back to your place," he asks in a less-harsh tone.

"If you want to come with me, you are more than welcome to, but you're riding in the passenger seat." I move past him, open the driver's side door, and jump in. Starting the car, I wait as Emmanuel continues to stare at me through the window.

He rakes an aggravated hand through his hair, mumbles something in Spanish, and then he walks around to the passenger's side door and jumps in. Without a word, I reverse out of Rachel's driveway.

"You know, you don't have to come with me if my driving bothers you that much," I tell Emmanuel, who is sitting still next to me. Silently stewing.

"That's not what bothers me," he grunts.

"What *is* bothering you then?" I ask him.

"The fact that I can't seem to say no to you, or force you to obey me how I can with anyone else," he says. "See how easy that is? You ask me what's bothering me and I tell you the truth."

"You can say no. That's easy too." I smile and look over at him, ignoring his accusation.

"Keep your eyes on the road. You're driving precious cargo here, mi alma." Emmanuel points towards the windshield.

"You're not that precious," I tell him.

"Not me, *you*," he says.

"I'm not precious either."

"You are the most-precious thing I have, Evie. Don't do anything risky." He seems so genuine when he says things like that. Maybe he actually believes I'm special.

Once I'm back at my house, I park the car. Paz pulls in directly behind me. "He did that on purpose, didn't he?" I ask Emmanuel. "Blocked me in? Are you scared I'm going to drive off without you or something?"

"Or something," Emmanuel replies, getting out of the car. "You need a new car," he adds when he reaches me on the other side.

"There's nothing wrong with my car." I'm quick to defend my little BMW convertible.

"It's a death trap," Emmanuel counters.

"Everyone dies, E. If I die in a car accident, then at least it's in the car I love." I shrug.

"No." He shakes his head. "You're not dying on me, Evie. I can't do that again. I'm buying you a new car," he grunts and walks over to where Paz is standing on my front lawn.

"No, you're not!" I yell after him before turning and walking inside my house, letting the door slam behind me.

My mind is whirling. What does he mean he can't do that again? Did he lose someone he loved? Is he still in love with her? Whoever she is—*was?* Why the hell am I jealous of a person I'm not certain even exists?

I head into my bathroom, open the drawers, and start applying my makeup. I need to look my best. I'm feeling off-kilter. Being around Emmanuel does that to me. But, damn, does he know how to make me feel good too. I can't believe I fucked him again. *After* swearing it was only going to be a onetime thing. But the moment I saw him waiting for me to wake up... The fact he was outside the bedroom and not in it...

I melted, and all of my common sense went out the damn window. Because I wanted him. I wanted to feel his arms wrapped around me. I was so relieved to see him in person. I didn't realize how attached I'd grown to the man over the last couple of weeks. We've talked daily, but that shouldn't be enough to build an attachment.

After I'm satisfied that my face is perfect, I walk into my bedroom and find an outfit that will make me feel just as good as my face looks. Deciding on a light-pink bodycon dress with black lace cutouts that curve around my sides, I smile. I love this dress. I pair it with cute little black ankle boots. Then add some bracelets, a necklace and earrings, before I find a hair tie and pull my hair back into a high ponytail. I don't really have time to do much else to it.

I open my bedroom door and stomp out into the living room, where I find both Emmanuel and Paz standing together.

"Just so you know, it's rude to speak in a language I don't understand," I chastise them.

"Ah, I'll be outside." Paz shakes his head. "Good luck," he whispers to me as he passes.

*Good luck? What the hell do I need luck for?*

I watch him walk out of the house. And when I turn my eyes back to Emmanuel, his face is hard, his jaw clenching. "You look stressed," I tell him.

"You always go to work dressed like that?" he asks, waving a finger up and down my body.

Self-consciousness washes over me. "What's wrong with my dress?"

"My cock went from half-mast to fully erect the second you walked into the room—that's what's wrong with it. You look too fucking fuckable," he grunts.

"So it's my fault you can't control your dick?" My hands land on my hips. Now I'm mad. "That's the same as saying if I walk out of the house and get raped today, it's my fault, right? I was asking for it, because I looked so good, right?"

"No, that's not what I'm saying at all. Don't put words into my mouth, Evie. If anyone ever tried to... I'd fucking kill them before they could even touch you. I'm saying it's going to be real fucking hard for me to keep my hands to myself. It's no fun walking around all day with a boner." He steps towards me, and I take a step backwards.

"That's not my problem," I tell him.

"No, it's mine. But, you know, being my girl-friend and all, I thought you might care about my problems a little."

"Still not your girlfriend, Emmanuel. And I don't not care, but I'm not changing just because your dick gets hard a little too easily." I shake my head. "Now do you want to show me this thing or not?"

"Come with me." He holds out a hand. "You really do look fucking gorgeous, Evie. But that was true before you went and put all that on your face."

"I know," I tell him. Because I do. I'm not fishing for compliments.

# Chapter Eighteen

Evie isn't one of those women who needs constant reassurance about their looks. She knows exactly how beautiful she is. Sometimes I get the feeling she resents it.

Evie places her palm in mine. I use my other hand to adjust my pants. I wasn't lying when I said my cock is fucking hard. I can't look at this woman without finding myself in this predicament—regardless of what she's wearing. The more I get to know her, the worse my need for her becomes. I'm ready to say *fuck it* and take her home, find a way to never let her leave without her hating me for it.

I'm not usually one to tiptoe around someone. I know what I want and I take it. Evie is different. I *want* her to *want* to be with me. I don't want to have to coerce her or force her hand. Doesn't mean I won't if I have to, but I'd prefer if she chose me.

I lead her to the garden outside the property next to hers. "Remember how I said I bought a house?" I ask her.

"Yeah." She nods.

"This is it." I gesture in front of us.

Evie's head snaps towards me. "You didn't!" She gasps. "Emmanuel, why on earth would you buy my neighbor's house? That's insane."

"Because I don't like the idea of strangers being so close to you. I bought the one on the other side and the one behind yours as well," I tell her.

"You're surrounding me," she whispers. "Why? Seriously, this is a small town. The worst thing to ever happen here was one year when the Christmas tree went up in flames. Turned out some kids put fireworks in it and set them off when the tree was being lit."

"That's... I want to know who is close to you. I

want to know that you're safe, especially when I can't be here with you," I explain.

Evie shakes her head. "I need to go to work." Turning around, she tugs her hand out of mine and walks back over to her car. She glares at Paz as she slides into her driver's seat. "You can either move your car or I'm going to ram it."

He looks to me. "She took that well, jefe."

"Seems that way." I shrug. "Follow her. I have some calls to make."

With a nod, Paz climbs into his car and reverses out of the driveway. Before Evie can do the same, I open her car door and lean in. My lips press against hers. "I don't like you being angry at me."

"You should probably get used to it if you plan on sticking around, because you have this way of annoying me, Emmanuel," she says.

"I'll catch up with you later. I have some errands to run. Paz is following you."

"Thanks for breakfast. I forgot to mention that," she says. I can tell she's really struggling with whether she wants to punch or kiss me right now.

"Anytime, mi alma." I kiss her forehead and then straighten up, closing her door. I watch as she drives away, Paz following behind her.

I head into the house to the left of Evie's. I made

the owners offers they couldn't refuse, then arranged for them to be relocated while Evie was still in Vegas.

When I walk in, I find the boxes I had Alejandro send me. I could have had Paz do it, but I don't want anyone other than me knowing this stuff exists. Some things are best kept to yourself. With the boxes in my arms, I head back to Evie's house. She didn't lock up, so maybe I'll install a self-locking door.

Starting in her living room, I open the boxes of surveillance equipment and get to work installing cameras and microphones throughout the room. I don't just want to be able to see what she's doing. I want to know what she's talking about, if she's talking to anyone.

Once the living room is done, I move on to the kitchen, and then the bedrooms. I don't plan on having her stay here without me a lot, but if she is, at least I'll be able to see with my own eyes that she's safe.

There's also the fact that I might catch her talking about her past. I haven't been able to find shit out yet, no matter how many pageant fucking judges my men have interrogated. It's really starting to fucking piss me off that I don't know what happened to her. That I can't fix whatever it is that haunts her.

One way or another, I will find out, and I will erase her nightmares. I'll enjoy delivering her the heads of whomever the fuck hurt her too. I just need some fucking names. It's frustrating not being able to force her to do things my way. I love her fire, though, and won't do anything to douse that flame. She's going to need it to survive in my world.

After I've bugged the entire house, I put all the trash away, and then sit on her sofa and call Alejandro.

"Jefe, how are things stateside?" he asks.

"Did you get anything out of the judges yet?" I fire back. He picked up two more pageant judges yesterday.

"Not yet, but I've gone a different route. There's a local girl who competes in Vegas. I'm going to talk to her father, see if he's heard anything," Alejandro says.

"Someone has to know something," I grunt.

"If they do, they're all keeping tight-lipped about it," Alejandro says, "But don't worry, jefe. I'll find out. It's only a matter of time before someone breaks."

"I'll be back in Vegas tonight, so make sure nothing is at the compound." I don't want to give Evie any reason to try to run. She knows what I do. I don't hide it from her. Knowing and seeing are two different things, though.

"The place will be spotless," he says.

"Tell everyone to conceal carry. Evie's not a fan of guns in her face," I tell him.

"Most people aren't, jefe. I'll make sure your girl doesn't see a thing." Alejandro will get it done.

"Thanks." I cut the call and look around. This is Evie's space. There could be something here, something that could narrow down my search for answers.

I could look. She'd never know I did. Instead, I walk out and lock the door behind me. I peer up and down the street. I should have thought about how I was going to get to Evie's store before I sent Paz to follow her. I pull out my phone and call him.

"Jefe?"

"Is she still at the shop?" I ask him.

"Yep," he tells me.

"Good. I need you to come pick me up." I've been here too long. I need to see her. I hate being away from her, which is a fucking problem because she's not going to allow me to hover over her 24/7.

---

I watch Evie through her shop window as she helps customers and talks to her employee. "What do we know about this Amy?" I ask Paz.

"Not much. She lives with a boyfriend. Doesn't do much other than come to work," he says.

"I don't like the way she looks at Evie," I grunt.

"Jefe, most women look at Evie with envy, I'd say."

"I don't like it. Have the girl looked into further." I get out of the car when I see the last customer exit the store. I don't want to interrupt Evie's work, but I can't sit here and watch her all day either. I need to be closer to her.

A bell on the door jingles when I push through, and Evie looks up, a wide smile on her face that morphs into something a lot more genuine when she sees me. And then she glances around the room and the smile falls.

"Amy, can you run down to the bakery and grab me a coffee, please? And one for yourself too?" she directs her employee.

"Ah, you sure?" Amy asks Evie, who looks at me warily.

It's on the tip of my tongue to tell the girl not to fucking question her boss. She's been given an order. She needs to just fucking follow it.

Evie glares at me while answering Amy. "Yep, I'm sure."

I walk over to the counter, leaning forward and pressing my lips against her cheek. "Mi alma, I missed you."

"It's been three hours, E. You can't have missed

me," she says with a small smile. The bell on the door indicates Amy's departure.

"And yet I have, immensely." I walk behind the counter, my hands cupping each side of her face and my lips hovering over hers. "I'm not used to this," I admit.

"Used to what?"

"Missing someone. Caring if I see someone again or not," I tell her.

"Have you never been in love before, Emmanuel?" Evie asks. "I mean, not that you are now, but you're not exactly young. Surely, you've had girlfriends before me. Not that I'm your girl-friend either," she's quick to clarify.

"You are mine. I don't care what label you put on it. You are mine, Evie Carter," I tell her before slam-ming my lips on hers. My tongue pushes into her mouth. Evie's arms snake around my neck as she pulls me towards her.

By the time we pull away, she's breathless. "You didn't answer my question," she says.

"What question?" I ask, even though I know the answer. It's not a conversation I want to have, espe-cially with Evie.

"Have you had a girlfriend before?" she repeats.

"Once, when I was a teenager," I say. "You know,

this shop looks amazing, mi alma. You ever thought about franchising?"

"Who was she?" Evie presses.

"It was a long time ago and it's the past. It doesn't matter. What matters is the future. And you, mi alma, are my future."

"The fact you don't want to talk about her tells me she matters, E. I'm not going to get all hurt or jealous over some teenage girlfriend, you know. I've dated people before too."

"I don't want to talk about the men you've dated, Evie. I want to rip their heads off. I don't like the idea of knowing other people have tasted you, that other people know what you feel like. You are mine. Everything about you is mine," I growl. My arm wraps around her, and I pull her body flush against me.

"Emmanuel, you're shaking," Evie whispers.

"Because the thought of you being with other men makes me murderous."

"You should probably get a shrink." She laughs. "That's not normal."

No, it's not normal, but it's who I am.

"I'll keep that in mind." I chuckle and press my lips to the top of her head. "You know I was serious about you franchising this place," I tell her. "You have created something very unique here. It's amazing."

"I don't have the capital for that kind of investment, E. And, honestly, it's a lot to keep up with one store. I couldn't imagine doing more."

I did a wire transfer into her bank account two days ago. She hasn't seen it yet, because if she had, she'd know she had the *capital* to do whatever the fuck she wanted. The fact she's not screaming bloody murder at me is also a dead giveaway she hasn't noticed it.

# Chapter Nineteen

Lying in bed with Emmanuel's arms around me, I feel safe. That feeling tells me I've lost my damn mind. There is nothing safe about this man. I can't seem to stay away, though. I'm drawn to him in a way I've never been drawn to anything in my life. It's both suffocating and like being able to fully breathe for the first time.

Confusing is what it is. And I have no idea what to do about it. Which is why I'm giving him the week he so desperately wants. After this week, I'll return to my life in my small town, and he'll go back to Mexico. Sure, our paths will probably cross again. Our best friends are married to each other.

My fingers trace over the letters that spell out my name on his arm. It's insane that he tattooed this on him. Truth is, I secretly love it. I can't recall a time someone has wanted to memorialize me to the point of having my name permanently on their skin.

I wonder if he has the other girl's name on him. The one he so clearly did not want to talk about? I should make a point to inspect every inch of this man's body, just to find out. I didn't want to press him about her, because there are plenty of things in my past that I never want to tell him either. It would be hypocritical for me to push him to open up if I'm not prepared to do the same. There's also a small part of me that is jealous, no matter how stupid that is.

I close my eyes and inhale, loving the warmth that surrounds me. Emmanuel's arms tighten around my body. He's been asleep for the last thirty minutes. I don't want to move, because I don't want to wake him. Also, I like being right here. Next to him.

---

*"No, don't touch me!" I cry out, struggling against his hold.*

A scream jolts me and my eyes pop open. I look around the room. Emmanuel is sitting next to me on the bed, his jaw tense. Something's made him angry. I want to reach out and pull him into my arms, comfort him. But then he opens his mouth.

"Who?" he growls. His voice deep, cold. His eyes are darker than I've ever seen them.

"Did I fall asleep?" I ask. That never happens. We're still on the plane, so I couldn't have slept for long.

"Who the fuck touched you, Evie? I want a name."

"I don't know what you're talking about," I lie.

"You cried out *don't touch me*. Don't lie to me, Evie," he says.

"Then don't ask me questions I can't answer." I get out of bed and find my discarded clothes. "Were you watching me sleep? How long was I asleep?" I really don't like people being in the room with me when I'm asleep.

"I don't know. I woke up when you started thrashing around, crying out for someone not to fucking touch you. I got off the bed, thinking you were afraid of me, but you were asleep, Evie. Who were you dreaming about?"

"It was a nightmare, not a dream, and it wasn't real," I argue as I get dressed.

Emmanuel stares at me. Watching me. His jaw ticks and his eyebrows furrow. I know he's frustrated, but I need air. I need to get away from him before I cave and tell him everything... before I ruin everything. I want this one week, damn it. Just let me have this man for a week so I can look back when I'm old and say I once lived for myself.

"I need some water," I say, walking out of the bedroom. The plane is still in the air, so it hasn't been long.

"Ma'am, can I get you anything?" the flight staff, whose name I've forgotten, asks me.

"Can I get a water, please?" I reply.

"Sure, ma'am. Would you like me to bring it to the bedroom for you?" she offers.

"No, I'll sit out here. Thank you." I take a seat on the closest recliner. How on earth did I fall asleep?

A minute later, a body fills the seat next to mine. I don't need to look to know it's Emmanuel. "You know I only want to kill the people who haunt your nightmares, Evie."

I turn to look at him. "I don't want you to kill anyone for me, E. Let's just forget it and enjoy the week."

Emmanuel's eyes scrutinize me. "If you think I'm

letting it go, think again. Someone hurt you and I will find out who it was. You might not want me to kill them, but I promise you I'm going to. And when I do, you'll be able to sleep knowing they can never hurt you again. *No one* will ever hurt you again."

It's a nice thought, a lie I could easily see myself falling into. I'm not going to be that person. I'm not going to be so insanely stupid to let myself believe that he can keep me safe from the monsters in this world.

"I know violence is your thing. It's how you run your business, but it's not mine, E. I don't like guns. I don't like blood, and I don't like the idea of people dying because of me."

"I'm going to teach you how to fight, how to shoot, and how to use a knife. Once you're familiar with them, you won't fear them as much."

*That's what he got from me saying I don't like violence?*

I shake my head. "I don't want to be familiar with weapons, E. I just want..." I pause, because I don't know what it is I want anymore. I was content living my boring, small-town life. I have good friends. I have a great business. I didn't need or want anything else.

Now, there's Emmanuel. I want him in ways I never thought I'd want someone. I also want it to be temporary. I can't do the forever thing. I'm not girl-friend material. I can't even fall asleep next to him without waking him with my nightmares.

"I want you to be safe. That's all. I want to be able to protect you, Evie. I can't fail you. I won't fail again," Emmanuel says.

"What do you mean *again*? You haven't failed me at anything, Emmanuel."

"I couldn't protect you from whatever happened in your past, but I can make sure those who caused your nightmares learn their mistake," he says. But I don't think that's what he meant when he said *again*.

"You didn't know me in the past."

"I should have met you sooner." He's serious. I can't help but laugh.

"Yeah, okay, that's not really how life works, E. You might be used to controlling everything that happens in the world you live in, but that's not normal. And unless you have a time machine, not even you can change the past."

"I could hire a team of scientists to get working on that time machine." He smirks.

"That would be a complete waste of money. I'm sure you have more important things to spend your money on."

"I do have a niece now."

"You already gave her a ten-million-dollar trust. What else could you possibly give her?" I ask him.

"Whatever she wants." He shrugs.

"So what are you planning while we're in Vegas? You have me for one week."

"My plan is to keep you naked and in my bed for as long as possible, stopping only for food breaks."

"And here I was, thinking you were going to wine and dine me." I wasn't, but I wouldn't say no to seeing just how Emmanuel Lopez wines and dines a lady.

"You want to go out?" He looks at me curiously. "Like on dates?"

"Well, isn't that what people do when they're getting to know each other?"

"I wouldn't know. I've never dated anyone," he says.

"I thought you had a teenage girlfriend."

"We were kids, Evie. It's not the same." At the mention of her, Emmanuel's whole persona changes. He looks away from me and something flickers in his eyes. Pain maybe?

Now I'm more curious about who this mystery girl is and what she did to hurt him so much. "Do you have her name on you too?" The question is out of my mouth before I can stop it.

"No, you are the only person I've wanted to imprint on my skin, on my soul, mi alma."

"You don't even know me. I still think it's insane you did that." I look down at his arm, and a small smile spreads across my face. "It is pretty, though."

"It's a reminder of what I have to lose if I fail," he says, following my line of sight.

I don't have it in me to tell him that he can't fail, because I won't be sticking around long enough for him to fuck anything up. It's a week. What could possibly go wrong in a week?

"Are you planning on seeing your friends while we're here?" I ask, changing the subject to something lighter.

"I'd prefer not to have to share your attention with anyone else," he grunts.

"Okay. I haven't told Charlotte I was coming to town. I don't really want her to know that this is a thing. I'd rather we keep it between us."

"You ashamed to be seen with me, mi alma?" Emmanuel quirks a brow.

"No, it's not that. It's just... it's a week. We don't need to have the world involved in what you and I do," I explain.

Every time I mention the timeframe, Emmanuel's jaw ticks. He doesn't like it. But it is what it is. We live in different places. He's a cartel boss. I'm a dress shop owner. We might be compatible in bed, but that's where it ends.

"We will do this your way until your way doesn't work anymore," he says. I have no idea what he means by that. I also don't really feel like arguing about it either, so I drop it.

I look around the plane. A girl really could get used to living in luxury. "This is a really nice jet."

"You want one? I'll buy you your own." Emmanuel shrugs.

"Don't you dare do anything stupid like that." After seeing how generous he is with his friends and new niece, I wouldn't put it past him. "I'm not here because you have more money than you know what to do with, E. I'm here because you have a really nice dick." I smirk.

"My really nice dick thanks you for being here." He laughs.

# Chapter Twenty

Waking up to my girlfriend screaming out in pain isn't a fucking walk in the park. I thought someone was actually in the room. I was ready to get my hands bloody. When I realized she was asleep, my first thought was why the fuck can't I see into her brain? It'd make this so much easier if I could see her nightmares.

My second was... I don't care what I have to do. I will get her to tell me what I need to know.

I've been patient. I've been biting my damn tongue when I want to yell and scream at her for keeping this shit from me. We've been back in Vegas for two nights now. She hasn't slept since, and I'm fucking drained, only catching an hour here and there myself. Because I don't want to leave her alone longer than I need to. I've had to go out and deal with shit when it's come up, but mostly I've been right by her side.

"Why do you look like that?" Evie is sitting across from me. We're playing chess. Well, I'm teaching her how to play anyway.

"Like what?"

"Like you've already lost the game," she says.

"Trust me, mi alma. I never lose."

"You think I can't beat you?" She raises a challenging brow.

"Even if you did beat me, I'd still be winning," I tell her.

"How do you figure that?"

"Because you are my queen, and when the queen is winning, so is her king," I explain.

"You know, for someone who's supposed to be a big scary cartel boss, you do say the sweetest things." The smile on Evie's face makes me want to tell her so many more sweet things.

"Supposed to be? Are you doubting the fear I

instill in people?" I raise my brow at her this time. As much as I don't want her to fear me, I also don't want her to forget who I am.

"I've yet to see you do anything scary, E. For all I know, you're just some bored rich guy who made up a story." She shrugs.

"It isn't my goal to have you fear me, Evie, but don't forget who I am, what I'm capable of. If there ever is a time you have to see me do something... less than favorable, I need you to know that I would never be that person with you." I don't know if what I'm telling her is the truth. There is still a part of me that will kill her if that's the only way to keep her. Because letting her go isn't an option.

"I know who you are," she says, moving one of her pawns, which opens my next move.

"Checkmate." I smile.

"Again? Seriously? I hate this game." Evie pushes the board towards me. "I quit."

"You can't quit just because you're losing. You change your strategy. You learn and you improve. We never quit," I say.

"It's just a game, E. It's not that serious." She shakes her head from side to side.

"Maybe." I shrug again. "But we're not quitters."

My phone vibrates on the table, Sammie's name flashing on the screen.

SAMMIE:

I need you in Innes. Now. She's here.

His mother turned up a couple of days ago, around the time I came back to town with Evie. Sammie has a complicated relationship with his mother. She's an addict. Always has been, but she's his mother and he has trouble saying no to her when she wants something.

ME:

On my way.

"We need to go to the Strip for a bit," I tell Evie.

"I can wait here if you need to go and do something," she offers.

"I'd prefer if you came with me," I tell her. "I just need to help a friend with something. It won't take long and then we can go out and grab some dinner. You know, that whole wine and dine thing you wanted."

"Okay." She smiles. "But can I change first?"

"No need. You look fucking gorgeous just how you are." I stand and hold out a hand to her.

Evie places her palm on mine and follows me. "You say that even when I'm naked without makeup on, E. It doesn't mean I don't want to look my best if you're taking me out in public."

"You look your best when you're completely naked without makeup on, mi alma. But I'm not about to ever let anyone else see you looking like that." I lead her out of my office and through the house. She really does look fucking perfect. She always does.

It takes my driver fifteen minutes to pull up out front of the Wild Card. I have ten men surrounding us as I guide Evie through the casino floor, heading straight for Sammie's nightclub.

I see both the relief and questions on his face when he spots me.

"Fancy seeing your ugly mug here." I smile at Sammie before turning to his mother. "Ms. Russo, I had no idea you were in town. It's been a long time." When I hug her, she makes a point to press herself up against me. I step back almost immediately, never having let go of Evie's hand.

Ms. Russo turns her attention to Evie next. "And who is this beauty?"

My shoulders straighten. Friend's mother or not, I will fucking slit her throat if she tries to mess with my girlfriend. Ms. Russo likes to play mind games with her son, so I wouldn't put it past her to try them with me. I'm hoping she's not that fucking stupid, though.

"This is Evie." I squeeze her hand a little tighter when I say her name. "I was about to take her home. I just bought a new house close by. You want to come and see it?" If I can get the woman away from here for at least one night, it will give Sammie some peace.

When I look to my friend, I find his glare bouncing around the bar, until it lands on no other than Lailani.

"Fucking hell," I mutter as I stare at Lailani, who doesn't appear too thrilled at the moment. "I gotta use the restroom. Finish your drink, Ms. Russo. I think you're going to love my new house."

"I have a room here," she replies.

"You'd rather stay in this cesspool than the comforts of my home?" I give her the *don't fucking say no to me* look. "Now, I'm offended."

"Well, okay. Just for one night. I do need to grab some things, though. I'll wait for you in the lobby." Ms. Russo downs her drink before sliding off her barstool. "Sammie, we will continue this chat," she directs to her son before walking off.

"I'll be right back." I drop Evie's hand as I turn to her. "You want a drink?"

She doesn't say anything, just shakes her head, and I lift a hand, indicating for my men to step closer. Five of them are within reaching distance.

"I'll be quick," I whisper before moving towards the bar.

"Follow me," I tell Lailani as I pass her. By the time I turn the corner, she's right behind me. "Whatever you're thinking, don't."

"Why would I be thinking anything?" she asks.

"Because I know you, Lai. Just don't do anything without talking to me first," I tell her.

"Sooo, you want me to call you before giving Sammie a blow job? That kind of thing?" She peers up at me with that innocent look on her face.

"Cute. You know what I mean." I step around her and make my way back towards Evie. I hated leaving her, but I needed to check in with Lailani. I know what she's capable of and I don't want her doing something she'll regret later. Like killing her boyfriend's mother.

My friends are trying to keep whatever it is they're doing on the down-low. I don't know why, but it's not my problem.

"You ready to go?" I ask Evie.

"Yep." She hops off the stool.

"Thanks for coming," Sammie says.

"Don't mention it," I tell him. "I'll see if I can get

her to go home." I don't know what his mother wants. Usually it's money so it shouldn't be hard to coax her out of town again.

Ms. Russo is waiting for me in the lobby. She gives Evie a very disinterested glare before smiling at me.

"You ready?" I ask her.

"Lead the way, Emmanuel. You know, you always were my favorite friend of Sammie's." Her hand lands on my arm.

I step aside. "Thanks, Ms. Russo. Paz will drive you to the estate. Evie and I will be in the car behind you." I nod to Paz, who moves forward to lead the way.

"Okay, but you're going to give me the tour yourself, right?" Ms. Russo asks me.

"Of course." I smile, having absolutely no intention of spending any more time with the woman than I have to.

***

"Jefe, she's at the Paris Hotel," Paz says. Lailani disappeared after the club, while I've had a hell of a night trying to escape Ms. Russo's claws, which Evie found amusing.

I just left my girlfriend in a bathtub to come

downstairs and get some work done. "Go and get her, bring her back here, and make sure she's not seen," I tell him. The last thing I need is for people to know Lailani works for me.

By the time Paz returns with Lailani, I've just stepped in to check on Evie. "I'll be back in a second. Wait here. Paz needs something," I tell her.

"Where would I go?" she asks me.

"Nowhere I wouldn't find you," I say as I walk out of the room.

I jog downstairs to my office. The quicker I deal with Lailani, the quicker I can get back to my girl.

"Enjoying yourself?" I ask when I find Lailani sitting on my desk, drinking my tequila. Anyone else would already have a bullet between their eyes.

"Sure," she says, kicking her feet back and forth.

"Get off my fucking desk, Lailani," I grunt, as I maneuver around the furniture and drop into my chair.

Lailani jumps off and plops into one of the seats opposite me. "You summoned me?"

"No one summons you," I say.

"You seem to. Quite often actually. What do you need?" she asks.

"Can't a friend just want to check in with a friend?"

Lailani rolls her eyes. "E, are you lonely? Do we need to schedule lunch dates or something?"

"The woman you saw tonight. She's his mother," I explain.

"I know."

"Then why the fuck are you hiding out in a hotel room?"

"Because I like my peace." *She's lying.*

"Right, well, I'm gonna need you to find him tonight and make sure he's not falling apart."

"Why?" Lailani narrows her glare at me. "I mean, why would he be falling apart?"

"He has a... difficult relationship with that woman," I tell her.

"I'm not going to bother him when he's spending time with *his mother*." She shakes her head.

"He's not spending time with *his mother*. She's here. For tonight anyway." I don't know how I'm going to convince Ms. Russo to leave town, but I will find a way.

"Why is she here?" Lailani asks.

"Like I said, he has a difficult relationship with her and it stresses him out. A distraction, such as yourself, is exactly what he needs right now," I suggest.

"Yeah. I'm not a whore, E. I'm not going to go

and find your friend to distract him from his mommy issues," she snaps at me.

"No, you're going to find *your boyfriend* and distract him from his mommy issues, because that's what good girlfriends do," I correct her.

"I'm not. He's not." Lailani shakes her head back and forth until she relents, huffing out a breath. "Fine. I'll find him."

"Great. Now, pretend you've never been here," I tell her.

"Gladly." Lailani stands and smooths out her clothes.

"Oh, and Lailani," I call out before she makes it to the door. "When Sammie asks you to babysit for Carlo's kid, accept the offer."

"What? I am not babysitter material, E." Lailani's eyes go wide.

"You are the only person I want protecting my niece when her own father can't be there," I say. "Her safety comes before any of them. Hers and Evie's."

"How long are you staying in town?" Lailani asks.

"Until I don't need to be here."

"Right. Okay, how long am I staying in town?"

"Until you don't need to be here," I repeat.

"Helpful," she groans.

"If you want to quit the job, Lailani, you can. I'm not forcing you to be here." I'm not forcing her to do anything she doesn't want to do.

"I know. I happen to like this job. It comes with benefits." She smiles. "You should see how good Sammie is with his tongue."

"We're friends, but we are not those kinds of friends. You really need to find some women to gossip with. Paz will drive you back to the city. I believe Sammie is waiting for you in your apartment."

I stand and follow Lailani out of the office, leaving her to exit through the garage while I head up the stairs in the opposite direction. I need to get back to Evie.

# Chapter Twenty-One

When I agreed to come and stay with Emmanuel for a week, I honestly thought I'd get bored. I figured he'd be off working all the time and I'd be left to my own devices. I was wrong. He has left me a couple of times, but it's never for long. When he said he wanted us to get to know each other, he really meant it.

We've talked about everything—well, everything

except for the one thing he really wants me to talk about. My past. I can't do that. Not yet. I'm not ready to ruin whatever it is we have. My week is coming to an end, though, and I know I have to go back to reality. Back to my life.

Will it hurt? Probably. But I'll be okay. I've survived far worse.

"Penny for your thoughts?" Emmanuel asks.

We're both completely naked under the covers. He also wasn't lying when he said he wanted to keep me naked and in his bed as much as possible. Again, I'm not complaining. The man knows how to give an orgasm. The world could be ending, and I wouldn't care, because nothing else matters when he's touching me. My only thought is *more*. I want more of him.

"I was thinking about how our time is almost up and I have to go back home," I admit.

"Our time is only just beginning, mi alma," he says.

"I have to go home, E. I have responsibilities." I also have no intention of staying in this cocoon. As good as it is, it's not something that can last.

"I know. But you going back home doesn't make you any less mine." His eyes bore through me. When he looks at me like this, I feel like he can see right into my soul, like he can see all the ugly beneath the beauty and looks right past it.

Wishful thinking on my part. No one would look past the ugliness I carry within me. I wouldn't expect him to either.

"Long-distance relationships don't work, Emmanuel."

"Says who?"

"Statistics for every long-distance relationship ever."

"Fine. I'll move to your little country-bumpkin town." He smirks.

"You're going to move your entire empire to a small country town? That's not going to work." I laugh. I can just picture it now. My little neighborhood surrounded by Emmanuel's men.

"I would give it all up for you," he says quietly.

My eyes widen. "I would never ask you to do something like that." I wouldn't. He might not have chosen his life, but I do know he doesn't hate what he does.

Emmanuel looks at me pensively. "You wouldn't?" he asks, appearing almost puzzled.

"Why would I want to change you? If I did that, you wouldn't be you, who I happen to like. A lot."

Emmanuel smiles at me. It's a genuine smile I never see him give anyone else. It's purely mine, and every time I see it, my heart melts a little more for this man.

"You like me, huh?" He quirks a brow.

I roll my eyes. "If you tell anyone I said that, I will deny it until my last breath."

Something shifts in Emmanuel's mood. His entire face hardens in an instant. "Your last breath isn't something I want to think about." He places a hand over my heart. "I don't want this to stop," he says, looking down at my chest.

"Want what to stop?"

"Your heart, your life. I don't want to end it," he says cryptically.

I don't understand what he means. "Are you planning on killing me, Emmanuel? Because if you are, can you at least give me a few more orgasms first?" I roll over and straddle him.

I'm joking. I don't actually believe he is going to kill me. If I did, I wouldn't be in bed with him. Do I believe he's capable of it? Sure. But I'm not afraid of him.

"Not planning on it, no," he says, his hands moving to my hips as I grind my pussy down on his cock. I swear the man is a walking hard-on. He's always ready to go.

"Well, thank god for that because I'm not ready to die yet. I have a long list of shit I need to do before

I go," I tell him. My fingertips trail over his pecs, down across his abs, tracing each dip between the muscles.

"What's on this list?" Emmanuel asks. His own hands start moving up my torso until they're cupping each of my breasts.

"It's a long list."

"I've got time," he urges.

"I want to go to Paris fashion week. I want to spend my birthday in a villa overlooking the ocean in the Maldives. I want to be able to do charity work for orphanages and help children. I want to be able to make a difference in someone's life that has been dealt a shitty card. I want to live," I rattle off.

"I want to be the one to make all of those things possible for you, Evie." Emmanuel reaches higher and grabs behind my neck. He pulls me forward until his mouth is crashing onto mine.

My lips part, allowing him the access he's seeking. I've always enjoyed kissing when I've had a man who is decent at it. But I fucking love kissing Emmanuel. I can't get enough of him.

My pussy grinds on his cock before I lift slightly and move one of my hands between our bodies. Wrapping my fist around his shaft, I line the tip up with my entrance and slide down on him.

"Fuck, you feel so good," he says, breaking away

from the kiss. His hands grip my hips, holding my body still as he thrusts upwards. My clit grinds against his pelvis when he bottoms out inside of me.

"Oh, fuck!" I grunt out as he repeats the movement.

"Fuck, I love fucking you, Evie. You're so fucking wet, so fucking warm. Your cunt was made for me. It wraps around my cock like a glove."

"Oh god, don't stop." I know I'm going to miss this, the connection I feel when he's inside me. The way my body heats up. I'm almost certain I'll spend the rest of my life reminiscing about the week we've had.

"Fucking you is my new addiction. One I don't plan on curing." Emmanuel rolls me over, pulling out and then flipping me until I'm on my stomach.

He moves my body as if I weigh nothing, until I'm on my knees. His cock slams into me from behind, fast and hard.

"I want you to come all over my cock. I want to feel your juices running down my fucking balls."

*Oh god...*

My body shakes. Goose bumps cover my skin, and a light sheen of sweat forms on my forehead. Emmanual slows his movements. Positioning a hand underneath me while his fingers find my clit, pinching my most sensitive part and sending a tsunami of pleasure through me.

"Are you going to be a good girl for me, mi alma? Are you going to come? Drown my cock with everything you have?"

"Yes!" I cry out. My legs shake, and if it weren't for Emmanuel's hold on me, I wouldn't be able to stay upright.

He picks up his pace, hitting that spot that no one else has ever found. "Oh, fuck! I need you to come now, Evie," he grunts.

Seconds later, my entire body tenses up as I come apart for him. I've never experienced orgasms like the ones he manages to draw out of me, and I doubt I ever will again.

He pulls out quickly, and then he's spilling his seed all over my ass.

Rolling me over so I'm lying flat on my back, Emmanuel covers me with his body as his lips press against mine. "I will never tire of fucking you, mi alma," he says. They're not the sweetest words, and yet, they have a way of making me feel more cherished, more loved than I ever have before. "I'm going to run a bath."

I then watch as Emmanuel climbs off the bed and walks naked into the adjoining bathroom. "You know, you spoil me. Who is going to run my baths when I go home?" I call out after him.

Emmanuel's head pops around the doorframe. "Easy. Don't go home."

I laugh off his suggestion. Because, unfortunately, *not going home* isn't an option for me. He'd get bored with me eventually or find out the secrets he's desperate to know.

Emmanuel disappears into the bathroom, and I lie here staring up at the ceiling. I don't know what to say to him. I have no doubt he's serious, and if I said I wanted to stay, he'd make it happen. I can't put that on him, though. It's best that we end this thing after the week I promised him.

I shift onto my side, reach for my phone, and scroll through my emails. When I find my latest bank statement, I open it. It's not something I check often. Bookkeeping is the worst part of my business and my personal finances—well, they're not much better. I hate anything to do with budgeting and accounting.

I do, however, make sure there's always enough money in my account for a rainy day and that my bills are paid. That is what being an adult is all about, right?

When I open my bank statement, I blink and then zoom in on the document. *That's not right.*

Closing out of my emails, I log into my banking

app and, sure enough, the number with all the zeros remains on my balance.

"What the fuck?" I mutter as I sit up and click into the account. This money isn't mine. Someone's made a mistake.

But when I scroll down a little, and see a deposit from Lopez Enterprises, I know it's not a mistake. Well, not a bank mistake. It's an *Emmanuel mistake*. Jumping off the bed with my phone in my hand, I storm into the bathroom.

"What the hell, E? Is this for real?" I yell at him, turning my phone screen around so he can see it.

"Yeah, I was wondering when you were going to notice that." He smiles proudly, as if he's done something good.

"I don't know what kind of woman you think I am, but I am not a whore. You can't pay me for services rendered. I'm not some trophy you can pay to go along with whatever the fuck you're doing." I'm yelling. I have no doubt that the entire estate can hear me.

"When have I ever treated you like a whore, Evie?" he asks me.

I wave the phone in the air. "Right now. This," I say. "I don't want your money. I don't need your money. You can shove it right where the sun doesn't shine. I'm sending it back."

Emmanuel closes the distance between us. His hand snatches the phone from my grip and he throws it onto the counter. "You. Are. Not. A. Whore," he repeats, emphasizing every word. "You. Are. Mine. *My girlfriend.* And if I want to give my girlfriend access to fucking money, I will."

I shake my head back and forth. "I don't want it."

"Too fucking bad. I'm not having you need for a single thing, Evie. Try to send it back. I dare you." He smirks.

Does he really think he can threaten me into keeping his money? Yeah, that's not happening. One way or another, the twenty-five million dollars currently sitting in my bank account will be returned to sender.

# Chapter Twenty-Two

The look on Evie's face tells me she's not at all intimidated by me. Which I both love and hate. It's fucking frustrating as hell that she won't just do what I want her to do. That money in her bank account is hers, though. I don't care what she does with it. Let her try to send it back to me. She won't be happy with the outcome.

"You know what? I think I want to have a bath by myself," she says.

I look her up and down. Her nipples are hard. Her thighs are pressed together. "You sure about that?"

"Yep." Moving to the side, Evie holds the door open for me. "Thanks for running the water."

"Anytime, mi alma." I don't argue with her. If she wants to bathe alone, she's welcome to do so. "Don't touch yourself. I will know," I warn as I step out.

Evie grumbles something that I don't catch as she slams the door behind me. I hear the lock click into place and chuckle. She should know by now that no lock is going to keep me out if I want to get in.

I walk into the closet and get dressed. Evie loves her baths. Which means she'll be in there for a while. I head downstairs and message Paz to meet me in my office. Ten minutes later, he arrives.

"Jefe?" He walks in and sits across from me on the sofa.

"Anything yet?" He knows what I'm asking.

"I've just picked up three girls. The judges aren't talking, so I thought I'd change tack," he says.

My brows raise. "For the love of God, tell me you're not torturing fucking pageant girls." He also knows I'm trying to switch things up in the organization, and not targeting innocent fucking women is the start of that.

"No. I'm trying out other methods of persuasion." Paz smirks. I suppose using his charm is better than torture.

"Heard anything from Alejandro?"

"Not yet," he says.

I stand and start pacing the room. "There has to be something. I know something happened and I want to fucking know what it is," I growl, my fingers combing through my hair. "Someone has to know something."

"She still won't say?" Paz quirks a brow.

"No," I tell him. "I'm not pushing her to open up about something that causes her so much fucking pain."

I've thought about it, but whatever happened to her was bad enough to be giving her nightmares years later. And I'm guessing it's why she doesn't sleep as well.

"She wants to go home," I grumble. Evie is determined to go home now that our week is coming to an end. "Have the jet ready tomorrow night."

"Will do. You going with her?"

"I'll fly with her, but then we both have to return to the estate. I need someone else on her," I say, hating that I need to take Paz back with me. But he's the most trusted man in my organization and there's a lot of shit to sort through back home.

"I'll send Enrique. He's the closest to her town," Paz says.

"Make sure he knows what will happen to him if a single hair on her head is touched." I hate having to leave Evie, but I can't force her to stay with me. I need to give her the opportunity to want to stay first.

My phone pings with a message from the front gate.

**Front Gate: Mrs. Lopez is here. She wants to see you.**

"Fucking hell," I groan. My parents never officially married but that didn't keep my mother from taking my father's name or him from considering her his property.

"What?"

"My mother is here." This is the last thing I want to deal with right now. Don't get me wrong. I don't hate my mother. I'm just not ready for her to know about Evie.

"Want me to do anything?" Paz asks.

"No, I'll deal with her. Hopefully, I can get her to leave before she finds out I have a... guest." I choose my words carefully so Paz understands my meaning, then send a message to the gate, instructing the guards to escort my mother to the front door.

Paz follows me out to the foyer. The door flies open right as we approach. "Emmanuel, why on earth am I being stopped from entering my own son's house?" My mother kisses my cheek at the same time she's chastising me.

"Because we've increased security," I tell her.

"Mrs. Lopez, it's good to see you," Paz greets, and my mother gives him one of her disapproving looks.

"I hope you're keeping my son out of trouble in this god-awful city. Why have you two been hanging around so much lately?" she asks.

"I have a call I have to make. It was good to see you, Mrs. Lopez." Paz walks away, likely trying to avoid the interrogation.

"Ma, come into my office." I hold my arm out towards the hall, leading the way.

"I'm not here on business, Emmanuel. I'm your mother," she replies, crossing her arms over her chest while digging her heels into the ground.

"Fine, come to the sala then." I turn, knowing she'll follow me. "Want a drink?" I walk over to the small bar trolley in the corner and pour myself a tequila.

"I'm good. What are you really doing here, Emmanuel?"

"I'm not discussing business with you, Ma." I pivot to face her again. "You know that's not how this works."

"Okay then, why are you avoiding me?" she presses.

I shrug. "I'm not. I've just been busy."

"You are never too busy for your mother," she says, lowering herself down on one of the sofas.

I don't bother arguing with her. She will just keep talking in circles. "How've you been?"

I haven't seen her much. Not since my father's death and the release of the confinement that he kept her in. She's been making the most of her newfound freedom. Traveling and doing fuck knows what else.

When I get a notification on my phone from my bank, it takes everything in me not to react. *She didn't... Yes, she did.*

Evie fucking transferred the entire twenty-five million dollars back to me. How the hell did she manage to get that done so fast?

"Give me a sec," I tell my mother, putting my phone to my ear and walking out of the living room as I wait for the call to connect to my banker.

"Mr. Lopez, what can I do for you?" Grant asks.

"I need fifty million transferred into Evie Carter's account immediately. If she returns it again, I want you to double the sum and resend it back," I instruct. "As many times as it takes."

"Ah. Sure. Okay, I can do that," Grant says. "You want me to call you or just make the transactions?"

"Just make the transactions," I tell him before cutting the call. When I walk back into the living room, I find my mother exactly where I left her. "Can we do this another time? I really do have other things I need to do."

"You know, I heard a rumor that you had a girl hanging around," she says, rising to her feet. "I would hope that you're not pushing me out of your house for a woman, Emmanuel."

"Where'd you hear that?"

"Around." She shrugs. "Is it true?"

Before I can answer, I hear Evie's shriek coming down the stairs. "Seriously, E, this is insane even for you!"

My mother's eyes widen and she's immediately heading towards the foyer, where all the commotion is coming from.

"Where are you?" Evie yells out.

"Right here," I tell her.

Evie spins towards me. Her mouth opens and then closes when she notices I'm not alone. "Oh, I thought... I didn't know you had visitors. Sorry." She glances between me and my mother.

"This is my mother," I explain, taking a few short steps towards Evie.

"Oh, hi. It's a pleasure to meet you." Her features all fall into place as she gives that well-practiced, polite smile she has down pat.

"You're supposed to be dead," my mother says, her face pale.

My head snaps towards her. "What did you say?" I ask her in Spanish.

"She was supposed to die," my mother replies in English.

"What?" Evie looks to me.

I keep my expression neutral as I turn to face her. I do not need her to know just how unhinged I feel right now. "Evie, can you go wait for me upstairs? I'm going to see my mother out."

The sound of a gun cocking has me peering over a shoulder to find my mother aiming a barrel at my girlfriend. Without a second thought, I have my own pistol trained on my mother.

"Drop it," I grind out between clenched teeth.

"She isn't good for you, Emmanuel. She was supposed to be dead. Your father said he took care of her."

"How the fuck do you know about Laura?" I ask, my barrel still fixed on my mother as I step in front of Evie.

"Who do you think told your father about her? I was looking out for you. She was a distraction you didn't need."

"Drop the gun, or I will fucking blow your brains out," I warn.

"I did it for you, Emmanuel. That girl is going to get you killed," my mother insists. "Move out of my way."

"That's not going to happen. This isn't Laura. Laura's dead. But it wasn't Papa who did it. It was me," I admit. "And if you don't drop that gun, I will end you too."

"I'm your mother," she says.

"You, I can live with losing. Her, I can't."

"Emmanuel, don't do this," Evie whispers from behind me.

I don't give my mother another warning. She's not dropping the gun and I'm not giving her a chance to take a shot at Evie. My finger presses down on the trigger. A hole forms between my mother's eyes and then her body drops to the floor.

Paz, along with five other men, all come running into the foyer. He looks from me to my mother.

"Clean this up," I say. Then I turn around and take hold of Evie's hand, leading her upstairs and quickly closing us inside my bedroom.

Before I say anything, I pull her body tight against mine. She's shivering. I never wanted her to see who I really am. A man capable of killing his own parents without remorse.

"I'm sorry you had to see that." I press my lips against the top of her head.

"You..." Evie takes a step backwards, shaking her head. "Who is Laura?"

*That was not the question I was expecting.*

I inhale a deep breath. "She was my girlfriend, when I was sixteen. It was a long time ago, Evie."

"Why would your mother think I was her?"

"Because you look like her." I shrug.

"What happened to Laura?"

"I killed her," I say, waiting for her to run, to scream, for any sort of reaction. What I'm not expecting is for Evie to step towards me and wrap her arms around my waist.

# Chapter Twenty-Three

When the man you've been sleeping with tells you he killed his teenage girlfriend, the last thing you should be doing is hugging him. I do it anyway as I held on to Emmanuel tight. I needed one more hug from him because now I know this really is ending.

I just watched him shoot his mother. He pulled the trigger without blinking, and here I am, still wanting comfort from him.

"I'm sorry," I whisper. I'm sorry he had to do what he just did. For me. Someone who is a temporary fixture in his life.

Inhaling a lungful of air, I step out of his arms. When he tightens his grip on me, I shake my head.

"Let me go," I plead.

"I'm never letting you go, Evie," he says as he drops his hold from me. "You are mine. You will always be mine."

"I can't do this, Emmanuel. I'm going home," I tell him.

"No. We need to talk about this. We need to work through this," he insists.

"You just killed your mother. You shouldn't have done that. Not for me." The shock of everything that just transpired is finally hitting me.

"I don't need her. I need you, Evie. I will not live without you again. It's not happening."

I tilt my head to the side. *That's it.* Everything clicks. He's using me to replace her. The girlfriend he claims he killed.

"I'm not her," I remind him.

"Not who?"

"I'm not Laura," I clarify.

"I know," he says.

"You need to let me go. I can't do this." I don't

want to cry. I can't fall apart, even if my heart is breaking.

"No." I hear the determination in his voice. The hardness too.

"You don't want me, Emmanuel. I'm not worth this kind of trouble. I'm sure as shit not worth killing your mother over. You don't even know me! You don't even know—"

"Then tell me," he cuts me off. "Why the hell wouldn't you be worth it, Evie? Because I can guarantee there is no one I would ever put before you."

I shake my head again. I have to tell him. He's not going to let me go unless he knows the entire truth. He has to see all the ugly, broken parts of me. When he does, he won't want to keep me.

My throat goes dry. This isn't something I've ever talked about. I hate thinking about it, let alone talking about it.

I move towards the bed and sit on the edge of the mattress. "It started when I was twelve..."

Emmanuel's body stiffens. "What did?"

"I don't remember falling asleep. I remember winning a pageant and being in the car in my dress. When I woke up the next day in the hotel room, I was naked, and there was pain. But I didn't know what happened. But there was blood on the white sheets. I told my mom and she said I'd gotten my period. That's all it was." I shake my head. "I was twelve, so I believed her."

I take another deep breath and close my eyes.

"But it kept happening. After every pageant I won, I would wake up naked, sore, and there would be bruises." My voice is quiet. "One time, I remember waking up and someone was on top of me. A man," I admit. "He yelled at me and then something pricked my arm. When I told my mom about this incident, she said it was just a nightmare and that I needed to forget it."

I don't know what Emmanuel is doing. I can't look at him. I open my eyes and stare at the carpet.

"It just kept happening. It wasn't until I was sixteen that I really understood what was going on. I mean, I knew, but I wanted to believe everything my mom said. It was easier if she was telling me the truth."

"What happened when you were sixteen, Evie?" Emmanuel asks, his voice hoarse.

When I glance up at him, his jaw is tight and his palms are clenched. I've never been afraid of him, never saw him as the scary cartel boss I know he is, not even when I witnessed him kill his own mother. But right now, he looks every bit as scary as he is supposed to be.

"I... I was pregnant," I say quietly. "I told my

mom. I didn't know how it had happened. I never had a boyfriend. I didn't even remember ever having sex... The next pageant I went to, a Vegas event, I won. And the following day, I woke up in a hotel room and I wasn't pregnant anymore. My mom told me that they took care of it." I look down at my hands as they twist around the bedsheets. "They gave me an abortion while I was passed out."

Emmanuel kneels in front of me. His hands cup my cheeks. "I'm going to kill every single fucking one of them. I will deliver their heads to you on a silver platter. I promise this will not go unpunished, Evie."

"It won't matter. It won't fix anything, E. Now you know. Now you can see all the ugliness that's underneath the pretty skin. I'm not ever going to be normal. You need to let me go," I tell him.

"No." Emmanuel's voice is firm. "There isn't a part of you I don't love. You are mine. Even the broken parts, every last shard. They're mine and I'm not giving them back."

"I need to go home. I can't stay here." I peer down at where he's still kneeling in front of me. I don't want to leave him. I have to. We are not good for each other.

"I'll take you home," he says.

"Thank you." I sigh in relief. Maybe what I told

him is finally sinking in. I'm not the kind of complication he needs.

---

When Emmanuel said he'd take me home, he meant he would literally escort me home. Which is why he's currently standing in my living room, after helping himself to a tour of the place. He went through each room, inspecting every crevice. What he is looking for, I have no idea. This is a small town where nothing happens. I could leave my door unlocked and not feel like anyone was going to come in. It's why I've never moved away.

"Thank you for bringing me home. Now that you own the three houses surrounding me, I'm sure you can find somewhere else to sleep tonight," I tell him.

"You don't want me to leave, Evie," he says confidently.

"Maybe not. But I need you to," I say. He's right. I don't want him to leave. But I do really need to be alone. And the sooner I rip this Band-Aid off, the better.

Emmanuel's head tilts to the side as he stares right through to my soul. "I'm going to leave, but don't mistake this as me leaving *you*, mi alma, because that is never happening. I'm going to give you the space you need right now, but I will be back." Emmanuel leans forward and presses his lips to mine. Then I watch him turn and walk out my front door.

I twist the lock in place and lean my back against it as the first tear falls down my cheek. I wipe it away with the back of my hand and inhale a deep breath. Once I'm composed enough to move, I push off the door, walk into my bedroom, and fall onto my bed. My legs curl up, and I let the rest of the tears fall.

I knew letting him go was going to hurt. But this pain...? It's worse than I expected. I watched the man kill his own mother. He admitted to killing his girlfriend as a teenager. Why am I so hung up on him? There is something seriously wrong with me...

Emmanuel didn't let go of me for the entire flight home. He was either holding my hand or had his arms wrapped around me. It's as if he knew our time was coming to an end too. I know he says he'll be back, but when reality sets in and he realizes we're not good together, that I'm really not girlfriend material, his infatuation with me will die.

*You look like her.*

My mind can't get that one phrase out of my head. I look like the girlfriend he killed. How did he kill her? I'm so confused, with so many emotions that I don't know how to handle. Is that really the only reason he's so determined to be with me? Because he's replacing a love he lost with a lookalike?

A fresh wave of tears falls and my chest heaves as confusion, hurt, and loss surround me.

My phone pings from my pocket. I pull it out and immediately wish I hadn't.

CABRÓN:

If you need anything, call me. Day or night. I will be back, Evie. I don't care what you're thinking right now. This is not the end. Don't let your own fears hold you back from something great. I won't let you break us.

Why is he doing this to me? He needs to let me go. He needs to forget about me. I don't believe his words, as nice as they are. I need to be the one living in reality. The fact is, we are too different. We are not compatible. He is a murderer—I've seen it with my own eyes. It's also something that should be high on my list of Emmanuel cons versus pros.

The sound of my front door unlocking has me sitting up. *Please don't let it be him.* I don't move from my bed, but I do breathe a sigh of relief when Rachel appears in my doorway.

"Oh, Evie." She climbs onto the mattress and drags me into her arms. "I'm sorry."

"What are you doing here?" I ask her through my tears.

"Emmanuel messaged me and told me you needed me," she explains. "He didn't say why. What happened?"

He had her come here. He knew I wasn't okay, and because I didn't want him here, he sent my best friend. I hate how perfect he is.

*Nope, murderer. Not perfect. Far from perfect.*

"I told him what happened," I say through hiccups.

Rachel stills. "You told him. Everything?"

I haven't even told *her* everything. She knows that.

I nod my head, unable to look at her. I thought telling him would make him as disgusted in me as I am in myself. I thought seeing all the broken parts of me would make him not want me. I'm not sure it worked, though.

"What did he say?" she asks.

"That he'd deliver the head of every person who ever hurt me on a silver platter."

"That's, um, it's something," she says. "At least he means well?"

There is so much more I wish I could tell her. Somehow I can't bring myself to say the words. I trust Rachel. I do. But telling her I just saw

Emmanuel kill his mother could get him in a lot of trouble. I don't want to risk anything happening to him.

*Oh my god! I'm protecting him.*

The reality of that is not lost on me. I might not be able to keep him, but that doesn't mean I want anything to happen to him.

"I can't let him do that for me. It won't fix me anyway," I tell Rachel.

My phone pings with another message. I sit up and look at it.

CABRÓN:

You are not broken, mi alma. There isn't a part of you that needs fixing. Don't forget how fucking perfect you are.

My brows draw down. Why would he send me that right now? After what I just admitted to Rachel?

I shrug it off as a coincidence. What else could it be? I also tap on his contact and change the name from *Cabrón* to *E*. He really isn't an asshole. At least he hasn't been one to me.

# Chapter Twenty-Four

I left her. And ever since, all I've wanted to do is go back and fucking get her. She's not happy. She also won't fucking message me back. It's been two days. I know she'll reply eventually. She returned the fifty million I put in her bank, so I had no choice but to double it again. She hasn't said anything about that yet, but I know she won't be able to stop herself from cursing me out when she finally notices.

I look forward to it.

Until then, I'm going to straighten shit out as much as I can. I need it to be safe enough to bring Evie home. She can think we're through but we are far from it. We're never going to be done. Not even death will keep her from being mine.

"Jefe, you good?" Paz asks from beside me.

We're standing outside one of our factories, about to do a walk-through. I've been gone too long and these assholes need to know I'm still around, that my word is still fucking law. There hasn't been too much trouble since I cleaned house a few weeks ago, but you never know when cockroaches will want to come out of hiding again.

I've made it my mission to instill more fear than ever into the people within my organization over the last couple of days. The more they fear me, the less likely they're going to be to try to go against me. I've been using a different tactic on the civilians. I want them to adore me. I want them to want to please me. This is why I've been donating an obscene amount of money to schools, charities, etc.

It will work. People around here won't bite the hand that feeds them. And right now, that hand is mine. I might be the devil, the thing nightmares are made of, but when money is involved, they tend to overlook the horns.

"Yep," I tell Paz, pocketing my phone.

I was watching Evie. She's at home, looking fucking miserable. I want to call her but she's not answering. I have Enrique stationed in one of the houses next to hers, keeping an eye on her from a distance. She didn't like it when she noticed he was around yesterday, but I'm not leaving her without protection.

I meant what I told my mother. I can't live without this woman. I won't. I have no doubt the heartbreak I felt when I lost Laura will be nothing compared to losing Evie. I don't plan on fucking finding out either.

I open the door and am immediately hit by the smell of sweat. The heat is fucking ridiculous. The warehouse is set out with four rows of long tables, workers lining each side, weighing and packing product. As soon as my presence is felt, everyone freezes.

"Continue," I grunt, waving a hand in the air as I walk right down the middle of the rows.

I search every table, looking for any inconsistency that I could use as a teachable moment for these fuckers. I have a lot of frustration to get out, and my fists are exactly how I've been doing that over the last couple of days.

I wanted Evie to tell me what had happened to her. I needed to know. And when she did, it was worse than even my imagination could have conjured up. I figured something happened in her sleep, and that's why she doesn't sleep now. But what she told me, what those fucking assholes did to her... it's kept me fucking awake at night too.

Evie thinks she's broken, scarred, damaged beyond repair. I think she's fucking perfect. I just need to find a way to get her to see herself the way I do. As a strong, fiercely independent woman.

I stop in the middle of the warehouse and look around. Everything appears fine. Everyone is working while trying to ignore my presence, which I can understand isn't an easy feat.

I turn to Paz. "Think this is all going to be ready for the next shipment going out?"

"It will be," he says.

With Louie doubling his order, and another buyer wanting more, we need to increase production without dropping the quality. "I want it all tested before it gets packed up," I tell Paz.

"Already got it covered." He nods.

"Let's get out of here." I turn to leave and spot a man on the far side of the room staring right at me. It's not out of curiosity either. I walk towards him and his stare doesn't waver, nor does his obvious disdain for me.

Paz follows right behind me and barks out, "Who the fuck are you?"

The guy's attention moves from me to Paz. "Carlos," he replies.

"What the fuck is your problem?" Paz asks while stepping up next to me.

I tilt my head to the side. I don't know what's up with this guy, but I don't like it. I also don't need it.

"No problem." Carlos shakes his head, but his face betrays him again. He also looks somewhat familiar.

"Do I know you?" I'm already reaching for my pistol.

"You killed my cousin. Jenna," the asshole spits out. *Big fucking mistake.*

"I thought you looked familiar. Family resemblance, I guess." I smile, leaning forward to get closer to his face before that smile widens. "I enjoyed every fucking minute that bitch suffered."

"Fuck you," he hisses.

"Sure, you can try to fuck me... when we meet again in hell." My fist wraps around the collar of his shirt. The barrel of my pistol presses into the skin under his neck. "You really didn't think this one through," I tell him before pulling the trigger.

I let go of his shirt and shove his body backwards. The guy next to him quickly jumps out of the way.

"I want Jenna's entire fucking bloodline erased by the end of the week," I tell Paz.

Fucking bitch is haunting me from the pits of hell. I don't need any more cocky assholes thinking they can get revenge for their dead relatives. That's not how this fucking works.

---

I have the CCTV footage of Evie's house on my computer. I'm currently in a meeting with my top enforcers. Alejandro Cru and Los Cuervos. I want the fuckers who touched Evie to pay. And I want to be the one doing it. I also don't have time to just go out and round them all up, which is where these men come in.

"I want her mother picked up. She knows who and she knows when," I tell them. I haven't explained exactly what Evie suffered, but these guys aren't stupid. They know the evils that lurk in the darkness. "I want a list of names."

I turn towards my screen. Evie's lying on her sofa reading a book. She looks fucking sad. I've had a package sent to her. I'm hoping it will bring a small smile to her face when she receives it.

"There's a doctor. Her mother will know who he is. I want that fucking asshole too," I add.

Alejandro raises a brow but nods in agreement. "We will get the list and the doctor, jefe."

"These sick fucks preyed on an innocent girl. They're going to pay for it," I grunt.

I can't even begin to imagine what Evie went through at sixteen, finding out she was pregnant while knowing she'd never willingly had sex. And then waking up after an abortion was performed, without her consent. That's fucked up, and I've seen some fucked-up shit in my time.

"Contact Paz when you have them. I want to be the first to talk to this doctor," I tell them. "Keep the mother alive. For now."

As much as I want to kill the woman for what she's done to her daughter, what she let happen, I won't unless Evie asks me to do it. I can't risk pushing her farther away.

My attention returns to the screen. Evie's walking towards her front door. I smile.

"That will be all." I dismiss my men, then watch as Evie opens the door and takes the delivery of tall red roses.

The delivery guy hands her a box next. Evie smiles politely and shuts the door. She places the vase on the ground and picks up the box before she steps into her kitchen and sets it on the counter.

It's a gift that will keep on giving. But it's her

face when she opens it that I wanted to see the most. After cutting the box open, Evie pulls out the card. A small laugh escapes her lips. She quickly stops herself and frowns at the contents. She hesitates, hovering the box over the trash can until she finally decides to let it drop.

I swipe up my phone and send her a message.

ME:

Pleasuring you is my favorite thing to do. Just because I can't be there doesn't mean I can't give you pleasure. Wear the gift, Evie.

# Chapter Twenty-Five

I stare at my phone screen. *Wear the gift.* He can't be serious. But it's Emmanuel Lopez. Of course, he's serious. My gaze goes to the trash can. Who sends someone vibrating panties? Emmanuel, that's who.

He told me that he was the only one who would ever give me pleasure again. I guess this gift is his way of controlling my pleasure. Well, screw that. I don't plan on wearing those panties, and if I want to pleasure myself, it'll be with my trusty vibrator that has never let me down.

Before I can stop myself, I type out a reply to him.

ME:

> Thanks, but no thanks. Don't send me gifts.

E:

> You can't tell me what to spend my money on, mi alma. If I want to shower you with gifts, I will.

ME:

> I threw it in the trash. I don't need anything from you.

E:

> I know. BTW, those roses by the door need water.

My brows draw down. *How does he know I left the vase there?*

I look around the kitchen as if the answer is going to just jump out and hit me in the face. Surprise, it doesn't. But now that I'm talking to him, I don't want to stop, which is a problem.

Emmanuel is like a bad drug habit I can't break. It's been two days since I've spoken to him. He's messaged me and tried to call, and I've ignored all of his attempts. I figured he'd stop eventually and that it would all get easier.

ME:

How do you know the roses are by the door?

E:

I put cameras in your house.

My eyes widen. One thing I'll give Emmanuel? He doesn't lie to me. No matter how much I won't like the truth, he still gives it to me. It's refreshing and somewhat comforting.

Where the hell has he put the cameras? I search through the kitchen and can't find anything that looks out of place. I don't see any flashing red lights like they show in movies either.

ME:

Why would you put cameras in my house? That's creepy and an invasion of my privacy.

E:

So I can watch over you. Protect you. You are mine, Evie. You don't get to hide from me.

I stop the smile that started to form on my lips. I really do need to find a shrink because the fact that I find that endearing and hot is problematic.

An idea comes to mind. I don't understand why he's still showing interest in me, but one thing we've always had is sexual chemistry. I honestly expected that to die down the second he found out about my past, and it might still. But right now, while he's still interested, I'm going to beat him at this little game.

ME:

Where are the cameras, Emmanuel? Do you have them in my bedroom?

His response comes fast.

E:

No, I wouldn't do that to you.

A wave of relief washes over me. He knows how I feel about being watched when I sleep. I know it's stupid to be grateful that he didn't put cameras in my bedroom when I should be livid that he has them in my house at all. But honestly, this could be fun. He's in Mexico. That's a long way from here.

ME:

Where are they?

E:

Foyer, living room, kitchen, study, laundry, and by the back door.

ME:

So if I'm sitting on my sofa, you
can see me?

As I wait for his reply, I walk into my bedroom.
Rummaging through my drawers until I find what
I'm looking for. *Perfect.*

E:

Yes.

After changing into a little white silk slip, I
remove my panties and dig out my trusty vibrating
friend. I message Emmanuel on my way back out to
the living room.

ME:

Are you the only one who can see?
Is anyone else watching this?

E:

You think I'd let other people look
at you? Fuck no. It's just me.

ME:

Good. You might want to tune into
the living room. I hear the show's
about to start.

I leave my phone on the counter and walk out. I
don't want to be distracted by his messages. I want to

show him that I own my pleasure. Screw him and the whole bullshit thing with him being the only person that can pleasure me. I've been doing it a lot longer than he has. Sure, he might be better at it, but I'm good too.

I plop down on the sofa and look around the room. I have no idea where the cameras are located. It doesn't matter, though. He said he can see me. With my vibrator in one hand, I lie down and pull the straps to my slip over my shoulders, just enough so that my breasts tip out.

I cup one of my breasts with my free hand while the other moves south. I let my legs fall open as the vibrator reaches my core. Then I switch it on and close my eyes. The first thing I see is him. Emmanuel. His smirk, that one dimple I love on his cheek. Then it's his eyes. Dark, full of lust and sinful promises. The way Emmanuel looks at me—like I'm something special—that's what gets me every time. I've had men look at me with desire. But with Emmanuel, it's different. It's not just desire. It's like he needs me as much as I need him.

I squeeze my eyes closed tighter, rubbing the vibrator over my clit before moving towards my entrance and pushing it inside. My teeth bite down on my lip as I smile. The thought of him watching me do this is making me wetter. I start to pump the vibe in and out. Slowly at first, but it doesn't take long for my speed to increase as I chase that peak. I picture Emmanuel fisting his cock, his hand wrapped around the base. I can see my name on his wrist as his hand slides up and down.

Damn it. Now I want to taste him. Feel him fill my mouth.

I imagine myself on my knees, his hands wrapped around my hair as he feeds me his cock. I greedily take all of it, every single inch he gives me. I can taste him. I can feel his warm spurts down my throat as he fucks my mouth. That's when my orgasm hits me. My thighs clench closed, my pussy contracting around the vibrator.

When the last of the pleasure leaves my body, I open my eyes, disappointed when I don't find Emmanuel staring back at me. Holy shit, I can't believe I just did that.

Standing on wobbly legs, I fix the straps of my slip and make my way back into the bedroom. Swiping up my phone along the way. It's ringing, and I'm not at all surprised that it's him on the other end.

I decline his call dead turn on the shower. I can't stop myself from looking around the room, searching for cameras. Of course, nothing stands out, so I message Emmanuel again.

Seriously? I don't want to talk to him. It's one thing to message him, but to hear his voice...? I don't think I'm that strong. I can't fall back into him. I just got him to leave. He might be in Mexico but I have to wonder how much work he actually gets done, because he's constantly messaging and calling me.

I waver between calling him and telling him to *fuck off* over a text message. Curiosity gets the better of me, though. I need to know where these cameras are. Which is why I find myself pressing the green call button next to his name.

"Mi alma, that was some show you put on." His voice comes through deep, raspy.

"Are there cameras in my bathroom, E?"

"I miss you," he says, instead of answering my question.

I sigh into the phone. "I don't like being watched, E."

"You just made yourself come, knowing full well I was watching, Evie. I think you like being watched," he says, sounding cocky and self-assured.

"I was proving a point," I tell him.

"What point was that?"

"That I don't need you to give me pleasure. I am more than capable of making myself feel good. And if I wanted to, there are plenty of men in the world who would be willing to pleasure me too, so you can stop sending me gifts of the vibrating kind."

"Mi alma, any man stupid enough to touch what's mine will find themselves missing a head," Emmanuel growls. "As for the gifts, it's my money and I'll spend it how ever I please. Spending it on you just happens to be what pleases me the most. There's also the fact that I know you were picturing me while you were shoving that dildo up your cunt."

I gasp. There is no way he knows what I was thinking. "Nope, I was not thinking about you at all. Your ego really is too big, E." I turn the phone on speaker, set it on the vanity, and slide the slip down my body. "Are there cameras in this bathroom or not?"

"No, there isn't," he says.

"Thank you. I want all of them removed. And that lackey you have following me around, send him home."

"Enrique is one of my best lieutenants, Evie. He is not a lackey. He also won't be going anywhere unless you want me to come back already?" There's hope in Emmanuel's voice. He wants me to say yes.

"No. We can't keep doing this, E. We need to stop. You need to stop," I whisper.

"I would, if I truly believed you wanted me to. You don't want me to stop, Evie. You just need time to come to terms with what we are."

"And what are we?" I ask.

"Endgame, mi alma. You are my ending."

I cut the call, because I don't know what to say to that. Step into the shower stall, fall to the floor, and let the water wash over me. I never should have gotten involved with Emmanuel. Charlotte warned me and I didn't listen. I thought it was harmless flirting that would lead to one night of really great sex.

This... It's so much more than that. It's too much, and I'm scared I'm going to break more than I already have.

By the time I get out of the shower, there's a new message on my phone.

E:

You can run, but you can't hide from me. I see you, Evie. I see all of you, and you're fucking amazing.

# Chapter Twenty-Six

The image of Evie fucking herself with a dildo won't leave my mind. It has to be the most erotic thing I've ever seen. I know she was trying to prove a point to me, insist that she didn't need me. It failed on her part, though, because I know she was thinking of me when she came. I didn't need to be there. She closed her eyes and pictured me.

I wish I could see just what she was picturing so

I could make whatever fantasies run through her head come true. For now, I'll have to wait. I've had to fly back to Las Vegas. Alejandro called and said he was able to get the list out of Evie's mother without much fight.

I was surprised it was that easy for him. I honestly thought she'd deny any wrongdoing. According to him, she seemed broken and lost. Quickly rattled off the names of everyone who paid her to have her daughter—her words.

I said I wouldn't kill the woman, but fuck do I want to. What kind of mother does that to their child?

When I think about what Evie went through, a rage like I've never felt before courses through me. It's feral. Which is why I'm starting my vengeance for her with the fucking doctor who took her rights to choose away. I know that sounds hypocritical coming from me, considering I'm not giving her the opportunity to choose a life without me in it. I've never pretended I was perfect, though.

I've been sitting at the opposite end of the room, watching the man currently strapped down to an operating table. He's squirming, doing his best to get free. It's pointless. Even if he did manage to loosen his bindings, he'd find himself back on that table before he could take three steps.

Paz and Alejandro are here with me. Each just as eager to get the show started. There's a reason Alejandro is my top enforcer. He's a goddamn psychopath. He lives for this torturing shit. Me? I do it out of necessity. Usually.

Right now, excitement fills me at the thought of causing this fucker pain.

I stand and slowly make my way over to the table. A bright surgical light shines right above his face. I made sure it was flickering just to fuck with him. He's been here for five hours now, not knowing why or what was going to happen to him. It's time he learns.

"Hello, Dr. Venn. I've been waiting to meet you." I lean over the table. I want to see his eyes. I want the fear, the moment he realizes he fucked up.

"Who are you? Untie me!"

"Tsk, tsk, tsk." I shake my head. "I don't know why you think you're in a position to be making demands right now," I tell him. "From where I'm standing, you're in no position to be telling anyone what to do."

"What do you want?" he asks, his body going limp. Has he given up already? I hate when they have no fight in them.

"You did something to someone I happen to care about. A girl, a few years ago, right here in Vegas.

You performed a procedure on her without her consent or knowledge," I explain.

The asshole shakes his head again. "No. I wouldn't do that."

"Let me refresh your memory." I pull out my phone and show him a picture of Evie. It's one I found online from her pageant years. Evie has a face no one is forgetting. The woman is fucking beautiful.

The doctor's eyes go wide in recognition. "Her mother told me she wanted the procedure," he says.

"But she didn't," I hum. "You helped the people who abused this girl. You took something from her she will never get back. Now, I'm going to take from you."

"I didn't know!"

I wave a hand in the air, indicating for Alejandro to bring in our surprise guest. "The way I see this, you took a child from her, so it's only fair for me to take one from you."

Alejandro drags in a punk-ass college student who just happens to be the good doctor's twenty-year-old son. He's screaming but stops when he sees his father.

"What the fuck?" the kid yells, trying to pull away from Alejandro, who delivers a swift kick behind the knees, forcing the fucker to the ground.

"No! He had nothing to do with this. Take it out

on me! Leave him out of this," the old man pleads, his eyes tearing up as he stares at his son.

"I would, but I want you to feel every single bit of pain she felt when she woke up and discovered her baby had been killed by you," I tell him. "The difference is... you'll be able to see your child killed. You will know it's happening. She didn't."

"She was sixteen. A child would have ruined her life," Dr. Venn insists. "I was helping her!"

"You helped the people who abused her. You did not help her," I correct him.

Walking over to the table that hosts several surgical knives, I grab one. These little blades are sharp. I step behind the son, grab the back of his skull, and dig the blade into the side of his throat.

"You feel that? The fear? The loss? Now imagine you're a sixteen-year-old girl." I look the doctor directly in the eye as I make a clean slice right across his son's throat. "That..." I sweep out a bloody hand, aiming the tip of the knife in the doctor's direction as he screams out in agony. "That is a fraction of what she felt. Of what she feels every single fucking day," I hiss. "Do me a favor. Don't go anywhere."

I turn around, letting the kid's body drop to the concrete floor, and walk out of the basement. I want to leave the old fuck in that room for a few hours. I want him to stare at his dead son before I end him. I don't want his suffering to be over just yet. Evie has had to suffer for years. A few hours are nothing in comparison.

I head into the bathroom, wash my hands, and glare at myself in the mirror. I've never shied away from the monster glaring back at me. I've embraced it. This was my father's doing. He created this man. And for the first time in my life, I'm thankful to him for it. Because being *him* means I can do what I have to do to get vengeance for Evie.

A few minutes later, I'm heading down to my office, Maria following close behind me. "I have lunch," she says, placing a tray of food on my desk. "You need to eat. You're looking skinny."

"Thanks?" I ask with a raised brow.

"When is Miss Evie coming back?" Maria nods. "I like you better when she's here."

"As soon as I can convince her she wants to come back." I shrug.

"Well, don't make me wait too long," Maria says before walking out again.

I shake my head at her. Maria has always been like a second mother to me. Which then has me thinking about Laura. I never suspected that my mother was capable of doing that to me. Of taking something away from me.

I was never going to let her do it a second time. I didn't want to kill her, but when it was a choice between her and Evie, I chose the woman I want to spend the rest of my life with. I chose the woman I need more than I need my next breath.

Leaving the tray of food, I stand and pick up my car keys. "Going somewhere?" Paz asks from where he's now standing by the door.

"Out. I'll be back in a few hours," I tell him.

"Need me to come?"

I shake my head and make my way to the garage.

---

I haven't been back here since I first saw Evie. I've been avoiding her. Laura. I felt like I'd replaced her and I didn't want her to know. But I haven't replaced her. Evie isn't Laura.

"I wish I had known what was going on back then. I wish I could have saved you," I tell Laura.

I don't wish for her to be alive now, though. I don't want the life we could have had. Because the life I want now isn't with her. It's with someone else.

"I met someone. You would hate her." I chuckle. "But I..." I stop myself short. I don't want the ghost of my ex-girlfriend to hear those words before the woman who earned them does. Evie needs to hear them first. "I'm sorry, Laura," I say as I stand and leave, messaging Evie as I walk back towards my car.

ME:

I miss you.

Three simple words but they couldn't be more true. I fucking miss her. I need her to hurry the fuck up and come back to me. I don't know how much longer I can allow her to believe that I've left her alone.

EVIE:

You can see me anytime you want.
Just turn on your creeper cameras.
The ones you STILL haven't
removed from my house.

I laugh to myself. I have no intention of removing those cameras.

As I jump in the car, another message comes through from Lailani.

KILLER WOMAN:

Someone took a shot at Carlo in
front of the Royal. He had Jazzy
with him. Both are unharmed.

A red haze fills my vision. Someone took a shot at one of my friends and his six-year-old daughter? My fucking niece? Today is not the fucking day to be that someone.

I immediately dial Louie.

"E, now's not a good time," he answers it on speaker.

"It usually isn't when you're being attacked. What do you know about the shooter?"

"We're handling it," Louie says.

"That's not what I asked. Someone took a shot at my niece. I want to know who it was," I growl.

"We're tracing the plates now. We will find the fucker," Carlo chimes in.

"Not if I find him first," I say before cutting the call. And I will find them first.

As soon as I get back to the house, I head down to the basement. I need to finish the doctor off and then move on to finding my next fucking victim of the day.

The old man looks defeated. He's accepted his fate, his gaze locked on his son's lifeless body.

"I hope it fucking hurt like hell. Because that's exactly where you're going, motherfucker." I wanted to draw out his suffering. Right now, I just want to send him to hell.

Picking up the blade I used to slice his son's

throat, I step up to the table. I don't bother saying anything else as I slice Dr. Venn's throat from one side to the other. Then I pick up a vial and hold it under his jaw until it's full to the brim before securing the cap and pocketing the whole thing.

Alejandro and Paz are both standing behind me when I turn around. "Someone took a shot at Carlo and Jazzy. I want their fucking head now," I grunt. "No one takes a shot at my fucking niece."

I haven't known the kid for long. She just recently turned up on Carlo's doorstep with a note. But she's his daughter, which makes her family. And honestly, she's the sweetest fucking little girl I've ever met. I will do anything to protect her.

# Chapter Twenty-Seven

Skimming through a catalogue and circling items that I want to stock is a part of my job that I love the most. It's been a quiet day in the store, but the lead-up to prom means I know the busy season is fast-approaching.

Staying on top of the latest fashion trends is a must. Like I said, I love it, though. It's what I've missed about the pageant world after I left. The dresses, the glamor. That shine was only disguising the monstrosities underneath it all...

I shake my head, trying to get those memories out of my mind.

"Oh, that's hot," Amy says, peering over my shoulder and pointing to a black evening gown I just circled in red pen.

"It really is," I agree.

It's been good to be back at work, back to my normal life. Well, as normal as it can be when you have a member of the De La Sangre Cartel following you around whenever you leave your house. I do my best to pretend he's not there. Enrique. That's who Emmanuel says he is, anyway. I've never spoken to the guy. Personally, I like Paz better.

My head pops up when the bell on the door jingles and a very tired-looking Rachel walks into the store, still wearing her scrubs.

"Hey, I didn't know you were stopping in today." I drop the red pen onto the counter and walk around. My arms pulling my friend into a tight hug.

"I came to see how you were doing," she says.

I squint at her. "Did Emmanuel send you?"

"No." She laughs. "I don't need your boyfriend to tell me how to be a good friend."

"Not my boyfriend. But thank you. I'm fine." I turn as I say this because she will know I'm anything but fine. I miss him. I don't want to, and a part of me hates myself for it, but I want to see him. I want his arms wrapped around me. I want his lips on mine.

"Sure. You got time for lunch?" Rachel asks.

"Ah, I shouldn't." I look around the empty store.

"Go. It's quiet. I'll be fine here," Amy tells me with a smile on her face.

"Are you sure? I've left you alone so much lately," I ask her.

"I'm sure. I've got this." She nods.

"Okay. Call me if anything comes up. Anything at all."

After getting my purse and phone from behind the counter, I follow Rachel out of the store. We walk arm in arm down the quiet street. Neither of us needs to tell the other where we want to go for lunch because we have our favorite little diner just around the corner.

I turn and glance over a shoulder. Enrique is exactly five paces behind us. "You know he's kinda hot, in that look but don't touch way," Rachel whispers.

"Who is?" I ask her.

"The bodyguard who's following us." She smirks.

"Look but don't touch. Where was that advice when I met Emmanuel? I could have saved myself a lot of heartache." I sigh.

"Pretty sure Charlotte said something along those lines," Rachel reminds me.

I give her my best unimpressed side-eye. "Have you seen the man? He could have come with a warning tattooed on his forehead and I still would have ignored it."

"Probably, but I'm sure it wasn't all bad. You went back for more. That says something."

I'm not a relationship kind of girl. I've done my best to avoid them. I went with Emmanuel for the week because I told myself it was only *a week*. Prior to that, when we were talking daily through messages and phone calls, it was new friends chatting. Or at least that's what I like to tell myself. Now, I can't seem to go an hour without thinking about the man...

"Do you regret it?" Rachel asks after we squeeze into our favorite booth.

"Regret what?"

"The week you spent in Vegas with him?"

"No." I shake my head. "Well, there are parts I'd like to change, but I can't." *Like the fact that he killed his mother to protect me. Or that he admitted that he'd killed his girlfriend.* "But also, I think spending time in Vegas has been therapeutic. I put so much on that city when really I should have dumped all of it on the people who did it, not the place where it happened."

"That's something to take away then, I guess, along with all the orgasms that man gave you."

"How do you know he gave me orgasms?" I raise a brow at her.

"Because only an idiot would go back for more if he didn't deliver the first time. And you, my friend, are no idiot." Rachel smirks.

"Why thank you, Doctor." I smile at my friend. "How's everything at the hospital?" I ask, because I don't want this whole lunch to be about me.

"I thought I knew tired. Then I became a resident. It's busy, so busy. But..." She pauses.

"But what?" I urge her.

"I've applied for a position in Seattle," she says quietly.

"What? Seattle? Why? That's so far away. First Charlotte and now you. I'm going to die old and alone," I groan.

"Don't be so dramatic. You're going to end up with Emmanuel. We both know that man is not leaving you alone. And you love him. Whatever he's done to make you want a break, I'm sure it will work itself out," she tells me.

I wonder what she'd say if I told her I watched him kill his own mother? That's out of the question, though.

"Maybe you should talk to Charlotte about him? She just married one of his friends."

"I'm not bothering her with my relationship—or should I say non-relationship? She's enjoying her time being a new wife, and I want her to be happy and carefree," I say.

"It's your choice, but I would not want to be you when she finds out you're hiding this from her." Rachel laughs.

"Pfft, I've got a bodyguard hanging around me 24/7. Not even Charlotte could penetrate that." I gesture a thumb over my shoulder towards Enrique.

"Maybe, but I bet she'd give it her all," Rachel counters, and we both laugh out loud, picturing our friend going berserk on a Mexican cartel member.

"I think it will all blow over soon," I say at the same time my phone starts ringing from inside my purse. I frown when I pull it out and see Amy's name on the screen. "Amy?" I answer.

She never calls. I always tell her to call if she needs me but she never does.

"I'm so sorry. I don't know what to do!" she shrieks.

"It's okay. What's happening?" I ask her.

"I was steaming some dresses. One of them caught fire and I couldn't stop it. I'm so sorry. I ran out of the store," she explains, and I hear fire trucks zooming past the diner.

I look up to Rachel, and without a word, I pick up my purse and run for the door. Before I can get there, Enrique is blocking the entrance. "Why are you running?" he asks me.

"Get out of my way!" I yell at him. "My store is on fire. I need to go." I shove at his chest, but he doesn't budge.

"What do you mean on fire?" Enrique grabs my wrist. He's holding a pistol in his other hand, and then he's dragging me out of the diner.

"Put that thing away. You're going to draw unwanted attention to us. And let go of me!" I hiss. The moment I walk outside, I can spot the smoke billowing in the sky.

"Stay behind me. We need to get you out of here," Enrique says.

"No! I need to put that fucking fire out." Managing to twist out of his hold, I kick off my heels and then I run barefoot down the street.

I round the corner and come face-to-face with my store. Two firetrucks are blocking the entrance, their hoses already spraying water onto the building. I can't look away.

An arm wraps around my waist. "Don't ever fucking run off on me again. I'm trying to protect your ass here," Enrique growls in my ear from behind me.

"If you don't remove your hands from me right now, I'm going to scream bloody murder," I tell him.

"You think that scares me?" he asks. "You need to get in the car. I need to take you home."

"You can fuck right off." I shove my elbow into his ribs. He hunches over, his hold on me loosening, but not enough for me to get away from him again.

"Fucking hell. Calm down," he grunts.

"My store is on fire and you're telling me to calm down? Fuck you." The next time I try to elbow him, he manages to move out of the way before I can make contact.

"I'll let you go, but you need to stay by my side," he says.

"Sure," I agree in a sugary-sweet voice, having no intention of following through.

"I'm calling jefe," he says.

"Don't," I tell him. "He's busy, and this..." I wave a hand towards my shop. "...doesn't concern him." I walk over to a fireman who is talking to Amy. She doesn't appear hurt. I'm glad she got out okay.

"Oh my god, Evie, I'm so sorry. I don't know what happened. One minute everything was fine and then..." She shakes her head, tears running down her cheeks. "It's all my fault."

"No, it's not." I pull her into a hug. "It's okay. It's going to be okay," I say, unsure if I'm trying to convince her or myself. I'm lost. I don't know what I'm supposed to do.

"What happened? How much damage will there be? Is anything salvageable?" These questions all come from Rachel, who has finally caught up with me. She's looking at the fireman, waiting for answers.

"We won't know for a while yet. Who's the owner?" he asks.

"I own the shop but I rent the building. I can get you my landlord's details if you need them," I reply.

Shit. Am I going to have to pay for this? I don't know how I will even replace all the stock that I've just lost. How the hell am I supposed to repair a whole building? This is going to ruin me financially.

I could sell my car. Who needs a car anyway? Maybe my house too? I don't need that either, right?

"Okay, this is what we're going to do. We are going to take Amy home. Then you're coming to my place. We will contact your insurance provider and find out what we need to put in a claim for the losses," Rachel says, taking charge of the situation.

*Insurance. Yes. I have insurance. Why didn't I think of that?*

"Okay." I nod my head and follow Rachel and Amy to the car that's parked across the street.

My phone rings. I'm not surprised when I see Emmanuel's name on the screen. "I'll catch up with you. I need to take this," I tell the girls before answering. "Hello."

"Mi alma, are you okay?" Emmanuel asks.

"Physically? Sure," I tell him.

"I'm sorry. What do you need?"

"I need to not have your guy manhandle me for a start, and then I need to not have my store burned to the ground. I'm sorry. I'm a little busy. Can I call you later?"

"Enrique manhandled you? How?" Emmanuel growls through the phone.

"I'm fine. I ran. He didn't want me running towards a burning building. It was a misunderstanding." I try to smooth over the situation. I don't think Emmanuel would do anything to the workers he's instructed to protect me? I mean, the man is just trying to do his job.

"I'm done waiting. I'm coming to get you. I'll be there tonight. Pack a bag. You're coming home," Emmanuel says, and then the line goes dead. *He's not coming here.*

Shit, he is. Emmanuel Lopez doesn't say anything he doesn't mean. Darn it. What do I do?

# Chapter Twenty-Eight

"Paz, we gotta go get Evie. I need the jet and a new fucking lieutenant for the western region because I am going to fucking kill Enrique!" I yell out through the house. I have no idea where Paz is, but I know he's close. He's always close.

As expected, he rounds the corner. "What'd he do? Is Evie okay?"

"Her shop is currently burning to the ground.

She said something about Enrique manhandling her," I grind out between clenched teeth.

"He touched her?" Paz's brows raise in surprise. "Fucking moron," he adds in Spanish before heading towards the garage. "Let's go. I'll contact the pilots on the way to the hangar."

"I'll meet you at the car. I need to grab something." I run upstairs. Opening the safe in my wardrobe, I retrieve the small velvet box I've stored there for Evie.

A few minutes later, Paz jumps into the back seat of the car with me. I have my laptop out as I search through the CCTV footage of Evie's shop that I have stored on the cloud. How the fuck does a dress shop go up in flames? In my experience, fires are never an accident.

I watch as Evie leaves with Rachel. Enrique messaged me earlier, saying that they'd stopped at a local diner. I watch as Evie's employee walks around the store. There's something about this girl I don't like. Amy maneuvers around the counter. She taps a key on the computer and then the cameras cut out.

"Someone turned her cameras off," I tell Paz. "At the dress shop."

"Who would target her?" Paz asks.

"Anyone on that fucking list we got from her mother." *If they know we're coming for them...*

Fuck, I should have considered how this could come back to her. I don't care what I have to do. I will be taking her back to Vegas with me. At least I have more men there, more secure properties.

"Have you spoken to Enrique?" Paz asks. "He see anything?"

"No, I don't want him to know I'm coming for him. He was at the diner with Evie when the store caught flames," I explain.

"When you say manhandle, what exactly did he do?" Paz questions.

"Does it matter? He fucking touched her. He was instructed not to fucking touch her," I grunt.

"I'll find someone suitable for promotion on his crew." Paz scrolls through his phone. I close my laptop and message Evie.

ME:

It's going to be okay.

I know what that shop meant to her. The fact she's just watched it burned to the ground will be breaking her heart. Whoever fucking did this will pay.

EVIE:

How? I've lost everything.

ME:

You will never lose me. I will build you a new store, anywhere in the world you want it. I will fix this for you.

EVIE:

I don't want your money, E.

ME:

You don't need my money. You have your own.

I know she sent the fifty million I put into her account back. I had my banker double it again. She either hasn't noticed or is choosing to ignore it until she figures out her next move.

Evie reads the message but doesn't respond. A few minutes later, she's calling me.

"Hello, mi alma," I answer.

"Don't *mi alma* me, Emmanuel. What the hell did you do? One hundred million? Are you freaking kidding me? Are you trying to get me arrested or something? How do I explain the sudden deposit of a hundred million dollars into my account?" she screams down the phone. "I have enough to worry about right now. Your crazy ass isn't something else I want to add to the list. Take it all back."

"Are you done?" I ask, waiting for her tirade to end.

"No," she huffs.

"I know you're stressed, Evie. I understand how you feel. But you haven't lost everything. That will never happen. It's just a hiccup. You will get your shop back. I promise you," I tell her. "Whoever is responsible for the fire, I will find them and I will make them pay."

"It was an accident, E. Amy was steaming a dress. She said the fire started. She didn't know what to do and ran out of the store," Evie says.

I don't want to put more stress on her than she's already under, so I don't question her employee's story. I'll ask the girl myself. I don't believe for a second that the CCTV was accidentally cut minutes before the fire started, or that a fucking garment steamer could ignite such a large blaze.

"I... I need to go. I'm sorry. Just... forget I said anything. This isn't your problem, E. It's mine, and I will deal with it."

"Evie, your problems are mine. You are mine," I remind her because I feel like she purposely forgets that fact.

"I'm not anyone's. You need to forget you met me. Go and find someone who's not as much of a mess as I am," she tells me.

"You really want me to go and find another woman? Take her to bed?" I ask.

Evie hesitates, but then she says, "Yes." It's quiet, soft, broken. But she uttered the word.

"Too bad. It won't work. You wanna know why?"

"Why?"

"Because she wouldn't be you. I'll see you in a few hours. Stay with Rachel. And don't mention anything to Enrique. I don't want him to know I'm on my way," I tell her.

"He's gone," Evie says.

"What do you mean *he's gone?*" My back straightens.

"He overheard me tell you he manhandled me, mumbled something about getting a bag from his car, and then he got in it and drove off. I haven't seen him since. I thought you finally listened to me and sent him home."

"Evie, I need you to walk around Rachel's house. Lock every door and don't stand in front of any windows. Does Rachel have guns?" I ask her.

"No. What's going on, E? You're scaring me," she says.

"It's nothing. I just don't like the idea of you being alone. Unprotected. Find a knife, a weapon, and hold on to it. Remember to always choose yourself," I tell her. "I'll be there soon."

"What's happening?" Paz looks to me when I drop the phone onto my lap.

"Enrique left. He knows I'm coming for him. Bastard. She's alone," I grumble.

"I'm sending Tomás. He's only a two-hour drive away. He will get there in half that time," Paz says.

"Gracias."

---

The pilots made it to the small airfield just outside Evie's town in record time. Paz informed me that Tomás was outside Rachel's house, where Evie is staying. I feel a little better knowing she's not alone, but I'm keen to get to her.

I want her to know that she can rely on me. That when life throws curveballs at her, I will be there to shield her from the blow. I want her to turn to me for anything that she needs, because I will make sure she fucking gets it.

The car pulls to a stop out front of Rachel's house. I walk over and say a quick hello to Tomás, asking him if he's seen Enrique. I will find him, no matter where he's hiding.

My fist rises to knock on the door right as it swings open. "Where is she?" I ask, pushing my way past Rachel.

"Well, hello to you, Emmanuel. Gee, why don't you come right on in. Can I expect the rest of your entourage to drop by too? I don't think I have enough tea for everyone," Rachel snarks at me.

I glare at her. "You're a surgeon. I'm sure you know just how quickly a tongue can be removed from someone's mouth."

"Sure, threaten the best friend. That's how the villain ends up with the girl in all the stories." Rachel rolls her eyes at me—fucking rolls her eyes—and then slams the door behind us. "Evie, your boyfriend's here!" she yells out through the house.

"I don't have a boyfri..." Evie's words stop when she sees me enter the living room. "E, what are you doing here?"

"Please finish that sentence, mi alma." I tilt my head to the side.

Evie stands, walks right up to me, and presses up on her tiptoes to glare in my face. "I don't have a boyfriend."

My hand cups the back of her neck and my lips claim hers. My tongue pushes into her mouth, circling around. *Fuck, I missed her.*

When I pull away, I keep my hold on her. "You do have a boyfriend, Evie," I remind her.

"What I have is an obsessed stalker with psychotic tendencies. That is not a boyfriend. A boyfriend is someone who takes me out on dates, brings me dancing. Not someone who installs cameras in my house and watches my every move."

"We can agree to disagree. It doesn't change the fact that you're mine," I say. "Get your things. We're leaving."

"Um, where on earth do you think you're taking me?" Evie steps back, quickly folding her arms over her chest.

"Your house. I'm sure Rachel has better shows she can watch than the one you and I are giving her right now." I look to her friend, who hasn't left the room.

"I'm sorry, Rach," Evie tells her.

"Don't be. This is entertaining." Rachel shrugs.

"I'll call you tomorrow. Thank you for your help with the insurance company and everything." Evie hugs her friend, whispering something into her ear that I don't catch.

I wait for Evie to pick up her bag, and then I take hold of her hand. "Thanks for taking care of her, Rachel." I nod and lead my girl out of the house.

"Paz, how are you? Sorry you got dragged back here." Evie smiles at my second-in-command. I'm not sure I like the friendship these two have developed.

"Miss Carter, it's not a problem at all. Sorry to hear about your store." Paz nods politely before climbing into the driver's seat.

Evie and I climb into the back. Once she's settled, I lean over and whisper into her ear, "I missed you."

"It's been three days," she states.

"And?"

"You need help." She shakes her head but smiles at me. "So do I, apparently, because my first thought when I saw you was relief that you came."

"I will always come when you need me," I tell her.

Evie wants to be wined and dined, and I've been fucking shit at giving her that. I'm going to change it right now. I take out my phone, search for five-star restaurants on Google, and make a reservation for tonight. I want to take her out. I want to show her that I can be that guy. The one who listens and gives her what she asks for.

"We're going out tonight. I've made a reservation for dinner," I tell Evie.

"Really? Where? And what if I don't want to go on a date with you?" She lifts a questioning brow at me.

"You do. And it's a surprise," I say.

"You know, your ego is too big for your own good. You're not as hot as you think you are, Emmanuel." She smirks.

"I only need to be as hot as *you* think I am, mi alma. I don't care what anyone else thinks."

"Guess we should book a plastic surgeon then. 'Cause, honestly, you could use some work." She laughs.

If I didn't have confidence in bounds, her words could cut. They don't, though. I know the effect I have on this woman.

# Chapter Twenty-Nine

I think I need my head examined. Excitement fills me. I have butterflies at the thought of going on an actual date with Emmanuel. He wouldn't tell me where he was taking me, just that it was a nice restaurant. It's been a good reprieve from thinking about the store and everything I've lost.

I also haven't had a reason to get this dolled up in a while. I might have gone overboard on my appearance tonight, but I don't want to embarrass

Emmanuel in public. I want him to be proud to be seen with me. I also need to feel good about myself, and looking good always helps me stay calm.

I was surprised and excited when he showed up at Rachel's house. I know he said he was coming, and I didn't doubt him. I just didn't expect him to make it so quick. I don't know how to not want to fall into the comfort he offers me. Right now, I need someone to be a brick of support, and he's doing that. Without me having to ask him to.

I've given this man plenty of opportunities to leave me. And he won't.

*Because you look like her.* That nagging voice in the back of my head keeps popping up, reminding me that I'm not Emmanuel's true love. I'm her replacement.

"Holy shit." Emmanuel walks into my bedroom.

I'm sitting on the end of the bed, tying the straps of my gold heels around my ankles. Emmanuel squats down in front of me, pushing my hands out of the way. He takes hold of the strap of my shoe and fastens the buckle. His hands linger on my ankle.

"You look fucking breathtaking, mi alma," he says while his fingers travel up my calves.

I'm wearing a red bodycon dress that ends just above my knees. There's a small split in the back and the neckline is square-shaped, showing a good amount of cleavage in a non-trashy way. I curled my hair, leaving it to fall over my shoulders.

"Thank you." I look Emmanuel up and down.

His dark hair is styled to perfection, almost too good. I want to run my fingers through it just to mess it up a bit. I love when his hair falls over his forehead. And he's wearing a fitted-to-perfection three-piece suit. Then again, he always is.

"You don't scrub up too shabby yourself," I tell him.

"Thanks. You ready?" Emmanuel stands and holds out a palm to me.

"Sure. But this is our first date. Don't expect to be getting into my panties tonight." I smirk as I accept his hand.

"It's not your panties I want, Evie," he says.

"That's good, because I'm not wearing any." I laugh and walk out of my bedroom.

"What? Fuck. Wait. Stop!" Emmanuel calls out after me. I'm halfway down the hallway before he catches up. His arm wraps around my waist and he tugs me towards him. "Seriously, Evie? No panties?"

I nod. Emmanuel's hand snakes up the inside of my thigh. My back is flush with his chest. When his fingers reach my bare pussy, he groans. I almost tell him to forget the date when he slides those fingers through my folds, only to pull them away again.

Without another word, he straightens my hem and lets go of me. I turn to look at him over a shoulder, watching as he sucks those two fingers clean.

It's hot. Damn it! Why do I have no self-control around this man?

"You know, if you play your cards right, I might just invite you in for a nightcap."

"Mmm, I'm looking forward to dessert," Emmanual says, his eyes dark and full of lust. "Let's go, and keep those legs closed. If anyone gets even a glimpse of your pussy, I will kill them."

"I know you don't usually do this whole dating thing. But most girls aren't impressed by threats of murder, E." I pat his chest.

"Good thing you're not most girls," he replies, taking hold of my hand. "And that wasn't a threat, Evie. It's a promise."

Why does his possessiveness make me so insanely horny? He knows my worst secrets, the darkest part of my life, and he still wants me. Why?

*Because you look like her.* I shove that voice down a second time. I don't want to let doubt ruin tonight.

When we walk into the restaurant, I'm relieved I went overboard on dressing up. This place is swanky as hell. It's probably the nicest restaurant I've ever seen. I'm nervous. I plaster on my pageant smile and grip Emmanuel's hand as we're led through the posh interior.

When the waiter opens the private room, I look around, stopping at the entrance. Emmanuel glances back at me. "You okay?" he asks, eyeing me up and down.

"Uh-huh." I nod, that same smile still on my face.

Emmanuel frowns but continues to follow the waiter into the room. His hand wrapped around mine. When the waiter goes to pull a chair out for me, Emmanuel steps in front of the kid. "I've got it," he grunts.

"Of course, Mr. Lopez. We have wine and entrées ready for you as you requested. I will be back to collect your orders for the main course." The waiter lowers his head and walks out of the room, closing the door behind him.

I sit down and look around. The entire room is lit by candles. There are vases of red roses everywhere. The table is a small two-seater. Emmanuel sits across from me.

"This is really beautiful," I tell him. I've been on dates before, but this is next level.

"It was last minute. I can do better. I will do better for you," he says as he inspects the room.

"This is perfect. I don't need better, E."

"Why did you have that fake smile on your face, then? When we walked in?" he asks. "I don't ever want to be the recipient of that smile, Evie. I only want your real emotions looking back at me."

"I'm nervous. It's not you, or this place. I swear this is the most romantic date I've ever been on, and it's only just started. I just don't want to embarrass you. I don't want to do the wrong thing."

Emmanuel laughs. "You think you could embarrass me, mi alma? Never." He shakes his head. "You are the best thing I've ever owned. There is nothing you need to do other than be yourself."

"First, you don't own me. And second, I'm the second best you've dated. I'm not her, E," I remind him, already hating the fact that I'm jealous of a dead woman.

*A woman he killed*, I need to remind *myself* of that.

Emmanuel fills my glass with red wine. He doesn't say anything, just stares at me. It's not until he finishes filling his own glass that he looks away. "I know you're not her. I don't want you to be her, Evie. I want you to be you." His eyes meet mine again. "I love you, every single part of you. I love you more than I ever thought it was possible to love another person."

"Did you love her?" That's the response I give after having him declare his feelings for me? I'm a bitch, but I can't say those words back to him. Fear has a grip around my heart, and I can't bring myself to let go that much.

"I thought I did. I guess in a young, teenage way, I did. I wanted to save her," he admits.

"What happened to her?" Why would he want to save someone he killed? And why am I okay with the fact that he killed her? *Okay* is a strong word. I'm not *okay* with it, but I'm also not running for the hills.

"When I was sixteen, my father ordered me to kill her. He told me love was a weakness that needed to be killed before it killed me," Emmanuel says.

I gasp. "That's awful."

"I thought I could get her out, give her a new identity, money to leave town and never come back. I was going to lie to my father and tell him I did it," Emmanuel says. "I'd put her up in an apartment. She was a street kid, like Louie, Carlo, and Sammie. I was taken to live with my father, but I came back to Vegas as much as I could to see her. I thought I hid her well. The only people who knew about her were my mother and my friends."

I don't interrupt. I get the feeling he hasn't had this conversation before.

"I finally had her papers ready and went to the apartment to tell her my plans. I was too late, though. I found her on the bathroom floor with a needle in her arm. She overdosed. On purpose. I tore the needle out of her arm, and she looked up at me and said she killed my weakness so I could become the greatest."

Emmanuel doesn't appear sad when he recalls the events, but there is something about the way his face changes. I can't pin it.

"I thought it was my father's doing. That he got to her somehow. I never once thought that my mother would have been the one..."

"I'm sorry," I tell him. "You should not have had to go through that kind of loss, especially at such a young age." I breathe in a lungful of air. "Do you still miss her?"

"I..." Emmanuel stops. "I like that she's dead, Evie. It's fucked up, but I buried her in an unmarked grave. No one knows where she is. No one could take her from me again because she's dead. I liked that."

I blink, unsure what to say, what to do. "Why did you tell me you killed her? You didn't kill her, E."

"I failed her. It's the same thing." He shrugs.

"No, it's not," I tell him. "I failed my baby. I

couldn't protect the baby growing in my own body. Is it my fault it got killed?"

"What? No. You had no choice. Nothing that happened was your fault, Evie. You didn't fail. You were abused," he says between gritted teeth.

"Then Laura dying wasn't your fault either." I'm relieved I know the full story now. I'm not consciously dating someone who killed their girl-friend. Makes me feel a little less insane.

"I won't fail you, Evie. I will always protect you," Emmanuel says.

"I don't need you to protect me. I just need you to listen and give me space when I need it. And maybe be patient with me. I'm broken in so many ways I don't think I'll ever be whole."

"I will be the glue that holds your broken pieces together," he says. "I have a gift for you."

"A gift?" I smile, only to drop it when he pulls out a small velvet box. No, this isn't happening. Is it?

*No. He's not that crazy.*

"Relax, it's not a ring." He chuckles.

"I wasn't worried," I lie.

"Yes, you were. But just so we're clear, it will be a ring one day soon, Evie," he says.

I take the box from his hands, expecting a pair of earrings or a necklace. My brows furrow when I open it to find a small vial filled with red liquid.

"What is this?" I ask, plucking the little glass bottle from the box's lining.

"The blood of the doctor who performed that procedure on you when you were sixteen," he says.

I drop the vial back into the box. "What did you do?" I look up at him. My hands shake.

"I killed him, and I have a long list of names who will be joining him in hell soon."

I shake my head. "I don't want you to do this, Emmanuel. I don't want you killing people for me. No."

"There is nothing I wouldn't do for you, Evie. This, getting vengeance on your behalf, is something I need to do. I enjoyed it, seeing the pain on his face, seeing the life drain from his body. He deserved so much worse for what he did to you."

"You can't do this. Please just let it go." I shove the box back towards him. "I don't want this."

"Would you have preferred a ring?" He lifts a challenging brow.

"Yes," I deadpan. "Because I don't want people's deaths on my hands. I don't want people to die because of me."

"They're not. They are dying because of their own actions, not yours," Emmanuel says. "Try the wine. I think you'll like it."

"Why? Is the cup filled with the blood of my enemies too?" I mumble.

"No, but it can be if that's what you want."

"I don't," I say quickly. I pick up the glass and take a sip of the sweet liquid.

*Damn it. He's right. I do like it.*

# Chapter Thirty

"You can sleep, you know. I won't creep on you," Evie says. We're currently cuddled up on her bed, watching some shitty romance movie. Well, she's watching the movie. I'm struggling to stay awake.

"Are you saying I'm not pretty enough to creep on, mi alma?" I ask her.

"No, you are. I'm just not a creeper." She chuckles.

"I wouldn't mind you creeping on me," I tell her. "In fact, I'd welcome it."

"Good to know. But seriously, you look exhausted," she says.

"It's been a busy couple of days. Add that to the fact I didn't have you with me, and it just made it hell." I truly have never missed anyone the way I miss this woman when she's not with me.

"E? How did you find the doctor? How did you know who he was?"

I've been waiting for her to ask this. I continue to twirl my fingers through her hair. "I sent someone to talk to your mother. She gave us a list of names, every asshole who touched you. I started with the doctor."

Evie sits up, moving away from me. "Did you... did you kill my mother?"

"No," I answer quickly. "I sent someone else to talk to her. Because if it had been me, knowing what she did to you, I probably would have. And I won't do that unless you want me to."

Evie shakes her head. "I don't," she says. "I don't want to see her again, or talk to her, but I also don't want her to die."

"You are too good for this world, Evie Carter," I say, pulling her back into my arms. It feels right, being with her, holding her. "I want you to come to Vegas with me."

"I can't," she says.

"Why not?"

"Because my store just burned down, E. I need to sort it out. I need to be here to rebuild. There are probably a million things I need to do that I don't even know about yet. I've never had a business burn down."

"You didn't own the building, Evie. All you have to do is submit your insurance claim and find a location for a new store. Order your stock and go from there. You can do that from Vegas," I tell her.

The shrill ringtone of her phone interrupts us. "Shit, it's Charlotte," she says. "Be quiet. You are not here."

I raise a brow but don't say a word as Evie answers her friend's call.

"Charlotte, hey, how's married life?" I don't hear the other side of the call, but Evie responds with, "I didn't want to bother you. You are finally happy, Charlotte. You don't need to be bothered by my problems."

Their conversation continues for about five minutes before there's a knock at Evie's front door. Standing, I pick up my pistol from the bedside table. Evie's eyes widen at me.

"Um, Charlotte, someone's at my door. I'll call

you back," she says, dropping the phone while glaring at me. "What are you doing?"

"Seeing who the fuck is knocking on your door at seven in the morning," I tell her. "Wait here."

"No. Put that away. It's probably Rachel." She barges past me.

"Evie, don't open that door," I growl behind her. She looks back over her shoulder at me.

"You are overreacting." She rolls her eyes. "But by all means, open the door if it means that much to you." She steps to the side and gestures in front of me.

Blocking her body with mine, I swing the door open. "Who the fuck are you?" I ask the man who has his fist raised halfway as he prepares to knock again.

"Ah... is Evie here?"

"Who the fuck are you?" I repeat.

"Oh my god, E, stop." Evie shoves her way through the small gap between me and the opening of the door. "Phil, what are you doing here?"

"I... ah... There was an update on the investigation at your shop. Thought you'd want to know," *Phil* replies, his eyes bouncing between Evie and me.

"What update?" she asks.

"The fire wasn't an accident. They found evidence of arson. I shouldn't even be telling you this. I just wanted to give you a heads-up, because the cops will be here soon asking questions," the asshole says what I already suspected.

"What? I don't understand. Amy said she was steaming a dress and the fire just started. Why would she lie about it?" Evie questions.

"I don't know. But I figured you didn't know anything about it. I'm sorry, Evie." Phil shakes his head from side to side. "I'll catch you around," he says as he turns to leave.

"Who the fuck is Phil and why is he so concerned about you?" I ask Evie as soon as the door is closed.

"You need to get a grip, Emmanuel. Phil is Charlotte's ex. He's also a firefighter at the local department." Evie walks towards the kitchen. I follow her.

"Your friend has some seriously awful taste in men," I grumble.

"She married one of your best friends," Evie retorts.

"My point exactly," I tell her. "I'm going out for a bit. I'll have Paz stay here with you. If the cops come, let Paz talk to them. You don't tell them shit."

"Where are you going?" she asks.

"I have an errand to run." I lean in and kiss her cheek. "I won't be long."

Evie frowns. "Okay."

Paz knocks on the front door. When I open it, I tell him what I'm doing in Spanish and mention that the cops could turn up to question Evie. What I'm about to do, well, it will be easier to ask her for forgiveness than permission.

Tomás is waiting for me out on the street. "Ready for some fun?" I ask him.

"Always, jefe." He smirks. The bastard is twisted in ways I'll never understand. Then again, to make it up the ranks, you need to be twisted as fuck.

It takes ten minutes for us to stop four houses down from Amy's. She shares a place with her boyfriend, Hugh. As Tomás and I get closer to the property on foot, we can hear the screaming coming from inside the house.

"You're a fucking idiot, Amy! I told you it would be okay. You had to go and burn the fucking place down," a male voice yells.

"She was going to figure it out, Hugh. I couldn't hide the fact that money was missing." Amy replies.

I wave my hand towards the back of the house. Tomás follows my lead. I turn the doorknob and it opens. I walk through the kitchen, following the shouting until I find both Hugh and Amy in the living room.

Amy gasps when she sees me. The boyfriend puffs out his chest. "Who the hell are you?" he asks.

I tilt my head to the side, raise my arm, and pull the trigger. The fucker drops to the ground with a thud. I'm not here for him. Amy lets out an ear-piercing scream.

"You fucked up," I say, pointing the gun in her direction.

"No. He made me do it!" she cries out. "I didn't mean to."

Tomás walks behind her, covering her mouth. "You know I can make her pay in ways you won't, jefe," he tells me in Spanish.

"No." I shake my head. "You stole from my girl-friend. Burned down her store, her dream."

I walk around the room. I don't want her death to be easy. Fuck this girl. She fucking broke Evie's heart.

"You got a light?" I ask Tomás.

"Yep." He reaches into his pocket and hands me a lighter.

"Bring her here." I walk down the hall, opening each door until I find the bedroom.

Amy kicks and screams against Tomás's hold. It doesn't do her any good, though.

I pull the sheet from the bed and twirl it around, creating a makeshift rope before tying it around Amy's body. I return my attention to Tomás. "Keep her there. I'll be right back."

I head into the garage, glancing around until I find what I'm looking for. A bottle of starter fluid. This will work. When I make my way back into the bedroom, I pour the liquid over the sheet.

Tomás smiles at me, knowing exactly what's coming next. "You torched her dream. I'm going to torch you," I tell Amy.

"No... please. Don't do this. I didn't mean to!" She screams when Tomás lets go of her.

Amy attempts to stand up, but stumbles back to the ground. I flick the lighter and toss it in her direction. The sheet ignites. Her screams get louder, her body thrashing around on the carpet.

"Damn, jefe. If I'd known we were barbequing, I would have bought s'mores." Tomás chuckles.

"You have issues." I laugh, watching as Amy's body finally stops moving. "Let's go."

Tomás follows me out the back of the house. As we climb into the car, the sound of sirens can be heard in the distance.

"They're quick to respond here," Tomás says, starting the engine.

"Small fucking towns," I grunt. I hate them. But I don't plan on being here much longer.

When I get back to Evie's, the cops are on her doorstep with Paz.

"Is there a problem?" I ask, stepping up behind the pigs in uniform. I could have taken them both out and they'd be none the wiser. Fucking idiots are too comfortable with the locals.

"You are?" The taller one looks me up and down.

"Emmanuel Lopez. Why are you at my girlfriend's house?"

"We have some questions for Miss Carter, regarding the fire at her store yesterday," he says.

"She was at lunch with her friend when that fire started. From what we understand, her employee, Amy, told her it was an accident. She was steaming a dress when the garment burst into flames," I tell him.

"We have reason to believe the fire was deliberate," the other officer chimes in.

"Deliberate? What would anyone have to gain by burning down a dress shop?" I counter.

A voice comes over the radios they're wearing. They pause to listen to it before adding, "We will be back." Then they both rush away.

"Guess they have more burning matters to attend to," Paz says with a slight smile on his face.

"Guess so," I agree, watching the police car pull out of the driveway. "Get the jet ready. She's coming home."

# Chapter Thirty-One

Emmanuel walks into my house like he owns the damn place. The man really does know how to take up a room. He exudes power and authority wherever he goes. I'm sitting on the sofa, watching as he walks through the house, and then he finally comes back to me.

"Guessing you didn't find the boogeyman under the bed, then?" I ask him.

"Why didn't you want your friend to know I was here?" he says, totally ignoring my dig.

"Because I'm already lying to one of my friends when it comes to you. I don't want to add another," I tell him.

"Why are you lying?"

"Gee, I don't know, Emmanuel. Maybe because when I'm asked why I'm crying and why I told you to leave me, I didn't think the right answer was that I just saw my boyfriend kill his mother." I stand and wave my hands around.

"You don't need to lie, Evie."

"Yes I do, because what if I did say that, and then that friend went to the cops, Emmanuel? I don't want you to get into trouble. So not only am I lying, I've become an accomplice to your crimes."

"Nothing I do will ever come back on you. I guarantee you that," he says.

"You can't guarantee anything, Emmanuel. You aren't the law."

"Wanna bet?" He raises a brow.

I shake my head. "You should probably go. I'm pretty sure the cops are coming back to talk to me, and you shouldn't be here when they do."

"You think I'm leaving you to deal with any of this on your own? You're out of your fucking mind," he growls. "We're leaving for Vegas tonight. You are coming back with me."

"Excuse me?" My arms fold over my chest. "Who the hell do you think you are, ordering me around?"

"Your boyfriend," he replies.

"Pfft, you are not my boyfriend. And I'm not going back to Vegas!"

"I am your boyfriend, and you are coming back to Vegas. If I have to gag and tie you up to get you there, I will," he grunts.

The idea of him tying me up isn't totally unappealing. But having him order me around? Yeah, that's not happening.

"I'm not your pet, Emmanuel. You can't just bark orders at me. I have a life of my own." The ringing of my phone interrupts our argument. I snap it up off the coffee table. "Rachel, now's not a good time," I answer when I see my friend's name on the screen.

"You hear about Amy?" she asks.

"No. What about her?"

"There was another fire. At her house. Two bodies were found inside," Rachel says.

"What?" My eyes go to Emmanuel. *He wouldn't.* But before that thought leaves my mind, I know deep down that he absolutely would.

"I'm not sure what's going on, Evie, but it might

be a good idea for you to go and visit Charlotte for a while. Get out of town."

"Yeah, I think I might," I whisper into the phone. "I'll call you when I get there." I hang up and stare at Emmanuel. "What did you do? Actually, don't tell me. I already know too many of your crimes. I don't want to add another one." I bring my phone back to my ear and call Charlotte.

"Hey," she answers.

"Hey, you got time for a visitor for a week or so? I think I need to get out of town for a while, get my mind off everything," I tell her.

"I always have time for you, Evie," she says. "And I'll have a room for you. Oh my god, it's going to be so much fun. Want me to book you a flight? When are you arriving?"

"I'll book it." I laugh. "I'm not sure, but I'll let you know when I'm getting in. Thanks, Charlotte."

"See you soon," she says.

"I'm booking a flight to Vegas. I'm going to be staying with Charlotte. And you and I... this isn't a thing in front of anyone," I tell Emmanuel.

"You're not booking a flight. We have a jet. And as for staying with Charlotte, I'd prefer you to come home with me," he says.

"I can't go back to your house, Emmanuel. I watched you kill your own mother. I can't go back there," I tell him quietly. "All the guns, it's just... I don't like it."

Emmanuel looks at me silently, appearing to consider his next words. "Okay. You will stay with Charlotte, and I'll go along with this whole *we aren't dating* bullshit you've cooked up. For now."

"Thank you." I sigh in relief. I don't know why I'm not ready to tell Charlotte, probably because she will try to talk some sense into me. Whereas Rachel is a diehard *love conquers all* kind of girl.

"Pack what you need," Emmanuel says before sitting on the sofa. He pulls out his phone and starts scrolling.

I don't know what it is, but something feels really unfinished about our argument. Or maybe it's the fact he's getting his way. I'm going back to Vegas.

***

About an hour into the flight, I feel it, the tiredness catching up with me. It always starts with dizziness. Not now. I cannot fall asleep here.

"E?" I call out, my voice wobbly as I reach for his seat.

"What's wrong?" He's on his feet and in front of me within seconds.

"I think I'm going to crash out," I tell him. My

eyes are wide. "I can't fall asleep here." Now I'm panicking.

Emmanuel picks me up and carries me into the bedroom. He lays me down and curls up next to me. "You are safe here, Evie. You can sleep."

"I can't," I say, already knowing I'm losing the battle. "Don't let anyone in, please."

Emmanuel holds me tighter. "No one is ever going to get to you. I promise. I will be right here when you wake up." His lips press against my forehead, and then I feel my body relax.

---

I wake with a jolt. My eyes spring open. A pair of strong arms wrap around me. "It's okay. I've got you," Emmanuel whispers into my ear. "It's just the jet landing."

My body relaxes slightly, but I do a mental take of every part of me. Trying to see if anything hurts. My hands run over my jeans. They're still on, and I sigh. Emmanuel's arms loosen their hold on me, and he slides off the bed.

I roll on to my back and look up at him. His jaw is tight, ticking, and his eyes... He looks... hurt. That can't be right. Am I still dreaming?

"What's wrong?" I ask, sitting up on the bed.

"We've landed. I'll have Paz take you to the Royal. Call me if you need anything," he says and then leaves the room.

*What on earth just happened? Did I say something in my sleep again?*

I continue to lie on the bed for about five more minutes. When I realize Emmanuel isn't coming back, I get up.

Paz is waiting for me in the main cabin. "Miss Carter, you ready to go?"

"Sure." I look around, expecting to see Emmanuel but he's not here.

"He had an important meeting to attend," Paz tells me.

"You don't need to lie to me," I say, walking past him.

I climb into the front passenger seat. Paz sits in the driver's seat. "Whatever he did, I'm sure he meant well," he says as he pulls out of the airstrip.

"I think this time it's something I did," I admit. "I just don't know what."

"I doubt you could do anything that would piss off jefe, Evie," Paz says, dropping all formalities. "I've never seen him like anyone as much as he likes you."

"He seemed pretty pissed off when he left. But It's fine. I'm not here for him anyway." I sigh. "I'm going to spend time with my friend, figure out how I'm going to rebuild my store. Deal with the insurance company and all that."

"Your insurance is going to be denied," Paz tells me.

"What? How do you know that?"

"It was arson. They won't cover it."

I lean my head back and groan. "Great, so I'm screwed. I literally have nothing."

Paz laughs, literally laughs out loud. "You're the girlfriend of Emmanuel Lopez. You definitely do not have *nothing*."

"I'm not, and whatever he has is his. Not mine. I don't want it." I still need to figure out a way to return the hundred million he deposited into my account. I'm afraid if I send it back, he will double it again like he has the two times before that.

"Sure, you're not," Paz mumbles.

The rest of the drive is quiet. I can't get the look on Emmanuel's face out of my head, though. I need to know what I did. I need to know why he was so pissed at me. I shouldn't care. I wanted him to leave me alone and he finally is. I should just go with it. But I can't. My stomach is turning.

"Where did he go?" I ask Paz. "Emmanuel—where is he?"

"Ah, I'm not sure," he replies.

"Yes, you do. Can you take me to him? Please."

"I can't."

"I can always tell him I needed to see him and you wouldn't let me." I shrug and dig my phone out of my purse.

"Fucking hell, you are more evil than he is." Paz smiles at me. "I like it." He picks up his own phone and types a message to someone. No doubt Emmanuel. "Okay, I'll take you to him," he says. "But don't let the place get to you."

I don't know what he means by that. Well, not until he drives into a cemetery. "Whose buried here?"

"I honestly have no idea." Paz shrugs.

It clicks. Laura. She's here. This is where he comes to talk to her. And all of a sudden, I don't want to be here. Is it because of her? Is that why he ran out of the room and left me there?

"I shouldn't have come," I whisper.

"You absolutely should have. Whatever you two are fighting about, fix it," Paz says.

"You know, I think I'm starting to appreciate the fact that Enrique never spoke to me," I mutter as I get out of the car.

I walk over to Emmanuel. He doesn't look up. He's sitting in front of a grave. I drop down next to him on the grass. The words "I was loved" are written in script on the stone. That's all. No name, no dates, just that one phrase.

"I don't know what I did," I whisper. "But I don't want to cause you pain."

This gets him to finally look at me. "You don't trust me," he says.

My brows furrow. "Yes, I do."

"No, you don't. The first thing you did when you woke up was check your clothes. You thought I'd do to you what those sick fucks did," he grits out.

"It's a habit. I do that even if I'm alone, E. It wasn't because you were there. I trust you more than I should. I've never fallen asleep with anyone besides Charlotte or Rachel. If I didn't trust you, I would never have fallen asleep in your arms," I try to explain. "I warned you that I was messed up. I told you I was broken. You didn't listen."

# Chapter Thirty-Two

Having Evie check herself after falling asleep in my arms made my stomach fucking sink. She doesn't trust me. She thought that I'd do to her what they did. The sick fucks who drugged and took advantage of her. I've gone above and beyond to show her that I'm not that kind of fucking monster. Despite being who I am, I don't want to be that person to her. I never want her to fear me.

She's saying it's all in her head, that she's broken. I don't believe it. She's not fucking broken. I know she doesn't trust me. I know the first thought that went through her head when she woke up was: *Did he touch me?*

"It's okay to not trust me, Evie. It's smart even," I tell her. "Because I am a monster far worse than those who hurt you."

"You aren't a monster, and I trust you more than most people," she says.

"A few days ago, I ordered the extinction of an entire bloodline. And just this morning, I burned a woman to death because she purposely burned your store down. Don't fool yourself into thinking I'm anything but who I am."

"You... what? Amy?" Evie gasps. "Emmanuel, I didn't ask you to do that."

"I know, and I also know you wouldn't. But I'm not the kind of guy who just lets things slide. I will always put you first, and if someone fucks with you, they will have to deal with my full wrath," I tell her.

"The body count is getting out of hand, E. We are not good for each other. Whatever this is, we should stop."

"We can't stop," I admit. "You are mi alma. I found you and that's not something I'm going to forget or let go of. The only way this ends is with one of us right here. Dead and buried."

"You want me to die? Like she did?" Evie asks. There's no fear in her voice, more curiosity.

"If I wanted you to die, you would be dead," I say. "I prefer you alive."

When it's just the two of us talking, everything seems almost normal. I've never been able to talk to anyone the way I can with Evie.

"Okay, because I'm not really ready to die yet." She smiles. "And if I do, I'm going to come back and haunt your ass forever."

"I'd welcome the company." I laugh. "You'd be the fucking prettiest ghost there ever was."

"I know," she says, not in a conceited kind of way, more like she's bored with hearing about her looks.

"You don't like people telling you you're beautiful," I state.

"I've heard it my entire life." Evie shrugs. "I know I'm pretty, but sometimes, I wish I weren't."

"Your looks are not what make you beautiful, Evie. It's your heart. It's the goodness that shines right from your soul." I get a message from Paz telling me they found the guy who shot at Carlo and Jazzy. I quickly pocket my phone, stand, and look to Evie again. "You should go and see Charlotte. I'll find you later."

"Are you still pissed off at me?" she asks. "Not that I care. You can be as mad as you want. It doesn't bother me one bit."

I smirk. She cares. If she didn't care, she never would have asked Paz to bring her to me. "I was never pissed at you, mi alma. I'm pissed at myself for not being enough for you." I press my lips to hers. Then I turn around and walk in the opposite direction.

"Wait!" Evie calls out.

I pivot and look at her. Waiting for her to continue speaking.

"Take me with you," she says.

"I can't do that. There's something I have to do, and I would prefer you didn't see me do it."

"You are enough. Take me with you," she repeats. As much as I want to give in to her, I'm not about to let her see me remove a man's head from his body.

"Come on, I'll take you to the Royal." I grab hold of Evie's hand. As we make our way over to my car, I message Paz and tell him to have the fucker's head on a platter for me.

"You don't trust me to see whatever you're doing?" Evie asks once we're locked inside my car.

"I don't want you to see horrors you will never forget. It has nothing to do with trust," I explain. I start the engine and drive away from the cemetery. I'm not even sure why I came here. Habit, I guess.

"I don't care, just so you know. If you want me to help you dig holes all over Nevada, I will." Evie smiles at me. It's easy to say but I saw the look in her eyes when I told her that I'd burned her employee alive.

"I will never let you get these hands dirty like that, Evie." I grab her palm, bring it to my mouth, and kiss her knuckles.

"What if my hands aren't as clean as you think they are? How do you know I haven't already killed someone?" she asks.

I laugh. "You haven't."

"Well, I could have. You don't know that," she huffs.

"I know you. I want to say that I'm sorry about your employee."

"You want to say sorry or you are sorry?" Evie counters.

"Does it matter?"

"Two very different things. Why do you think she'd burn the store down? I don't get it."

"Her boyfriend was making her steal money from the shop. She got worried you'd figure it out and thought a fire would destroy any evidence of her wrongdoing," I say, and Evie appears taken aback.

"She told you that?"

"I heard them arguing." I shrug. "You know you can open a store up anywhere. A fire isn't going to keep you from having your dream, Evie."

"I don't think the insurance will pay me anything. Since it's not an accident."

"I happen to know you have a fair sum of money in your account. Use it to build a new store."

"I'm returning your money. I don't want your money." Evie glares at me. "As soon as I figure out a way to return it without you doubling it again, I will."

"Is it a bad thing for a boyfriend to want to make sure his girlfriend never wants for anything?" I ask her.

"Yes. When said boyfriend gives said girlfriend an obscene amount of money."

The shrill of my ringing phone blasts through the car. If it weren't Paz, I'd ignore it. "Hola," I answer.

"Jefe, I've got the head. On a silver platter for you. Where do you want it?" he asks in Spanish.

"Meet me at Carlo's," I tell him in English before switching to Spanish and adding, "Did you get any intel?"

"Joey Marciano," Paz says.

"Fucking hell," I curse under my breath. Carlo's father-in-law is trying to take him out? I've done business with Marciano a few times. Never liked the slimy fuck. Now I have a reason to kill him. Cutting the call, I look over to Evie. "We're making a pit stop at Carlo's before the Royal. You mind?"

She shakes her head. "Nope."

When we arrive at the Wild Card, I hand the keys to the valet and open Evie's door.

"I can wait down here," Evie suggests as we walk into the casino lobby a few minutes later.

"You're not waiting down here." I meet Paz at the bank of elevators, and he hands me the silver tray.

"Are you delivering food?" Evie asks, looking at the tray.

"Something like that." With my free hand on her lower back, I lead Evie into the elevator. I know she wants to keep us secret, but I don't give a fuck who sees her with me. She's mine. I want the fucking world to know it.

The moment we walk into the penthouse, little feet tap against the marble floors. "Tío E!" Jazzy yells out excitedly. I catch her with one hand around her waist when she jumps at me.

"Hey there, princesa. How are you?" I ask as I set her down on her feet again.

"I'm good. Daddy and Antonia are in the office. Want me to get them?" she replies.

"It's okay. Can you do me a favor and show Evie where the kitchen is? She needs some water. I'm going to talk to your daddy real quick."

"Sure, come on, Evie. We have lots of things to drink." Jazzy takes hold of Evie's hand before leading the way through the foyer. Evie looks back at me in question. I don't need her seeing what's under this silver dome.

I walk into Carlo's open office, and he and Antonia stand. "You go into catering, Emmanuel? I didn't know times were that tough," he asks with a raised brow while eyeing the platter in my hand.

"I didn't know you were a comedian," I fire back at him, then turn to smile at Antonia. "Mrs. Bianchi, pleasure as always."

"Emmanuel, nice to see you again," she replies. She is always polite. Her father raised the perfect mob wife.

"Evie is out there with Jazzy," I tell Antonia, knowing they've met once before.

"You brought Evie with you?" Carlo asks.

"Just making a quick pit stop. We were on our way to the airport but I wanted to deliver this," I lie because, well, I like to keep these fuckers on their toes. They do not need to know my plans to stay in town for a while. I set the tray down on his desk. "You might want to wait till your wife is out of the room before you open it," I add under my breath.

"Babe, can you find out what Jazzy wants for dinner?" Carlo asks Antonia.

"Sure." Antonia leaves the office and closes the door behind her. Not a single question.

Carlo pulls the lid back from the serving platter to find a dismembered head sitting on a bed of lettuce. "Artful," he says, scrutinizing the face, probably trying to recognize the asshole.

"Thanks. I thought so." I smile.

"Who was he?"

"Call the boys. Put 'em on video. I want you all to hear this." I smirk, knowing Louie is going to be pissed I beat him to the guy.

Carlo calls Sammie and Louie on video chat. Sammie is the first to answer. "What's up?"

"Emmanuel has something he wants you to hear," Carlo says.

A few seconds later, Louie joins us. "Carlo?"

"Yeah, I've got Emmanuel here. He brought a gift." Carlo then turns the camera around and shows them the severed head.

"Creative." Sammie chuckles at the same time Louie asks, "Who is it?"

"Glad you asked. This is the guy who shot at Jazzy." I grin. "Told you I'd find him first."

"Did you get anything out of him before you decided to cut off his head?" Louie grunts.

"Yeah, I did," I reply as my glare shifts to Carlo. "This part you're not going to like so much."

"What?" he asks.

"The name he gave me. Joey Marciano," I say.

"Fucking hell." Carlo slams the lid down on the platter with a loud *clank*. "Thank you," he says. "But I'll handle it from here."

"You think she knows?" I nod towards the door Antonia disappeared through.

"Not in the slightest. She'd tell me," Carlo insists with a confidence he probably shouldn't have.

"How sure are you about that?" I press him.

"She just had lunch with him, came home, and immediately told me the fucker ordered her to steal something from me," he says.

"What he want?" Louie chimes in.

"This," Carlo picks up a flash drive and holds it in front of the camera. "It has enough evidence to earn the fucker five life sentences."

"You turning rat?" I ask.

"Fuck no," Carlo hisses. "I wanted his daughter, and I was going to get her how ever I could."

I had a feeling there was more to their relationship than a quick arranged marriage between strangers. They are way too close, too in sync with each other to have just met.

# Chapter Thirty-Three

Sitting in the car next to Emmanuel as he drives is starting to become one of my favorite things to do. There's something sexy about the way he drives, or maybe the vibrations of his fancy car are what's turning me on. I look at Emmanuel's hand on the steering wheel. His other one is on the gear stick. Nope, it's definitely him. Those dark, tattooed hands are hot.

Then again, it could be the memories of how

those hands work their magic on my body. I'm not sure it matters at this point. I'm almost ready to tell him to pull the car over and let me jump on his dick for a while.

Before I can make the suggestion, he turns onto the circular driveway and stops out front of Charlotte's casino. "Thanks for the ride," I tell him.

Emmanuel looks at me, really looks at me. Then he draws out a card and flicks it in my direction. "Room 666. Go straight there," he says.

"Why?" I ask, looking at the card.

"Because you are mine, and right now, you need something that only I can give you. What kind of boyfriend would I be if I let you go... unsatisfied?" he asks.

"Still not my boyfriend. And I'm more than capable of satisfying myself. Pretty sure you've seen proof of that." My cheeks heat, but I fake the bravado I don't feel.

"Go to the room, Evie," Emmanuel says.

"Go to hell, Emmanuel," I counter. I don't know how many times I have to tell him I'm not a dog.

"I'm already on my way there, but before I arrive, I'm going to enjoy heaven as much as I possibly can." He winks. "Just in case that wasn't clear, heaven is your pussy."

"Yeah, I got that." I roll my eyes and get out of

the car. I take the card. Because as much as I like to give him shit and want to stand my ground, he's right. I am horny, and I know if I meet up with him, I will be leaving one very satisfied woman.

As soon as I walk through the front doors of the casino, any plans of meeting up with Emmanuel go out the window when I'm jumped by an overexcited Charlotte. "Oh my gosh, I've been waiting forever for you," she says. "I can't believe you're finally back."

"I only just left." I laugh. Honestly, if it weren't for the store burning to the ground, I wouldn't be back here. The thought of everything I've lost hits me, and I hold on to my friend a little tighter.

"Are you okay? I'm so sorry about the shop. I know it was your dream, but we can rebuild, right?" Charlotte asks. "And you are safe. I mean, you weren't in the store—*thank God.*"

"It's going to be okay," I say while wiping a stray tear from my cheek.

"Oh, Evie, shit. Okay, we're going to work through this together. We're going to find you a new location, and I'll even help you go through catalogues for more stock," Charlotte offers.

"You hate looking at dresses," I remind her.

"But I love you, so I'll suffer through it." She smiles.

Charlotte's gaze falls behind me, and I turn my

head to see Emmanuel walking through the glass door with Paz right by his side. His eyes immediately find mine, and I give a little shake of my head.

"Do you think he has a tracker planted under your skin or something? That man is always wherever you are," Charlotte says under her breath.

I wouldn't put it past Emmanuel. I mean, if he could, he probably would put a tracker on me.

"Or *that man* is your husband's friend so that's why you see him around a lot?" I suggest. Linking my arm through hers, I lead Charlotte towards the elevators, walking straight past Emmanuel and Paz. "Besides, I think the sidekick is way hotter," I add loud enough for both men to hear and then give Paz a smirk. He just shakes his head at me.

"Shh... they can hear you," Charlotte hisses.

"That's the point," I tell her. When I look back over a shoulder, Emmanuel is glaring at me. I give him a smile and I see his face soften ever so slightly. But I know he's mad, and probably has a case of blue balls because he thought he was about to get laid.

Maybe Rachel was right. Maybe coming to see Charlotte is exactly what I need. When we get up to Charlotte's penthouse, she shows me to the guestroom. "Are you sure you don't want me to get you your own suite? Louie won't mind."

"Do you not want me here?" I ask her.

"Of course I want you here," she says.

"Does your husband want me here?"

"My husband wants me to be happy, and you being here makes me extremely happy. So, yes, Louie wants you here." She smiles. "Now, want to get drunk and forget the world?"

"Absolutely." I nod. I need that. To forget the world, and day-drinking with my best friend is just the way to do it.

I throw my bag down on the bed and take out my phone. A text from E is already on the screen. I open it and skim the message.

E:

I'll destroy anything that competes with my ability to have you completely.

My brows furrow. Is he talking about Charlotte? He better fucking not be threatening my friends. But then, like a lightning bolt, it hits me. An awareness that he is legitimately insane sends me into a panic. It was only a few hours ago that he told me he had burned Amy alive. I shoved that deep down, because for some reason, the man has a hold on me and it seems my morality knows no bounds when it comes to him.

ME:

> My friends are off-limits,
> Emmanuel. Do NOT touch them.
> That is one thing I will NEVER be
> able to forgive you for. Also, don't
> fucking threaten them again,
> because I might be tiny, and I might
> not like violence. But when it
> comes to those I love, I will
> become the person who digs holes
> all over the desert.

My fingers tap across the screen in rapid succession. "You okay?" Charlotte's concerned voice has me looking up.

"Uh, yeah, just some asshole who has the wrong number," I tell her, putting the phone back in my pocket.

I feel the vibration of another message. As much as I want to ignore it, I can't stop myself from looking.

E:

> Flawless and fierce. And MINE.

I roll my eyes as I shove my phone back into my pocket. He can sit and read for a while. "Whatever is bothering you, I hope you know I'm here for you, always," Charlotte says.

"I do know," I tell her. "Ditto."

I follow Charlotte into the kitchen, where she

retrieves a bottle of chilled white wine and two glasses. We then head to the living room. Charlotte pours us both a very healthy serving of wine.

"So, tell me, how is it being married to Las Vegas's bossman?" I ask her.

Charlotte blushes and smiles. "It's... amazing."

"So, aside from his dick, what else is amazing about him?"

She appears to consider my question while taking a sip from her glass. "I've dated a few guys. But I've never felt loved the way Louie loves me."

"I'm really happy for you, Charlotte," I say.

"You know, one day, it's going to happen for you too," she tells me.

I look away. I hate lying to my friend. But I'm already dumping my problems on her. It's not fair to add my dating life to that list. "Mhm, maybe.'

"Who is he?" she asks.

"Who is who?"

"The man you've been fucking. I know you better than you know yourself, Evie Carter. I know you're seeing someone," Charlotte insists.

"*Seeing* isn't really the term I'd use." I shrug, taking a huge gulp of the wine, followed by another and another, until the glass is empty.

"What's the term you would use, then?" she presses.

"I don't know. It's... complicated."

"How so?"

I sigh. "I've been a horrible friend, and I've been lying to you," I admit.

Charlotte's eyebrows draw down in confusion. "About what?"

"About the person I'm seeing."

"As long as it's not my husband, I don't care who you're dating, Evie. I just hope he makes you happy," Charlotte says.

I laugh. "Definitely not your husband."

"I know." Charlotte nods. "I trust Louie."

I raise a brow at her.

"And I trust you," she's quick to add.

"Good, because I would never do anything to hurt you," I tell her.

"Yeah." Charlotte gets a distant look on her face. She caught her sister fucking her ex-fiancé the day before the ceremony. She ended up running off to Vegas and then met Louie. The rest is history, as they say.

"So, you really don't care who I've been sleeping with?" I ask her.

"No. Why would I care?"

"It's Emmanuel," I whisper, like saying his name out loud might just make him appear.

"WHAT!" Charlotte jumps up, her voice rising

with her. "Are you insane? Emmanuel, as in *the cartel boss* Emmanuel?"

"Wait... You just said you didn't care who it was," I remind her as I refill both of our glasses.

"That was before I knew you were in bed with a madman," she says.

"He's not mad," I huff.

Charlotte tilts her head and stares at me.

"Okay, fine, he's a little insane. But he has good qualities too," I tell her.

Charlotte plops back down next to me on the sofa. "I'm sorry. I just... I want you to be safe. I want to keep you alive for as long as possible. We have old people plans, remember?"

"I remember. We're going to get houses next to each other, with rocking chairs on the porch, and we will watch our grandchildren play together." It's the same scenario we've dreamed up for years.

"Exactly. Do you really see Emmanuel sitting in a rocking chair on a porch?" Charlotte asks.

"Do you see Louie doing that?" I fire back at her.

"Yes, in a perfectly-fitted three-piece suit." She smiles wistfully.

Can *I* see Emmanuel in my future?

"I'm not saying he's going to be the forever guy, Charlotte. I'm just saying he's the right now guy."

"From what I hear, if Emmanuel Lopez wants to

keep you forever, he will, and there's not a damn thing anyone can do about it," she tells me.

"I'm more scared of the fact that I might actually want him to keep me," I whisper. "He knows."

"He knows what?"

"Everything. I told him. I thought it would push him away. It didn't."

"Of course it didn't. Nothing that happened to you is your fault, Evie," Charlotte says. "It does not deter from the beautiful soul you are. Not one little bit."

"Can I tell you something? You can't tell anyone. Not even your husband." I look at her.

"Anything," she says.

"He found the doctor who did the procedure on me when I was sixteen. He killed him," I whisper into her ear, not wanting anyone else to hear me.

"I think I just found a reason to like Emmanuel." Charlotte smiles.

"He's determined to find them all..."

She nods. "And another reason to like him. Good."

"Like I said, you can't tell anyone about us. I told him I wanted to keep it on the down low here. And I don't want to take away from your honeymoon bliss. This is your time to shine, Charlotte."

"Don't be ridiculous. We can shine together. But

I won't tell anyone," she says, holding up her pinkie finger.

I link mine through hers, and we shake on it. I couldn't even count the number of secrets we've shared like this. But none of them have ever been about murderous boyfriends.

# Chapter Thirty-Four

I haven't seen her in hours. I'm eager to get back to her. I left Evie at my house because I had to deal with a last-minute complication with a drop. I would have preferred to stay in bed with her. It's where I always want to be lately.

I told her I wouldn't be gone long. I've been gone for hours. Evie hates being at the estate, especially without me. She says the place feels haunted and doomed. I know she has trouble getting past the *memories of my mother. Of when I had to kill my mother in front of her.*

*It wasn't my finest moment, and somehow I need to get her to be able to be in my house without remembering that incident. Or I need to find a new house.*

*I run up the stairs and push through the bedroom door. She's not in the bed where I left her.*

*"Evie?" I call out, walking into the bathroom before I stop at the scene in front of me. "No!" I scream at the top of my lungs. "No. Fucking no!"*

*I drop to the floor. Evie's body is covered in blood. A knife is on the tiles beside her. I reach up for towels and wrap one around her wrist.*

*"What the fuck have you done?" I yell as I shake her unresponsive body.*

*A shadow forms in the doorway. I pull out my gun, aim, and shoot. I don't care who it is. No one is taking her from me. I hold her body against my chest. When someone else comes into view, I shoot again.*

"Fuck, Emmanuel. Stop!" Paz yells at me. Something slaps my hand and the gun falls. My eyes snap open and I'm staring at my second-in-command.

"Where is she? Evie?" I call out, shoving the blankets aside and jumping to my feet.

"E, you were having a nightmare. Whatever happened, it's not real," Paz says calmly.

"Where is she?" I repeat.

"Call her." He hands me my phone.

I sit on the bed and dial her number, hitting the camera function because I need to see her. "You know I'm starting to think my insomnia is contagious. Why aren't you sleeping?" she asks me.

"Show me your wrists," I tell her.

"What? Why?"

The click of the door lets me know Paz has walked out of the room. "Evie, please. Just show me your wrists," I plead with her.

Evie sets the phone down on the bed and then holds her hands over the camera area. "Do you have some kind of wrist fetish, E? Because I gotta admit that's a little odd, even for you."

"I have a *you* fetish, Evie. Anything you is my fetish," I tell her. "Show me your face again."

"Bossy," she says as I watch her scribble something down on a piece of paper.

"What are you doing?" I ask her.

"I'm making a pros and cons list on you," she says.

"Really? What's on this list?" I can't shake the image of her on the bathroom floor... "Wait, Evie have you ever tried to kill yourself or had thoughts of doing so?"

"No. Why?"

"Just needed to make sure. Okay, now tell me what are the pros on your list?"

"Are you okay, E? You seem a little stressed."

"You're not in my bed. So, no, I'm not fucking okay," I grunt.

"Grouchy," she says as she scribbles on the paper again.

"Did you just write down that I'm grouchy?" I quirk an amused brow at the phone.

"Yep, it's on the cons list too," Evie tells me.

"Yeah, what else is on this list of cons?"

"You really want to know?" she asks.

"The list of items you're creating to talk yourself out of falling for me? Yes, because I will find a way to cross every single one of them off," I tell her.

"Okay, well, first you're a..." She pauses.

"A what?" I urge her to continue.

"I don't think I should say that part on the phone, E. What if someone is listening?"

I laugh. "Mi alma, no one is listening. Say whatever it is you want to say."

"How do you know the feds haven't bugged Louie's apartment or something? You don't know," she insists. "You'd think someone in your position would be more careful with their phone calls."

"Louie has scramblers everywhere. There is no bug that would survive them," I explain.

"Oh… okay then. Con, you're a cartel boss. Pro, you have a job," she says.

I can't help but laugh. "Keep going."

"Con, you're bossy. Con, you're grouchy. Con, you think you own me."

"I don't think I own you, Evie. I know I do. Continue," I tell her.

"Pro, you look really good in a suit. Pro, your dick is really impressive. Pro, you make me come—always. Pro, you make me feel less broken." Her voice quietens as she says the last one. "Pro, you are loyal to your friends. Pro, you're protective of those you love. Pro, you worship me."

"I'm feeling like this list is heavy on the pro side, Evie."

"Con, you make me forget my own morals. Con, I can't seem to stay away from you."

"That one seems like it should be on the pro list." I laugh.

"What would be on your list? About me," she questions.

"I don't have a single con to list about you, Evie. You are fucking perfect in every way," I tell her.

"That's bullshit. There has to be something about me that aggravates you," she says.

"The fact that you're not already my wife," I mutter, shocking both of us. Where the fuck did that come from? Do I want to keep Evie? Fuck yes. Does that mean I want to get married? It would seem that way.

"Um... I didn't thank you. I should have. Thank you," she whispers.

"What are you thanking me for?"

"For the first time, I walked around here without looking at the faces of strangers and wondering if they were the one. You know... the doctor," she says.

"Evie, you don't need to thank me for that. I will erase all of your monsters from this earth. That's a promise," I tell her. "When can I see you?"

"You just saw me today... or yesterday."

"It was too long ago," I grunt.

"Charlotte is going to help me search for a new shop location tomorrow. I also need to try to contact the insurance company and see what, if anything, I can get out of them," she says.

"Evie, you don't need an insurance payout. Use your bank account. I will see you later today," I remind her before cutting the call.

***

I've been keeping busy, trying to give Evie space and time. It's a good thing I've got a list of targets to hunt down and kill—otherwise I would have caved and gone to her already.

I've gone through two names on the list of ten. The fucker in front of me is number three. I wasn't expecting his family to be home when we breached the property. I'm not deterred by that fact either. None of them will be able to talk once I leave here.

Is it fair for his family to pay a price for his crimes? No, but the world doesn't revolve around fairness. When it comes to the fucking assholes on this list, I have no empathy for them or their families. What they did to Evie, and God knows how many other girls just like her, makes me fucking sick to my stomach.

"Bruce, Bruce, Bruce." I shake my head at the fucker on the ground in front of me. His hands up in surrender, as if it's going to make a difference. "You want to be the one to tell your wife and daughters why they're about to die? Or should I do the honors?"

"I don't know who you are or what you want. Take it. Just let them go," he says, looking at his two teenage daughters and then their mother.

"You don't know me. But you know *her.*" I hold out my phone with a photo of Evie on the screen. The weak fuck wets his pants, literally.

"No." He shakes his head.

"Oh, but you do. Do you want to tell them what you did?" I ask him.

Bruce shakes his head again.

"Fine, I'll do it," I say, turning my attention to the group of women. I show them the picture of Evie. "Bruce here drugged and sexually assaulted this girl after she won pageant shows. That's why I'm here."

"No, he wouldn't do that. You have the wrong person," his wife says, her voice calm.

"You have too much faith in your sick fuck of a husband," I tell her while aiming the barrel of my gun at her head.

I pull the trigger. She falls backwards and blood splatters all over her daughters. Their screams are high-pitched and honestly? Fucking annoying.

"See what you did, Bruce? That could have been avoided had you not been a sick fuck who takes advantage of young girls." I sigh.

"I'm sorry. I didn't mean it. I'm sorry!" he cries out. "Just let them go."

Holding up two fingers, I indicate for my men to collect the girls. "Take them upstairs, do whatever you want with them, but make sure they're not breathing afterwards," I instruct.

With a nod, my guys drag the girls kicking and screaming up the stairs. Bruce seems to find his balls, because he stands in an attempt to grab for his daughters. To save them. It's no use. There's no saving anyone.

"You fucked with the wrong woman," I say as I send a bullet into his kneecap.

"I said I was sorry!" he screams at me.

"You see, I don't need your apologies. I'm just here to send you to hell. There's a special place there for fuckers like you." I pull the trigger. Another bullet lodges in his shoulder. I'm drawing this out, because, well, it's fun.

"Please, let them go. They don't have anything to do with this!" he cries out again.

"The thing is... I didn't get to where I am today by leaving witnesses. Their deaths are on your head," I tell him. "Not mine."

After hearing two consecutive shots from above, Bruce shrieks in agony.

"Huh, who would have thought my men would have better morals than you do? They let your daughters off easy," I hum before putting a final bullet between his eyes.

As I walk out of the house, I instruct one of my soldiers to burn it.

I slide into my car and skim my phone. Paz went back home today. One of us needs to be there. He hasn't checked in yet, which is odd for him. He always checks in when he lands.

I send him a message.

ME:

You land okay?

Pocketing my phone, I tell my driver to take me to the Royal. I don't care what Evie is doing right now. I need to see her.

# Chapter Thirty-Five

I've been on the phone for half an hour with a representative from the insurance company. I feel as if I'm going around and around in circles. "Ma'am, first you have to submit a copy of the police report, then your claim can be processed," he says.

"Thank you. I guess I'll contact the police for that report then." I hang up without saying goodbye.

"What's wrong?" Charlotte asks.

"They won't do anything without a police report." I sigh.

"Okay, so let's get the report. The fire was an accident. They can't *not* pay you out," she says.

I shake my head and whisper, "It wasn't an accident."

"What do you mean? Did you do it?" she whispers back.

"No, it was Amy. And why are we whispering?" I ask her.

"You started it." Charlotte shrugs. "I just went with it. Amy? Why would she burn down the store?"

"Remember that fireman you dated? Phil? He came by my house the morning after everything happened and said they had evidence it was arson. Amy was the only one in the store and she said it started from the garment steamer."

"Oh my gosh, I hope you told the police. Have they arrested her?"

I shake my head again. I don't know how to tell my friend they can't arrest anyone because Emmanuel got to them first.

"Why not? You don't owe her anything, Evie," Charlotte presses.

"She's dead," I tell her. "There was a house fire the day after the store burned down, and Amy and her boyfriend were caught inside."

"Really? That's... a strange kind of karma and a waste of eye candy. Her boyfriend was hot." Charlotte smirks.

"Who was hot and what karma?" Louie's voice from behind us has me jumping out of my skin.

"Holy shit, don't sneak up on a girl." I gasp, a hand firmly planted on my chest.

"Evie's store fire wasn't an accident. Her employee did it. And then, the next day, the girl's house burned down with her and her boyfriend inside it," Charlotte explains. "Karma, right?"

"Karma or a psychotic Mexican," Louie mumbles under his breath before repeating, "Who was hot, Charlotte?"

"Amy's boyfriend." Charlotte's smirk widens.

"Good thing he's already dead then," Louie grumbles.

"Phil was looking rather fine still," I chime in.

"Who is Phil?" Louie asks.

"Oh, just the fireman Charlotte dated a few years back." I smile at my friend.

Louie looks to his wife. "You dated a fireman?"

"Mhmm." Charlotte nods.

"I've been told she has shitty taste in men." I chuckle as I relay what Emmanual said.

"*Had,*" Louie corrects me.

Something on the television screen catches my

attention. "Wait! Can we turn up the volume?" I point to the screen. "I know those men."

Charlotte picks up the remote and the reporter's voice starts recalling the three home invasions resulting in multiple murders and fires.

"This happened today?" I ask.

"Seems that way. How do you know them?" Charlotte replies.

"They were all judges, at the pageants." I swallow, my throat dry. Then the reporter mentions one of the homes included a man, his wife, and two teenage daughters.

"Oh..." Charlotte's eyes bulge out of her head.

"I feel sick." I run from the room, straight into the bedroom I've been using, and then into the adjoining bathroom.

Falling in front of the toilet, I empty the contents of my stomach. This is my fault. People are dead because of me.

"Evie, I'm so sorry. You shouldn't have to see that." Charlotte rubs a hand up and down my back. "Louie, get some water!" she calls out.

Once I'm sure I'm not going to throw up again, I grab some toilet paper and wipe my mouth. "It's my fault."

"It is *not* your fault. You didn't do anything to those men," Charlotte insists.

"Here, drink this." Louie hands me a bottle of water. He looks from his wife to me. "Why would you think this is your fault?"

I can't tell him. I shake my head as more tears fall down my face.

"Thanks. Can you make me some coffee?" Charlotte asks. "We're fine in here."

"You sure?" Louie appears undecided. He doesn't want to leave his wife with me. I don't blame him. People have been dropping like flies around me.

"I'm sure. It's girl stuff," Charlotte tells him, her voice firmer. He nods once and turns down the hallway.

"I'm sorry, Charlotte. I'm going to pack my things and go home. I shouldn't have come here. I shouldn't have brought my problems to you." I choke down a sob.

"Nonsense. You are not going anywhere. You are my best friend. Your problems are my problems," she says.

"You're supposed to be enjoying the honeymoon stage."

"Trust me, Louie and I are getting plenty of honeymoon time in." She waggles her eyebrows up and down. "You think he did this?"

I shrug. "Who else?"

"I don't know. But I mean, it could be anything

and not even linked to you. How many other girls do you think they're were?" she asks.

"I have no idea." I've thought about it. Often wondered why no one had come forward. But what can you say if you don't remember anything that happened? "I'm really sorry."

"Why are you apologizing again?" Charlotte says.

"Because I'm a mess." I push myself up and look at my reflection in the mirror. I'm horrified by the woman staring back at me. She's ugly. Inside and out. "I think I'm just going to have a shower."

She's the reason two teenage girls are now dead. She's the reason three homes were burned down today. This woman isn't a good person. I'm not even sure why Charlotte hasn't kicked me out already.

"Evie, look at me." Charlotte forces me to turn around. She brushes my hair away from my face. Then she wipes her fingers under my eyes. "You are a good person. This is not your fault. You didn't choose what those men did to you. Just like you didn't choose what happened to them."

"I told him. I knew what he was capable of and I told him. I should never have said anything..."

"I disagree. Your telling him freed you from carrying the burden alone, and it proved that what happened to you doesn't define you, Evie. I know you thought you were unlovable, but if the actions of that man aren't love, then I don't know what is," Charlotte says.

Emmanuel has told me that he loves me more than once. I've never been able to bring myself to say it back because I'm too scared to let myself. Can I really love someone capable of such brutality? The better question is can I allow myself to love a monster? Because I'm not so sure I don't already.

"He murdered innocent people, Charlotte," I mumble.

"One, we don't know the facts. And two, *we don't know the facts*. Did he maybe go a tad overboard? Yes. But I mean, you have met him, right? He's a little... unhinged at the best of times. But I feel like, when he looks at you, that level reaches all new heights."

"You didn't even know we were seeing each other until yesterday." I roll my eyes. "And now, suddenly, you're all Team E?"

"So it's *E*, huh? I'm Team *Evie*. Always. And I saw the way you came to life when you were talking about him yesterday. He's good for you, hon."

"He's a murderer..." I whisper.

"So is my husband? Does that mean I love him less? Or that he loves me less?" Charlotte shakes her head. "No."

"It's different," I tell her.

"How so?"

"Louie isn't out killing innocent people, is he?" I counter.

"Not that I know of," she admits. "Have a shower. It will make you feel better. I'm going to order pizza and find a whole lot of wine."

"Okay." Before Charlotte leaves, I grab on to her and pull her into my arms. "Thank you."

* * *

I spent over an hour in the shower, and then another fixing my appearance. I blow-dried and curled my hair. Reapplied my makeup and put on a cute little yellow sundress. I stand by my theory. If you look good, you feel good. And I do feel better. Or at least I feel like my mask is back in place and I can face the world again.

Do I want to? No. But I need to. I can't hide in the bathroom forever.

The moment I walk out of the bedroom, I wish I could turn back around and hide. The hushed voices of Louie and Emmanuel stop the moment they notice I'm standing in the doorway.

Emmanuel's eyes run up and down the length of my body. Slowly. From my toes, up my legs. He takes a moment to look at my hands twisting in front of me before his eyes continue their perusal.

"I'm going to help Charlotte with setting the table. Pizza just turned up. Evie, you good?" Louie asks me.

I nod and give him a polite smile. Something tells me if I said no, he'd stay and wouldn't leave me with the ruthless monster I can't seem to find a way to truly hate like I know I should.

As soon as Louie's gone, Emmanuel takes a step towards me. Instinctively, I take a step backwards. His eyes squint and his jaw ticks but he continues stalking forward as I continue to move in the opposite direction. Until he closes the bedroom door and I realize I've just locked myself in a room with him. That's not good.

"I should go and help Charlotte," I say.

"Why have you been crying?" E asks. He reaches out, grabs my chin, and tilts my face upwards.

"I haven't."

"Don't lie to me, Evie," he says.

"Why?" I shake out of his hold. "What are you going to do? Kill me like you did those two innocent teenagers?"

"I would never hurt you."

"That's not true and we both know it. If I gave you a reason, you wouldn't even blink an eye before killing me," I fire back at him. "You'd probably keep me in some unmarked grave like Laura. Visit me when you feel bad about your life choices."

"You're angry," he states.

I laugh. "Now he's a genius."

"I didn't kill those girls."

"You might not have been the one to pull the trigger, but you were the one who gave the orders. It's the same thing, Emmanuel," I tell him.

"Those assholes don't deserve to breathe," he seethes. "I will not let them live their lives like they've done nothing."

"Their families didn't do anything to me, Emmanuel. The men? I can overlook them. Nothing I say is going to stop you from doing whatever it is you want to them. But teenagers, Emmanuel? Really? I thought maybe I could get over this whole cartel lifestyle thing. But I don't know if I can. Actually, I can't." I shake my head. "I can't live with knowing that I'm the reason innocent people are dead."

# Chapter Thirty-Six

The nightmare from last night still haunts me, especially when I hear Evie say she can't live with people's deaths on her hands. I look down at her wrists, perfectly intact, my thumbs stroking the smooth skin there.

"Nothing that I do or give orders to do is on you, Evie. That falls on me. You are clean. You will always be clean," I tell her.

"It doesn't work like that, E. The only reason

you're going after these men is because of me," she says.

"It's because I can't live in a world where people who hurt you exist. Not because of you. That's on me," I assure her. "I need to know that you're not going to do anything you can't undo."

"Like what?"

"I won't have anyone take you away from me, Evie, not even you. So if you're having thoughts like that, you need to tell me. I will find a way to help you."

Evie steps back. "You think I'm suicidal. Why?"

"Are you?"

"No. I'm confused. I'm upset, but I've survived shit all my life. I'm not a quitter," she says.

"Good, then fight. For your happiness. For me. I know you feel this. I know you want this. I also know you're scared." I sigh. "I don't ever want to see you break, Evie. I don't want to lose you."

"Then stop killing innocent girls," she hisses.

"I will do my best to ensure there are no witnesses in the future. But this line of work, it's messy, and I can't make guarantees. I also won't lie and tell you what you want to hear." I run a hand through my hair as I lower myself onto the edge of the bed. "I've had this conversation before."

"What conversation?"

"The one where you don't want me to continue the job, the one where you want me but not the lifestyle that comes with me." I look up at Evie.

"You had this conversation with her?" she asks.

I nod my head. Laura wanted us to run together.

"I'm not her, E. I would never ask you to leave your lifestyle... or your job. I just don't know how to come to terms with it in my own mind," she says.

"I know you're not her. Losing her hurt, Evie. But losing you? That fucking tore me apart and it wasn't even real," I admit.

"What are you talking about?"

"Last night, I had a nightmare. I found you on the floor. Your wrists were slashed. There was so much blood." I try to shake the images from my head. "It was so real."

"E, I'm not going to do anything like that. I promise. Like I said, I might be broken, irreparably so, but I'm not going to give up," Evie says.

"You are not broken. You are fucking perfect." I stand and walk over to her. Wrapping my arms around her, I pull her into my chest. "My father was right."

"About what?"

"Love does make you weak. I'd lose it all for you. If I had to go to war, I would wager everything. Every single fucking thing, for you."

"I'm scared of how much I'm falling in love with you."

I pull back. Evie has never uttered those words. I've said them to her, but she has never said them back. I smile down at her. "Well, that won't do. We can't both be scared."

"Pfft, nothing scares you. You're the leader of the De La Sangre Cartel," she says.

"You scare me."

"Maybe we can just be scared together?" Evie suggests.

"Together," I agree. I lean down and press my lips to hers. When I pull back, I push my luck. "So, will you come home with me now?"

"I can't. Charlotte got pizza and wine. And we have plans for tomorrow," Evie says.

"I don't like it when you tell me no," I grunt.

"That's because not enough people in your life tell you no, E. Don't worry. You'll get used to hearing the word." Evie smiles.

"Don't ever cry over something I've done again." I take hold of her hand. "I don't want to be the reason for your tears."

"Then don't give me a reason to cry."

I left Evie to have pizza with Charlotte, while Louie dragged me into his office. I'm waiting for whatever bullshit he has to say, but the fucker likes to make a show and dance about everything. He takes his time pouring two glasses of whiskey.

Handing one to me, he walks around his desk and sits down. "When she saw what you did, it made her sick. Physically. She ran to the bathroom to throw up," he says.

*Fuck. I knew she had been crying. I didn't know she'd been sick.*

"It had to be done," I tell him.

"There a reason you're going after pageant judges?" he asks.

I tilt my head to the side. He doesn't know. "There is always a reason I do anything." I lower myself down onto one of the chairs across from him.

"Want to share that reason?"

"It's not mine to share." No fucking way am I telling anyone Evie's business. My men have educated guesses. They know better than to question why I'm doing something, though.

"This whole thing with Evie, it's not going to end up with her disappearing, is it?" Louie presses.

"You know, I don't recall you being her father," I retort. "Or mine."

"She's my wife's best friend. If anything happens

to her, it would make my wife extremely upset. I won't allow that to happen," Louie says.

"Good. Remember that while she's choosing to stay at your house and not mine," I grunt.

Louie, the fucking smart-ass that he is, smirks. "I never thought I'd see the day a woman could resist your charms, E."

"Fuck off. She just wants to spend time with her friends. She lost her shop. She needs the distraction," I mutter.

"Sure, that's it." He laughs.

"Speaking of stores, I want you to offer her a spot at Royal's mall. I want the rent to be controlled and half of what the going rate is," I tell him.

"And why would I do that?" Louie asks.

"Because if you don't, I'll make sure no one wants to rent a space in your mall," I threaten.

"You do know we are friends, right? You don't threaten your friends, E."

"You are my oldest friend, Louie, but don't mistake friendship for weakness. Make it happen for her. She needs this. I also prefer her here, where you and the guys can keep an eye on her when I can't."

Louie quirks a brow at me. "You planning on moving back stateside?"

"No, but I can't take her home yet. I need to make sure shit is sorted out there first."

"I'll draw up a lease. I'll get Charlotte to make it seem like her idea. She'd love to have Evie around more permanently."

"Her and me both," I grunt. I down the rest of the contents in my glass before I slam it on the table. "We have another drop coming up in two weeks."

"I'm aware," Louie says.

"Good, make sure you're there for it. I won't be collecting my own shit again," I tell him.

"Wouldn't miss it," he says with a smile. "Pleasure doing business with you, E."

"Always." I push to my feet and walk towards the door.

"Where are you going?" Louie asks.

"To say goodbye to my girl and then go visit my niece," I tell him.

"You're going to Carlo's? I'll come with you."

"Why?"

"Because you're not stealing uncle cred from me," Louie says.

"You have some serious fucking issues."

I find Evie in the dining room. There's a slice of pizza on her plate that looks like she's picked at it at best. "Evie, a word," I call out to her.

"Emmanuel, not a dog," she counters.

Louie chuckles from behind me. His hand slaps my shoulder as he passes.

"Evie, can I have a moment of your time?" I try again.

"Sure. See? That wasn't hard." She jumps up off her chair, takes hold of my hand, and drags me towards the guest bedroom. She closes the door behind us before she looks up at me. "Your moment has started."

"Why aren't you eating?" I ask her.

"I'm not hungry," she says.

"I want you to eat."

"And I want you to not be so bossy and controlling. We all want things in life, E."

I almost smile. She has to fight me every single step of the way. I know how to get her appetite to make an appearance, though. I pull Evie over to the bed, pushing her backwards so she falls flat on her back. My hands separate her thighs, pinning them open.

"What are you doing?" Evie asks.

"You might not be hungry, but I'm fucking starved," I tell her as I position myself between her legs. My shoulders open her wider. Using one hand, I move her panties to the side, revealing her smooth pussy. "You're fucking wet." I groan as I run my tongue right up the slit.

"Well, you have your head between my legs. What do you expect?"

I continue to lick her, from bottom to top, circling my tongue around her hardened bud. Evie's hands land on my head, her fingers pulling at my hair.

My free hand moves to her opening and I push two fingers inside her. I curl them, finding that sweet spot. Her thighs tighten around my head as they attempt to close. With each thrust of my fingers, my tongue circles her clit.

"Fucking hell, you're delicious," I growl into her pussy.

I don't stop until I feel her pussy contracting around my fingers. Flattening my tongue on her clit, I push down. Evie's hips lift as she grinds against me, her orgasm causing her body to shake. I continue licking her until she relaxes fully.

I look up at the very satisfied grin on her face. "Again."

Evie shakes her head, but I'm not taking no for an answer.

"Again," I repeat before I push my tongue into her opening, circling it around. My fingers press against her back entrance.

"Shit, E," she grunts.

I don't stop my assault on her cunt until she's coming all over my tongue. Evie grabs a pillow, pulls it over her face, and screams. I smile, peppering her pussy with little kisses as she comes down from her high.

"Best fucking meal ever," I say as I make my way up her body. I shove the pillow aside.

"Now I'm hungry." She smirks.

"Good, you've got pizza on the table. Go and eat it." I climb off her.

"That's not what I want." Evie pouts as she stares at my very obvious erection.

"Sorry, mi alma, I gotta run. I'll see you later." I lean down and kiss her lips. Then I move towards the door before I say *fuck it* and fuck her.

Louie is waiting for me in the foyer. "You've got something... here," he says, wiping at the side of his mouth.

"Fuck off." I shove at him and press the button for the elevator.

"Good chat, then?" I hear Charlotte ask from behind me. When I turn around, Evie's face is flaming red.

"Meh, I've had better," she tells Charlotte, causing Louie to laugh his fucking ass off as we step into the elevator.

*Better, my ass. I'm going to make her eat those fucking words later.*

# Chapter Thirty-Seven

"What!" I scream at Rachel through the phone. She just told me she got the job in Seattle. She's moving next week. "I can't believe I'm going to be the only one left," I groan. "My social life is over."

"Says the one who's currently in Vegas while I'm stuck at the hospital working my third consecutive fifteen-hour shift," Rachel counters.

"You chose to be smart," I remind her. "We can't

all be surgeons. But I'm happy for you. Sad for me, but happy for you."

"Thank you," she says. "So, how's Vegas been? Seen Emmanuel?"

"I have, a little. But mostly I've just been hanging out with Charlotte."

"I'm surprised he's leaving you alone at all. The man is the definition of obsessed."

"You have no idea." I roll my eyes. I know Emmanuel comes off really strong, but I've kinda grown to love it. I like the way he makes me feel like I'm the most important person in the room. As if he'd do anything for me. Then again, he's proven that he really would do anything for me. Over and over.

"Just don't go running off and getting married without me," Rachel says.

"I have no plans of getting married." I laugh at her.

"Does Emmanuel know that?" Charlotte asks as she walks into the room with a cup of coffee in her hand

"Oh, I love you!" I moan as I pass her the phone and take the coffee.

"I know." Charlotte smiles.

"Rach, tell her!" I call out.

"Tell me what?" Charlotte looks at the screen.

"I'm moving to Seattle," Rachel says.

"What? When? Why? How?" Charlotte fires off question after question.

"I applied for that job there and I got it. I'm moving in a month," Rachel explains.

"I'm so excited for you. Look at us all getting out of our little small town and moving to big cities. Who would have thought?" Charlotte squeals.

I raise a hand. "Ah, I still live in that small town."

"About that." Charlotte looks to me. "Rachel, help me out here," she adds while eyeing the phone. "I have a proposition."

"I don't think I'm cut out for being a sister wife, babe." I laugh.

"Not that kind of proposition." She shakes her head. "I happen to know there is empty retail space in the mall downstairs. I want you to have it."

I laugh harder. "Yeah, because my little burned-down boutique can afford a prime storefront in Vegas's most popular casino."

"It's rent controlled. And it's perfect for you. At least come and look at it. For me." Charlotte gives me that pout of hers that always gets her what she wants.

"Fine, I'll look. But I'm telling you I cannot afford it."

"Yay! Keep an open mind, Evie. If Charlotte says you can afford it, then you can. She's the most frugal of all of us," Rachel chimes in.

"I'll keep an open mind," I agree before narrowing my eyes suspiciously. "Wait... Was this plan cooked up by Emmanuel?"

"No, it was actually Louie's idea. And when he told me, I got so excited at the thought of you moving here. He then went on to say it's a done deal and that he'll have the lease drawn up by the end of the day." Charlotte smiles dreamily. "He wants me to be happy, and having at least one of my best friends is what's going to make me happy."

"Why would your husband be thinking about location spots for my shop?" I ask her.

"Because he has an empty store, and he doesn't want an empty store." Charlotte shrugs. "Just come and look at it."

"Fine. But I need to shower first," I say, sipping at the coffee.

"Deal, but let's not make it a two-hour shower. Time's a wasting, Evie." Charlotte walks out of my room, taking my phone with her as she starts talking to Rachel about something else.

I follow her out. "Hey, you have your own phone. I need that one!"

"Why? Expecting a call?" Charlotte teases.

"No," I lie. I have no doubt Emmanuel will call or message soon, and like the fool that I am, I'm waiting for him to do it.

I know! Yesterday I was ready to put distance between us, but he has a way of getting me to forget the outside world. I get it. And honestly, if any of my friends were dating him, I'd be kidnapping them and running away with new identities. But me? No, I'm the idiot who runs towards the dangerous man, despite knowing that it will likely be my undoing.

"Okay, not a call, but he did just message you. Damn, who would have known the man could be so sweet and cute." Charlotte smirks.

"Give it to me." I swipe for my phone, but she raises her hand.

"What's it say?" Rachel asks.

"Mi alma..."

"Charlotte, I will find a way to drain that rooftop pool that you love so much. I don't even care if I drown the city," I say, threatening the one thing she loves most. Swimming.

"Pfft, you wouldn't." She squints her eyes at me.

"Maybe not, but I do happen to know one man insane enough to do it for me if I asked." I shrug.

"You wouldn't!" Charlotte gasps as she drops my phone back into my open palm.

"Sure I wouldn't." I laugh. We both know I would never do anything like that or ask someone else to. But the threat alone is enough for me to get my hands back on my phone.

"You play a dirty game, Evie," Rachel says. "I gotta go. My break is over."

"Bye, love you," all three of us say in unison, and then the call cuts out.

I look to Charlotte. "I'm going to shower."

"Tell Emmanuel I say hi," she hums in her sweetest southern accent.

I don't respond, but on my way to the bathroom, I do open his message.

E:

Mi alma, my bed is cold without you. I need you to come home.

ME:

Home would indicate we live together, E. We do not.

I set my phone down on the counter and turn on the shower. As I'm pulling my pajamas over my head, the phone vibrates across the marble.

E:

We do live together. You just haven't accepted that fact yet. Doesn't make it any less true, though.

ME:

You need serious mental health help.

E:

No, what I need is you.

ME:

I'm getting in the shower.

E:

I want to watch. Video call me.

Before I can respond, his face is flashing across the screen. I accept the call and place the phone back down on the counter, giving him a direct view of the ceiling.

"Evie, I want to see you," Emmanuel says.

"I'm naked," I tell him.

"That's the point."

"You're not watching me shower, E. It's weird. What did you get up to last night?" I ask as I step under the water.

"I went to see Jazzy. She asked about you."

"Why would she do that?"

"She saw your name on my wrist. Asked if I was going to marry Evie. I told her I was."

"You can't tell her things like that. She's a kid. You're going to get her all excited for something that's not even happening," I chastise.

"It's happening. How was your night?"

"Long," I groan. I didn't sleep. I haven't slept since I got here. I'm starting to feel it too. "Charlotte wants to show me a retail space today, at the Royal mall."

"Does she? That's good. It's a great spot," E says.

"Mhm, I can't afford a spot on the Strip. But I told her I'd look."

"How much is the rent?"

"I have no idea," I admit.

"Then you don't know if you can afford it or not. Want me to talk to Louie? I can negotiate the rate for you," Emmanuel offers.

"No," I tell him. "Don't do that. I'm not sure your negotiation tactics are suitable for my type of business."

"My negotiation tactics have proven results. If you want the store, take it. Believe in yourself like I believe in you." This man really does say the sweetest things.

"I will consider it." Turning off the water, I step out of the shower and wrap a towel around my body. Then I pick up the phone, finally getting a glimpse of Emmanuel. He looks tired. "Did you sleep last night?" I ask him.

"No, I had some things pop up."

"Everything okay?"

"Yes," he says, but the tick of his jaw tells me everything is very much not okay. "I despise that towel. Lose it."

I laugh. "You can't hate a towel. I gotta go. Charlotte is waiting for me." I cut the call to avoid the awkward goodbye.

---

I'm taking in everything that is the retail space Charlotte just unlocked for me. It's perfect, like insanely so. But I'm trying not to get too excited. I can't afford something like this. The place is already fitted out. I wouldn't have to do much.

"I'm going to leave you to look a bit longer. I'm getting coffee. You want one?" Charlotte asks.

"Ah, yeah, thank you." I spin around and try to take everything in.

There is another room off the back with a small kitchenette and then there's a bathroom. Who would have thought these spaces had their own bathrooms?

This shop is insane. It's huge, probably three times the size of my boutique. And there are four dressing rooms. *Four.* I had one. I know Emmanuel told me to believe in myself, but I feel nothing but doubt right now.

"Nice space." A low whistle has me spinning around.

"Can I help you?" I ask as my eyes instinctively flick towards the exit.

"Actually, I'm here to help you," the stranger says.

"How so?" The hairs on the back of my neck stand up. Something is wrong, very wrong.

"Agent Shawn Jerrerys. I've been waiting for an opportunity to meet you, Miss Carter." The man extends a hand to me. I don't take it.

"Why?" I fold my arms over my chest.

"Your boyfriend. I want you to look at these." Agent Jerrerys holds up a folder and then walks over to the counter and opens it.

I don't move. "You need to leave."

"You need to look at what the man you're fucking is capable of doing. You are in danger, Miss Carter. I can help you," he says.

I laugh. "I don't have a boyfriend. I have no idea who you're referring to."

"Emmanuel Lopez, leader of the De La Sangre Cartel? Ring a bell."

"No." I shrug a single shoulder.

"You do know... the crimes he's going down for, you'll go down right alongside him for them. Are you prepared to spend the rest of your life behind bars for this man, Miss Carter?"

"I have no idea what you're talking about. Please get out of my store." I aim a manicured finger behind the agent.

"Nice place. Tell me... how does someone like you afford a spot like this? From what I hear, your own store burned down just days ago," he says. "Arson is what they're calling it."

"Is everything okay?" Charlotte walks in, two Starbucks cups in her hands.

"This man was just leaving," I tell her.

"Mrs. Giuliani." The agent nods at Charlotte as he swipes the folder back up and walks out of the store.

"I'm sorry. I have to go," I tell Charlotte.

"Evie, what's happening?"

I hug her. "That was a fed. He wanted me to talk about E," I whisper into her ear. "Do me a favor? Ask Louie to text Emmanuel, tell him to meet me in room 666."

"Um, okay," she says.

I pull back to look her in the eye. "Go and find him, though. Don't call or message him."

"Okay." She nods and we both walk out of the store. I leave Charlotte to lock up and head towards E's suite.

# Chapter Thirty-Eight

I swipe the card against the door. The moment Louie called me, telling me I needed to meet Evie, I dropped everything I was doing to go and find her. I've been trying to call her the entire ride over to the Royal and she's not answering.

I was trying to find out where the fuck my second-in-command disappeared to. No one has seen or heard from Paz since he left me the other day. He should be at the estate back home. The jet didn't make it there and no one seems to know where the fuck it is.

When I walk into the suite, I find Evie pacing the living room.

"Evie?" I take my time, running my eyes up and down her body, checking for any injuries. My glare hones in on her wrists. They're intact. I still can't get the image of them sliced open out of my head. Seeing her unharmed calms my mind—a little.

"I want to get married," she says, stopping in the middle of the room.

I smile. But I don't approach her yet. "You do, huh?"

"Now," she says. "Will you do it?"

I tilt my head to the side. Part of me wants to take advantage of her momentary insanity. Another part wants to question her motives. *Why now? Why the fuck does she look desperate?*

"I sure as fuck am not letting you marry anyone else. So if you want to get married, it's going to be to me, Evie," I tell her.

Her body relaxes. "Okay. We can just go to a chapel, right? Like Louie and Charlotte did."

"We could." I nod. "But your wedding isn't going to be in a chapel. You deserve better than that."

"You don't want to marry me today?" she asks.

"I didn't say that. I will marry you right this second. I just said you're going to get the wedding you deserve. Not some cheap Vegas chapel."

"I don't care about the wedding. We just need to be married, Emmanuel," she stresses.

Now I really am curious. "Okay, I'll have papers drawn up. We can sign them this afternoon in front of a judge. It will be legal, but our wedding, that's something we will plan, and it will be fucking amazing."

"Okay." Evie nods a little too enthusiastically.

I take my phone out of my pocket and send Louie a message.

ME:

I need a judge to sign marriage documents between me and Evie. Today.

LOUIE:

Get the fuck out of here. Seriously? Does she know what she's signing?

ME:

She asked me.

LOUIE:

Why?

*That's a good fucking question.*

"You know, I don't really care why the sudden change of heart, Evie. Or about the urgency to get married. If you say that you want to be my wife, I will make you my wife. I am curious, though. Why now?"

Evie stares at me wide-eyed. "I... ah... it's not sudden," she insists. "I mean, it is. But really, we both know where this relationship is heading. I can't stay away from you, E. And when I think about something bad happening to you, well, I don't like it. At all. And I don't want to have to be without you." She sits down on the sofa. "I had a man approach me at the store today."

"What?" I walk over to her. "What man?" I ask, ready to tear *this man's* fucking head off.

"He said he was an agent. Shawn Something. I don't know. E, he had a folder he wanted me to look at and he wanted to talk about you. He mentioned you by name. He knew my name too, and he knew about my store burning down." Her words come out fast, rushed. She's panicking.

"Evie, mi alma, it's okay. Slow down. What did you tell him?" I ask.

She glares at me. Snatching her hands out of mine as she stands from the sofa. "I didn't tell him anything. Why would I tell him anything? I didn't even look at the folder. I said I had no idea who he was talking about. I said I didn't know you."

"Good." I sigh in relief.

"You think I'd talk to cops about you? Seriously? You were prepared to marry me and you don't even trust me." She waves her hands around the air.

"I *am* going to marry you. But not because you're scared of some douchebag agent. I'm going to marry you because you want to marry me, Evie," I tell her.

I message Louie.

ME:

Hold on the judge.

LOUIE:

She come to her senses already?

ME:

No, I did.

I pocket my phone and look over at Evie. "We're not getting married today. We will wait until you're actually ready."

"You just said yes. You said we could. What if they try to use me against you, E? What if I crack under pressure or something? If we're married, they can't use me to testify against you."

"You're not going to testify against me." I laugh. I don't tell her I know that because she'd be dead before she could. It's not something I want to happen. "I trust you, Evie. You don't need to worry about the feds."

"I can't go to jail, E. I don't even look good in orange," she says.

"You look good in any color. Come here." I chuckle as I pull her into my arms. "I really should have just taken you up on the marriage offer, despite knowing you'd regret it." I press my lips to the top of her head. "I want you to be my wife, Evie. And one day, you will be. But it's not going to be because you feel like you have to. It's going to be because you want to."

"You should have. I might not experience this level of insanity again," she mumbles against my chest.

"You know, we can start the honeymoon early. We have this suite and all," I suggest.

Evie pulls back to look up at me. "Yeah? What do you have in mind?"

"Come with me." I grab her hand and usher her into the bedroom. Walking behind her so I can unzip her dress before letting it fall to the floor. "Get on the bed."

Evie takes her time climbing onto the mattress... with that ass of hers on full display. *Fuck me.*

"How do you want me?" she asks while glancing over a shoulder.

"On your back, legs spread open. I want to see you." I step up to the edge of the bed.

Evie drops her thighs to the side, her pussy covered by a thin layer of pink lace. That isn't going to do. Bending down, I retrieve the blade from my ankle. I climb between her legs. Evie's eyes catch on the blade in my hand, watching me as I drag it up her inner thigh.

I bring the knife to the side of her panties. Evie doesn't flinch as I slice through the material, or when I repeat the process on the other side. Dragging the blade up her abdomen, I reach the front of her bra and slice through that too. Her breasts fall free as the fabric parts.

"You are fucking perfect. And mine."

"Mmm, what are you going to do with me?" Evie asks.

I push back from the mattress, removing my jacket, vest, and shirt. Then I unbuckle my belt. Evie doesn't move. Her legs are still spread wide for me. Her pussy glistening with her need.

I undo my pants, dropping them to the ground before toeing off my shoes while stepping out of the piled material. My fist wraps around my cock. I'm fucking hard as a rock. I need her.

"Look how wet you are. Your cunt is dripping all over the bed, Evie."

"Emmanuel, hurry up. Please," she begs.

"Please what?" I stroke my cock up and down.

"Touch me. Fuck me," she pleads.

"Not yet. I'm staring at a work of art. If your pussy needs petting, mi alma, pet it. Touch yourself. Show me."

Evie's hand quickly finds her clit. Her fingers start circling. It's fucking hot.

"Shove two fingers inside. Fuck yourself with those fingers as if you were riding my cock, Evie."

She groans, but follows my instructions, all while staring right at my cock.

"Fucking perfection," I tell her in Spanish. "I'm going to fuck you so hard you're going to be walking with a limp." She has no idea what I'm saying, but I do.

"Oh shit, E..." she moans, her fingers moving in and out of her wet hole.

"You coming is the best thing I've ever seen, Evie. I want to see it, now," I say, and her body quivers.

"It's better when you do it." She smiles shyly at me.

"Didn't you tell Charlotte that you'd had better?" I ask, turning her words back on her. I told myself I'd make her eat those fucking words. Her fingers continue to thrust in and out of her wet hole. I can't take my eyes off them.

"I lied. I've never had better than you. Please, E, I want your cock. I want to feel your cock inside me, E. I want you to make me feel the way only you can." She stares at me, hopeful that I'll put her out of her misery and fuck her the way she needs to be fucked.

"You want me to fuck you?" I ask her, my fist squeezing my cock.

"Please..."

"You want me to fill that greedy little cunt with this? It's ready for you." I look down at my cock.

"Yes. Emmanuel, stop teasing me and give it to me. You said you'd give me anything I wanted. What I want right now is you," she seethes. Her fingers don't stop fucking her cunt, though. Her hips raise off the bed.

"You have me, always, mi alma." I climb onto the bed again. I pull her fingers away from her cunt, bringing them to my mouth. I take my time sucking each one clean. "So fucking good," I moan as her taste dances across my tongue. I lift her ankles, placing them on my shoulders, and position my cock at her entrance. "Are you ready for me?"

"More than ready. Fuck me, E," she says.

One hard thrust and I bottom out inside her. I

don't give her time to adjust to the intrusion. I go all in and fuck her. Thrusting hard, fast. Evie's fingers claw down my back. I wouldn't be surprised if she's drawing blood. Within minutes, her pussy is convulsing around my cock as she comes undone. My name on her lips as her screams echo off the walls.

# Chapter Thirty-Nine

I don't know how I let Charlotte talk me into these things. I've just arrived at Carlo and Antonia's. They're having a dinner party with all their friends. I'm just the ringer in, also the only one that isn't part of a pair, which is glaringly obvious when I sit down at the table. There's an empty chair next to me. I always feel weird at these fancy dinners, but knowing these are Charlotte's new friends and Emmanuel's old friends makes me feel even more out of place.

"Fuck," Carlo hisses as the sound of the elevator rings out through the apartment.

"Pay up, fuckers. Ten G, each of you." Louie points from Sammie to Carlo.

"What'd you bet on now?" Charlotte asks her husband.

"How long it'd take for Emmanuel to show up," he replies. And sure enough, that's exactly who just walked through the door.

My back straightens. He messaged me about twenty minutes ago and asked what I was doing. I told him about this dinner.

"Thanks for the invite," Emmanuel directs to Carlo.

"I was hoping it got lost in the mail," Carlo grumbles. They have an odd friendship, these men.

"Tío E! Guess what? Guess what?" Jazzy bounces up and down in her seat.

"What, princesa?" The smile Emmanuel gives his niece melts my damn ovaries.

I've never once wanted to have children, even if Charlotte and I have daydreamed about our futures together. I don't deserve them. I'm not motherly material. It's an unfamiliar sensation I'm experiencing right now, though. Does Emmanuel want kids? I probably should have thought of that before I asked him to marry me. I'm thankful that he at least had the smarts to turn me down, or at least to tell me we had to wait.

"I get to go to a new school, and Daddy bought us a new house. And I'm getting a little brother or sister!" Jazzy announces to the room.

Antonia chokes on her wine. "Not anytime soon," she clarifies through a fit of coughing.

"You good?" Carlo rubs a hand up and down his wife's back.

"Uh-huh." Antonia nods, her cheeks now glowing red.

"And I'm getting cousins from Uncle Louie," Jazzy adds.

I look across to Charlotte. This is news to me. She shakes her head.

"Seems people have been busy," Emmanuel says, taking the seat right next to mine. His hand lands on my leg under the table, and I shake it off without sparing him a look.

"You moving back to town?" Sammie asks.

"I might." E shrugs. "If something keeps pulling me back here." As he says this, I feel the heat of his stare on the side of my face.

*Don't look at him. Don't look. Don't look,* I chant in my head.

I can't do this. Dinner with his friends, like we're a real couple.

*You just asked the man to marry you. You are a real couple.* The voice in my head pops up. I shove it down. I don't need rational thought right now.

"What's in the soup, Antonia?" Emmanuel asks.

"Vegetables," she says.

"You don't like vegetables?" he questions while eyeing her differently-colored soup bowl.

"They brought up carrot and coconut for Carlo. I swapped," she replies with a shrug. "Carlo doesn't like coconut."

"I'm not that fond of vegetables." Emmanuel reaches over the table and swaps bowls.

Now I do look at him. The man loves vegetables. I know. I've been forced to eat all kinds of them with him.

"Ah, I've already eaten some of it," Antonia says.

"How much?" Emmanuel asks her.

"Just a little," she tells him.

"It's fine. I'm going to get myself a drink. Louie, show me where the kitchen is." Emmanuel stands, taking his new bowl of soup with him.

Carlo shoves his chair back and follows Louie and Emmanuel out of the dining room. Odd. What the hell is his problem with that bowl of soup?

Sammie is the only male left at the table. "Any idea?" Antonia asks him.

"Nope, but this soup is real good, Antonia," he says with an easy smile.

A few minutes later, everyone returns to the dining room. I have no idea what's going on. There was some mention about the soup being poisoned and Jazzy got upset. Next thing I know Antonia is picking the girl up and walking out. Then Emmanuel, Carlo, and Louie start clearing the table of food.

Antonia comes back in with Jazzy still in her arms. She looks around in confusion. I'm with her. I have no idea what's happening, but I also don't want to be the one to ask.

"There was a problem in the kitchen. I ordered pizza. Should be here soon," Carlo says.

"Oh my god, I'm so sorry! What happened?" Antonia gasps.

"The cook had an accident, cut his finger and bled into the food," Carlo explains. "But everyone loves pizza."

"I love pizza!" Jazzy chimes in excitedly.

"Only monsters or aliens don't like pizza, Jazz," Sammie tells her. I agree. Pizza beats vegetables any day.

Emmanuel leans in and whispers in my ear, "Did you eat that soup?" he asks quietly.

I shake my head while frowning at him.

"Good. Don't eat anything. I'll get you something after we leave," he says.

"I'm just going to use the restroom." I push up from the table.

"Want me to show you where it is?" Jazzy offers.

"I'll show her." Emmanuel stands before I can protest.

"I'm sure you will," Louie mumbles.

Ignoring the stares, I let Emmanuel lead me out of the dining room, his hand on my lower back, because I don't want to cause a scene. As soon as we're out of view, I shake away from his touch.

"What's going on?" I ask in a hushed tone.

"What do you mean?" He takes me by the elbow, leading me into the hallway. He then opens a door and drags me into the bathroom.

"What was wrong with the food? You're acting strange," I ask him.

"I don't trust it. I think it was poisoned," Emmanuel says.

I frown. "Who would want to poison Antonia's dinner party?"

"Everyone at that table has a long list of

enemies," Emmanuel grunts. "But you're okay. It was the orange one that was poisoned, not yours."

"Wait... You didn't eat it, did you?" My eyes go wide.

Emmanuel smiles. "You worried about me, mi alma?"

"No, Emmanuel. Every girl dreams about their boyfriend being poisoned to death." I roll my eyes at him.

"Fiancé," he says.

"What?"

"I'm not your boyfriend, mi alma. I'm your fiancé."

"You are insane." I shake my head from side to side. A stupid smile spreading across my face.

"Why are we still not telling people about us?" he asks.

"Because I don't want to yet." Truth is... I don't know why. I guess it's because, when he does decide I'm not good enough and leaves me alone, I won't be as embarrassed? I have this fear that he's going to wake up one day and realize his mistake. No matter how much I might look like his dead girlfriend, I will never be her.

"We should get back in there. Remember, don't eat anything. I'll get you something when we leave."

"If you think the pizza is poisoned, why are you letting your friends eat it?"

"Because them, I can lose. You, I can't," Emmanuel tells me.

"You know, that's sweet in a really messed up way." But it's the same thing he said to his mother, right before he shot her. "Get out. I need to pee," I say as I shove him through the bathroom door.

Emmanuel walks out, and I turn on the tap. Because knowing him, he's standing right on the other side of the door. And that's exactly where I find him when I finish up and step into the hallway.

"You ready to get out of here?" he asks.

"Um, I'm going to leave first. You wait thirty minutes before following me," I tell him.

"Room 666. Meet me there," Emmanuel says.

"Why 666?" I ask, suddenly curious. It's the same room number he uses at the Royal.

"It's the room I book out in all of their hotels. Where else would the devil stay when he comes to town?" E adds with a wicked smirk.

"Ah, his own compound?" I laugh.

When I get back to the table, I make up an excuse that I have a migraine and I need to leave. Charlotte offers to come with me, but I manage to convince her that I'm fine. I think everyone was surprised when Emmanuel didn't get up and follow me out.

He didn't need to, though. As soon as I step off the elevator on level six, two of his men are there waiting for me. "Miss Carter." One of them nods politely at me.

"Evening," I mumble and then make my way to the room that says 666 on the door. I tap the magic card across the panel and it clicks open. This suite is nice. I wonder how often Emmanuel stays here? Has he brought other women here?

Five minutes after I arrive, there's a knock at the door. That's weird. I knew Emmanuel wouldn't wait the full thirty, but I didn't expect him to knock either.

"Did you forget your key?" I open the door. A gasp leaves my mouth, and my hand rises to cover it. "What happened?" I ask a bruised-and-bloodied Paz.

"Where's E?" he questions.

"He's not here. What happened? Shit, come in." I hold the door open. The guy has seen better days.

Paz limps his way inside. When I go to help him, he flinches. "Don't touch me," he hisses.

"I'm sorry." I close the door and look around the room. "What can I do?" I have no idea how to actually help him.

"Call E. Don't tell him I'm here, just insist that you need to see him."

"Okay, I can do that." I look at Paz as he falls on to the sofa. One of his eyes is swollen shut, his lip is cut, and there are scrapes and bruises all up his torso. Did he walk through the casino like that?

I grab my phone out of my purse and dial Emmanuel's number. "Mi alma? Did you get to the room okay?" he answers.

"Uh, yeah. C-can you meet me now?" I stutter.

"What's wrong? Who's there?" I hear his footsteps. There's an echo on the phone.

"I, ah, I just need you to come, E," I tell him.

"I'm going to be right there. I'm on the elevator now. Do not hang up," he says.

"Okay."

Paz groans as he tries to get into a more comfortable position.

"Shit." I walk over to the bucket of champagne on the table. Obviously Emmanuel was planning to come back here tonight.

"What was that?" he asks.

"I stubbed my toe," I lie.

"Evie, what's going on? Come on! Why won't this thing move faster." He sounds like he's hitting a door.

"I'm okay, E. It's not me," I whisper as I walk into the bathroom and find a hand towel.

"I'm almost there."

I can hear the sound of the elevator opening. When I make it back out to the living room, I pick up some ice and wrap it in the towel. Just as I'm handing it to Paz, the door bangs open, hitting the wall with a loud thud. Paz jumps up, shoving me behind him.

Emmanuel runs into the suite with his gun raised. "What the fuck?" he grunts, his voice calm when he turns to me. "Evie, come here."

I step around Paz. "You need to sit down. Put some ice on your face. And both of you need to lower your damn guns."

"Evie, come here," Emmanuel repeats, his tone leaving no room for negotiation.

I walk over to him. I have no idea what's happening, but Paz is his most trusted man, so why is his being here sending Emmanuel into a frenzy?

# Chapter Forty

I reach for Evie and shove her behind me. "Where the fuck have you been?" I ask Paz. No one has seen him for days.

"I got picked up." Paz drops his gun onto the table. I don't lower mine. Not even when he falls back onto the sofa with a pained grunt.

"Picked up by who?" I press him.

"Feds," he says.

"Did you talk to them?"

"Does it look like I fucking talked? I am not a goddamn rat," he says that last part in Spanish.

"Why'd you come here?"

"Followed your GPS location to the casino," he says. "Figured you'd eventually show up to your usual room."

"The police did that to you? They're not allowed to touch you. You need a doctor." Evie steps in front of me.

I lower my gun but I don't let go of it. "Evie, can you go into the bedroom? Call Charlotte and have Louie send his doc up." I need to get her as far away from Paz as I can right now.

It's not that I don't trust him, but I didn't get as far as I have by letting my guard down. I'm not going to start now.

"Sure. Here, wait." She digs around in her purse. "It's not much but it's all I have," she says, handing Paz a small packet of Tylenol. I don't have it in me to tell her that's not going to help him.

"Thanks." Paz accepts the pills from her.

I watch as she walks into the bedroom. Then I sit on the coffee table, moving Paz's gun out of reach. He doesn't miss the action.

"If you're going to kill me, do it. I didn't fucking talk, jefe," he says.

"What'd they say to you?" I ask him.

"They were talking about things they shouldn't know. About drops, about Giuliani." Paz nods towards the bedroom. "And they mentioned Evie."

"What the fuck would they want with her?" I grunt. I know Evie said an agent talked to her, but I figured they'd seen her with me and took a shot.

"Someone is talking to them, jefe," Paz says. "There is no other way for them to know the things they know."

"They have no concrete proof of anything. Otherwise I'd already be in cuffs."

"We need to flush out the fucking rat," Paz says.

"Anyone heard from Enrique?" My money is on that little fucking weasel. I never should have trusted him with Evie's security.

"No. You think it's him?" Paz raises a brow. "Makes sense."

"If he's gone rat, they're hiding him somewhere." I stand and walk to the small kitchen area. I pull down a glass, fill it with water, and hand it to Paz. "I'd take those before she comes back out and forces them down your throat," I tell him, nodding towards the pills.

Paz's one eye widens. But he doesn't say anything, just pops the Tylenol into his mouth and sips at the water.

"What was the agent's name?"

"Agent Shawn Jerrerys," Paz sneers. "Fucker cuffed me to a chair so I couldn't fight back."

"He approached Evie yesterday."

"What she do?"

"Asked me to marry her." I smirk at the memory.

"That's... Really?" Paz asks.

"Why is that so hard to believe?" I counter.

"It's not. It's just... not what I expected." He shakes his head before dropping it onto the back of the sofa. "I hope you said yes."

"I'm not an idiot." There's a knock at the door, and Paz tries to stand. "Stay there," I tell him. I have no idea who it is yet. "You see the two men I stationed on this floor when you came in?"

"No one was there," Paz says.

The knock sounds out again. I stick my head into the bedroom. "Evie, were there two men on this level when you came in?" I ask her.

"Yeah, they were waiting by the elevator. Why?"

"No reason. Stay here," I tell her, closing her inside the room as I make my way to the front door of the suite.

Stepping to the side, I pull it open, my gun raised and my finger ready to pull the trigger.

"Fucking hell," Louie grunts as he shoves past me. "That's one way to welcome friends."

Sammie laughs as he follows Louie inside.

"You look like shit," Louie says to Paz.

"Yeah, feel it too," Paz groans.

When Louie goes to say something, I place my finger to my lips and nod towards the still-closed bedroom door. "Evie?" he says, and I nod. Then he looks to Paz. "What the fuck happened?"

He doesn't say anything, just lets his head fall back onto the sofa again. "You should see the other guy."

"You call a doc?" I ask Louie.

"He's on his way."

"Take her home," Paz tells me.

"Don't move." I walk into the bedroom and close the door. Then I turn around and look to Evie.

"What happened? Did the cops really do that to him? Oh my god, E, what if they pick me up for questioning?" She's panicking.

"That's not going to happen," I assure her.

"You can't control that."

"I'm going to take you home," I tell her. "Louie and Sammie are here. They'll stay with Paz."

"I don't need you to take me anywhere." Evie shakes her head. "Help your friend. I can find my own way home."

"Like fuck, you can. You are not walking out of this room alone."

"You're not my father, Emmanuel. You cannot boss me around." She folds her arms over her chest defiantly.

"No, I'm your fiancé. And right now, I am telling you what to do because it's for your own goddamn good, Evie. You can hate me all you want. I don't care. I'm not letting you put yourself at risk." My hand runs through my hair. I'm fucking frustrated. "Seriously, why do you feel the need to fight me on everything?"

"Why do you feel the need to control every aspect of my life?" she fires back.

"Because I'm trying to fucking keep you alive!" I yell.

"You do know you're not God, right? I'm going to die one day, and there's not going to be a thing you can do to stop it."

"Watch me," I seethe. "You are not fucking dying."

"You need to sort your shit out, E. I don't know how many times I need to say it. *I'm not her.* I'm not going to hurt myself. I'm not going to be the cause of my own death. You need to figure that out. You can't use me to undo the past if that's what this is," she says. "I'm going home. Don't you dare follow me!"

Before Evie reaches the door, I grab hold of her arm and pull her back towards me. My hand cups her jaw, tilting her head upwards. I slam my lips onto hers. Pushing my tongue through her closed lips until she willingly opens for me. My tongue delves into her mouth, swirling around. Hard, fast.

When we pull apart, I don't let go of her. "You're right. You're not her. I'm not worried about you being her, Evie. Because I never loved her the way I love you. I've never loved anyone the way I love you. With you, it's different. It's more. It's fucking every-thing," I admit. "So forgive me for wanting to fucking hold on to that for as long as I possibly can."

There's a knock at the door. "E, we gotta get back up to Carlo's. Antonia's sick," Louie says.

"I'll meet you up there," I call back without letting go of Evie.

"Go. I'll wait here," she says.

I laugh. "Yeah, that's not fucking happening." I step back and then take hold of her hand and drag her out of the bedroom behind me. Paz is on the sofa. There's an older doctor looking him over. "You good?" I ask.

Paz gives me a thumbs-up. "Never been better, jefe."

"I'll be back. Stay here," I tell him. When I walk out into the hall, the two guys I had stationed outside the door are actually fucking there. "Where the fuck were you two?" I grunt in Spanish.

"We went for coffee," one of them says.

"*You went for fucking coffee.* You had orders. Do not let anyone in that fucking room, got me?" I growl.

"Yes, jefe." They nod at the same time.

If I didn't have Evie with me, they'd both already have holes in their heads. But I'm trying to shield her from the reality of who she's stuck with for life. Although I'm almost certain that she's not going to try to run. She would have done that already, or she would have talked to that fucking fed.

Evie doesn't say a word as we make our way back up to Carlo's. When we get there, I find Charlotte in the living room. I pull Evie back out to the foyer and hold her against me. I don't care who the fuck sees her with me anymore. She needs to get used to us being public.

"Don't leave without me," I tell her.

"Sure thing, Daddy." Evie rolls her eyes at me, and then looks down when she feels my cock twitch at her words. "Don't get any ideas. I'm not role-playing that with you."

I smirk. "We'll see." I kiss her on the forehead before I leave to go in search of Carlo. He's in his bedroom freaking out. I mean, I get it. His wife was poisoned when she ate that fucking soup.

Sammie clears his throat. "I'm going to take Jazzy to my place for the night. Lailani is there."

"She's already asleep. Someone needs to sit in her room. She's going to wake up. She has nightmares, and she can't wake up alone," Carlo says.

"I'll go," I tell him and walk out.

I step into Jazzy's bedroom and sit on the floor, resting my back against the wall. I've heard about her nightmares. Lailani says they happen daily.

Not even ten minutes later, the sweetest little girl I've ever met wakes up screaming. I jump to my feet. "Shh, princesa, it's okay. Tío E is right here," I tell her.

She looks over, jumps out of bed, and runs for me. I catch her as she wraps her tiny arms around my neck and sobs onto my shoulder. "I thought they found him," she cries.

My hand rubs at her back. "You thought who found who?"

"The bad men, the ones that were looking for daddy," she whispers.

"Princesa, I'm not going to let anyone hurt your daddy or you. I promise," I tell her. "Whoever these bad men are, I will find them and I will make sure they can never hurt anyone."

"I love you, Tío E. Don't tell Uncle Louie, but you are my favorite." She hugs me tighter.

I smile. I knew I was the favorite, and as much as I want to rub it in Louie's face, I'd never break Jazzy's trust like that. "I won't tell anyone. I love you, princesa. Now, tell me everything you know about these men? Did they hurt you?"

I already have a long-ass list of names I'm hunting down. What's a few more?

# Chapter Forty-One

Something feels wrong. I can't put my finger on it, but I have this feeling of dread. Emmanuel left me in Carlo's apartment with Charlotte and Lailani. He went out with Louie, Sammie, and Carlo to do God knows what. I didn't ask, because let's face it, ignorance is bliss sometimes.

I'm not naïve. I know the man I'm in love with.

God, that feels weird to admit, even if it is to

myself. Truth is, I've fallen for Emmanuel. At this point, if he said he wanted to skin me alive so he could wear me like a coat, I'd probably not bat an eyelash.

Okay, maybe I wouldn't go that far, but I feel real fear for him... Not myself. *Him.* I'd do anything to be able to make sure he's okay. I totally get why Charlotte jumped in front of that bullet for her husband now. Although I think if I ever did do that for Emmanuel, he'd likely kill me himself in a fit of rage at my carelessness for my own safety.

These feelings are giving me whiplash. As hot and cold as I've been, Emmanuel has been nothing but patient. Obsessively demanding but patient. He is so used to always being in full control of every situation. And yet, when it comes to me, he's prepared to give me a little of that control. Or... should I say that he gives me the appearance of control.

I'm not stupid. I'm fully aware that if I were to leave, if I ran, he'd find me and he'd drag my ass right back into his orbit. I don't think there is any way out of this thing with Emmanuel. Not that I want there to be an out. At least not right now. Ask me again when he does something else to piss me off. I'm sure it won't be long. He has a knack for it.

"I'm going to go check on Antonia." Charlotte

stands and walks out of the living room. Leaving me alone with Lailani.

The woman keeps looking at me very intently. As if she's trying to figure me out. I'm used to people staring at me. I've had to deal with it my entire life. But this is different. It's as if she knows something I don't.

"You know he's going to be okay. You shouldn't worry," she says.

"Who?" I ask her.

"Your boyfriend." She smirks. "I get the feeling that one is like a cockroach, impossible to kill."

I scrunch up my nose. "Emmanuel is not a cockroach. He's more like a... phoenix."

He's far too good looking to be called a cockroach.

The sound of the elevator pinging has me standing. They're back.

Lailani jumps up, shoving me aside. "Stay there," she hisses as a loud bang erupts through the apartment, followed by another and another. Lailani runs out of the living room with two guns in her hands.

*Where did those even come from?*

It's at that moment that I realize those bangs... are gunshots. There's three more and then silence. What the hell is happening?

I walk out and find Lailani digging through a man's jacket. Blood is pooling all over the white marble floors around him.

"Evie?" she calls out.

"Yeah," I whisper. I'm right behind her..

She spins around, pinning me with a disapproving look. "I told you to stay there."

The sound of footsteps coming from the hallway captures her attention. She stands in front of me, relaxing when she sees Antonia.

"Where's Jazzy?" Lailani asks.

Shit, Jazzy! She's just a kid. She should not be seeing or hearing any of this.

"Why?" Antonia stands straighter, a defiant look on her face.

"Because we need to get out of here, Antonia. We don't know how many more of them are out there," Lailani replies.

"Who are you?" Antonia asks.

"I work for Emmanuel," Lailani says, and I spin around to look at her. *She what now?*

"What?" Antonia looks just as confused as I feel. She quickly turns to me. "Are you okay?"

I nod my head. Physically I'm fine. But I'm far from okay.

"Did you know she works for Emmanuel?" Antonia asks me.

I shake my head, as I look from Lailani to the bodies on the ground. Before I can say anything, a phone starts ringing. Lailani's. She answers it on speaker.

"Where's Evie?" Emmanuel's voice booms out, sounding panicked.

"Here, safe," Lailani answers while looking at me.

I feel cold. My hands are shaky, and a light sweat is forming on my forehead. I don't know what to do. What am I supposed to do right now?

"Jazzy?" is Emmanuel's next question.

"She's okay. We all are," Antonia answers.

"Lai, get them to the compound. Now!" There's a sense of urgency to his voice. And then, ever so quietly, he adds, "Thank you," before cutting the call.

I'm stuck on the part where he called her Lai. Just how well do these two know each other?

*Now is not the time to be jealous, Evie. Damn it, the girl probably just saved your life.* But why the secrecy? Why would they pretend not to know each other?

"Go get Jazzy. And where is Charlotte?" Lailani looks to Antonia.

"She's in the panic room with Jazzy. I pushed her in there and shut the door," Antonia replies.

"Good. Let's get them." Lailani nods approvingly.

Once Antonia returns with Jazzy in her arms and Charlotte behind her, I breathe a sigh of relief. This is what I need, my best friend. I go to step towards Charlotte, but Lailani takes hold of my hand.

"Stay behind me," she tells everyone before turning her glare my way. "I need you to be right by me."

"Why?" I ask her.

"Because I like my head attached to my shoulders, and your boyfriend won't think twice about *un*attaching it if I don't get you out of here in one piece," she says.

"He's not my boyfriend," I whisper. I'm not sure who he is to me anymore. What else isn't he telling me?

"Yeah, well, he doesn't know that," Lailani mutters under her breath. She steps into the elevator and tugs me behind her again.

My phone vibrates in my pocket. I pull it out and read the message from Emmanuel.

E:

Do whatever Lailani and Paz tell you, Evie. Don't argue.

*Don't argue? Does he even know me at all?*

ME:

> Is it Lailani or Lai, Emmanuel? It's not a good look to have hidden girlfriends, even if they are in plain sight.

E:

> She's a contractor. Not a girlfriend. Now is not the time for this conversation.

The moment we step into the garage, five men start walking in our direction. They quickly surround me. I spot Paz.

"Miss, boss wants you to come with us," he says.

He looks slightly better than he did a few hours ago. He's standing upright and doesn't look like he's in pain. There's a little bit of comfort in seeing him. I know it's stupid, but Emmanuel trusts him. Which means I should too, right?

"I bet he does." I roll my eyes and pocket my phone. "I'm staying with them."

"You're all coming with us," Paz says.

I remind myself that Emmanuel trusts these men, and no matter what happens, I know Emmanuel wants me to be safe. He wants me alive. He also trusts Lailani.

I'm on autopilot as I climb into the back of an SUV. Paz eyes me with concern but doesn't say anything. It's such a stupid thing to focus on, but right now, this jealousy is giving me the distraction I need to avoid thinking about the bodies we just stepped over.

Thirty minutes later, we are pulling through the large iron gates of Emmanuel's estate. Guards line each side—although, this time, they don't seem to have rifles. Until I look closer and see that they do. They're just hiding them behind their backs.

As soon as I'm out of the car, I'm ushered into the house, once again surrounded by men in black suits.

"Miss Evie, welcome back. I have a bottle of your favorite wine on the table in the conservatory along with a tray of your preferred snacks," Maria greets us.

I smile at the woman. I like her. She's always so nice to me when I'm here.

"Thank you, Maria," I say before turning to Charlotte. I see all the questions on her face. *"Don't ask,"* I hiss at my friend. I am not in the headspace for an inquisition right now.

"Oh, you can bet your sweet ass I'm asking," Charlotte replies.

"Now, you must be Miss Jazzy. I've heard all about you, and your Tío E requested that a plate of banana pancakes be waiting for you upon your arrival. I have those on the table too," Maria says, bending down to Jazzy's height.

"Pancakes, yes! That's a good surprise." Jazzy smiles while bouncing with excitement.

"Call if you or your friends need anything else, Miss Evie." Maria looks to me before she disappears.

"Miss Evie?" Charlotte whispers.

"Not now. Come on, I don't know about you girls, but I need some wine." *I really, really need some wine.*

"I'll, ah, catch up with you. I have something I need to do," Lailani says.

I know I'm being a bitch, but as I watch her turn and walk her way through Emmanuel's house, I'm hit with a deeper sense of jealousy. Why the hell am I jealous?

"It's always the quiet ones," Charlotte mutters under her breath.

"Did you know?" Antonia asks Charlotte.

"Not the slightest clue," she replies, looking at me. I shake my head. I had no idea either.

I find a bottle of white wine in an ice bucket on the table. Four glasses around it. There's also a charcuterie board filled with cheeses and meats. I pick up the bottle of wine.

"We're going to need more than one," I grumble to myself.

"I'm good with water. My stomach still isn't a hundred percent," Antonia says, as she gets Jazzy settled in front of a plate of pancakes.

"I'm good with wine," Charlotte says, holding out an empty glass to me.

Once we're topped off, I sit down.

Charlotte sits right next to me. She reaches over and holds my hand. "You doing okay?" she whispers.

"No. But I will be," I whisper back.

My friend gives me a concerning look. "This really is good wine," she says. "Just how does Emmanuel's housekeeper know you love it?"

"Is that the front door?" I ask, knowing we are nowhere near the front door. I swallow the cold, sugary liquid in my glass. "I'm going to the restroom."

I'm lying. I need space. I know Charlotte means well, but right now, I need time to think, time to process what the fuck just happened.

As I'm walking back towards the front of the house, Carlo comes running in. I pass Maria, who gives me a polite smile. As soon as my feet touch the foyer, I'm taken back to that day when Emmanuel's mother was here. Emmanuel is in the doorway. He's talking to a few of his men in Spanish. But his eyes are on me.

Without a word, I walk past him and head upstairs. There's one room in this house that I feel peace. His bedroom. We spent most of our time there during my brief stay. That's where I want to be right now.

# Chapter Forty-Two

Ⅰ'm ready to burn this fucking city to the ground. Some asshole with a hard-on for my friends put Evie in the line of fire. That will not go unpunished. Louie wants me to let Carlo get his revenge on Antonia's father. I don't disagree. Doesn't mean I have to like the idea.

I'm in the doorway of my foyer with my men. I know Joey Marciano doesn't have the resources to breach the boundaries here, but I don't ever make the mistake of underestimating anyone. Which is why I've instructed my men to increase security, making sure they know Evie is their only priority when she's in this house. I don't give a fuck if anyone else makes it out alive, as long as she does. Okay, Evie *and* Jazzy —that little girl isn't going anywhere either.

I never would have thought that one of my best friends having an instant family would mean I would too. When I heard Jazzy was dropped off to Carlo without him having any prior knowledge of her, I didn't think too much of it. Until I met her and knew I would do anything for my niece. She's Carlo's, which makes her mine.

Once my men disperse, I head into my office and pick up my laptop. I open it and do a quick Google search for the best bridal stores in Milan. The first thought that popped into my head when Lailani told me they were hit was that I didn't marry Evie yet. I need to marry that woman. I was a fucking idiot to tell her we should wait.

I know Evie, though, and a wedding dress is more than just an outfit to her. It's why I want her to have the fucking dress of her dreams. Finding a few listings, I save the tabs and head upstairs with the laptop.

Evie is sitting on the edge of the bed when I walk in. We stare at each other, neither saying a single word. I close the door behind me and walk over, stopping a few steps away from her.

"Let me have it," I tell her.

"Have what?" she asks, clearly confused.

"Yell at me, tell me how much you despise me and this life. Whatever it is you want to say, do it. Because I have something to say also, but you're going first," I clarify.

"I'm not going to yell at you," Evie says. Then she stands. "Actually, I am. Are you fucking her?"

My eyebrows jump up in surprise. That is not what I was expecting.

"Fucking who?" I ask. "Actually, don't bother telling me. Either way, the answer is no. I'm not fucking anyone who isn't you, Evie. You should know that."

"Lailani? Or Lai?" she says sarcastically. "Why hide that you know her if you're not fucking her?"

"Because she's a contractor, Evie. A hired gun. A hitwoman. Whatever the fuck you want to call it. I have a job. She takes it on. That's all there is to it." I shrug. "I had her here keeping an eye on Louie, Sammie, and Carlo. To protect them from a threat they had no fucking idea was lurking in their backyard."

"Why not just tell them? Why keep her a secret?" Evie asks.

"Because that's not how people stay safe. I'm not sorry I brought her here. Because if it weren't for her, you'd be on the fucking floor of Carlo's penthouse with a goddamn bullet between your eyes. Is that what you would prefer?" Now I'm the one yelling. I take a deep breath. I need to calm down. I do not want to yell at this woman, but fuck, she frustrates the shit out of me.

"What I'd prefer is not being in a situation where I'm at risk of being shot at in the first place."

"I... That's never going to be our reality, Evie. I can put in as much security and safety protocols that money can buy into place around you. I can do everything I know to keep you safe. But I can't guarantee that you'll never be put at risk again. I'm not going to lie to you and give you false hope that our lives are going to play out in some little cottage with a white picket fence," I tell her.

"No, they're going to be in compounds surrounded by men in black suits who carry rifles everywhere," she says.

"I'm sorry." I'm at a loss for words. "I know that you deserve better than this. I want to give you that, but I can't."

Evie frowns at me. "Are you dumping me? Because you don't get to do that. You don't get to make me fall in fucking love with you, Emmanuel Lopez, and then break up with me."

I laugh, because the mere thought of me dumping her is absurd. "No, Evie, I'm not dumping you. I came in here to give you this." I wave the laptop in the air.

"Why?"

"I've saved some stores on the Google page. I want you to go through them and pick out a white dress." I hand Evie the computer.

"A dress for what?" she asks.

"Open the laptop, Evie. Have a look." I sit on the edge of the bed.

Evie comes and sits next to me, opening the laptop and then clicking on the first tab in the Google browser. "E... what? These are wedding dresses," she says. "In Milan."

"I know. We're going to Milan, and we're getting married," I tell her.

"What? Seriously? When?"

"Tomorrow," I say. "Pick a dress. You are going to be my wife."

"Are you sure?" Evie looks me in the eye. She can't be fucking serious right now.

"Am I sure? Evie, I don't know what else I have to do to get you to trust me. I don't know what I can say to reassure you that you are it for me."

"I know," she whispers.

"You don't know. If you did, you wouldn't have just asked me if I was fucking another woman," I tell her.

"Deep down, I knew you weren't. But I got jealous, okay? You have a damn pet name for her, E. And she knows her way around your house. I don't like that another woman is so comfortable in your space. It was jealousy, not mistrust. If I really thought you were fucking someone else, I wouldn't be here."

"You have no reason to be jealous, Evie." I cup her cheek with my hand, my thumb stroking up and down the smooth skin. "You are the only person I see in a room. You are the only one I want."

"Be honest. When you look at me, is it really me that you see? Or is it her?" Evie asks.

"It's you," I reply quickly. "I haven't compared you to her since that first night we met, Evie. I swear it's you."

"See? I'm even jealous of a ghost. Something is wrong with me." She shakes her head.

"Nothing is wrong with you," I tell her. "I was jealous of a fucking towel, Evie, because that fabric was touching your body when I couldn't."

"Well, yeah, but we already know you're insane. One of us has to have all of our screws tight, E. We can't both be nutty."

"You are not nutty or insane or anything else of the sort. You might have very questionable taste in men, but I'm not here to point that out." I laugh.

"Can we... Can you lie down with me." Evie moves up the bed and slips under the blankets.

"Are you tired?" I ask her.

"Maybe. It's been a while since I've slept and today was... a lot."

"I'm not staying if you're sleeping, Evie. I'm not having you wake up and look at me like I'm a monster again."

"I won't," she says.

"You will, and you won't be able to help the questions that run through your head. I get that, but I can't see it," I admit.

"Can you just stay until I fall asleep then?"

"That I can do." I lie on the bed, and Evie curls up into my arms. My lips press onto the top of her head.

"E? I don't like fighting with you," Evie says.

"I fucking hate it when you do too." I chuckle. "I love you. I don't care what you throw at me, Evie. I'm not going anywhere."

"Can you lock the door when you leave so no one can get in?"

"I will make sure no one comes in here," I tell her. "Promise."

"Get Alejandro here," I tell Paz. We've been sitting in my office for the past three hours, searching through every database we could get our hands on. I haven't found him yet. But Enrique cannot outrun me. I will find him and show the fucking world what happens to rat bastards.

"Anyone else?" Paz asks.

"No." I've been over every question the agents asked Paz, the things they claimed to know, and he was right. There is no possible way they knew it unless they have Enrique. "That agent, he wants Evie to turn."

"You worried she will?" Paz lifts a curious brow.

"No." I shut that idea down real fucking quick. "But he doesn't know that."

"What are you suggesting?"

"He's going to try to contact her again. He just has to think she's alone," I say.

"You're going to use your wife as bait?" Paz attempts to clarify.

"No. She's also not my wife. Yet," I remind him.

"But she will be. Might as well get used to the term now." He shrugs. "So what's your plan?"

"Evie's going to go back and start writing up ideas for that retail space. She'll take Charlotte with her, and when I have Louie drag Charlotte away, the dirty fucking cop will show his face again."

"And let me guess... you'll be there?" Paz says. "Bad idea, jefe. It's you he wants to pin."

I laugh. "If he had anything concrete, I'd already be in cuffs." We can do this and have a couple of guys tail him when he leaves.

"Let me dig through the night. If I can't come up with the asshole's home address, we go with your plan," Paz says.

I raise a brow at him.

"I'm not using our queen if we don't have to," he adds.

I smile. He likes Evie. Good. It means he'll do whatever it takes to protect her. "Fine, you find him before morning, and we follow him from there. If not, we draw him out," I tell Paz. "I need to go find Lailani."

"Good luck." Paz sighs. "By the way, I see our little queen isn't a fan either. She has great instincts. We should get rid of Lailani."

"We're not getting rid of Lailani. And Evie likes her just fine," I lie.

I'm in the garage when Lailani walks in. I heard her arguing with Sammie and knew she'd be looking for a quick escape.

"You need to let Carlo deal with him." I step out of the shadows. Probably not the smartest thing to do considering she's fucking lethal with that gun of hers.

"Jeez, E, why are you hiding in the shadows? I could have shot you," she points out.

"You're far too smart to try to shoot me, Lai." I chuckle. She's quick with her trigger finger, but she's not reckless.

"I need to borrow a car."

"Did your yelling match with Sammie blow out an eardrum? I said you can't touch this." I shove my hands into my pockets, because I don't want to accidentally strangle the woman, and glare at her.

"They could have gotten Jazzy," she says.

"I know. Which is exactly why her father needs this."

She knows I'm right. This is Carlo's fight. He needs this kill.

"Okay, but I still need a car," she grunts.

"Take the Merc." I nod towards a black G-Wagon.

"Thank you," she says. "I'm assuming now that my cover is blown, the job is finished?"

"The job is finished, but that doesn't mean you

need to leave town," I tell her. As much as she likes to remind me we're not friends, we both know that we are.

"I don't really have a reason to stay." Lailani looks away from me.

"Don't you?" I question.

"He hates me. He doesn't understand me. People never do." She shrugs as if she doesn't care. She does. "It's okay. I knew this would happen."

"For what it's worth, I think you should give him a chance to understand you," I tell her.

"I... My dad asked me to visit. I need to deal with that and Sammie needs time."

"Time for what?"

"Time to miss me, time to realize what a chauvinistic ass he's being." Lailani rolls her eyes.

"Okay, call me if you need anything," I tell her.

"Why would I do that?"

"Because that's what friends do, Lailani," I groan.

"Yeah, we're still not friends. But thanks for the car. I'll return it in one piece." She smiles as she climbs into the Merc.

"If you don't, you're paying for it. I'm not running a charity here," I tell her, then watch as she pulls out of the estate. She'll be back. No way Sammie is letting her go for long. There are also other jobs she'll want from me. She's the best. I'm not letting her off my payroll anytime soon.

I send her a message.

ME:

Be safe, Lai, and thank you for what you did for Evie.

KILLER WOMAN:

Your wife hates me.

ME:

She doesn't know you.

KILLER WOMAN:

Don't die, E. I might need a job again one day.

I laugh, pocket my phone, and head upstairs. I told Evie I wouldn't stay in the room with her when she slept. But I can't stay away either. I sit in the chair in the corner and watch as her lips part ever so slightly, the rise and fall of her chest giving me a sense of peace. Knowing her heart is beating is what keeps mine beating too.

# Chapter Forty-Three

When I wake up, I'm in a pitch-black room, and I'm alone. My first thought is where is Emmanuel? And then my second is... this feels different. I woke up and I didn't automatically think about what could have happened to me when I was asleep. No, my first thought is where the hell is my boyfriend? Fiancé...

Shit, that is a little odd to say. Emmanuel Lopez is my fiancé. I'm going to marry that man.

A huge smile crosses my face. I'm really going to marry him. I know I've had my doubts about Emmanuel, about us. But something clicked. I realized that I don't want to be without him.

Does that mean I have to marry him? No, but I want to.

Pushing the covers aside, I reach over and switch on the light. I don't know why I'm disappointed he's not here. He specifically said he wouldn't be. He told me no one would get into this room, and I know when Emmanuel says something like that, he will do everything in his power to make it happen.

I open the bedroom door and look up and down the hall. It's empty. Weird. He usually has men everywhere, even on this level of the house. The place has that eerie quiet to it. I don't know where he is, but he is here. I hope.

As I make my way downstairs, that quiet disappears. Replaced by footsteps, people talking. I listen. But whoever's speaking, they're doing it in Spanish, and it's not Emmanuel's voice.

His office. It's the most logical place for him to be. I walk towards that room, passing four guards who smile politely at me before turning their attention away. I know this is something I have to get used to. I'm just not sure I ever will.

When I reach the office, the two guards standing

at the door give me a nod. One of them knocks on the door twice.

"Is he in there?" I ask.

"Yes, ma'am. You can go in." The one who knocked opens the door.

"You don't have to call me *ma'am*. Evie works just fine. Thank you." I smile as I pass him to enter the office, but he doesn't say anything. He just closes the door behind me.

"Mi alma, you're awake." Emmanuel stands from his desk and walks around. Why does it feel like he's walking in slow motion?

Deciding he's not moving fast enough, I meet him halfway and throw my arms around him. "I woke up and my first thought was where were you?" I admit, hugging him tight against me.

Emmanuel's arms wrap around my waist. He holds me flush against his chest and his warmth envelops me. This is what I woke up wanting. This man wrapped around me.

"I wanted you to be there," I whisper.

Emmanuel pulls his head back, staring down at my face. "We will discuss this later," he says before briefly pressing his lips to mine. Way too briefly. When he pulls away, he lets go of me. "Evie, you know Paz. This is Alejandro and Rafael," he says, nodding to the three men I didn't even notice.

My face heats up. "Um... I'm sorry. I didn't know you were busy. I can... I'll be..." I don't know where I'll be.

"Right fucking here," Emmanuel grunts, leading me over to the sofa. "They were just leaving."

"Nice to meet you, ma'am," Alejandro says. The greeting is repeated by Rafael as they both leave the room. Paz comes over and sits across from me. His face still looks like crap.

"Are you okay?" I ask him. "I mean, that kinda looks like it hurts."

"I've had worse." He chuckles. "You okay?"

"What day is it?" I rub at the side of my head, trying to ease the sleep fog.

"Thursday," he says.

I jump up. "What? Why didn't you wake me? We were supposed to get married yesterday. You didn't even wake me. I missed my own wedding because I was sleeping." I look to Emmanuel.

"I'm not waking you up when you need to sleep, Evie. And we can get married any day. The date isn't important," he tells me. "I do have some papers for you to sign, though." He walks over to his desk.

I follow him. "Papers for what?"

"Louie had the retail lease delivered, and there're some... financial documents we need to sign before we can tie the knot," E explains.

"Like a prenup? E, if you want me to sign a prenup, just say so. I don't want your money." I laugh, because I really don't.

"It's not a prenup, Evie. The documents are to add your name to all of my businesses, homes, and other assets," he says. "It's security for you. To make sure you will always have whatever you need."

"Again, I don't want your assets," I tell him, then smile as my eyes drift lower. "Well, there is one asset you have that I want, but that's not a financial one."

"And that's my cue to leave." Paz coughs from behind me before I hear the door open and close.

"I would rather sign a prenup, E. I would rather you and the world know that I'm not marrying you for your money. I'm marrying you because I can't think of a single reason not to anymore, and because I love you."

"Say it again," he grunts.

"I'm marrying you because I want to."

"Not that part." He squints his eyes at me.

"I love you," I repeat without breaking eye contact.

"I fucking love you more than I ever thought possible. What I have is yours. That's how marriages work. We combine assets. That's how *our* marriage will work," he says.

"I don't have assets." I laugh. "I have a house I

still owe a mortgage on and the rubble of a dress shop."

"You don't have a mortgage on your house. I paid it off. And you have a new store lease right here." He holds up the manilla folder and hands it to me, followed by a pen. "Sign it and I'll send the paperwork back over to Louie.

I walk around E's desk and plop myself down in his chair. Emmanuel gives me a weird look as I open the folder and click the pen. "What?" I ask him.

"People don't sit in my chair, Evie," he says.

"Well, first, I'm not people. I'm your fiancée. And second, I like this chair." I grin.

Emmanuel laughs, like full-belly laughs, and the sound vibrates through me. I like it. He's always so serious. I often worry he's going to die of a heart attack at a really young age, just from stress.

I start skimming the papers.

"I've already read through them all. You can sign," E says.

"I like to read what I'm signing," I tell him. "Also, I don't even know if I can afford this lease."

Emmanuel comes over, stands behind me, turns to the next page, and points to a number. "That's the monthly rent. I've read every single page. I would not let you sign anything that didn't have your best interests in it."

"How can it be that cheap? That's less than my rent back home."

"Friends rate. Don't question Louie's shitty business decisions, mi alma. Just... take advantage of them," Emmanuel says.

I shake my head. "I am not taking advantage of our friends."

"He's hardly doing it tough." Emmanuel chuckles.

He's right. I pick up the pen, turn to the last page, and scribble my signature across the line.

"Congratulations, you have yourself a new store."

"Oh my gosh. I can't believe this is actually happening!" I squeal. "Wait... I'm going to have to move to Vegas. I can't live in Georgia and have a store in Vegas. What was I thinking?"

"Then we move to Vegas."

"You live in Mexico."

"We live wherever the fuck we want to live, Evie. That's the benefit of being the boss." Emmanuel winks at me. "Speaking of Mexico, we need to make a quick detour before Milan."

"Okay, I've never been. What do I need to pack? What do I need to wear?" I ask as the options fire through my head.

"Whatever you want to wear."

"Helpful," I groan.

"Here. Sign these." Emmanuel shoves another stack of paperwork in front of me. "It's for the joining of our assets."

"Okay. But you do know I'm not in this for the money, right?" I look over my shoulder at him.

Emmanuel leans down and presses his lips to mine. "I'm well aware."

There're ten different spots that need my signature. I sign them all, without reading them. I trust Emmanuel. The notion is ridiculous. I'm fully aware of that, and the very real chance that this decision may just come back and bite me in the ass. But I'm deciding to take a leap of faith.

Emmanuel picks up the folders and puts them on the other side of the desk. "Now, let's go eat. You haven't eaten in days."

"I was asleep."

"I know. But now you're not. What do you feel like having?" he asks.

"I can cook for us," I offer.

"Maria will cook whatever you want, Evie."

I frown. "You don't trust me to cook for you?"

"I don't want you to have to cook for me. There's a difference," he says.

"But what if I want to?" I counter.

"Then the kitchen is all yours."

"Good. Because I actually don't hate cooking." I smile. I don't do it often, but I do like it.

"Can you cook Mexican food?"

"Ah..." *Shit, I can't.*

"I'm kidding. Relax." Emmanuel taps the tip of my nose with his finger. "Make whatever you want."

"I can learn how to cook Mexican food. I'll take lessons," I tell him.

"You don't need to do that."

"I want to," I insist.

Emmanuel stands in the kitchen watching me make pasta. It's simple, but it is delicious. Well, at least, I hope he thinks it is.

"I know it's not fancy like you're used to," I say, handing him a bowl full of Carbonaro. "But I figured you must like Italian food too if you want to get married in Milan so bad."

"It smells fucking great," he says as we settle into the small dining table. "I've never had anyone cook for me before."

"You have Maria cook for you all the time," I remind him.

"That's different. She's paid to do it. I mean, I've

never had anyone cook for me just because they wanted to," he clarifies.

I don't know what to say to that. "You're welcome. So, why Milan?"

"There's a church I saw once, and it's the perfect place for you," he says. "Fit for a queen."

"I'm not a queen, E."

"Yes, you are," he argues.

Then I remember what I told Rachel. I promised I wouldn't run off and get married without her. Shit. "Um, can we invite friends to Milan?"

"We can take whomever you want." Emmanual shrugs.

"Just Rachel and Charlotte." I don't have any family to invite. Those two girls are my everything.

"I will make sure that they're there for you."

"I'll call Rachel... when we know proper dates. She might not be able to make it with her work schedule."

"Evie, if you want to go back to Georgia and get married there, so your friend can attend, then we can," Emmanuel says.

"It's just... after Charlotte got married in Vegas without her, I promised Rach I wouldn't just run off," I explain.

"So we nix Milan and go for Georgia." E shrugs again.

"Let me talk to her first," I tell him. She might be able to swing it.

"Okay," he says around a mouthful of pasta. "This is fucking delicious, by the way."

"Thank you." I smile.

Who would have thought I'd love cooking for a man so much? Certainly not me.

# Chapter Forty-Four

I've been busy before. There's always something or someone to deal with in my line of work. At the moment, though, it's fucking insane. Not only am I crossing names off the list I obtained from Evie's mother, I'm also looking for the rat bastard Enrique and that fucking agent who beat the shit out of Paz and approached Evie.

Paz was able to find the agent's home address but

the asshole hasn't shown his face there yet. We've got men stationed on his street waiting for him. He has a wife and a ten-year-old son—pawns I would usually use to my advantage—but I promised Evie I would avoid the killing of innocent people where I could.

And then there is the whole getting married thing. Which, believe me, I fucking want to marry that woman. I just can't fly out to Milan or Georgia or wherever the hell we're getting married right now. I need to deal with these threats before we can do that.

The plan is to use Evie to draw out this agent. I know assholes like him. He's watching her, and as soon as he thinks she's alone, he's going to try to approach her again. When he does, I'll fucking be there. First, I have a meeting that Paz and Alejandro set up. One that can't be missed.

I just left Evie at Louie's. She's talking to Charlotte and Rachel about the wedding. Really, I just wanted her somewhere with someone I could trust to look out for her. Not that I haven't left twenty guys around the Royal. If she leaves that penthouse, she will be surrounded. Everyone protecting her like the queen she is.

As soon as I walk into the conference room, the faces of the six men sitting at the round table pale. I smirk. I like having that effect on people. One of the men goes to stand. I hold out a hand and then someone else is pushing him back down in the chair.

"Please, don't stand on my account," I say.

"Who are you?" another asks with a bravado he really shouldn't have.

"Watch your fucking tongue. I'm the one asking questions here. Not you." I point to him.

"Why would I answer anything you have to say?" he sneers at me.

My fist connects with his jaw. The asshole goes flying backwards in the chair and then he's on the floor. "Get him up," I tell my men, and two soldiers drag the guy to his feet.

"What the fuck?" the asshole cries out.

I take my phone out of my pocket and hold it up to him. "You know this girl?" I ask.

The asshole's eyes widen.

"Thought so." I nod my head to the table. "You all fucking touched the wrong girl. Now, I'm here to collect the things you touched her with."

Paz walks up behind us and passes me an axe. Just the tool I need for this job. "You're last." I point to the asshole with the sore jaw.

It's worst being last, because you get to watch everyone else's punishment, knowing your time is coming and there's not a single thing you can do about it.

I have two guys holding down each of the others, their arms spread out in front of them. I had a marble table put in this room for this purpose. I don't need the axe going through fucking wood or glass.

Walking around the table, I assess my targets. "Duck, duck... goose." I tap the head of the third man and stop behind him. "Guess you get to be first."

"No! I didn't do anything!" He shakes his head while lies spill from his lips.

I lift the axe and bring it down on his right wrist, his hand detaching in one clean cut. The asshole screams, his head swirls, and I hurry to bring the axe down on his left arm.

"You don't get to pass out. You're going to feel every single fucking bit of pain," I hiss into his ear. "Now, let's continue the game, shall we?" I step up behind the next guy. "Duck, duck, duck, goose."

The fourth fucker jumps or at least attempts to. They're all trying to get out of their seats at this point. But it's useless. Their old, scrawny asses are no match for the soldiers I've got holding them down. The axe bites into his left hand and then his right.

I continue this with all five of my targets before stopping at the sixth guy. "You know what? I think

I'll start by taking something else you touched her with."

At my suggestion, my men lay him flat on the table that's now covered in blood. The others passed out shortly after their arms were removed. Only one remains cognizant of what's to come for him.

"Blowtorch," I tell Paz, who just laughs and shakes his head at me.

I fire up the torch and hold it over the asshole's crotch. It doesn't take long for the fabric of his pants to incinerate, and then the smell of burning flesh fills the air as his dick and balls melt away. His screams are music to my ears.

Once I'm satisfied his dick is nothing more than mutated flesh, I hand the torch back to Paz. "Time to go, boys."

At my command, my men all straighten and follow me out. Once we're in the parking lot, I hit the button on the little controller in my hand and the building is engulfed by flames.

"That was some show," Paz comments as we slide into the car.

"Good. Let the word spread. I want everyone to know what happens to the fuckers who touch her," I grunt.

"I'm sure it will be widespread through the cities before the jet hits the ground," he says.

"Make sure everything is set up there. I'm bringing her home tomorrow morning. I want her to feel safe," I tell him.

Our compound in Mexico isn't like the one here. It's on a much larger scale, with a lot more men. It's also where our factories are. It's where most of our business is done. Once the drugs cross the border and I have my cash, I don't have anything to do with the product.

By the time I make it back to Louie's penthouse, news of the explosion is on every media outlet. "Have a party?" he asks, meeting me in the foyer.

"Something like that," I tell him.

"You know, most people invite friends to their parties."

I tilt my head. "And if I had any, I'd invite them," I deadpan.

"Ouch." He rubs his heart. "You know, one of these days, I'm going to actually believe you hate me."

"Where is she?" I ask, looking around for Evie.

"They went up to the pool," he says.

"Alone?" I'm already hitting the button for the elevator.

"We both know my wife is never without security," he says. "There are five of my men up there."

His reassurance does nothing to relieve my

stress. It's not until I step out onto the rooftop deck and lay eyes on her myself that I relax. I clock five of my men within feet of her and nod at them. They move back slightly but stay close enough, so that if they need to, they can reach her.

"Having fun?" I pick up a towel and lay it over Evie's body. She's sprawled out on a sun lounger in a fucking bikini. There are way too many men up here.

She goes to brush the towel aside.

"Don't you dare take that off," I warn in a low growl.

"Oh yeah? What are you going to do about it?" Evie raises a defiant brow at me as she plucks the towel off her back and throws it my way. And then, she's on her feet. Her hands on her hips as she glares at me. "You are not my father, Emmanuel."

"I'm your husband. That trumps father." I drape the towel around her shoulders and pull her against me, holding her tight. "There are men all over this rooftop and they're all looking at your pretty little ass that's on full display for them. You can yell at me all you want. Behind closed doors, Evie. Not in front of the men who work for me. Never in front of people."

She stills in my arms and looks up at me. "You're serious."

"They can't get ideas in their heads that I've gone soft. It's how we stay in power."

"It's how *you* stay in power," she corrects.

"*We.* You are my queen. You are my equal, Evie," I tell her.

"Just not in front of anyone, right?"

"Just once, I would love it if you could just say: *Yes, E. Whatever you want, E,*" I grumble.

"No you wouldn't." She shakes her head and laughs.

She's right. I would hate if she turned into that person. But, fuck, it's tiring fighting with her about every single topic.

"We have the rest of our lives to figure out shit. Let's not fight about it now," I suggest.

"That sounds like a solid plan, because I'm going swimming and you're coming."

"I'm not dressed for the pool," I state the obvious.

"Drop the suit, E. I'll meet you in there." Evie winks and then wiggles out of my hold—and the fucking towel. I watch as she jumps right into the water.

Fuck me. Guess I'm going swimming. I remove my jacket and nod to one of my men, handing him my pistol and knife. I remove my shirt next. Evie's head pops out of the water, and she watches me with a devious smirk on her face.

As soon as I'm down to my black briefs, I jump into the pool. My arms circle her waist and I pull her body up against mine. My lips find hers and I fucking devour her.

"I love you," I whisper against her lips.

Evie's legs wrap around my torso, and her arms tighten around my neck. "Good, because I like being loved by you."

# Chapter Forty-Five

I cannot believe this is mine. Charlotte hands me the key to the retail spot I just signed a lease for. I unlock the door and we walk in. "This is really happening," I tell her.

"It's happening." She smiles. "I'm so happy you're moving here. I'm not going to be alone anymore."

"You are never alone." I roll my eyes at her. "You have a husband and a whole new family, Charlotte."

"*We* have a new family," she corrects me. "You're marrying into this crazy-ass family too."

"I am." I smile. "It's insane, right? I mean, I thought you were totally looney when you married Louie, but I get it now. I think maybe when you find your person, you really do just know."

"Yeah." Charlotte gets that dreamy *Louie* look on her face. "I still pinch myself when I look at him and think... that is my husband."

I've known for longer than I've been willing to admit that I love Emmanuel. I never believed he would be able to love me back, though. Not until this last week really. He's shown his obsession, his need to possess me. But now, I understand that's his way of showing love. Especially because he doesn't give that side of him to anyone else. When we're alone, he's not as guarded. When he's around his men, or his friends, he has walls up so high I doubt anyone could climb them. And then he'll look at me and those hard eyes soften ever so slightly.

"So, I'm thinking pink," I say, changing the subject back to the store.

"Baby pink?" Charlotte suggests. "Oh, Evie, we're going to have babies together, and our kids will be best friends, and we can have a boy and a girl each. Imagine if they fall in love and then we get to share grandbabies." She sighs wistfully.

"Okay, that's a lot to take in, Charlotte. And I'm not sure I want kids," I admit.

"Yeah, you do," she tells me.

"We'll see." I shrug. "What do you think about green?"

"I think pink and green. And gold!" she says. "I also think, before we really get into this planning, we need more coffee."

"I'll go get it this time. You stay here. Start looking through these. We need so much stock." I hand her catalogues from my suppliers.

"Okay, but don't judge the ones I pick if they're not what you're looking for. I'm not the fashionista here," she warns.

"It will be fine," I tell her. "Be right back."

Starbucks is just around the corner. Another perk of this store's location. I do love my coffee. After placing my order, I stand to the side and wait. Those little hairs on the back of my neck lift. I look around. Someone is watching me, but I can't see anyone.

It's probably Emmanuel's men hiding in the shadows. I'm pretty sure. He always has me followed, even when I don't know they're there.

"Evie!" the barista calls out my name.

"Thank you." I take both cups and turn to make my way back to the store. Stopping when someone steps right up in front of me, blocking my path.

"Miss Carter, nice to see you again," Agent Shawn Something says.

I look up at him. "I'm sorry? Have we met?" I feign disinterest.

"Cute. We need to talk. I need to show you this," he says.

"I don't need to see anything you have to show me. Excuse me." As I try to step around him, he steps to the side, blocking my exit again.

"Do you have any idea why your boyfriend is going around killing old pageant judges? Cutting their hands off?" he asks. "Just this morning, six more judges were killed, brutally, before the building blew up. Know anything about that?"

"I have no idea what you're talking about," I tell him.

"You see, I think you're lying. Considering you're an ex-beauty queen, who happened to be judged by every single man who's now being slaughtered. Hell of a coincidence, don't you think?" he asks.

"There are millions of girls around this country alone who compete in the pageants. Is every single one of those girls suspects?" I ask him.

"Not every one of those girls is fucking a known cartel leader," the agent retorts while staring down at my cleavage. Gross.

I smile. "I'll let you in on a little secret." I'm really tired of men thinking they can intimidate me. "I don't fuck Emmanuel. I let him fuck *me*—something you'll never get to do."

The agent smiles back at me. "I wouldn't be so sure of that. When I lock your boyfriend away, you will be back to being a no one, having no one. You'll need a shoulder to cry on." His hand reaches out to touch my face.

On instinct, I push one of the cups into his open palm. The lid comes off and hot coffee pours all over him. Okay, maybe I helped the coffee spill out a little.

"I don't let scum like you touch me," I tell him.

"Evie, you okay?" Emmanuel's voice comes from right beside me.

*When the hell did he get here? Where the hell did he come from?* Then panic sets in. He should not be here. This cop wants him.

"Take me home," I tell Emmanuel.

The agent drops the cup on the floor, his expression frozen like he's seen a ghost, but then that shock turns into a nasty glare. "Don't worry, Mr. Lopez. I'll take real good care of her once I lock you away," he sneers.

Emmanuel's jaw ticks. I take hold of his hand

and start to walk away. Emmanuel doesn't budge, though.

"E?"

At the sound of my voice, he seems to snap out of his stare-off with the agent and then he lets me drag him out of the coffee shop.

My hands are shaking. I do not like confrontation. I hate it. I will stand up to anyone who is threatening someone I love, though. And that asshole was threatening Emmanuel. I don't care what they think he's done.

Okay, I'm pretty sure he did cut the hands off those judges, but I'm not asking him. And I don't care. They deserved it. They were not innocent men. Emmanuel has stuck to his word by not putting innocent family members in the line of fire. For that, I'm thankful.

He pauses me in the middle of the mall. "Evie, stop."

Turning to him, I blink away the tears. I don't want to cry, but I'm so frustrated and emotional right now. I feel helpless. I want to be able to make sure no one can touch Emmanuel. I just have no idea how to do that.

"I'm going to fucking kill him," Emmanuel growls. His finger wipes under my eye. "I'm sorry."

I shake my head. "You can't kill him, E. He's a cop."

"I will kill anyone who brings tears to your eyes, Evie. I don't care if they're the fucking Pope."

"Okay, pretty sure the Pope is never going to make me cry. But it's not him. It's me." I shrug. "I'm just… frustrated. I feel helpless, E. You are out there doing all kinds of unspeakable things to make me feel safe, and what am I doing? Getting coffee and planning a new store with my friend. I want to be able to make the world a safe place for you too, and I can't."

Emmanuel gives me a puzzled look. "Evie, you do more than make the world a safe place. You make it a better place. You give me peace," he says. "Besides, I like doing unspeakable things to anyone who threatens to hurt you, or has in the past. It's become my new favorite hobby."

"Is the list done?" I ask.

"It's done." He nods.

"Thank you. Now, can you take me home?"

"Yes."

"Wait… I need to get Charlotte. I left her at the store."

Emmanuel's hand grips mine firmly as we walk back towards the store. This is the first time he's seeing it. "This is a nice spot," he says.

"It is," I agree. "I still can't believe it's mine."

"Hey." Charlotte looks up from where she's sitting on the floor. She's got catalogues spread out in front of her. "What happened?" She jumps to her feet. "I don't care how scary you think you are, Emmanuel. I will gut you if you make her cry." She's in his face within seconds.

"Okay, calm down. It wasn't him," I tell her.

"Why were you crying, then?" she asks me.

"I wasn't. It was one tear that escaped. It's nothing," I say, carefully wiping under my eye.

"There's a fed sniffing around. He's approached Evie twice now when she's been alone. Don't let her be alone again," Emmanuel explains.

"What? Why am I always the last to know these things?" Charlotte throws her arms in the air before pointing an accusatory finger at me. "You should have told me."

"You're honeymooning. I'm not ruining your happiness with my shit any more than I have," I tell her.

"Fine. I call an end to the honeymoon stage. Right now. It's over. From now on, you tell me everything," she says.

"You can't just call an end to the honeymoon stage. That's not how it works." I laugh.

"Yeah, well, I just did," Charlotte says. "I mean it, Evie. I want to know what's happening with you."

"Okay," I agree, for no other reason than to end this.

"Can this be done remotely?" Emmanuel eyes the pile of catalogues on the ground.

"Um, yes," I tell him.

"Good. We're going home. To Mexico. Today," he says.

"What? Today? I don't even have anything to wear!" I start rummaging through the clothes I packed to come to Vegas. I didn't exactly have a lot of notice.

"Evie, we can buy whatever you need when we get there," Emmanuel says, as if that's the solution to my problems.

"You can come and raid my closet. Louie keeps having shit delivered to me that I don't even need," Charlotte adds.

"Oh my, how horrible your life must be that your husband constantly gives you gifts." I roll my eyes at her.

"It really is." Her lip tilts up in mock disgust.

I turn back to Emmanuel. "How long do I have?"

"How long do you need?" he counters.

"Mmm, three hours?"

"Okay, I'll take you to Louie's and then come back and collect you in three hours," he says.

"I don't need you to escort me upstairs," I tell him.

"You might not need me to, but I need it," he counters, and I melt a little.

———

As soon as we're in Charlotte's penthouse, she disappears, leaving me alone in the foyer with Emmanuel.

"Three hours," he says. "Don't leave this apartment until I come back."

"Why?"

"Because I don't like the idea of you being anywhere without me right now."

"Okay." Usually I'd tell him where to go, but I feel like he needs this. And it's not like *I* need to go anywhere.

Once Emmanuel leaves, I walk into Charlotte's bedroom, finding her in her closet.

"Holy shitballs." My mouth drops open in shock. She wasn't kidding when she said Louie keeps having stuff delivered for her.

"I told you it's excessive."

"It's amazing, Charlotte. This is literally a dream

closet," I say, walking in and spinning around. "I'm almost too afraid to touch anything."

"Don't be. Take whatever you want," she says.

"I've never been more thankful that we are the same size than I am right now," I say while ogling her floor-to-ceiling shoe rack that is stacked full of all the latest designer heels.

# Chapter Forty-Six

Once I'm in the car, I call Paz. "You on him?" I ask.

I know my men are good at what they do. I didn't want to have to use Evie as bait, but I knew the second that asshole thought she was alone, he'd pop up.

She was never alone. I was watching her the entire time. She just didn't know it. But I couldn't have been more proud of her. She stood her ground, didn't let the fucker intimidate her at all.

The moment I saw him reach for her was when I stepped out of the shadows, not that I needed to. Evie poured an entire cup of coffee on his hand. I heard what she said to him, what he said to her. And, well, that tongue of his will make a great fucking trophy when I rip it out of his head and put it in a glass jar.

I'm not usually the collector type, but I think I might just become one. I will hunt down and collect a body part from every single person who tries to cross my wife,. Although I doubt many will be stupid enough to try. Not now that I've set the tone for what happens to those who do.

This cop thinks he's untouchable because he's a fed. Newsflash, the law can't touch me. I don't give a fuck who he is.

"Sending you the location now. He just walked into a house. Quiet street. My money is this is where Enrique's hiding out," Paz says.

"On my way." I have three fucking hours before I'm picking up Evie and taking her home with me. I put the location into the car's navigation system. "Fifteen minutes."

"Fuck," Paz hisses.

"What?"

"They're leaving. The pig and Enrique both just walked out," he says. "They're getting into a car."

"Follow them. Don't fucking lose them," I grunt.

"On it," he says.

"Stop the car. I'm driving," I call out to the front seat.

My driver pulls over and gets out. I jump out of the back and slide in behind the wheel. Then I slam my foot on the pedal. I don't have time to wait for him to get back in.

I have three SUVs behind me, or at least they're trying to catch up with me as I weave in and out of traffic.

"They're turning onto Paradise Road. Just got off Hidden Well," Paz says.

I throw the car left, heading towards Paradise. This little weasel is not fucking getting away from me. Fuck that. "They clocked you yet?" I ask Paz.

"No," he says.

"Good."

"They're heading for the fucking airport. Gray Honda sedan."

"Almost there," I say.

They are not going to make it to the airport. There are fucking concrete barriers blocking me from getting onto the other side of the road. Fuck. But then I see an opening. I yank the steering wheel to the right and the car swerves, just missing the barrier as I guide it across the road.

"What the fuck?" Paz curses.

I don't respond, because as the cars I'm heading towards honk and veer out of the way to avoid collision, I see my target. "I'm ramming the front. You got the back?" I ask Paz. I'm headed straight for the fucker.

"Got it," he says right as the front of my SUV hits the Honda.

Paz rams the back seconds later. The car spins, and I accelerate and ram into the driver's side, sandwiching them between two SUVs. They can't fucking move.

The cop doesn't quit, though. I see him draw his weapon. I climb out and walk behind the car. My own pistol rises and I fire a shot that goes through the windshield and then the back of his head.

Paz is pulling open the passenger side door and then dragging out an unconscious Enrique.

"Get him on the jet, in the back. I don't want Evie knowing he's there. We're taking the fucker home," I instruct.

"Got it." Paz nods.

"Two hours," I add as I walk away from the wreck. The sound of sirens can be heard in the distance as I climb into one of the waiting SUVs. "Get me back to the Royal," I tell the driver.

"Sure thing, jefe." He nods.

---

I can't believe I'm finally taking her home. To Mexico. I've done everything I can to make sure her arrival is smooth and accepted. Anyone stupid enough to go against me doesn't tend to keep breathing for long anyway.

"I'm excited to see where you live," Evie says.

"I live wherever you are," I tell her.

"You know what I mean." She turns her attention back to the catalogues she's got spread out on the table in front of us. "Do you have a pool?"

I chuckle. "*We* have a pool. Yes."

"Is it bigger than the one at the Royal?" she asks me.

I nod. "Yes."

"Good. I can't wait to send Charlotte pictures. Will you swim with me again?"

"I'll do whatever you want, Evie." How does she not already know this?

"So, if I want to go shopping in the city, you'll come with me?"

I turn to look at her. "I don't want you leaving

the house without me. So, yes, if you're going shopping, I'm going to be with you."

"Why can't I leave without you?" She squints her eyes at me.

"Because it's fucking Mexico, and you don't speak Spanish. Also..." I lean in to whisper in her ear. "I hear the cartel is really bad. They like to kidnap pretty little girls like you and sell them."

Evie's eyes widen. "Please tell me you don't actually do that."

"Me? No. But it happens." I shrug.

"Well, why don't you stop it from happening?" she says.

"Because I can't change how everything works overnight," I explain. "I've been the boss for two years, Evie. I'm still working my way around everything. And my father, he wasn't a good man. None of us are."

"That's not true. You are a good man, E. You just... do some bad things sometimes."

"Whatever helps you sleep at night, mi alma." I lean forward again and kiss her forehead. "But I'm serious. I don't want you going out without me."

"Okay, I won't. Besides, your translation skills might be useful. I should learn to speak Spanish," she says.

"We will work on it. Besides, our kids will be

bilingual. You're going to have to know the language," I tell her.

"I don't think I can have kids, E," she whispers.

"What do you mean? Is there something wrong with your... uterus?" I ask. "Because it's the twenty-first century, and we can afford whatever medical intervention we need."

"No. Well, I don't think there is. It's me. I'm not a good mother."

"How would you know that? You've never been a mother."

"I was." Evie looks down, and I feel like an ass. Of course she's talking about when she was sixteen. That choice was taken away from her, though.

"Evie, would you have kept it?"

"No... I don't know... Probably not. I mean, what kind of child wants to live knowing they're here because their mother was raped? But it was still my fault they took it. I should have protected it more. I could have given it to a family who wanted a child," she says.

"That was not your fault. That choice was stolen from you. There is nothing you could have done, Evie. You were fucking sixteen." My jaw ticks. Hearing her say that she was raped so bluntly...

I know that's what happened. I wish I could

bring all the fuckers back alive. They got off way too fucking easy.

"What if I don't want to, E? What if I don't want kids?"

"Then we won't have any." I want kids. I'm expected to have an heir. But fuck expectations, because I'm not going to make the woman I love give me a child out of obligation or expectation.

"Will you hate me for that, though?"

"There is nothing in this world that could ever make me hate you, Evie." I pull her against me. "We don't need to decide right now. We have so much time."

"Yeah."

I hold the door open, waiting for Evie to climb into the car before I follow her. "What are they doing?" she asks, looking out the windshield.

"Fucking hell," I curse and jump back out. "What the fuck are you doing? I said to wait until we were gone before you brought him out!" I yell at the two fucking soldiers dragging Enrique from the jet.

"Sorry, jefe. We thought you left," one of them says as they back up and retreat into the jet.

"I'll deal with them." Paz follows after them. I

hear the sound of two gunshots before he comes back out and nods at me. "I'll meet you at the compound."

"You good?" I ask him.

"I get to play butcher. I've never been better," he says.

"She cannot see any of this shit," I tell him.

"I know." Paz nods. "She won't."

I jump back into the car. Evie stares at me. "I don't want to know," she says.

"Good, because I wasn't going to tell you." The car pulls away, and I slide up the black divider that separates us from the driver. "You weren't supposed to see that."

"I figured. Was that Enrique?"

"It was," I tell her.

"I'm not going to pretend to be okay with every-thing you do, E. That's not me. But I will find a way to not let every little thing bother me," she says. "I want this to work. I love you."

"I love you, and this is working, mi alma. There's no other possible scenario. Now, are you ready to see your new home?"

"Part-time home. I already have a home, and I need to find a place in Vegas too. Shit... I have so much to do to organize a store opening," she mutters under her breath.

"You should hire an assistant," I tell her. "Delegate the shit you don't want to do."

Evie laughs. "My business isn't as lucrative as yours, E. I can't just hire people."

"I'll hire one for you, then." I shrug. "We also have a wedding to plan."

"We do." Evie smiles. "I spoke to Rachel. She has a week off before moving to Seattle, so she could make Milan if that's what you want still."

"I want whatever you want. Where did you dream about getting married?"

"I never let myself dream about getting married because I didn't think anyone could love me."

I'm shocked by her confession. "Evie, you are the easiest person in the world to love," I tell her. "Why wouldn't anyone love you?"

"Because I'm not whole."

"You are. You are fucking beautiful inside and out. There's nothing about you that I don't love." I lean in and press my lips to hers. "I love you."

"I know you do," she says.

"Good. Don't ever forget it."

As the car pulls into the estate, the gates open and Evie's attention fixates on the view outside her window. "Oh my gosh, it's gorgeous!" she exclaims.

"Beyond words," I agree. When she turns around to look back at me, I'm holding out a small black box.

"This is for you." I open it to reveal the four-carat, oval-shaped solitaire diamond.

Evie's eyes widen. "E... really? That's... huge."

"I've heard that before." I smirk. I take the ring out of the box and slide it onto her finger. "I never want to see this hand without this ring on it."

"Are you kidding? I'm going to be buried with this rock. It's so beautiful. Thank you." She throws her arms around me.

"Let's not talk about you being buried, Evie. I don't like the thought," I grunt.

"I really do love it. Thank you," she says, pressing her lips to mine.

# Chapter Forty-Seven

I wasn't exactly expecting Emmanuel to live in a straw shack. But this house, mansion, palace... I'm not sure what this place is even classed as. Whatever it is, it's not what I was expecting. It's nice, excessively so. Then again, with all the men he has around the place, I'm not surprised it's so huge.

"Do they all live here?" I ask Emmanuel as he guides me through the interior.

"No," he says. "The only one who lives on the compound is Paz, in a separate house. Everyone else is here on shifts."

I look around, taking in as much as I can while keeping up with Emmanuel's pace. "You know, I remember how it feels. To see this place for the first time. I was fourteen when my father made me move here."

"Did you like it?" I ask.

"No," Emmanuel says.

"Was there anything about your father you liked?"

"His money wasn't the worst." Emmanuel chuckles. "When you spend the first part of your life with a single mother struggling to make ends meet, it can be blinding. But nothing in life comes without a price, Evie."

"What price did you have to pay?"

"Freedom," E says.

I can't begin to imagine the pressure he's under. I don't want to add to it. "*Sooo*, have you ever brought a girl here?" I smile.

"No," he says.

"Good. That means we have a lot of rooms to christen." I waggle my eyebrows at him. "If this is going to be my home too, then I want memories in every single room. The naked kind of memories, E. I mean, that's if you're up to it."

"If I'm up to it? Are you trying to poke the bear, mi alma?"

"Maybe?" I laugh.

The next thing I know, my feet are leaving the ground and I'm dangling upside down over Emmanuel's shoulder. His palm comes down across my ass, while also holding my dress so no one sees my butt. Ever the gentleman, right?

"You know, if you didn't have to show off and have such a massive house, you'd have me on a bed already," I taunt.

I hear a door open, and then I'm flying through the air before I land on something soft. A mattress.

"Wait," I tell Emmanuel when he goes to climb on top of me. I want something, and I want it now.

"What's wrong?" he asks. "Did I hurt you?"

"No." I crawl off the bed. "Just... stay still. I want to do something."

I unbutton his suit jacket and slide it off his shoulders until it hits the floor. I remove the cufflinks from his shirt—they're gold with the letter E on them. After removing his vest, I loosen his tie and yank it over his head. Emmanuel bends to make it easier for me. I feel like a kid on Christmas morning, unwrapping the best gift. The first three buttons of his shirt are undone, but then I get impatient. I want to see all of him. Grabbing the fabric between my fingers, I tear at it. Buttons go flying across the room, but I get my eyes on his entire torso.

"Sorry," I tell him as his now-ruined shirt hits the floor.

"Don't worry about it. I have plenty more," he says.

I run my lips over his pecs, then drag my tongue right down the middle of his body. Every hard groove under my fingertips. I need him, so bad I can feel my thighs quivering.

"You really are carved to perfection," he says as I drop to my knees.

"I bet you say that to any girl who gets on her knees in front of you." I smirk.

"I would never allow another woman to be in this position, Evie. It's only going to be you," he tells me. And I believe him.

I undo his belt, flick the clasp of his pants, and lower the zipper, sliding the material down over his ass. His cock bounces free, proud and hard, right in front of my face. I wrap my hand around his length, watching as precum leaks from the tip. My mouth waters at the sight. As much as I want to tease him, draw it out, I need this more than I need air right now. I flatten my tongue along the underside of his shaft. His salty flavor explodes on my tastebuds, and my moan vibrates around him. Emmanuel's hand wraps around my hair and he tilts my face upwards slightly.

My eyes connect with his lust-filled gaze. Dark. They're always darker when he's turned on. Which is a lot of the time. Emmanuel never takes his eyes off my face as I continue to suck up and down his shaft. I keep one hand wrapped around the base, pumping with the motion of my mouth, while I use my other hand to cup his balls, rolling them around, gently massaging them.

"Fuck. Fuck!" Emmanuel's fingers tighten in my hair. His hips jerk forward, pushing more of his cock down my throat, until I'm choking. He pulls back slightly. "Breathe through your nose and relax," he says before shoving it all the way back in. He takes over the movements, holding my head still as he fucks my face. And I let him.

My hands cup his ass cheeks. He has the best ass. I love watching him walk in front of me.

"Fuck, I'm going to come." Emmanuel goes to pull out of my mouth.

I stop him with a slight shake of my head. I want everything he has. Seconds later, ropes of cum are squirting down my throat. I swallow as much of it as I can, proud when Emmanuel does pull free and not a single drop leaks out of my mouth.

"I fucking love you," he says.

"I know." I smile.

---

After we showered and ate together, Emmanuel sat me down and turned on some rom-com. He knows I love them. My fingers aimlessly roam around his bare chest. "I like touching you," I say.

"That's good." He chuckles. "Don't ever stop doing it."

"I won't, not even when you're old and lose all these muscles," I tease.

"That's never going to happen," he grunts like I've offended him.

"We all get old, E."

"Old, yes, but I'm never going to get fat, Evie."

"What if I get fat?" I ask him.

"I will love every single pound of you," he replies without missing a beat.

"Okay. Let's hope that never happens. I don't know what I'd do if I weren't pretty," I admit. "I mean, when you spend so much of your life focused on always being perfect, always being the pretty one, what happens when that prettiness fades?"

"Evie, your beauty goes far beyond surface level."

"That's what you say to ugly people, E." I roll my eyes.

"I've never lied to you, Evie, so why would I lie about your beauty?"

"I don't know." I shrug. "It's shallow. I get that. But it's just how I was taught to be. I've tried not to be so focused on how I look, but I feel better if I look better. So I gave up on fixing that part of myself."

"There isn't anything wrong with wanting to look good," E says. "Do you think I like wearing fucking suits all day? In the heat? No, I do it to maintain an image."

"Mmm, you do wear them really well." I grin.

Emmanuel's phone rings. He picks it up, holds it to his ear, and listens. He says something in Spanish before setting the device down. I really do need to learn this language. "I have to go deal with something. Make yourself at home. Maria is here. Anything you want, just ask her."

"Maria is here? Did you clone her or something?"

"No, I had her flown out. I thought you could use a friendly face, and she wanted to visit family," he explains.

"Thank you." I lean forward, straddle Emmanuel's hips, and press my lips to his. "I'm going to do some work, start ordering things for the store. I'll need the Wi-Fi password."

"Your devices are already connected. I won't be long," E says, rolling us over so he's on top of me. "There are shirts in the closet. You should put one on and cover these." His lips then latch on to one of my nipples.

"Okay. Take your time. I'm not going anywhere," I tell him.

Five minutes later, Emmanuel is walking out of the bedroom, fully dressed in a custom suit. How does he look so good in such a short amount of time? It's really not fair. It takes me hours.

I decide to get up and put on some clothes. Then I'll find the kitchen and make a coffee before settling in and ordering things to fill a new store. It's a big project, but I'm glad I have something to keep me busy. I can't make Emmanuel feel like he needs to babysit me 24/7. That's not me. I'm not clingy. At least I wasn't until I met him.

I walk into his closet and pause. What the actual hell? Spinning around in a circle, I feel like I just stepped into a department store. Everything is so neat, organized. And this closet is the size of some people's entire homes. Who lives like this?

Emmanuel apparently.

I don't even know where to start, but my fingers

trail along the fabric of jackets, then shirts. I open a drawer and find neatly-laid socks. Another drawer houses ties in a range of colors. All folded to perfection. I pull down a white dress shirt and throw it on. I swim in it.

Once I have it buttoned up, I fold the sleeves up to my elbows. I'm about to walk out when something catches my eye. A drawer that's not fully closed. It's on the opposite side of the room. I walk over with the intention of closing it, but then I see a picture frame. I slide the drawer open and find many more pictures. My hands shake as I pick up the first one, then the next.

"What the fuck?" I whisper, dropping the photos to the floor.

I keep digging through the drawer. These images are of all the same person. Me. They start from when I was a teenager, and go all the way through to this year. Why does Emmanuel have these?

# Chapter Forty-Eight

The thing about torturing members of the cartel? They know the deal. They know they're not getting out of here, no matter what they say. Which is why Enrique is staying silent. He's accepted his fate.

"I just want to know why?" I ask him. "You, of all people... I wouldn't have thought you would turn rat."

"You were going to kill me anyway. I touched

her, and I knew in that moment that it didn't matter what I said," he grunts.

"So you went to the feds?"

"They came to me. They were already following her," he says.

I nod to Paz. He sticks a needle into Enrique's arm. The drug will paralyze him, keep him still as I do what I have to do.

"You know this could have been avoided. The punishment for touching her would have been far less than that of total betrayal." It's a lie. I wouldn't have gone any fucking easier on him.

Even if he was trying to protect her by stopping her from rushing into a burning building, he should have found another way to do it. He didn't have to touch her. He also didn't have to run to the fucking cops.

I walk over to the wall and pick up a pair of coveralls. This job is messy. I don't need to go back into the house covered in blood and bodily fluids. Evie does not need to see that. Once I step into the coveralls, I pick up two filleting knifes, handing one to Paz. We stand on each side of the table. Enrique's completely naked and strapped down in front of us. He knows what's about to happen. Hell, he's delivered this punishment to more than enough people himself.

"My family..." he says.

"You should have thought of them before you became a rat." I glide the knife just under the skin of his shoulder. It takes time, finesse, to remove someone's flesh from their body. But when you do it enough, it becomes like muscle memory. The knife slides from side to side, almost as if I were filleting a fish.

Once we are done with his arms, we move onto his chest. Enrique hasn't said a word. He can feel it, but he's not going to show us that it's bothering him. The drug keeps his body still, but it doesn't erase all the pain.

An hour later and we have one skinned rat.

"I want him hung in the middle of fucking town," I tell Paz, dropping the knife and shaking the cramp out of my hand. "Make sure it's known that I'm back in town and this is what will happen to anyone else that steps out of line."

"Will do." Paz nods.

I step out of the coveralls, open the oven that will be used to burn the removed skin, and shove them inside. That was very anticlimactic. I wanted him to scream. I wanted to hear his pain. But when I saw the determination mixed with the acceptance of his fate on his face, I knew I wasn't going to get that out of him.

I head to the sink and scrub my hands, the water turning red as the blood washes away. By the time I'm walking out, Paz has three guys dragging Enrique from the warehouse. I get in the car and head back up the hill. It's about a five-minute drive from the main house. Somewhere I don't ever plan on showing Evie. This property is huge. The only part she needs to know about is the main house and gardens. The rest, well, nothing good ever happens on the outer edge of the property.

I walk into the house and find Maria in the kitchen. "Did Evie come down?" I ask her.

Maria shakes her head. "No, she hasn't come out of the room."

"Okay, I'll take something up to her." I open the fridge, and pull out a bottle of water and a prepared bowl of mixed fruits. Evie hasn't eaten in a while, so she has to be hungry.

When I walk into the bedroom, my heart sinks when I don't see her on the bed. I drop the water and the fruit bowl on the dresser and run into the bathroom. I expect to find her on the floor. Surrounded by blood. Thank fuck I don't. She's not in there. The light in the closet has me heading in that direction.

That's where I find her. On the floor, surrounded by pictures. Pictures she was never meant to see.

"Evie?" I call out to get her attention.

"W-what are these?" she asks, her voice shaking as she picks up some of the photos.

*Fuck. How do I even explain this to her?*

I run a hand through my hair. "You weren't supposed to see those."

"I figured that much, Emmanuel. Why do you have all these photos of me?"

I sit down in front of her. Taking a deep breath, I try to find the words to explain to her just how deep my obsession with her goes. I don't want to lie to her, but I also don't want to lose her either. Fucking hell.

"I first saw you when you were sixteen," I explain. "It was a year after Laura died, and I—you were there. In Vegas, in an evening gown with a crown on your head. The most beautifully haunting image I've ever seen." I pick up a photo, the one photo that isn't of her. "I thought you were Laura. I followed you that night and waited outside the hotel. But when you came out the next morning, something had changed. You looked even more like her, broken. Troubled."

I shake my head, trying to clear the memory.

"I was only sixteen. I didn't have a lot of power at the time, but I hired someone to follow you, just to make sure you weren't her. They assured me you weren't."

"I'm not Laura," Evie whispers.

"I know that. At the time, I was convinced I was losing my mind. I kept my distance. But I printed out every picture I could find. I wanted to believe so bad that you were her. That she got out and was alive somehow. It's why I didn't try to learn your name. I didn't want to let go of the possibility. I also didn't want to put you at risk by getting too close," I admit. "But then you showed up in Vegas again. The night we met."

Evie looks up at me, her eyes wet with unshed tears. She's hurt, and it's because of me. Fucking hell.

"I couldn't let you go a second time."

She shakes her head. "I'm not her," she repeats.

"I know."

"Do you?" she asks. "You're using me to replace someone you lost. That's not love, Emmanuel. That's... you trying to erase your grief."

"I'm not fucking using you for shit, Evie. I love you. Evie Carter, soon-to-be Evie Lopez. I don't want you to be her. She was weak. She wasn't strong enough for this life. She wasn't a fighter. You know why I know you're not her? Because you are strong, the strongest person I know. You don't quit. You fight for your happiness and you fight for those you love. Laura didn't fight, Evie. You do. Besides looks, there is nothing similar about you and Laura." I wave the photo around.

"Do you have pictures of her?" Evie asks.

"This is the only one."

Her brows furrow. She squints at the image in my hand. Then she shakes her head. "That's me, Emmanuel."

"No, it's Laura. You look just like her, Evie, eerily so. But I took this photo myself. I know it's Laura."

"I don't understand," she says. "My mom has that exact picture of me in her living room."

"That's impossible," I tell her. Her mother cannot have this picture. "There were only two copies. I kept one, and Laura had one."

I don't remember what happened to Laura's copy. I left all her things. I couldn't deal with any of it. I wanted to move on. I wanted to start my plan of revenge against my father. It took years, but I got it eventually.

"It's me, Emmanuel. I'm telling you my mother's house is covered in pictures of me. This one is in her living room. I haven't been there in years, but I know my mother had an obsession with my looks. She loved displaying her beautiful daughter all over her house. I doubt that would have changed now," she says.

"How?" *How could her mother have a photograph of Laura? Why would she have it?*

"I don't know," Evie says.

"I'm sorry. I should have told you. I didn't want to scare you away. I can't lose you, Evie. I know this looks bad. Fuck, I get it. But I need you. Don't take the one thing in the world that I actually love." I'm begging her. I really can't lose her.

"You don't love me, E. You love her," she says.

"No." I shake my head. I reach out and pick up her hands. "I love you. It's you, not her."

"I can't spend my entire life wondering if, when you're looking at me, you're thinking about her."

"I don't. The only thing I think about is you, Evie. You. I think about us, our future. I will never let anyone come between us, especially not a fucking ghost," I growl. "I didn't love her. I thought I did, but I didn't know what love was until I met you."

"You've been following me since I was sixteen," she says.

"Only a few photos," I clarify.

"It's still creepy."

"I would never hurt you, Evie." I might have had the thought once, but I have not wanted her to die for a really fucking long time.

"I know," she says. "I need to go and see my mother."

"You want me to take you to the woman's house

who sat back and watched you get abused for years?" I don't know if I can do that.

"I need to know who she is." Evie looks at the picture of Laura again.

"She was a foster care kid, a street kid. She grew up in and out of homes, Evie. She didn't have family. She had me and the guys. She was an addict," I explain.

"You don't need to come with me, but I am going to go and speak to my mother." Evie pushes to her feet. She's wearing one of my dress shirts. "And after that, if you still want to marry me, you can take me to Milan."

"There is no *if*, Evie. I am marrying you." I stand and pull her into my arms.

"I'm not going to lie, E. It hurts. Knowing you've known about me all these years and you didn't even say hello? Not even a DM. *Like, hey, BTW, we're soul mates. Just thought you should know*," she says.

"I was an idiot. I thought I could keep you in a box. You were safe there."

"I feel safest right here, in your arms," she whispers, holding me tighter.

I don't know what I did to get this woman to love me so unconditionally, but I am not going to fuck this up.

# Chapter Forty-Nine

My mind is a mess. The only thing I know for sure is that I love Emmanuel. It hurts, knowing that he watched me, collected photos of me. That he lived in some alternate reality where his girlfriend didn't die at sixteen. I honestly don't know how to process it. I do know that I can't make any rash decisions based on being hurt. I knew that he loved her. I knew he grieved her loss. And I also knew I look like her.

I thought we had similarities. But I didn't think we looked exactly alike.

Emmanuel keeps eyeing me, as if I'm going to break down or run. Either is a possibility, but I'm not going to. Once I decided I was going to visit my mother, I went and got dressed. Did my hair and makeup to perfection and straightened my crown, so to speak.

I've spent all of my adult life pretending to be okay, when I was far from it. I can do it now too. He knows, though. When Emmanuel looks at me with concern, it's because he knows I'm not okay. He's literally the only person who has ever seen through my façade. The only person who stops and looks hard enough to see all the broken pieces inside.

It's not that my friends don't care. It's just that I don't like showing them the ugly parts of me. I don't want to be a burden. I glance back at Emmanuel and give him a smile. The kind that usually eases people's worries.

"Don't do that," he says.

"Do what?"

"Don't give me fake-ass smiles, Evie. I don't want them," he grunts. "I know you're upset. I want the real you. Give me whatever emotion you're feeling, because that's what I deserve."

"I'm fine," I tell him.

"You will be, but right now, you're confused and you're hurting. And you have every right to be. But don't sit here and lie to me," he says. "I never lie to you."

"No, you just keep truths from me, like the fact you were stalking me when I was sixteen, pretending I was your dead girlfriend," I spit out in frustration.

"I did." He nods. It's odd. He doesn't try to weasel his way out of this shit. He hasn't told some bullshit story. He told me the truth. Which is the only reason I believe him when he says he's in love with me. Not her.

Or it could just be me believing the truth I want. I don't want to lose him.

"Just so you know, I let myself fall for you because I thought... here is a guy who will never do anything to hurt me. Here is the guy I look for when I wake up, the one I want holding me when I go to sleep and the only person in the world who has ever been able to quiet the nightmares," I say. "I fell in love with you because you saw all of me and loved me anyway. You are so in tune with me that it's like you're in my head half the time. I love that. I do. But right now, it's just pissing me off. Get out of my fucking head, Emmanuel. Let me live in a fantasy bubble where everything is fine. Where I am fine. Where I'm not falling apart on the inside because I'm about to go and face my biggest demon."

"Okay." Emmanuel's arm wraps around my shoulders, and he pulls me against his side. "We will pretend everything is fine." He kisses my forehead. "I love you."

"I love you," I tell him.

"No." He shakes his head. "I love *you*," he repeats.

"I know."

"That's better." He smiles down at me and then presses his lips to mine. "I need you to never forget that."

"How many jets do you own, E?" I ask, looking around the luxurious plane.

"Two. Well, one now. We lost one," he says.

"How do you lose a jet?"

"When Paz was taken in, he was about to board the jet. No one has seen it since. So either the fed hid it somewhere or found a way to confiscate it."

"That's a lot of money to just lose." I frown. "Can't you find it. Like don't these things have GPS on them? Or an air tag or something."

"They do, but it was switched off. And it's not worth the hassle. I can buy another one," Emmanuel says, like buying a jet is no different from going to the store and buying a pair of shoes.

"That's insane," I tell him. "Maybe you should get a pink one."

"A pink one?" He laughs.

"Yeah, put everyone off the scent. What big scary cartel boss would be flying around in a pink jet?"

"None," he says. "Neither will I."

"Never say never," I tell him.

---

I look up at my childhood home. "It's exactly the same," I tell Emmanuel. My hand is gripping his tight. I haven't faced my mother in years.

"You don't have to do this, Evie. We can turn around right now," Emmanuel says.

"No, I do. I need to know," I tell him. "We can't start our marriage with unanswered questions."

"We can, because we don't need answers. We have each other. That's all I care about," he says.

"I know, but I want to know. Just... don't kill her."

"I'm not going to kill your mother, Evie," he grumbles.

"You killed your own mother, E," I remind him.

"She had a gun pointed at you," he says. "I will kill anyone who points a gun at you."

My mother doesn't have guns. She'd also never point one at me. I know it's fucked up, what she did. But in her mind, she does love me. That mind just isn't healthy.

With each step we take towards the house, my heart beats faster and faster. When we get to the door, I raise my fist and knock.

I hear the sound of heels clicking, and the door opens. My mother's smile falls when she sees me. "Evie?" Then that well-practiced pageant smile is back on her face. "Sweetheart, you look beautiful."

"Can I come in?" I ask her.

My mother frowns. "This is your home. Of course, you can come in," she says, stepping out of the way. She holds the door open and I walk through, pulling Emmanuel behind me. "This is Emmanuel, my fiancé."

"Oh." My mother gives me a once-over. "You look beautiful, Evie. Wait... Let me get the camera. I need to capture this moment."

"No," I say, my voice firm. "Not right now, Mom. Maybe after," I suggest, because I know my mother. Her pictures of me are more important than the actual *me*.

She nods. "Okay, come on in. Can I get you anything?"

"No," I say, following her into the living room. The space hasn't changed at all.

I sit on the two-seater sofa. Emmanuel sits next to me. I know the moment he spots the picture. It's in a frame on the table beside the chair my mother is sitting on. The entire room is filled with photos of me. Or at least I was always led to believe they were of me. I had such bad memory issues back then that I believed I just didn't remember having certain pictures taken.

"Who is she?" I ask my mother.

"Who is who, sweetheart?"

I stand and pick up the photo. "Her. Who is she and why do you have a picture of her?"

"It's you, Evie," my mother says without missing a beat.

I sit back down, the photo still in my grip. Emmanuel takes it from me. He undoes the back of the frame and pulls the picture out. "Laura, eternally beautiful," is written on the back of the image.

He hands it to me. "This was her copy of the picture," he says. "I wrote that."

I suck in a lungful of air. I will not let words he said to someone when he was sixteen hurt me. I will not let this hurt us. "Why do you have this, Mom?" I ask.

"How do you know Laura? Do you know where she is now?" My mom is looking at Emmanuel.

"The question is how did *you* know her?" Emmanuel counters, his voice hard.

"She's my daughter," Mom says.

"What?" both Emmanuel and I ask at the same time.

"She's your sister, Evie."

"I don't have a sister. I would remember having a sister, Mom. What are you talking about?" I'm so confused.

"There were two of you... when you were born. But your father wouldn't let me keep you both. So he took one. He took Laura, and let me have you," she says. "Then I found her, in Las Vegas, but she didn't want to know us." A sadness covers my mom's face. "She was so beautiful, just like you, Evie. She could have been a queen too. Together, you could have owned that stage. Two crowns."

Emmanuel squeezes my hand. "Mom, how did you get this picture?" I question.

"I followed her to an apartment, and I took it. She wouldn't come home with us. But I brought her here anyway." My mom looks at Emmanuel. "Do you know where she is? Is she still beautiful?"

Emmanuel looks at me before answering. "I

know where she is. She is still beautiful, Miss Carter. Laura will always be this version of herself." He passes the picture back to my mother.

"Oh, good. That's good. It's important to be beautiful," Mom says.

"We have to go." I stand and Emmanuel follows my lead.

---

Neither of us speaks until we get to the car. "Thank you." I turn to him. "For lying to her."

"Your mother needs help, Evie," he says.

"That's not my problem. I can't... It's not..." I don't know how to explain it to him.

"I know. It's okay." He grabs my hand. "Ready to pick up Rachel and head to Milan?"

"Emmanuel, you just found out I'm the twin sister of your dead girlfriend. You can't seriously want to marry me still," I say.

"No, what I found out is that you got stuck being raised by a sick woman. You had a sister who really didn't fare any better in the parent department. I love you, Evie. I am in love with you. Not Laura. You," he says. "I love your kindness. I love your loyalty, your strength. I love the way you look at me as if I can solve the world's problems. I love you. I love the way you love me. I love you."

"I know," I say.

"So, Milan?" he asks.

"Let's do it. Let's get married." I smile. I'm actually going to marry this man. I'm going to move on and live my life for the future and leave the past behind me. Those monsters can't hurt me anymore, and that's because of Emmanuel. He killed them all. He showed me that I can be loved, even the worst parts of me can be loved.

"You want to talk about it?"

"Not right now. But one day, I'm going to want you to tell me everything you know about my sister," I say.

"When that day comes, I need you to promise me one thing."

"What's that."

"That you remember that I love you. Don't forget that, Evie. It's important to me that you never forget," he says.

"I won't forget. How can I when you tell me every other minute? And you show me that you love me all the minutes you aren't saying it." I smile. "You know, we can always just go to Vegas and elope. It will be much quicker and cheaper."

"You are not having a wedding in Vegas. You are having a wedding fit for a queen," Emmanuel says.

"I think I'm going to like being your wife."

"Good, because you're going to be my wife, in this life and the next," he says. "You are mi alma. I will always find you."

# Epilogue

**T**his is happening. I'm actually marrying her today. When I saw this church on a trip to Italy a few years ago, I thought of her. I pictured her in a white dress walking down this aisle. And now she fucking is.

All those years of collecting photos, of thinking of the life Laura would have had if I hadn't failed her. Even then, I knew she wasn't Laura. I knew there was something different about this woman.

There was a pull towards her that was never there with Laura.

We still need to have to have a lot of real conversations about what her mother told us. I honestly don't know how Evie is able to go through with this, how she's not trying to run from me. When I saw her with the pictures, I thought I'd lost her.

Thankfully, by some grace of God, I get to keep her. Forever. Not that I ever would have let her run far. But the fact she didn't says a lot more than words ever will. I know she loves me in the same way I love her. It's not something logic can explain; it's deeper than anything I've ever felt.

"You doing okay?" Louie asks. He's standing up with me, along with Carlo and Sammie and Paz.

"I'm good. Why the fuck wouldn't I be?"

"Just checking." He chuckles.

The doors to the church open and then she appears. Evie. In a long white dress, with a smile that reaches her eyes. And when those eyes connect with mine, that's where they stay the entire time it takes for her to reach me.

"Hey." I smile as I take Evie's hands in mine.

"Hey."

It's on the tip of my tongue to tell her she's beautiful, but I don't think she needs to hear that word right now. I didn't realize just how desensitized she was. It's not that she didn't know she was beautiful. She did, because her mother never let her forget it. It's what her entire identity as a child was about.

"I love you," I whisper instead, because I don't think she's heard that enough.

"I know," she replies. "I love you."

"I know."

# Epilogue

I haven't told Charlotte or Rachel about Laura, about the fact I had a twin sister and Emmanuel was in love with her first. I'm not sure if I will. I don't want anyone else's doubt creeping into my mind.

I'm probably clinically insane. Seeing my mother again has made me realize it's also probably genetic. She's worse than she was even back then. Or I've just been out of that inner circle for so long now I forgot how bad it was to be in it.

I know Emmanuel loves me. I believe him when he tells me it's not her he sees. He's right. They were sixteen, puppy love. What we have is different. It goes beyond looks, beyond money. It's real. I feel it right down to my core. It terrifies me, because I don't know what will happen to me if I lose him.

When the priest says, "You may now kiss the bride," Emmanuel doesn't waste any time. His lips are pressed against mine.

"Fucking finally," he grunts. "I've been waiting for you to be my wife for weeks."

"Me too," I tell him.

"Let's get out of here. The things I want to do to you are not very holy." He smirks.

As soon as we're enclosed in a car, alone, he's on me.

"Fuck me, I need you now," he says. The divider screen is up, separating us from the driver.

My dress is long, form-fitting silk. I inch it up my legs and straddle him. I'm not wearing panties. I didn't want the lines to show. "I'm ready," I tell him.

Emmanuel unbuckles his belt and then his pants. I take hold of his cock. He might need me right now, but I need him more.

I line him up with my entrance and slide down. "Oh god."

"How?" he asks, his hands cupping my face. "How does it get better every fucking time?"

"I don't know," I moan as I move up and then fall back down on him. "But I'm going to spend a lifetime fucking you, E, so you better like it."

"This lifetime and the next." His hands move down to my hips, holding me still as he thrusts upwards, setting the pace as he fucks me. "Mrs Lopez, I fucking love you."

"I love you." I moan as an orgasm rips through me. I've never been more sure of anything in my life. "I love you," I repeat.

"I know," Emmanuel says, thrusting into me one, two, three more times.

***

## *THREE MONTHS LATER*

"Are you ready?" Emmanuel asks.

"No." I shake my head from side to side. How did I let myself get in this predicament? Then I look at my husband. *That's how.* "This is your fault, you know. If you weren't so damn sexy, I'd be able to keep my hands off you and we wouldn't be here right now."

He smirks. "Whatever it says, we are in this together. You aren't alone, Evie."

"I know." I take a huge breath. "Okay." Picking up the stick on the counter, I turn it over. The word *pregnant* flashes back at me.

Emmanuel smiles. "We're pregnant," he says in awe.

"How?"

"Really, Evie, I think you know how. It's because you can't keep your hands off me." He grins.

I laugh. "No, I mean. How am I going to do this, E?"

"*We* are going to do this together. We've got this, mi alma." He kisses my forehead.

"I wasn't enough to keep a child safe before. What if something happens? What if I fall asleep and, I don't know, someone takes them away from me again?" I ask him.

"I will increase security. I will stay awake whenever you're asleep, Evie. I'm not going to let anything happen to you... or him." He places a hand over my still-flat stomach.

"It could be a her, you know."

"It's a him," he says. "We need sons before a daughter."

"Why?"

"Because I'm going to need all the help I can get killing any boys who dare sniff around our daughter. And they're will be a lot of them," Emmanuel groans.

"You don't know that."

"With us as their parents, our children are going to be attractive, Evie. Trust me, when we have a daughter, she is going to need big brothers."

"Just how many kids do you think we're having?" I quirk a brow at him.

"We'll start with one and go from there." He smiles at me.

---

## TEN YEARS LATER

If he touches me again, I'm going to kill him. *We'll start with one and go from there.* That was five pregnancies ago. Every time, I ask myself how did this happen? And every time, I know how. My husband and I like sex.

"You need to push," the midwife says.

"E, I need a gun." I hold out my hand to my husband.

"Why?" he asks.

"Because I'm going to shoot everyone in this

fucking room!" I scream as a contraction hits me full force.

"Push," the midwife repeats.

I push down. Emmanuel stays silent, right beside me. He learned quickly the safest thing for him to do is not to say anything. A few more pushes and then I hear it, a tiny cry. Tears fill my eyes.

"It's a girl," the midwife tells me right before she places the most precious little bundle on my chest.

"It's a girl," Emmanuel whispers.

I glance over at him. He looks... scared. "Are you okay?" I ask.

"We don't have enough boys yet, Evie," he says.

"We have four," I remind him. "I'm not doing this again, E. You are getting fixed."

He screws up his face. "We can talk about that later." His hand covers the baby's back. "She's so precious," he whispers as he kisses my forehead.

"She is. Eliana Laura Lopez," I utter the name I've had picked for a girl through all five pregnancies.

"Eliana, you are going to be loved beyond measure." Emmanuel leans down and kisses her tiny head.

An hour later, a herd of elephants comes running into the room. Okay, a herd of Lopez boys. There's Elias; he's just turned nine. Then there is Esterio, who is seven. We have Ezekiel, who is five, and Emilio, who is three. And now that we have our little princess, Eliana, our family is complete.

549

# About the Author

About Kylie Kent

Kylie made the leap from kindergarten teacher to romance author, living out her dream to deliver sexy, always and forever romances. She loves a happily ever after story with tons of built-in steam.

She currently resides in Sydney, Australia and when she is not dreaming up the latest romance, she can be found spending time with her three children and her husband of twenty years, her very own real life instant-love.

Kylie loves to hear from her readers; you can reach her at: author.kylie.kent@gmail.com

Let's stay in touch, come and hang out in my readers group on Facebook, and follow me on instagram.